RAFE RYDER &

THE BRUSHSTROKE OF TIME

THE RAFE RYDER SERIES

The Well of Wisdom
The Brushstroke of Time

RAFE RYDER &
THE BRUSHSTROKE OF TIME

L. L. REYNOLDS

THE BRUSHSTROKE OF TIME

Cover design and art by Jenny Zemanek with Seedlings Design Studio at www.seedlingsonline.com
Editorial services by Quill Pen Editorial at www.quillpeneditorial.com
E-book production by Kella Campbell with Ebooks Done Right at www.ebooksdoneright.com
Print typesetting by Chris Bell with Atthis Arts LLC at www.atthisarts.com

Published by Ananiah Press
Brattleboro, Vermont
www.ananiahpress.com

ISBN (hardcover)   978-0-9969319-5-3
(trade paperback)   978-0-9969319-4-6
(ebook)   978-0-9969319-3-9

Library of Congress Control Number: 2018911011

First Edition: October 2018

Printed in the United States of America

For my daughter-in-law,
Lindsey L.
I adore you!

For my niece,
Jessica C.
One lovable little rapscallion!

In memory of:

Elsie Reynolds Ladd
Mary Reynolds Rich
Eva Reynolds Ames
Irene Ashe Reynolds

My crazy, quirky aunties who made my childhood so entertaining.
You are loved and greatly missed.

TABLE OF CONTENTS

THE RINGS OF MYSTFIRA

1
tHe islaNd of palades
Madri Ezekiel/Powers
The Amethyst Palace
Cloak of Purple

2
tHe sea of umbeR
Madri Omega/Carrions
The Palace of Umber Cascades
Cloak of Orange

3
tHe tRuviaN RiNg
Madri Typhicus/Administrator
The Javartan Village
Cloak of Stripes

4
tHe faiRy foRest
Madri Fey/Fairies
The Tree of Tuatha
Cloak of Yellow

5
tHe RiNg of Rocks
Madri Avalon/Cherubim
The Rose Quartz Palace
Cloak of Rose Pink

6
tHe weepiNg woods
Madri Roanin/Seraphim
The Red Beryl Palace
Cloak of Crimson

7
mukRot
Madri Keva/Dominions
The Palace of Turquoise
Cloak of Turquoise

8
tHe valley of wateRfalls
Madri Estel/Virtues
The Winter Blue Palace
Cloak of Pale Blue

9
tHe juNgle of equiNox
Archangel Michael
The Golden Palace
Cloak of Gold

10
tHe deseRt
Madri Isabo/Guardians
The Palace of Pearls
Cloak of Silver

11
tHe RiNg of asHlot
Madri Saniel/Thrones
The Emerald Sky Palace
Cloak of Emerald Green

12
tHe RiNg of ice
Madri Uriah/Principalities
The Sapphire Sky Palace
Cloak of Royal Blue

CAST OF CHARACTERS

◀◀◀ 1 ▶▶▶

Rafe Ryder
Grandson of Lady Jane Ryder
GROUP: Royal Rangers
COSTUME: Indiana Jones
HOME: England

Lady Jane Ryder
Headmistress of Ryder-Knight
Academy and Rafe's grandmother
COSTUME: Mrs. Santa
HOME: Maine

Baylor Wingate
Fraternal twin to Blake Wingate
GROUP: Royal Rangers
COSTUME: Peacock
HOME: Maine

Blake Wingate
Fraternal twin to Baylor Wingate
GROUP: Royal Rangers
COSTUME: Zorro
HOME: Maine

Deidre Dunn
Cousin to Blake and Baylor Wingate
GROUP: Royal Rangers
COSTUME: Cleopatra
HOME: Maine

Tahj Sharuk
Classmate of Rafe's
GROUP: Royal Rangers
COSTUME: Cowboy
HOME: India

Oliver Harper
Classmate of Rafe's
GROUP: Royal Rangers
COSTUME: Peter Pan
HOME: Texas

Ebon Lavey
Classmate of Rafe's
GROUP: Royal Rangers
COSTUME: Spock
HOME: South Africa

Gerand Rial
Classmate of Rafe's
GROUP: Royal Rangers
COSTUME: Firefighter
HOME: Maine

Audra Monroe
Classmate of Rafe's
GROUP: Royal Rangers
COSTUME: Christmas Caroler
HOME: Massachusetts

Parker Sutton
Classmate of Rafe's
GROUP: Royal Rangers
COSTUME: Red Riding Hood
HOME: California

Sullivan Cabot
Classmate of Rafe's
GROUP: Royal Rangers
COSTUME: Mobster
HOME: Vermont

CAST OF CHARACTERS

««« 2 »»»

Neil Trask
Classmate of Rafe's
GROUP: Thunder Stars
COSTUME: Ninja
HOME: Rhode Island

Mikiko Kaouri
Classmate of Rafe's
GROUP: Thunder Stars
COSTUME: Witch
HOME: Japan

Luke
First-responder on beach
and in corn maze
HOME: Araboth

Thomas
Luke's Jarvartan
HOME: The 3rd Ring of Mystfira

Seamus O'Shanahan
The Leprechaun
HOME: The 5th Ring of Mystfira

Poppe
Fairy who mixes up her words/
twin to Potts
HOME: The 4th Ring of Mystfira

Potts
Highly energetic fairy/
twin to Poppe
HOME: The 4th Ring of Mystfira

Prentiss
Librarian from Javartan village
HOME: The 3rd Ring of Mystfira

Zane
Librarian from Javartan village
HOME: The 3rd Ring of Mystfira

Simon
Baylor's red-tailed hawk
HOME: Wherever Baylor is

Leopold
Baylor and Blake's yellow
Labrador Retriever
HOME: Maine

Sion
Angel in dance class
HOME: The 10th Ring of Mystfira

Diadem
Student angel/famous for belching
HOME: The 10th Ring of Mystfira

Malachi
Student angel/most athletic
HOME: The 10th Ring of Mystfira

Haven
Student angel/most studious
HOME: The 10th Ring of Mystfira

Shar
Student angel/opinionated
HOME: The 10th Ring of Mystfira

THE BRUSHSTROKE OF TIME

Chapter One

No More Secrets

Thirteen-year-old Rafe Ryder scowled at himself in the full-length mirror. Staring at his Indiana Jones costume's reflection conjured up memories from six months ago—none of them good.

Slamming the closet door shut, Rafe strode across the room to peer at the family picture on top of his piano. The happiness captured in the photograph practically oozed out of the frame, but it was a picture of the old Rafe, the boy-who-didn't-know-his-father-was-sick Rafe, the before-someone-told-him-he-was-an-angel Rafe.

He pressed his lips together in a tight frown as he tapped the side of the frame with an index finger. If anyone had told him a year ago that he and twelve other Ryder-Knight Academy students would be stuck in Mystfira, an elite angelic training ground situated between the sixth and seventh heavens, he would have declared them absolutely barmy. But not anymore. Whether you like it or not, living in a place where impossible things happen on a daily basis changes you.

Stealing one last glance at the picture of his old carefree self, Rafe snatched it from the piano and hurled it with impressive force against his sitting room door. He didn't care what anyone said—his destiny lay on Earth, not the heavens, and he needed to find a way back home. The sooner, the better!

Gut knotted in anger, Rafe slumped onto the piano bench,

remembering his grandmother's words to him on the way home from the airport in Maine shortly after he'd subjected her to a particularly nasty rant about his parents' decision to send him away to live with her.

"You simply must learn to manage your temper, my darling," she had said. "Anger isn't always a bad thing, but it is a type of fire, and as with any fire, you must control the burn, or it will consume you."

Clasping his hands around the back of his neck and elbows resting on his knees, Rafe rocked back and forth, willing the white-hot fury to subside with slow deep breaths. He felt nearly back to normal when a staccato *thump, thump, thump* sounded on his bedroom door.

"Hey! What's going on in there?" called his friend, Blake, from the hallway. "Are you okay?"

"I'm fine!" Rafe shouted.

"Then open up."

Striding to the door, Rafe swung it open and frowned at the masked Zorro figure standing there.

"There you are," Blake said, poking his head into Rafe's room. His eyes came to rest on the broken picture frame and scattered shards of glass strewn about the floor. "Did you do that?"

Rafe stared at the floor. "So what if I did?"

"Okay. Okay. It's your picture. You can break it if you want."

Huffing out a sigh, Rafe lifted his eyes to meet his friend's gaze.

"Oh," Blake said, his eyes becoming wider and rounder. "It's because Madri Typhicus is telling the other Ryder-Knight students about you and Simon being angels today, isn't it?"

Rafe grabbed the hat for his Indiana Jones costume off the top of the piano and stepped out into the hallway without saying a word.

"I'm sorry you're spazzing about it," Blake said. "But, I've got to say I'm relieved. Baylor knows about Simon being an animal guardian, but I've kept *your* secret from her for the last two weeks, and it's *killing* me."

"That's not my fault," Rafe snapped. "We were told *not* to tell her until she felt better. Remember?"

"I know, and she'll eventually forgive me, but you . . . I'm not so sure. She's going to be furious, and trust me, she's terrifying when she goes ballistic. She gets really quiet, and then *boom!*"

Clipping his bedroom door shut, Rafe racked his brain for some childhood memory of Blake's twin sister "going ballistic." He couldn't come up with anything.

As Rafe opened his mouth to defend her, Baylor unexpectedly tripped out of her bedroom door and into the hallway behind them. Elbows pressed against her sides, she braced an elaborate feathered headdress against her head with both hands.

"That's not funny, Leopold! Get off!" she sputtered, yanking at the peacock cape she wore. "We're both going downstairs whether you like it or not!"

Bolting from behind Baylor with a yowl, the twins' yellow Labrador dashed down the hallway toward the boys sporting an indigo sweater and a smaller version of Baylor's cape.

"Slow down, buddy," Blake said, catching the dog by his collar. "What's got you so hot and bothered?"

"He's been acting spooked ever since I put that costume on him. I think he remembers what happened the last time he wore it," Baylor said.

Stooping, Blake brushed a hand through Leopold's fur. "I feel your pain, buddy. I'm not wild about wearing these duds again either, but you're going to be okay. I promise."

Leopold's doleful eyes laser-focused on Blake's face, and he managed a half-hearted tail wag.

"What are you guys still doing up here?" Baylor asked, shutting her bedroom door. "You should be in the ballroom."

Blake scrambled to his feet. "So should you. What's your excuse?"

Baylor walked toward the boys, patting her headdress. "I had to hot glue some more feathers onto this stupid thing so it would pass Deidre's costume inspection Are we late?"

"Not yet," Blake said, consulting his watch as they walked toward the stairs. "We've still got five more minutes."

Rafe groaned. "I don't know why I let your cousin talk me into this reenactment of hers. I'm not an actor."

"Seriously?" Baylor looked at Rafe with a bemused smile. "It's not like any of us really had a choice. You're the one from England. Aren't you familiar with queens?"

Rafe snorted at the thought of Deidre ruling England. Heaven help the poor British subjects who landed on Deidre's bad side. Heads would roll. Unfortunately for Baylor, since arriving in Mystfira, she'd spent a good deal of time on her cousin's bad side.

"And speaking of keeping our little queen bee happy," Blake said. "Try not to mention Rand. She's had a crush on him since she was six years old, and she is *not* handling the fact Rand is a dark spirit at all well."

Rafe pressed his lips together and pretended to zip them shut.

Scooting past her brother and Rafe in the hallway, Baylor broke into a run. "Race you guys to the ballroom!"

The three youngsters and Leopold sped down Cliff House's spiral staircase, through the majestic entrance hallway, and screeched to a halt outside the ornately carved ballroom doors.

Cracking one of the doors open as silently as he could, Rafe peeked inside. Shafts of morning sunlight cut through the stained-glass dome above the ballroom, casting richly hued streams of light over the polished parquet floors.

Overlooking the buzz of activity on the floor of the ballroom, the twins' cousin, Deidre Dunn, stood next to the magnificent pipe organ housed on the resplendent musicians' balcony that spanned the entire east wall.

With Deidre on the balcony, the twins and he would never be able slip into the ballroom unnoticed, unless—

Rafe spied one of their classmates, Parker Sutton, standing nearby. She was gazing into one of the gilded antique mirrors surrounding the four walls of the ballroom and trying to shape the thick strings of her Little Red Riding Hood cape into a fashionable bow.

"*Psst*. . . Parker. Over here," Rafe whispered. "Could you distract Deidre so we can sneak inside?"

Parker flashed one of her drop-dead gorgeous smiles and nodded. Flipping her long blonde hair over her shoulder, she strode towards the balcony. "Deidre," she called. "I cannot seem to tie a decent bow today. Could you please come down here and help me?"

"Coming," Deidre said.

Grabbing a clipboard, Deidre disappeared from the balcony and popped out from the musicians' staircase hidden behind the frame of one of the large ballroom mirrors. After that, it only took Parker a few moments to reposition Deidre's back toward the door.

Taking the cue, Rafe and the twins slinked into the ballroom with Leopold, but the clacking of the dog's nails on the floor might as well have been a series of short machine-gun blasts.

Deidre's head snapped up, and she spied the quartet in one of the mirrors. "I see you guys sneaking in here, and don't think for one minute I don't."

Blake tapped his wristwatch. "Chill, Deidre. We're right on time."

"Barely," Baylor whispered. "Stop antagonizing her."

"Okay, everyone! Quiet!" Deidre called, using her special stage voice, the one loud enough to slap the back row out of their seats at one of her performances. She tapped a pencil impatiently on her clipboard and waited for silence.

"As you all know, the fairies are having a festival celebration today, called the Festival of Fete-Reet—"

"Feadh-Ree," corrected a boy dressed as Mr. Spock. "It's called the Festival of Feadh-Ree."

"Thank you, Ebon. As I was saying, today is the Festival of Feadh-Ree—"

"Actually, for the sake of accuracy, the festival began last night," Ebon said. "I just finished reading a book about it. The children of Mystfira love this May holiday like no other. They sprinkle welcome mats of flowers outside the entrances to their homes and place baskets filled with homemade delicacies on their doorsteps before going to bed on the eve of Feadh-Ree. Early the next morning, the fairies collect the gifts and the children from their homes. Then the little fairies escort the youngsters to the Brume Amphitheater in the Fairy Forest for a full day of merriment, entertainment, and adventure. At dusk, the children are returned to their parents, exhausted and happy. Or so the book stated."

"Yeah. I don't know about any of that," Deidre said, "but I *do know* Madri Fey said everyone is super excited to see our performance today."

"Yay," said Blake, balling his fists up next to his head and shaking them in mock enthusiasm.

Deidre threw him a wilting glare and continued, "Our reenactment begins with Madri Fey reading a paragraph about how the best and brightest minds of Ryder-Knight Academy were assembled by co-captains Blake Wingate and Deidre Dunn to form our fabulous team, The Royal Rangers of Ryder-Knight Academy. She'll follow up with a few more paragraphs . . . *blah, blah, blah* . . . and then we'll begin the reenactment of how we ended up here in Mystfira."

"We've had eight rehearsals at eight different fairy mounds in the Fairy Forest. *We know,*" Audra said, her long red-gold curls bobbing as she tugged at the collar of her traditional Dickens Christmas caroler attire. "Can we speed this up? I'm roasting in this thing."

"Fine," Deidre said, looking down at her clipboard. "We'll move on to our costume review. When I call your name, line up in front of me so I can take one last look at your outfit before we go."

Sully clapped a hand to his head so hard it nearly knocked his mobster fedora off. "But why? We made all the changes you asked us to make."

"I'll be the judge of that," Deidre said. "First up for inspection is our math genius, Tahj Sharuk, playing the role of cowboy, and then after that I'll review our art aficionado, Oliver Harper, in the role of Peter Pan, and then our science genius, Ebon Lavey, playing the role of Mr. Spock."

"Come on, Deidre. Do we *really* have to do this?" Blake asked as Tahj, Oliver, and Ebon lined up in front her.

"Costuming is a very important part of the theater," Deidre said, examining the boys' outfits. "Besides, I didn't ask any of you to do something I wasn't willing to do myself. My Cleopatra, Queen of the Nile, outfit was such a wreck, I had to ask Baylor to completely remake it for me."

Blake turned to Baylor with a puzzled expression and whispered, "Have you lost your mind?"

Baylor shrugged. "She asked me nicely, and it gave me something to do while I was in bed resting."

"Well, that certainly explains why she's being so nice to you today."

"Okay, boys. Your costumes are good to go," Deidre said. "And thank you for lengthening those shorts, Oliver. I'm confident Peter Pan did not wear booty shorts."

"That's fabulous. Mock a person for having a growth spurt." Oliver said, crossing his arms and stomping away.

With a satisfied smirk, Deidre buried her nose in her clipboard. "Next, I need to see, Rafe Ryder, piano virtuoso and fencing expert in the role of Indiana Jones, then, Baylor Wingate, hotshot violinist, playing the role of a peacock, and finally, Blake Wingate, team captain, sports enthusiast, and *dancing fool*, as Zorro."

Rafe and Baylor scooted forward to have their costumes inspected, but Blake folded his arms across his chest, squatted on the floor and toe-kicked his way over to Deidre like a Russian dancer.

"Hey!" he yelled, suddenly springing to his full height and startling his cousin. "Dancing fool, at your service."

"Very funny," Deidre said. Reaching up, she adjusted the hat on Blake's head a little harder than necessary. "You'd better behave yourself today."

"Then you'd better remember not to call me any more names, missy."

Deidre brushed Blake aside with two dismissive waves of her hand. "Now, I'd like to see our literary genius, Audra Monroe, playing the role of a Christmas caroler. Then I'll check our computer whiz, Parker Sutton, in the role of Little Red Riding Hood, followed by our geography expert, Sullivan Cabot, playing the role of a mobster."

Linking arms with Audra and Parker, Sully dragged the girls forward with him. "Fine. Let's get this over with."

As Deidre looked over their costumes, she acknowledged each one of them with a smile and a nod. "Excellent," she said, checking boxes off on her clipboard. "Now, last but not least, I need the members of the Thunder Star team: Neil Trask, playing the role of a ninja warrior, and Mikiko Kaouri, playing the role of a witch. I'm sorry, but since you were on a different team, you'll have to tell me your areas of expertise."

"Are you kidding?" Oliver asked in an incredulous tone as Neil and Mikiko took their places in front of Deidre. "Haven't you ever seen Neil on the soccer field? He's one of the best junior athletes at Ryder-Knight, and Mikiko is in all my art classes. You must have seen her art exhibits. They're phenomenal!"

"No, I have not," replied Deidre, scribbling the information down on her clipboard. "My friends are all theater and performance arts students."

Neil Trask shook a head full of spiky brown hair. "That's not true, Deidre! Gerand Rial was one of your friends, and he wasn't a performance art student. And in case you've forgotten, he was with us when we got here. How do you expect us to do this reenactment without him?"

Deidre's clipboard slipped out of her hand and clattered onto the floor. Gasping, she dug the heel of her hand into her chest.

"Crikey, here it comes," whispered Blake, dropping his face into his hands.

"Not that it's any of your business, but my cousins and I were born and raised in the same town as Rand. We've been friends with him since we were babies! BABIES!" she screeched. "Don't you dare worry about Rand's part, Neil Trask! I've taken care of it! That little shape-shifting fairy, Potts, has volunteered to play Rand's role."

Rafe pressed a fist to his lips to keep from laughing out loud. Potts had been adamant that he didn't want to learn the shape of a dark spirit, but, just like the rest of the cast, Deidre had pestered him until he'd knuckled under and agreed to do her bidding.

"Baylor, I hope that hawk of yours is ready. Is he outside?" Deidre said, retrieving her clipboard from the floor.

"Simon's ready. He's up there." Baylor pointed to the balustrade of the ballroom balcony above them where a magnificent red-tailed hawk perched.

Deidre puckered her face in disgust. "*Ew!* That bird needs to stay in a cage when he's inside this house. There'll be bird poo everywhere, and I, for one, will not be cleaning it up!"

"I think bird poo is the least of our worries," Tahj said, pointing toward the ballroom doors. "What is the Sakal doing here?"

Heads pivoted toward the ballroom entrance to watch the council of eleven angels and one fairy, who oversaw training and instruction in Mystfira, slip into the ballroom.

"As if I don't have enough to deal with this morning," Deidre fumed. "I know I told you people we'd be meeting you at the Brume Theater. What are you doing here now?"

"Oh, my goodness. Look at their wings!" Oliver exclaimed.

Rafe and the other Ryder-Knight students stared at the Sakal in collective astonishment. They did have their wings, and they looked stunning. Although it wasn't unusual to see the madri-kim of the Sakal carrying their ivory scepters tipped with radiant crystals, they weren't wearing their usual colored robes or gowns which matched the tips of their scepters. Instead, they wore quilted white velvet robes nipped in at the waist and trimmed at the bottom with tiny feathers matching the color of their crystals and wing tips.

Deidre stamped her foot and pointed at the Sakal. "*None* of you are dressed in the right costumes for this reenactment."

"Forget about the costumes, Deidre," Sully said. "Why do they have their wings? They never walk around with their wings."

"And they shouldn't be walking around with them now, either," Deidre retorted. "I believe I made myself quite clear to everyone in this room which costumes I expected to be worn today. Did I not?"

Looking perplexed, the angel known as Isabo, surveyed the confused students. Normally, her thick brown braid flowed to her waist in a manner befitting a warrior princess, but today her hair was bejeweled and arranged in elaborate ringlets. A sudden look of understanding flashed in Isabo's eyes. The silver feathers of her robe swept the ballroom floor as she wheeled to face the administrator of Mystfira.

"Madri Typhicus, the children were being punished during our other high holidays and festival celebrations. They've not yet seen us like this."

"Ah, yes. Right you are, Isabo." Madri Typhicus turned to face the children. "The other members of the Sakal and I are attired in our jubilee robes, which are worn on angelic high holidays and festival days. On these special days, we are also permitted to have our wings."

"But . . . but . . . I was told Feadh-Ree was a fairy festival, not an angelic festival," said Deidre.

"You are correct, Miss Dunn, but Madri Fey is a member of the Sakal. Although she is not an angel, we respect her holidays and rejoice with her during her times of celebration," replied Madri Typhicus.

The tightness around Madri Isabo's eyes softened. "There is no need to fuss. I promise we will be appropriately costumed for your reenactment, but right now, we came to speak with you children regarding another matter."

"Can't it wait until the cast party tonight? We need to get to the theater," Deidre said.

Madri Typhicus beckoned the hawk from the balcony with his finger. "It cannot. It has waited long enough."

Uh-oh! Rafe's spine snapped ramrod straight, and his pulse thrummed in his ears as Simon landed on the ballroom floor next to Madri Typhicus. *Not now!*

"We know you are still grieving the loss of your friend, and we share your sadness. Even though he was a dark spirit, we were also fond of Rand," Madri Typhicus said. "That is why we are here today. The longer we allow you students to hold on to the belief that you really know who someone is, the more painful it will be when you discover you do not."

The Ryder–Knight students looked at each other in bewilderment. They had no idea what was coming, and Rafe wished he had the same luxury.

"Sion," Typhicus said, pointing to the hawk. "Please show yourself."

The hawk squawked as his body morphed and grew. Soon, a shirtless, muscular, dark-haired young man with a chiseled jaw and chocolate eyes stood before the Ryder-Knight students clad in a red and brown battle skirt and knee-high gladiator sandals. Two swords crisscrossed his back, peeping out over his broad shoulders.

With the exception of Baylor and Rafe, who had witnessed Simon's transformation once before, the students froze, eyes bulging and mouths agape.

"Simon, or Sion, as he is known in our world, is an animal guardian," said Madri Typhicus.

"That's so awesome!" Oliver said as he stared at Sion. "What about Leopold? And Audra's cat, Pebbles?"

"Leopold is just Leopold," Baylor murmured.

"That's correct, Leopold is not an animal guardian, and neither is Pebbles," Typhicus said, stretching his scepter out toward Rafe. "Now, for one last revelation. Touch the crystal on my scepter."

Looking around at the other Ryder-Knight students, Rafe scratched his cheek and frowned.

Typhicus reproached Rafe with a stern look and a sharp nod. "Raphael Guardian, please do as I have asked."

Stepping toward the madri, Rafe stretched forth a reluctant hand and touched the tip of the madri's multi-colored crystal. He felt his body changing, but the profound peace, joy, and love that he had had experienced during his first transformation did not return.

A strangled cry escaped Parker's lips and Audra gasped.

"You have *got* to be kidding me!" Deidre cried.

"I don't understand," Rafe whispered to the Sakal as the air behind him buzzed with sounds of alarm and astonishment. "This isn't like last time. I don't *feel* like an angel now."

Clutching her turquoise-tipped scepter, Madri Keva moved closer to Rafe. "We are not in possession of our angelic natures here in Mystfira—well, except in the Valley of Shadows. As we have told you in the past, every angel in Mystfira is required to experience human emotions for training purposes, even the teachers," she said in a hushed tone.

Reaching behind Rafe, Madri Typhicus plucked a feather from one of Rafe's wings.

"Oi!" exclaimed Rafe in surprise. "What was that for?"

The madri tucked the feather into his robe. "It is needed."

"For what?"

"I will explain it to you at a later time."

Jerking away from Typhicus, Rafe swung around to face the other Ryder-Knight students. His jaw dropped as he caught a glimpse of himself in one of the ballroom mirrors. Not only was he standing in front of his fellow classmates in the same scanty outfit Sion wore, but Rafe's thirteen-year-old body had transformed into that of a strapping young man of about eighteen years of age. Horrified, he rubbed his face in disbelief and tried to push it back into its proper shape, but it wouldn't budge.

"On Earth, your friend Rafe is an unaware guardian angel," Typhicus announced. "However, here in the heavens, he is known as Raphael Guardian."

The students stared, faces masked with a strange mixture of shock and confusion as they gawked at Rafe's great white wings edged in gleaming silver and the equally impressive muscles protruding from his bare chest and arms.

Rafe could hear all their hearts beating, but one of the children's hearts thudded in a wild, erratic manner. *Which one?* He scanned the group until his eyes settled on Baylor's neck where he could see her pulse throb as clearly as if he stood next to her. Her lips moved, but no sound escaped them. All at once, she swayed, and her knees buckled.

In a mere fraction of a second, Sion had flashed across the ballroom floor to her side. "I've got you," he whispered, catching her in his arms.

Deidre threw her hands in the air. "Oh, my gosh, and you all think *I'm* the drama queen!"

Baylor quickly found her footing and righted herself, shaking free of Sion's grip. Wrapping her arms around her waist, Baylor stared at Rafe as if she'd never seen him before in her life. Her look of betrayal rattled him to the core.

"That's enough. Change me back. Please," Rafe whispered.

The madri touched the scepter to Rafe's arm, and in an instant, Rafe stood before the Ryder-Knight students in his human form once again.

Unable to look at his classmates, Rafe hung his head. "I only just found out about this two weeks ago."

Madri Typhicus nodded in agreement. "That is correct. Rafe did not know he was an unaware angel, and neither did we. Although some of us did have our suspicions, none of us were certain of his identity until the seventh heaven of Araboth revealed the truth and insisted we inform the boy."

"An unaware angel in human form on Earth and now an aware angel in human form in the heavens. *Hmm*," Ebon said, stroking his chin. "That's bound to cause an existential crisis."

Blake threw his palms in the air. "Really, Ebon? What does that even mean?"

"It means he has an IQ bordering on annoying. That's what it means," Deidre thundered.

"Oh, dear!" Madri Fey said, peering into the crystal at the end of her scepter. "Do look at the time. We really must be getting to the Brume."

As if a switch had been thrown, Deidre snapped into theater

mode once again. Jamming her clipboard under an armpit, she clapped her hands and herded her classmates toward the door. "Yes, we do, and despite what we all just heard, the show must go on. Don't just stand there, people! Let's go!"

In uncharacteristic silence, the Ryder-Knight students filed out of the ballroom, and as they exited, Deidre twisted the upper half of her body toward the Sakal. "I will, of course, do my very best because I'm a seasoned performer," she said, "but I want you to know, I can no longer guarantee the caliber of performances you'll be getting out of the rest of them today. If we stink, it's on you!"

Tossing the long plaits of her Cleopatra wig, Deidre turned and strode to the ballroom door. "SIMON AND RAFE—OR WHATEVER THE HECK YOUR NAMES ARE," she bellowed. "MOVE IT! FAIRY FOREST! NOW!"

Coasting past Deidre, Sion winked. "By the way," he whispered. "You don't have to worry about me pooing inside of Cliff House, but I'd advise you to steer clear of me when you're outside. I'm really good at hitting things that agitate me out there.

As a muttering Deidre exited the ballroom, Madri Typhicus placed a hand on Rafe's shoulder. "All in all, I think that went rather well, don't you?"

Jerking himself away from the madri, Rafe stormed after Sion and Deidre. "No, Madri Typhicus," he spewed over his shoulder. "That did not go well. That most definitely did not go well."

Chapter Two
The Brume Theater

Rafe sped along a path in the Fairy Forest, mouth dry and stomach lurching. Normally, the brightly colored, cotton-candy-puffed trees of the Fairy Forest chased away the foulest of his moods, but not today.

He should have run across the other Ryder-Knight students by now. Either Madri Fey had magically transported them to the Brume Theater, or his classmates had decided to ditch him. Judging by the looks he'd gotten in the ballroom a few minutes ago, being ditched was a real possibility. In fact, he'd probably be lucky if any of his classmates spoke to him again. Ever.

A wisp of wind tickled the back of his neck. Swatting at it, Rafe quickened his pace. "Hello—lo—lo, Reef—eef—eef," the Parrot Wind whispered.

A cool blast of air lifted Rafe's Indiana Jones hat from his head and cartwheeled it down the path in front of him. "Stop it!" he shouted, chasing after the hat. "I've told you at least a hundred times to stop knocking things off my head, and another hundred times that my name is Rafe—not Reef."

Retrieving his hat and plopping it back on his head, Rafe heard two familiar giggles above him. Tilting his head skyward, he spied the twin fairies, Poppe and Potts, waving to him.

The little mischief-makers, renowned in the fairy world for flunking out of their beginner fairy classes and having to repeat them a second time, floated above him. Cradled by the wind, they wafted to and fro without moving their wings. The tiny drops of celestial light shimmering in their hair only served to accentuate their adorable faces.

"Don't be mad, Rafe. The wind is just playing with you," Potts called.

"In case you haven't noticed, I'm not in the mood."

"Are you trying to get to the Brume?"

"What does it look like to you?" Rafe said, glowering at Potts. "Of course, I'm trying to get to the Brume."

"Then you'd better come with us, so you're not late. We're riding to the theater on the wind."

"No, thanks. I'm good," Rafe said, doing an about-face and striding down the path in front of him.

"Kayo, but that is not the right way," Poppe shouted after him. "You are inggo to get lost."

Rafe scraped a hand over his face and groaned. He'd gotten used to the little fairy girl getting words with more than one syllable mixed up. More often than not, he found Poppe's speech pattern charming and rather amusing, but at the moment, it grated on his nerves.

"I'm not going to get lost. I'm following the signs," he said, continuing to trudge down the path.

"Um . . . yes," Potts called, "but the Fairy Forest is a big circle. If you go that way, you'll get to the theater, but not today, sometime next week."

Rafe stopped dead in his tracks. The twelve rings of Mystfira fit one inside the other, like a giant bullseye, giving the angelic training ground its unusual shape. How could he have forgotten? Clearly, his recent public humiliation had caused significant brain damage.

Rafe heaved a defeated sigh. "Fine."

Swooping to the ground, the Parrot Wind knocked Rafe's feet out from underneath him, and scooped him into the air, floating him upside down toward Poppe and Potts.

"Stop that! That's not funny!" Rafe said, swimming his arms around until he was right side up again, though still several feet above the ground.

Poppe giggled. "Yes, it is."

"Agree to disagree," Rafe snapped. "Why aren't you already at the festival with your children?"

"Don't rywor. We got our renchild hours goa."

"That's right, don't worry," Potts said. "We got our children hours ago. Madri Fey is watching them until we get back. She sent us to Cliff House to leave some gifts for you and the other Ryder-Knight students because you are helping us with the Festival of Feadh-Ree today. Just wait until you see. You're going to love what we brought you."

The Parrot Wind gave a shrill whistle, and Rafe felt the wind tighten its grip on him.

"Get ready," Potts squealed while the wind crackled and churned around them. "Here we go!"

With a sudden, exhilarating rush, Rafe blasted forward as if from a cannon, his legs flying straight out behind him. Clamping his teeth together and trying not to scream, he streaked through the air with the fairies at his side.

Plunging, dipping, and diving, the wind hurtled through the Fairy Forest twisting the twins' doll-like faces into grotesque caricatures. Ordinarily, the sight of the fairies' windblown faces would have had Rafe doubled over in laughter, but the unbridled power of the Parrot Wind left him stupefied.

Without warning, and just as suddenly as the wind rocket started, it stopped. The cushion of air dissolved beneath Rafe, and he found himself freefalling through the sky, flailing his arms and legs in a vain attempt to slow his descent. *"Whoa! Whoa! Whoa!"* he shrieked, plummeting toward the ground.

All at once, Rafe heard a whooshing sound, and he jerked to an abrupt stop, hovering spreadeagle mere inches above the forest floor. Grabbing him by his ankles, the Parrot Wind pulled Rafe up, flipped him into a sitting position, and deposited him on the ground with a thud.

"And you wonder why I never want to play any games with you," Rafe shouted into the wind.

Poppe and Potts fluttered to the ground giggling.

Glaring at the fairies and rubbing his backside, Rafe felt something stringy thrashing about his mouth and darting in and out between his teeth. He tried to catch hold of whatever it was, but it moved too quickly.

"Oh, my. He has a zort," Poppe said, her eyes growing large.

"Hold on. Put your teeth together like this and smile," Potts said, modeling a skeletal grin. "I'll get it out for you."

Rafe mimicked Potts' grin, and the fairy boy pulled what looked like a slimy, threadlike piece of dental floss from between his teeth. Potts flung it in the air and watched it wiggle out of sight.

Rafe uttered a disgusted snort. "What was that?"

"A zort," Poppe replied.

Taking his sister's hand, Potts skipped onto a nearby path. "It's a type of worm that lives in the air. Don't worry, they won't hurt you unless you swallow them."

"Why? Are they poisonous?"

"Yes," Poppe said. "They will make you ryve, ryve sick."

With his jaw sagging at the thought of what might have happened had he swallowed a zort, Rafe followed the fairies into a part of the forest he'd not yet seen. Giant red and yellow daisies grew along both sides of the path the fairies had chosen. Drooping and tilting their flowers like shields, the daisies outlined the way before them in brilliant color.

Stunned by the beauty of the footpath, Rafe shuffled along behind the fairies in silence. When they reached the last bend of the path, the scenery changed. A twenty-foot-tall thicket of brambles filled with barb-like thorns stopped them dead in their tracks.

"Okay, now what?" Rafe asked, folding his arms over his chest.

"Now we wait for a notgawo to let us in," Poppe said.

Potts nodded like a bobblehead doll. "Yes, now we wait for a woganot. Have you studied them yet?"

"No, but Madri Typhicus did mention something about a woganot to me a couple weeks ago. He said they protect the Mount of Mists."

"That's right," Potts said. "Woganots guard the entrance to the seventh heaven on the Mount of Mists, but they also guard the Brume Theater. Nothing gets by them. No sirree. If one woganot sees something, they all see it. If one of them knows something, they all know it. They're smart like that! You should see—"

Poppe slapped a hand over her brother's mouth. "You are a berjab jaw."

Jabber jaw? Rafe snickered. Potts did have a tendency to babble, and from time to time, it annoyed even Poppe.

"When I take my hand off your mouth, just tell Rafe why the notgawos guard the Brume. Kayo?"

Potts nodded, and Poppe removed her hand.

"There's a fairy portal inside the theater," Potts blurted.

"Really? Is that right?"

"Yes," Poppe said. "You can see it when we get sidein."

"What does your fairy portal do?" Rafe asked. "Does it take you to different places in Mystfira?"

"No. It's much better than that. It can move us through space and time to any universe, but only once a year—on the day you call Halloween. On that day, the Brume Curtain is thin enough for us to pass through it, and we're allowed to go any-where we want," said Potts. "It's how Poppe and I got to go to your Halloween corn maze last year."

Rafe couldn't believe his ears. *A portal? A magical gateway in the Brume Theater?* That meant, despite what the Sakal claimed, in five months there might just be a way for him and the other Ryder-Knight students to get back to Earth.

As Rafe's mind raced with possibilities, the hedge of thorns in front of him rustled, and a hulking winged figure with massive globular eyes stepped out. The eyes met in the middle of the crea-ture's face, reminding Rafe of a dragonfly, and a tuft of shocking pink hair wiggled where a nose should have sat.

The being lifted a flap from over its mouth and spoke. "Hello," it said in a deep voice.

Startled, Rafe stared at the bizarre creature. He couldn't help it. Sunk into every inch of the creature's body, including its wings, arms, and legs, were smaller compound eyes of different colors forming a pattern more beautiful than a peacock's plumage.

"Hello there," Potts said. "We're here for the Festival of Feadh-Ree. May we pass?"

The creature leaned in closer, and Rafe heard a whirring noise as the two massive eyes on top of his head focused on the fairies. "Poppe and Potts, fairies of the fourth ring, you may pass."

"Thank you, and what about our friend over there?" Potts asked.

The tuft of pink hair on the woganot's face twitched as the creature refocused its eyes on Rafe. "*Hmmm . . . how interesting,*" the creature mused. "You are the human child known as Rafe Ryder, but you are also—"

"No. No. No," Rafe said, increasing the volume of his voice with each 'no' and shaking his head. "I am Rafe Ryder. Just Rafe Ryder."

The flap over the woganot's mouth curved into a knowing smile. "As you please, Rafe Ryder. You may also pass."

The woganot waved a hand at the protective barrier in front of them. The thorns made a peculiar crackling noise and shrank away, revealing a long narrow fissure. Poppe and Potts hurried through the strange aperture followed by Rafe and the woganot. Hearing the thorns rustling behind him, Rafe swung around to see the sharp barbs growing back over the passageway and sealing it shut once again.

Inside the protective barrier, the thorny hedge continued, curving in a circle that extended out of sight. In the middle of the ring lay an enormous oval crater surrounded by eight towering stone cisterns. Rushing from the top and down the sides of the lofty cisterns, a smooth cascade of saffron-colored liquid poured into pools at their bases.

Stationed around the inside of the hedge stood an army of woganots and gargoyles at full attention.

Rafe gave a low whistle. "Is security always this tight here?"

"Yes," Potts said. "It has to be. The area above the Brume is a no-fly zone."

The woganot lifted his flap to speak. "The creatures from the Fairy Forest often forget and fly over the theater by accident. The gargoyles are here to keep the innocents from being harmed. We woganots are tasked with the disposal of the more, shall I say, malevolent characters who often try to gain access to the Brume."

Rafe raised his eyebrows and thumbed his ear in doubt. Gargoyles were the fiercest warriors in Mystfira and charged with protecting the angels. It was hard to imagine a woganot being a more serious threat to an enemy than a gargoyle, unless, of course, woganots were somehow capable of staring their opponents to death with their vast collection of eyes.

Poppe bounced up and down in front of the woganot. "Oh, oh! Can we show him how you do it? Can we show him?"

The woganot nodded. "Yes, but only a small demonstration."

Beaming, Poppe whipped a wand from her pocket and chanted,

"A cloth of glitz to the sky,
Zoom round and round, nice and high."

A bedazzled handkerchief shot from the tip of Poppe's wand and streaked about the sky with wild abandon.

Each of the eyes in the woganot's body vibrated and clicked, simultaneously homing in on the gaudy cloth. Without warning, one of the eyes burst from the woganot's torso, and flattened into a thin whirling blade. Bulleting through the air, the now razor-sharp eye struck the handkerchief at lightning speed. Shredded into sudden confetti, the material rained to the ground around Rafe.

"All the notgawo's eyes can do that," Poppe said.

"Impressive. How many eyes does a woganot have?" Rafe whispered.

"Nine dredhun."

Nine hundred eyes? Gulping, Rafe faced the woganot. "Sorry. I didn't get your name earlier."

"It's George."

"George?"

The woganot's eyes whirred and his pink facial hair quivered. "Yes. Is there something wrong with that name?"

"No, no. I was just expecting something a bit more . . . unusual. You know, like Slice, or Rip, or maybe even Shredder, but George is a fine name—a good solid name. As a matter of fact, where I'm from, we even have a little prince named George. I *love* the name George," Rafe rambled.

"A little prince that bears my name?" The flap above the creature's mouth curved upward again. "I like the thought of that."

Rafe returned a wary smile while composing a mental note to self. *Never mess with George.*

"Kayo. It's time to go," Poppe said.

The fairies yanked Rafe by his jacket sleeves to the edge of the gaping crater. Peering cautiously over the rim, Rafe's breath caught in his throat at his first glimpse of the Brume Theater. Like all things in the Fairy Forest, the oval amphitheater provided yet another lavish spectacle.

Three quarters of the luxurious theater showcased multicolored marble staircases, curved passageways, tiered fountains, and galleries filled with frescoed walls and pillars. The numerous seating sections featured giant clamshell chairs, glowing in vivid magentas, blues, and greens, and stuffed with elegant pearl accent pillows.

Potts pointed to the last quarter of the theater, which accommodated a gargantuan vertical ring outlined by a sumptuous green frame. A wispy, gossamer cloud shimmered from its depths.

"That's the Brume Curtain," Potts whispered.

"Your fairy portal?"

"Yes. Isn't it incredible?"

"Beyond incredible," Rafe said. *More like a dream come true.* He chewed the inside of his cheek to keep from smiling like a Cheshire cat as he ogled the portal, trying to memorize every detail.

The grating and scraping sound of stone against stone broke Rafe's concentration. Whirling, he watched as a hidden door slid open near the base of one of the towering stone cisterns, revealing the top of a lapis blue marble staircase leading down into the theater.

The fairies scrambled toward the staircase, and Rafe followed, anxious to see the wonders of the Brume Theater for himself.

Catching a whiff of vanilla and cinnamon, Rafe snuffled the air. "Is that . . . perfume?"

"It sure is," Poppe replied, skipping down the steps in front of him. "This one is made just for Ree-Feadh."

"Where's it coming from?" Rafe asked.

Potts pointed to the stone cistern above their heads. "Right now, the smell is coming from up there. Have you ever gone to the fairy store in Truvian called The Perfect Perfumery?"

"No. Never."

"Well, those perfumes are made here underneath the Brume Theater and stored in fairy vats down there. Some get bottled and sold in The Perfect Perfumery, but when we have special events here, like today, the perfumes get pumped up into the cisterns for delivery into the many fountains found inside our amphitheater. This one is my favorite. It's called Fairy Feadh-Ree. It smells *so* good, doesn't it?"

"It really does," Rafe inhaled another nostril full of the exceptionally light and crisp fragrance drifting about him before making his way down the marble staircase with Potts.

Seeing the variety of creatures milling about in the Brume Theater made Rafe feel like he'd wandered onto the set of a *Star Wars* film. No doubt, he had been accustomed to seeing these other life forms during his previous angelic training, but he had no recollection of that time in his life. Until now, most of them only existed in the pages of his *Not Necessarily Divine Creatures of Mystfira* textbook.

The class, taught by Madri Omega, had started last February with the study of rumbrumies, the large tree-dwelling creatures of the Jungle of Equinox, and one of the few friendly species inhabiting Mystfira.

Madri Omega had allowed the class to visit the ninth ring to observe the hairy orange beasties, known for their excellent sense of smell. Protruding from their wrinkly brown faces, the rumbrumies sported bloodhound-like noses that constantly sniffed the air for interesting scents. But the most intriguing thing about the creatures had to be the long, thick, bushy, stalk of hair on their heads, which concealed a hidden elephant-like trunk. The trunk served as the rumbrumies' second nose and third hand.

With final exams only three weeks away, Rafe wondered how many creatures he'd be able to identify in the amphitheater.

The zombie kids were, of course, easily recognized by their unsightly appearance, what with their skin peeling off in places, but they seemed surprisingly good-natured for the undead.

A group of vampire children congregated in a seating section covered by large light-blocking sails. In addition to that safeguard, they wore long black veils, which floated about them like protective bubbles. Rafe had learned, contrary to popular belief, vampires did not burst into flames when touched by the sun's rays; however, too much light did make them extremely disagreeable and difficult to manage.

Hearing a purring sound, Rafe looked down at his feet just in time to sidestep a baby yeti that had wandered onto the staircase. Since Madri Omega had said the adorable fluffy balls of fur had a tendency to bumble about and get lost in their youth, Rafe helped the yeti back to a seat beside the other yeti children. The fairy charged with the yeti's care promptly plopped into the child's lap to keep the little creature from getting up and running away again.

The next seating section was restricted to two rather repulsive-looking creature types: the muck monsters of Muckrot—with their tendency to leave slimy dirt and goo on everything they touched—and the flaming flignas from the Desert Ring, whose high body temperature often set themselves and things around them aflame.

Rafe quickened his pace as he passed a group of children known as patherics. With leech-like mouths, greenish-brown skin, no noses, no hair, and golden eyes that drooped out of their sockets, their looks could only be described as disturbing. Luckily, the patherics present in the theater today had puffy, distended skin. Madri Omega had advised a swift retreat if you met a patheric whose skin sagged. A famished patheric would not have one drop of remorse for draining your brain's electrical energy and leaving you behind on the ground, comatose.

"Look, Poppe found our children. We have onks this year. They live in the Ring of Ice like the yetis do," Potts said. Grabbing Rafe's hand, Potts pulled him down the steps toward Poppe. "One of the woganots is watching them for us until we finish acting in your play."

A short distance away, Rafe saw Poppe talking to two youngsters covered head to toe by a thick white coat of corded hair. Unless they moved, the onks's furry arms, legs, and facial features remained hidden under their dreadlocks. The creatures reminded Rafe of an oversized version of the mop he and his mother used to clean the kitchen floor.

"We brought some ice for them to sit on. Onks are very pleasant unless they're overheated," Potts said. "Not like the quarreling iffbees we had last year."

Potts stopped pulling Rafe and paused on a stair riser a few steps away from Poppe. "Iffbees are *not* nice," he whispered. "Did you know they like to slap people?"

"I did not," Rafe replied, "but I did hear they have twelve sets of hands."

"That's right, and unless you keep them all busy, they're slapping you with them," Potts said. "They're sitting up there in the way high up sections next to the angelic students."

"The angelic students are back from their spring break?" Rafe said, casting his eyes upward and scanning the crowd. The little rascal was right. The angelic students had returned to Mystfira.

"Is that where you're going to sit after you're done because you're an angel now too?"

A hoarse guttural sound escaped Rafe's throat. "What do you know about that?"

"Madri Fey told us about you and Sion this morning."

Rafe gulped in a deep breath. Madri Typhicus would certainly have told the angelic students about him and Sion *before* Madri Fey was allowed to inform her fairies, so that meant everybody knew.

Brilliant! Rafe stomped down the staircase with Potts and Poppe hot on his heels.

"What are you doing up there?" asked a nearby voice.

Rafe stopped and swiveled to eyeball the crowd around him.

He'd heard Blake's voice as plainly as if they stood next to each other, but he couldn't see his friend.

Potts tapped the back of Rafe's knee and pointed to the floor of the Brume. "He's down there. Every voice from the floor of the theater is amplified and translated into the language of the listeners in the theater. Pretty amazing, isn't it?"

"It is," Rafe said, shifting his gaze to the floor of the theater. He spied Blake and a leprechaun named Seamus standing near the bottom of the blue marble staircase, waving their hands in the air to get his attention.

"Get down here, buddy. It's time to start," Blake said, continuing to flap his arms at Rafe.

"*Keeean!*" Simon screeched, soaring into the air above the theater.

The red-tailed hawk plunged toward the ground in a daring death spiral. Pulling up at the last second, Simon winged his way around the Brume Theater as a cheer rose from the crowd. The hawk shrieked again and came to light on the replica of a fairy mound in the center of the Brume.

Oh, no! That was the signal for the Ryder-Knight students to assume their places. Rafe broke into a jog down the steps, as a smiling Deidre emerged from a tunnel next to the Brume Curtain, waving and blowing kisses to the audience.

One by one, the other costumed Ryder-Knight students appeared, parading along behind their fearless leader, smiling and waving to the crowd per Deidre's instructions.

"I'll be there in just a minute. Sorry," Rafe called down to Blake and Seamus.

Seamus tottered over to the bottom of the staircase and struck it with his shillelagh. "I tink not," the leprechaun said. "Yer comin' down now."

The stair risers tilted at a steep angle beneath Rafe's feet and disappeared, turning the staircase into a slick marble slide. Losing their footing, Poppe and Potts collided with the back of Rafe's legs, sending him into a headlong plunge down the slippery blue slope. Clinging to Rafe's legs like riders on a runaway toboggan, the little fairies hung on for dear life.

Sliding onto the floor at the bottom of the theater with Poppe and Potts still clinging to the back of his legs, Rafe landed with a mouthful of dirt. Spitting it out, he pushed his chest off the ground with his elbows and scrambled to get his knees underneath himself. The next thing he knew, a cold spray of water, accompanied by high-pitched wails and screeches walloped him to the ground again.

Coughing and sputtering, Rafe lifted his head, staring into the culprit—a splendid glass aquarium, which encircled the entire base of the amphitheater. Dozens of half-fish, half-human creatures with sea-foam green hair alternated between splashing the top of the water with their tails and screaming when their heads broke the surface.

Potts and Poppe sprang to their feet bowing and curtsying.

"Dat's da way da sea banshees express der appreciation fer a performance," said the leprechaun. "Stand up der and take yer bow."

Soaking wet and shaking the water out of his hair, Rafe rose, eyes probing the water tank in front of him. The aquarium held every water creature imaginable from the Valley of Waterfalls and the Sea of Umber. Besides the sea banshees, Rafe saw mermaids, mermen, selkies, sirens, water nymphs, kelpies, and naiads.

With his last bit of dignity seeping away, Rafe executed an awkward bow before sloshing his way over to the fairy mound.

As he took his place next to Blake and Baylor, a canopy of white mist formed above the Brume Theater, and a sudden hush fell over the crowd.

Dropping out of the billowing fog, a large luminous cloud with a glistening center descended, holding an orchestra of fairy musicians and their instruments. The maestro waved his baton and the fairy orchestra struck a powerful chord. The chord grew louder and louder until the center of the cloud burst open, showering the theater's awed spectators with fairy glitter.

"And dat's why dey call it da Brume. Ya never know what will be comin' out of da mist up der," Seamus said as the fairy orchestra began to play.

Since Rafe's father had been a world-renowned concert pianist, Rafe had been around orchestra instruments all of his life. He recognized the harps, lutes, wind chimes, tin whistles, recorders, celestas, glockenspiels, and drums hovering above him, but he had no explanation for the magical sounds the fairy musicians were able to produce with them.

The enchanting music began light, airy, and delicate, but then it changed, steadily building toward a mysterious and spellbinding climax. Just as the musical piece ended, a second cloud descended and exploded into a dazzling display of fairy fireworks.

In the midst of a spectacular rose-shaped fire flower, Madri Fey drifted to the ground, waving her scepter in greeting.

"Most honored guests," Madri Fey said, as her feet touched the floor of the Brume. "We welcome you to the Festival of Feadh-Ree."

A raucous cheer arose from the crowd.

Nodding and smiling, Madri Fey smoothed her gauzy yellow gown and waited for the children's excitement to subside.

"Thank you, dear ones. Thank you. We are delighted you have chosen to spend the Festival of Feadh-Ree here with us. We promise you all an unforgettable experience, and we've so much to share with you today. Activities, a sumptuous banquet, a magic show—"

"Ice cream?" shouted a voice from the crowd.

"Absolutely," Madri Fey said. "No visit to the Fairy Forest would be complete without a stop at our famous ice cream caves."

A wild roar of approval erupted from the children.

"Now, for your entertainment pleasure, we begin today's celebration with something very special—a reenactment of how the human children, whom you see standing here before you today, came to reside in our realm.

"Our story begins last October on the night all fairies and wee folk adore, the night of the Festival of Fajolie when we are permitted to visit other worlds. Many choose to spend this night visiting the realm of human beings, called Earth, to help them celebrate their festival of disguise known as Halloween."

The air around Rafe grew heavy, and he stopped listening to Madri Fey, or did she stop speaking? His body felt tingly and cold. Had it become windy? No, the air was still, but it puddled around him now, thick and suffocating. Something was wrong. He could feel it.

Sion and Leopold must have felt it too. With a raspy screech, the red-tailed hawk shot into the sky and hovered overhead, and Leopold raced away from the fairy mound, adding his guttural growl to the mix.

The ground beneath Rafe's feet vibrated, and an enormous splitting sound ripped at his eardrums. Turning his head, Rafe saw Mikiko, Neil, and Sully fall to their knees. The area around them shimmered and rippled, distorting his view of their images.

Without warning, the distorted area elongated and slowly folded down over the frightened, screaming children.

Breath suspended, Rafe turned ashen as Mikiko, Neil, and Sully vanished before his eyes.

"Time Tuck!" Madri Isabo shouted. "Safeguard the children!"

The Sakal's scepters emanated a weird lightning-like energy as the madrikim of the Sakal advanced toward the flickering anomaly, pointing the scepters over the heads of the Ryder-Knight students.

"Fairies, display your wands!" Madri Fey screamed.

Whipping out their wands, the fairies held them aloft. Madri Fey extended her scepter skyward as well, and a brilliant yellow light shot from it, leaping from one fairy wand to the next in a flash, lighting each one with blazing magic. She shouted:

> *"Send our guests home from this place.*
> *Move them now with utmost haste.*
>
> *Take them out of Theater Brume.*
> *Safely speed them to their rooms."*

With a mighty boom, every spectator in the stands disappeared from the theater.

Whirling, Madri Fey strode to join the Sakal, adding the power of her glowing yellow scepter to theirs.

"Those of you who are able to move, get behind us at once," Madri Typhicus commanded as the Sakal continued to approach the students.

Oliver, Tahj, Deidre, Ebon, and Parker bolted toward the protection of the Sakal, but when Rafe tried to move, he could not lift his feet. They were fused to the ground beneath him.

Baylor's body stiffened, and her breath hitched in panic. "I can't move."

"Me either," Blake said.

"Janey Mack! Tis got me shillelagh," Seamus bawled. "I can't use me magic ta save us."

Suddenly, the ground underneath their feet shifted and rippled. Then, without warning, it shimmered and levitated.

Instinctively, Rafe raised his arms as a quivering spongy mass tried to close over them. Searing pain ripped at his muscles and shot through his bones.

"That's it, Rafe. Hold it open for us!" Madri Typhicus said.

"Sion, can you help him?" Isabo called to the hawk overhead.

In the blink of an eye, the hawk changed into his angelic shape. Tearing from the sky, Sion hit the ground beside Rafe with a tremendous jolt, just as the shimmering bulk tried once again to fold over the children.

Sion raised his arms overhead, straining against the force above them.

"How do we keep holding this open?" Rafe asked through gritted teeth.

"You don't. I've got it now," Sion said. "I jarred you loose when I landed. Get Baylor out of here. I won't be able to hold this open much longer."

Rafe shuffled his feet. Sion was right; his feet were no longer stuck to the ground. Responding to a strange gut impulse, Rafe grabbed Baylor by the waist and pulled her out from under the fold. At the same time, Seamus discovered his feet were also free and leaped against Blake's back, rolling them both out of harm's way, next to Rafe and Baylor.

"Can you leave the fold, Sion?" Madri Typhicus shouted. "We're ready to close it."

His body bent from the weight and pain of the oscillating mass above him, Sion shook his head. "No. Do what you must."

The Sakal advanced toward the time tuck, the glowing lights from their scepters converging in vivid electrical patterns. The trembling mass exploded in a whirling vortex of light.

Turning, Madri Typhicus faced the Sakal. "Madri Isabo, get the rest of the Ryder-Knight students back to Cliff House where they are under the protection of the Blue Star. Then return to me at once. I'll need you. Madri Michael, find out who did this, and Madri Keva, find out where those children and Sion have gone."

"Hold on," Rafe said. "I'm not going anywhere until I know what just happened."

"Someone attempted to fold time, and I'm afraid your friends were caught in one of the tucks. I'm sorry," Typhicus said.

Baylor's breath caught in her throat, "Simon?" she whispered.

"Sion," Madri Isabo corrected. "He should be fine. He is an angel."

"What about the others? Are they d-dead?" Oliver asked.

"I certainly hope not. Generally speaking, one does not die in a time tuck. One is simply transported to another place and another time."

Fear crossed Ebon's face. "It's imperative that the place they land have enough oxygen and water in the atmosphere to sustain their lives," he said.

"Indeed," Typhicus replied in a solemn tone. "Indeed."

Chapter Three

Time Tucks

Madri Isabo accompanied the Ryder-Knight students to the grounds of Cliff House and gathered them around her. "I think it's best if you wait inside the house," she said.

"Aren't you going to stay with us?" Oliver asked.

Madri Isabo cupped the boy's chin in her hand and tilted his eyes to meet hers. "No. I have to return to the Brume, but you are safe here, little one."

Smiling in a reassuring manner, Isabo looked around at the remaining Ryder-Knight students. "You are *all* safe now. As long as you remain on the grounds of Cliff House, you are under the protection of the Blue Star. No harm can come to you here."

"But . . . but . . . but . . ." Oliver sputtered.

"Madri Typhicus and I will be back as soon as we find out what happened to your friends. Please, go inside and wait for us in the butterfly conservatory." As Madri Isabo spoke her last word, her body shimmered, and she vanished without a trace.

Deidre turned to Rafe with her hands on her hips. "What's up with that?" she asked. "Aren't angels supposed to fly away, not dissolve into thin air?"

"How would I know?" Rafe replied.

"*Duh*," Deidre said, snorting out a dismissive laugh, "because you're an angel."

Rafe felt the hair stiffen on the back of his neck, and he glowered at Deidre. "An unaware angel, and since I'm not allowed to remember anything about that, I'd say your guess is as good as mine."

"Can we all just please agree to be nice to each other? *Please,*" Audra pleaded. "This has already been a *terrible* day, and I don't want to end it with us fighting with each other."

"Fine. Whatever," Deidre said, marching toward the mansion's ornate pillared porch.

"What's all that stuff?" Parker asked, nodding her head toward the porch.

A large painting in a garish baroque picture frame leaned against the wall of the porch, and two large baskets piled high with fairy cakes sat in front of it.

"It's probably the thank-you gifts Poppe and Potts said they left here earlier today," Rafe said.

"Finally, something you do know," Deidre said, twirling to face Rafe.

Stepping between Rafe and Deidre, Audra shook her head at Rafe, imploring him with her eyes to remain silent.

Clenching his fists at his side, Rafe gulped in a deep breath and held it along with his tongue.

Zipping around the other children, Oliver dashed up the stairs to examine the thank-you gifts. "Oh, my stars!" he exclaimed. "Look at that painting! If I didn't know better, I'd say that was a Jackson Pollock original. Is it not fabulous?"

Oliver's eyes scoured the canvas as the other children joined him on the porch.

"It's a mess. A two-year-old could have painted it," Deidre said, her voice full of scorn.

Ebon cocked an eyebrow at Oliver. "I'm not as well versed in the subject of art as you. Who is Jackson Pollock?"

"Only the leading force in the abstract expressionist

movement of the art world in the nineteen forties and fifties. He'd drip, pour, splatter, fling, hurl, and smear the paint on his canvas using hardened brushes, sticks, and even basting syringes."

"As much as I hate to admit it, I have to side with Deidre. It looks bizarre," Blake said.

"I don't know. I kind of like it," said Tahj. "Look at the explosion of colors on the canvas. The greens, the blues, the purples . . . and the hint of yellow and red."

Parker squinted at the work of art. "Is that fairy glitter and some sort of thread stuck all over the painting?"

"That's what I meant when I said 'if I didn't know better, I'd think this was a Jackson Pollock painting.' He sometimes used things like sand, gravel, or broken glass to give his paintings more texture."

"Is there any way to know who the artist is?" Ebon asked.

"I don't think so," Oliver replied. "The painting's not signed."

Baylor threw an outraged glare at the group. "What is wrong with you people? We just lost Sion, and three of our classmates, and you guys are standing around here discussing art like nothing ever happened!" Stomping into Cliff House, Baylor slammed the door with a terrifying bang.

Rafe's jaw dropped. Despite what Blake had said to him earlier, he'd never known Baylor to glare, stomp, or slam anything. Maybe other girls did that sort of thing from time to time, but not Baylor. Never Baylor.

"Honestly, that girl has been such a drama queen today," Deidre said.

"Wow," Blake said. "That's the skunk calling the cabbage a stinkpot. You know how much Baylor cares about her hawk."

Standing toe to toe with Blake, Deidre delivered a smug smile. "Newsflash. Baylor doesn't have a hawk anymore," she said.

"Oh, snap," said Oliver.

"And furthermore," Deidre snarled. "I'm sure Sion can more than take care of himself."

Eyes narrowed to crinkled slits, Blake looked as if he might explode.

"Okay, you two. Break it up," Audra said, stepping between the cousins. She picked up the fairy baskets and handed one to Deidre. "We're all upset, but let's just get this stuff inside, change our clothes, and wait for the madrikim in the butterfly conservatory like Madri Isabo said."

"Agreed," said Parker, collecting Deidre's free hand and towing the girl toward the front door with her.

As soon as Deidre's back was turned, Blake stuck his tongue out at her.

"How mature of you," Audra said. "I hope that made you feel better."

"Much better," Blake said. "Loads and loads better."

Expelling the air left in her lungs with a whoosh, Audra rolled her eyes and followed the other girls into the house.

"They're girls, dude. Don't even try to understand them," Tahj said, giving Blake's back a supportive slap.

"I need a little help over here, mates," Rafe said, hoisting the edge of the painting. "This is a lot heavier than it looks."

"We can take it up to my room," Oliver said.

Walking over to the painting, Blake tried to lift the other end by himself. "I don't think we can get this up the stairs, Oliver. It feels like it's made of cement, not paint," he said. "Let's just stick it in the library for now. We'll decide where it lives later."

Tahj helped Blake pick up one end of the painting, while Rafe hefted the other end with Oliver and Ebon. It took all their effort to drag it into the library and lean it against a wall there.

Taking a few steps back, Oliver feasted his eyes on the painting again. "I cannot get over this piece of art. It's incredible! The canvas is full of energy and chaos, but yet, control. Every time I look at it, I see a different image taking shape."

Rafe's brows bumped together in a scowl. He could certainly see the chaos on the canvas. Helter-skelter brushstrokes, drips, and smears of paint, mixed with gleaming threads of some sort and fairy glitter.

"As a whole, the painting resembles a man with some sort of weird hair or headdress," Oliver said, "but when you look at it more closely, you can see so much more."

"I'll have to take your word for it," Blake said. "I'm pretty sure I could put a paintbrush in Leopold's mouth, and he could do just as good a job as that."

Oliver pointed to the midsection of the painting. "You can clearly see the rumbrumie and flaming fligna over here . . . and look, they're sitting right next to three onks."

"Yes. Yes. I see them too," Tahj said.

"*Hmmm.*" Blake inclined his head to the side and eyed the painting. "I don't, but I think I see a patheric in that corner over there. How about you, Rafe?"

Rafe tipped his head to the side and stared at the painting the same way Blake had done. "Sorry, guys. I've got nothing."

Hovering behind the other boys, Ebon cleared his throat before speaking. "I have to say I agree with Baylor's earlier assessment. Although this painting does offer an extremely interesting distraction, it does seem rather crass to be excessively admiring a painting when our friends have become casualties of a time tuck."

Oliver heaved a contrite sigh. "I know. I'm sorry. So, what's the plan now? Change out of these costumes and meet the girls in the conservatory?"

"Considering how wigged out those girls are acting right now, that would be the wisest thing for us to do," Blake replied.

Exiting the library, Tahj, Oliver, and Ebon headed up the spiral staircase, but Blake spotted the fairy baskets sitting on a table in the entrance hallway and snagged one of the small cakes.

Shoving half the cake into his mouth, Blake jabbed the other half in Rafe's direction.

Rafe shook his head. "No, thanks. I'm good."

"Suit yourself, but I don't know how anyone can say 'no' to a fairy cake," Blake said, cramming the other half into his mouth.

Thunk! A sudden, loud thud rang out from the behind the library door.

Blake startled. "What was that?" he asked with his mouth full of cake.

"I don't know. Let's find out." Striding to the library door, Rafe flung it open.

"Maybe the painting fell?" Blake said, stepping to Rafe's side.

The two boys stared into the room. Everything seemed exactly as they had left it.

"Do you think somebody's inside the passageway behind the bookcase?" Rafe asked.

Blake looked skeptical, but he walked over to the bookcase and turned a gold bird figurine at the end of one of the shelves. A hidden door swung open with a creak, revealing a hidden staircase.

"Anyone in here?" Blake called, snapping on a light inside the passageway and looking up the stairs. "Nope. Empty."

Scowling, Blake turned to face Rafe. "Why in the world would you think someone might be in there? Please tell me you didn't tell anyone else about the old servants' passageways in Cliff House."

"No, I haven't said a word to anyone. I promise," Rafe said.

"I guess I was thinking maybe Baylor or Deidre mentioned it to someone."

"Baylor would never tell anyone about the passageways, and Deidre doesn't know *anything* about them."

"What do you mean Deidre doesn't know about them?" Rafe asked, gaping at Blake. "Her mother grew up in this house with your Dad. Deidre *has* to know about the hidden passages here."

"She doesn't though," Blake insisted. "My Aunt Cecily got stuck inside one of them when she was six. I guess it did a real number on her, and she never wanted anyone to tell Deidre they existed."

"Wow," Rafe said. "So that's why your grandparents swore my parents and me to secrecy and told us we could never talk about the passageways or tunnels with anybody else."

"That's right, and the incident with Aunt Cecily is also the reason why Gramps wired the passageways with electricity and installed emergency bell knobs in the passageways and tunnels. That way, if anyone ever got stuck again, they'd just need to find one and keep cranking on it to be rescued."

"But the bells ring in a room in the basement," said Rafe. "How would your grandparents know someone was stuck if they weren't standing down in the basement?"

"The new bell system is wired to ring in the kitchen, the butterfly conservatory, Gram and Gramps' bedroom, Grams' sewing room, and this library."

"And even with all those precautions in place, your grandparents were never able to convince your aunt it was safe to use the passages again?"

"Nope," said Blake, flipping off the light and closing the hidden door. "Grams said it has to do with the psychological trauma Aunt Cecily suffered. Whatever that means."

"Do you think someone could have seen the bell room in the basement and figured out Cliff House has tunnels and secret passageways?"

Blake shook his head. "That room is always locked, and the only key to it is on a keychain in Gramps' pocket on Earth. Plus, I was down in the basement this morning looking for a screwdriver for the telescope Ebon is making. It's locked up tighter than a drum."

Frowning, Rafe knit his brow together. "Okay, so if no one is sneaking around in the passageways, how do you explain the noise we both heard in here?"

"I don't know. Maybe we only *thought* we heard something because we've been psychologically traumatized today, you know . . . like Aunt Cecily."

"There has to be a more logical explanation than that," said Rafe.

"A more logical explanation, *huh?*" Blake unbuckled the sword from around his waist and laid it on the library desk. "You want to know what I think? I think you've been hanging around with our friend Ebon, the boy genius, way too much."

"Me?" Rafe said with a chuckle. "You're the one helping the kid build his telescope. Not me."

"Good point. I should be the one that solves this mystery then," Blake said, staring around the room, "but I need to find some clues."

Crossing his arms and resting his chin on a fist, Rafe's eyes probed the room along with Blake's. After a few moments, Rafe's lips curved into a smile.

"What?" Blake said. "Have you figured it out? I don't see any clues in here."

"I don't either, and that's the point," Rafe said. "The painting was way too heavy for Poppe and Potts to lift, so that means they must have carried the painting to Cliff House using their magic."

"Yeah. So?"

"Remember last week when Baylor let them practice bringing some of the statues to life in the butterfly conservatory?"

"How could I forget?" Blake said, smacking the heel of his hand to his forehead. "The statue next to the banyan tree is still passing gas like it's her job."

"And the week before that, one of the store displays in Seamus's shop exploded half an hour after they tidied it up using their magic. I think the noise we just heard in here must have been a leftover side effect from one of their messed up magic spells."

"Those little boogers," Blake said, peeling off the black bandana mask covering his hair and eyes, and throwing it on top of the desk with his sword. "I should have known."

Rafe grinned. "There. The Case of the Mysterious Thump in the Library has been solved."

"Good, now we can get on with our lives," Blake said, throwing an arm around Rafe's shoulders and strolling out of the library. "Baylor really needs to stop letting those little fiends into this house every time they show up."

"Speaking of your sister—"

"Perhaps I should go check on her," Blake said in a fake British accent. "She seemed a bit out of sorts earlier."

Rafe evaded Blake's arm with an annoyed shrug. "Perhaps you should, and for the record, your accent is dreadful."

"Right-ho. Jolly good! Meet you in the conservatory in a few minutes then," Blake said. Grabbing another fairy cake from the hallway table, he bounced up the steps of the spiral staircase two at a time.

Hoping a snack might improve his mood too, Rafe collected a fairy cake and ate it as he climbed the stairs to his room, thinking about how the day had gone from bad to worse in a matter of hours.

Changing out of his costume, Rafe spun the day's events around in his head. His mind sifted through detail after detail until his brain felt like pudding. Nothing had followed logically since the moment he and the other Ryder-Knight students had landed on the beach in the first ring. In fact, he imagined being stuck in the middle of a black hole would be far more predictable than life here in Mystfira.

Staring at Rafe from the stand of his piano, Sergei Rachmaninoff's *Moments Musicaux* Op. 16 No. 4 in E minor beckoned him. It was a beast of a musical composition. However, concentrating on playing it would offer a welcome distraction. Seating himself on the piano bench, Rafe banged out the stormy piece in two minutes and a half.

Feeling somewhat better, he made his way to the spiral staircase. Halfway down the stairs, a thought struck him. As awful as it sounded, there had been an upside to the day's events: the time tucks would most certainly take the focus off his angelic origins.

Entering the corridor to the butterfly conservatory, Rafe felt a pang of guilt sweep over him. Supernatural or human, only the shallowest creature alive would be capable of thinking about himself after his classmates had been swallowed up by time and taken to who knows where.

It's official, he thought. *I'm a stupid git.*

Still berating himself, Rafe hardly noticed the shimmering stained-glass dome featuring ten beautiful angels above him as he entered the conservatory proper. Nor did he notice the hundreds of graceful wings fluttering about him as the butterflies flitted from plant to plant in the tranquil rainforest ambience.

He took his normal route over a winding grey-stone path that led to a waterfall feature and over a small arched bridge, barely aware of the buttonquail sharing the path with him.

Rounding the next bend, he spotted the other Ryder-Knight students seated under the white-pillared gazebo, their eyes fixed on the magical door connecting Cliff House to the Palace of Angels. It had just swung open.

Rafe sprinted to the gazebo and slid onto a bench next to Blake and Baylor as Madri Typhicus entered the conservatory followed by the other members of the Sakal.

"I won't keep you waiting," Typhicus said, approaching the children. "We have found two of your friends, and they are safe. The time tuck took Mikiko and Neil back to Earth . . . to the second year of their lives."

The children exchanged appalled looks.

"You're not going to bring them back here?" Blake asked.

"No, they may stay on Earth," the madri replied.

Deidre sprang to her feet. "That stinks, and it is not fair!"

"Did you miss the part where they're only two years old, Deidre?" Oliver asked. "They have to do the last eleven and half years of their life over. That's worse than staying here. At least we've only got four and a half more years to go."

"I don't understand," Parker said. "You said we couldn't return to Earth until our new guardians were trained to protect us."

"Yes, I did say that," the madri replied, "but when Mikiko and Neil were two years old, their guardians were alive and well. Thus, the guardians responsible for your friends have left the seventh heaven of Araboth and are protecting them once again."

"But what's the point of that? Won't they both just end up back here again when they're our age?" Audra asked.

Madri Isabo shook her head. "Their guardians have gone back in time with full knowledge of future events. They will keep their charges well away from last year's corn maze."

"But what about Sully . . . and Sion?" Baylor asked.

"We will not rest until we find Sully, and do not fear for Sion," replied Madri Ezekiel. "He found his way back from the planet Keptu and is safe in my angelic infirmary on the Mount of Mists. He had only minor injuries. I'm sure he'll be flying around the grounds of Cliff House within the hour."

Madri Ezekiel's expression turned grave. "However, it is very fortunate Rafe and Sion did not allow time to fold over you and your brother, Baylor. The atmosphere in Keptu is not hospitable to human life. You would both have been annihilated."

Blake cringed, and a small gasp escaped Baylor's throat.

Audra brought her hands to her mouth, and her eyes reddened. "Please tell us, Sully did not go to Keptu."

"He did not. He should be on Earth like Mikiko and Neil. In time, we will locate him," Typhicus said.

Deidre inclined her head sideways. "Wait just one minute! If time can be folded like we saw at the Brume, then you can send the rest of us home too. Just fold time back to a few hours before the corn maze began, and our guardians will be able to leave Araboth and keep us from going to the corn maze too."

"There is only one problem with that idea, Miss Dunn. Angels do not fold time," Typhicus replied. "We do not possess the knowledge or the ability."

Deidre glared at the Sakal as Typhicus continued to speak. "Angelic students are taught about time tucks and how to close them in the last year of their angelic training in a master class called Advanced Divine Physics. However, we seem to have no choice but to address them today. Madri Michael, would you do the honors?"

Brushing his long blond hair away from his face, Madri Michael stepped forward. "I'll need a few props. Madri Fey, may I have a piece of paper and three needles?"

The fairy madri waved her wand, and the objects materialized in the air beside him.

Grabbing the paper and needles as they floated past him, Madri Michael said, "I'll try to make this as simple as possible. The *paper* in my hand is meant to represent *time*. We were fortunate that time was only folded simply today. Like this." Madri Michael folded the paper in half. "The *needles* represent *things* pushed through *time* . . . like your friends," he said, pushing the three needles all the way through the paper at different points.

Cupping the needles in his hand, Madri Michael reopened the paper. Rafe could see six puncture marks where the three needles had passed through the paper, three on each half of the paper. "Only three things were pushed through time," Madri Michael said, "but you can plainly see here on this paper, that time was affected in *six* different places."

Ebon nodded in excitement. "I see what you're saying. When time was folded in the Brume, our friends left six openings in time, but if time had been folded in a more complex fashion, there would have been many more openings.

"Yes, excellent synthesis of the information," the madri said, giving Ebon a look of approval.

"So what?" Deidre asked. "Why is that important?"

"It is important because things become complicated when time is unfolded again. Using your friends as an example, you can see there are now six temporary openings left in the fabric of time. These openings are windows of opportunity for dangerous things to be pushed through into our time and space by any dark entity manipulating the folds."

Ebon leaned forward, gazing intently at Madri Michael. "Please elucidate. For instance, do dangerous things get pushed into Mystfira each time there is a time tuck?"

"No, not each time and not through each opening," Madri Michael said. "Usually things only get pushed through when the time tuck is specifically engineered for that purpose."

"That's how the sand whirlpools came to be in the tenth ring of The Desert," Isabo said.

"And that's also how the blanchilts came to reside in the ring that I protect," Madri Uriah said, tilting his head to the ceiling and heaving a sigh.

"The tiny insect-like creatures with a ferocious bite in the twelfth Ring of Ice?" Ebon asked.

"Yes," Madri Uriah said, punching out yet another sigh.

Tahj brightened. "Maybe nothing came through this time," he said.

"That is our hope as well, but at this point, we have no way of knowing if that is the case," Madri Michael replied. "The openings ripped into time's surface remain accessible for several hours, and those openings don't stay in one place. They have a tendency to bounce around."

Blake stared at the Madri with a puzzled expression on his face.

"It's hard to explain, and none of you will understand completely unless you plan to take the Advanced Divine Physics class sometime in the future," Madri Michael said.

"That may be true, but I believe what you're trying to say to us is there is no telling exactly where or when something new may have come through into our time and space here. You won't know until you encounter it," Ebon said.

Typhicus steepled his index fingers against each other. "That is accurate, and since we don't know who created this particular time tuck, we don't even know what we are looking for at this point."

Deidre scrubbed her hands over her face. "What *do* you know?"

"We know the art of time manipulation is known to Araboth and to a handful of other powerful dark spirits," Madri Typhicus said.

"Maybe it's Vexxon," Baylor said.

"No," Madri Isabo said with an emphatic shake of her head. "Vexxon cannot fold time, and he's a kitten compared to the dark spirits with that ability."

Rafe clenched his jaw. On Earth, the dark spirit Vexxon commanded the power of wind, water, rain, thunder, and lightning, but Vexxon was considered *a kitten* compared to the dark spirit that created the time tuck?

Madri Typhicus smiled. "It is also within the realm of possibility that this particular time tuck had nothing to do with the Ryder-Knight students. These things do happen here. It might just be that some of you were simply standing in the wrong place at the wrong time."

"Yeah, I believe that's why we're here in the first place. We were standing in the wrong place at the wrong time at the Halloween corn maze last year," Deidre snarled.

"Wow, great talk!" Blake said. "I feel better. Not!"

Tahj ran a hand across his forehead. "I hope nothing bad came through the time tuck. There are already more than enough dangerous things to deal with in Mystfira without adding anything else to the mix," he murmured.

"The Sakal and I share that sentiment with you, Mr. Sharuk," said Madri Typhicus, looking around at the students gathered under the gazebo. "Please, hear me when I say, we are committed to keeping you safe. Until we know more about the consequences of the time tuck that occurred today, you children will be staying in or on the grounds of Cliff House."

"But classes start tomorrow, and I was looking forward to them," Ebon said in a dejected tone, slumping on the bench.

"I'm sorry, but none of you, with the exception of Rafe, will be attending classes."

"We're stuck in Cliff House? What are we supposed to do around here?" Blake asked.

"It should only be a few days, while we are assessing the threat level," said Madri Isabo.

"Don't worry. We will provide a few classes and activities for you to do here," Madri Fey said cheerfully.

Deidre rose, holding her hands out like stop signs in front of her. "I can't believe you are going to confine us to this house like prisoners! I'm like . . . so . . . so . . . mad right now! I. Can't. Even."

Spinning on her heels, Deidre tramped out of the gazebo. Sporting sour faces and grumbling in loud voices, the other Ryder–Knight students trailed after her, except for Blake and Rafe.

When the others were gone, Rafe folded his arms over his chest, his eyes boring into Typhicus' with icy precision. "In case you're wondering, Madri Typhicus, that little talk you just had with all of us . . . that didn't go so well either."

Blake clenched his fist and stuck his thumb up in the air as he and Rafe turned to vacate the gazebo. "Mad props for consistency today, though, guys."

"I don't think I'll ever become fond of human sarcasm," Madri Fey said, glancing at the other members of the Sakal.

"That makes two of us." A thin-lipped frown played upon Madri Isabo's lips. "I can now see the value of your original suggestion when the children first arrived on the beach the night of the Summoning Ceremony."

"Oh, dear." Green eyes sparkling, Madri Fey covered her mouth with both hands to hide her smile, but her giggling could not be contained.

"Yes," Madri Typhicus agreed. "It would definitely have been easier to turn them into potted plants and keep them in the Presidio until their time in Mystfira had ended. I think it such a shame Araboth would not permit it."

Chapter Four

Alarm in the Palace

Half asleep, Rafe bent over the porcelain sink, slapping cold water over his face until he came to his senses.

He'd spent the night tossing and turning. Every time he'd managed to drift off to sleep, he'd woken, dreaming he heard the sound of servants' bells jingling on the indicator board in the basement of Cliff House.

Feeling a triffle less groggy, Rafe changed into his school uniform. Without bothering to look in the mirror, he ran a comb through his hair and raced out of his room to the Butterfly Conservatory.

Once there, he skimmed over the paths to the magical door connecting Cliff House to the Palace of Angels in record time. As he reached the door, a pins-and-needles tingle shivered through his body.

Not keen to face the curiosity of the other angelic students this morning, he'd come up with a simple plan to avoid most of them. He'd duck into Madri Estel's class before the other students arrived and leave his books on a desk in the back of the classroom. Then he'd hide behind one of the elaborate columns decorating the Angelology hall until class started.

Problem solved. Well, at least until class ended.

Turning the knob of the great wooden door, Rafe pushed, but the door resisted. He turned the knob again and bumped the door hard with his shoulder this time. The door still wouldn't budge.

Frustrated, Rafe reached for the hefty metal doorknocker. Just as he drew it back to rap, a decorative grill slid open above the knocker.

Clicking and whirring, a massive dragonfly eye focused on Rafe through the grill. "Raphael Guardian. You may enter," said the voice belonging to the eye.

"George?"

"Hello, Raphael Guardian." The pink tuft of hair on the woganot's face wiggled at Rafe through the grill before the door swung open.

"Striding through the door with an exasperated sigh, Rafe said, "Please. The name is Rafe Ryder, just Rafe Ryder."

The flap over the woganot's mouth tugged into an inane grin. "As you wish, Rafe Ryder," he replied.

"What are you doing here anyway?"

"I've been assigned to guard this door."

Rafe's brow furrowed. "Why?"

"I'm a precautionary measure."

"Against?"

George chuckled so hard all of the eyes in his body shook. "Against anything really."

"Touché, George. Touché," Rafe said, using a term he'd first learned to say in his fencing classes to concede a point to his opponent after his target jacket had been struck.

"Before you take your leave, I have been instructed to tell you to meet Madri Typhicus in the Presidio after your first class this morning. He says it's important."

"It always is," Rafe grumbled.

Offering George a quick wave of thanks, Rafe scooted through the stately hallways ahead of him until he reached Spokes, the massive circular dining room in the Palace of Angels.

It had earned the nickname of Spokes from the Ryder-Knight students because of the arrangement of the ten long tables, which reminded the students of spokes on a wheel.

"*Bur-ruuup, bur-ruuup, bur-ruuup!*" The palace trumpets blared.

Rafe paused mid step. This was not the usual short trumpet blast used to signal the end of angelic classes. The trumpets urgently sounded the two notes over and over again, one low and one high.

"It's the alarm!" screeched a startled voice from inside the dining room. "Go! Go! Go!"

In a state of panic, the angelic students poured out into the hallway. To Rafe's astonishment, most of them vanished into thin air the moment they set foot outside of the dining room.

Clutching a stack of books to her chest while looking over her shoulder, a girl with a brown ponytail slammed into Rafe, causing her books to scatter every which way.

"Oh, no," she cried, frantically groping to gather them again.

"Here," Rafe said, kneeling beside her. "Let me help."

"Haven, leave the books. We have to go now," said a blond boy scurrying up behind her.

Eyeing the children, Rafe gathered the books closest to him and stood. "Can you tell me what's happening?"

"No. No time to explain," Haven said, snatching the books from Rafe's hand. "Sorry."

Frowning, Madri Estel, the madri in charge of the virtue angels, rushed through the hallway toward the children, her pale blue gown sweeping after her. "What are you students still doing in this hallway?" she asked in a stern tone.

"It's my fault," Rafe said. "I was asking them about the trumpets."

"It's the Sea of Umber, isn't it, Madri? It looked really strange from my window this morning," Diadem said.

"Yes," said the madri, "and I don't have time for any more questions. I need the three of you to transport yourselves to your rooms at once."

Rafe head jerked back in surprise. He didn't have the slightest idea what Madri Estel was talking about. *Transport?*

Wrinkling her brow at Rafe's flustered face, Madri Estel placed a gentle hand on his elbow. "You don't remember how to do that, do you?"

"No. I don't."

"Never mind," the madri snapped. "Haven, Diadem, take him with you—to one of your rooms. Go."

Gripping her books to her chest with one hand, Haven grabbed Rafe's right hand, and Diadem seized the left one.

"My room," Diadem said, looking at Haven. "Now."

Haven's and Diadem's bodies shimmered and turned translucent. Looking down at his body, Rafe gasped. The same thing was happening to him, and it did not feel pleasant. In fact, it felt as if he were between the steel rollers of a coin press machine and having his breath squashed out.

Feeling disoriented and weak, Rafe found himself standing in a tower room with a high vaulted ceiling, a magnificent marble fireplace, a sitting area, and a four-poster bed draped with rich tapestries.

Giving Rafe a gentle push into a soft chair behind him, Haven placed her books on a nearby end table and crouched on the floor next to him. "Where's that bottle of amber your parents gave you?" she asked, twisting her head to look at Diadem.

"I'm on it. I'll get him a celestial spear too."

"Blimey!" Rafe whispered, still feeling dazed. "Where are we?"

"In Diadem's room," Haven replied, peering into Rafe's eyes.

Rafe rubbed his forehead. "How did the pair of you do that?"

"Wow, you really *don't* remember anything, do you?" Diadem said, handing Rafe a green bottle and something resembling a breadstick.

"Don't be dense, Diadem," Haven said. "If he did, it would defeat the whole purpose of him being an unaware angel."

Compassion flooded Haven's eyes as she gazed into Rafe's face. "We just thought of the place we needed to be and transported here with you. That's all. You can do it too. You just have to concentrate."

"I—what? I thought we flew places."

"We do, when we have our wings, but that's not the only way angels get around, silly," Haven said.

"I see." Rafe took a long swig from the bottle of amber.

That's what Madri Isabo must have done yesterday when she shimmered and disappeared in front of Cliff House.

"How are you feeling now? Better?" Diadem asked.

"A little. Does it always feel like you're being crushed to death when you're transporting someplace?"

"Only here in Mystfira while we have these human bodies, and only the first few times. You'll get used to it." Haven nodded reassuringly.

"This is excellent," Rafe said, pointing to the green bottle he held in his hand. "It tastes like honey and something else I can't quite put my finger on."

"The drink is called amber, and the ingredient you're not recognizing is aurora," Haven replied. "Amber helps us angels regain our strength. You'll learn about it when we take our Divine Healing classes."

"Amber's good stuff," Diadem said, planting himself on the

arm of Rafe's chair. "My parents always give me a few bottles to bring back to Mystfira when I'm home. I'm sorry about the celestial spear, though. I ate all the heavenly-flavored ones, so I had to give you an Earthly-flavored one."

Rafe chomped off the end of the strange-looking breadstick Diadem had given him. To his surprise, it tasted like he had placed a forkful of his mother's roast beef and mashed potato in his mouth, and it couldn't have been any more delicious.

"It's scrummy," Rafe said, forgetting not to talk with his mouth full.

Puzzled, Diadem quirked his eyebrows while Rafe continued to devour the celestial spear. "Does that mean you like it?"

Rafe swallowed another mouthful. "It means it's delicious," he said, taking the last bite of the spear.

"I'm glad you like it," Diadem said, striding over to the bank of palatial windows near his bed. Looking alarmed, he beckoned to Rafe and Haven. "Come over here, guys. You've got to see this!"

Sliding to the edge of his chair, Rafe wondered why Diadem appeared so unnerved by the seascape. Surely, it had to be the same view Rafe saw from the tower room in Cliff House, where he did the majority of his homework. Other than the Sea of Umber being a different shade of red every day, Rafe had never seen anything out of the ordinary going on out there, unless he counted the stunning panoramic view from the tower as exceptional, which he didn't, but probably should.

On Earth, the steep rock ledges at the edge of Cliff House's immaculate lawns descended spectacularly to the ocean shore below, but those cliffs paled in comparison to the height and glory of the jagged bowl of rock in Mystfira meant to contain the Sea of Umber. Far beneath the rocky heights, in the center of the sea, sat the small Island of Palades. There, surrounded by powdery red sands, the majestic Mount of Mists rose from its midst to touch the seventh heaven of Araboth.

Rising, Rafe stumbled over to the window with Haven by his side. He blinked in surprise and gripped the edge of the window frame to steady himself. He must be seeing things.

A brilliant orange Sea of Umber churned and bubbled like lava inside a volcano, occasionally spitting jets of viscous liquid upward. Rafe's jaw dropped at the water's new thick consistency and the dreadful grating and groaning noises issuing from the bowels of the sea.

Horrified, Rafe stared out the window with Haven and Diadem. Lost somewhere beneath the furious sea was the Island of Palades. Only the top half of the Mount of Mists could still be seen, wrapped in its usual swirl of gorgeous nacreous clouds.

"This is insane. Look how far the water has risen. It's even buried the Amethyst Palace and the Theoculus," Diadem said in a grim tone. "I'll bet the Sakal is not happy about this."

"What is going on down there?" Rafe asked.

"Hard to tell," Diadem replied, "but I'd bet my life that it has something to do with the Palace of Umber Cascades."

Rafe stared at the writhing sea. "The palace under the Sea of Umber?" he asked.

"Yes," said Haven, studying the scene below. "There is a passageway to the underworld beneath the sea, near that palace. The carrions use it to take the dark spirits they've captured back to where they belong."

"I bet they caught the dark spirit who opened the time tuck yesterday," Diadem said.

Haven shivered. "I can't wait to talk to Alspeth Carrion about what happened down there today. Let's find her right after the Jarvartan Joining and ask."

Tearing his gaze from the sea, Rafe gave Haven and Diadem a concerned look. "Will it keep rising?"

"It could." Diadem said with a solemn bob of his head. "My brother told me that when he was in training, the Sea of Umber flooded Truvian Village. Luckily for the jarvartans, they can transport themselves out of tight situations just like we can."

Haven scratched her cheek. "I wonder if we'll still have the Jarvartan Joining Ceremony today? If the sea level doesn't go down, Madri Typhicus isn't going to be able to move the Theoculus out of the Mount of Mists."

"What is this Jarvartan Joining thing you keep talking about?" Rafe asked.

Diadem looked at Haven with an incredulous expression on his face. "He *really* doesn't remember anything."

"Why do you keep saying that?" Haven said. "Of course, he doesn't."

Taking Rafe by the hand, Haven led him back over to the fireplace. "Sit," she said, pushing him back into a chair. Perching on a couch across from him, she continued to explain. "Toward the end of our first year here in Mystfira, we're assigned a jarvartan to assist us with our angelic duties. They are our helpers, healers, and partners for life."

"It's a little more complicated than that," Diadem protested.

"Shush," Haven said, giving Diadem a dirty look. "I'm getting to it. At the end of our training, if we are selected to be an unaware angel or go for more training as an animal guardian, we lose our jarvartans, and they are eventually reassigned to other angels."

"At the Jarvartan Joining?" Rafe asked.

"Exactly."

"But that's not all of it," Diadem said, pacing back and forth behind Rafe and Haven. "When a jarvartan dies, his or her angel is assigned to someone else immediately. That happened to my brother, Luke. His first jarvartan, Barnabas, died helping him protect Baylor, and then Thomas was assigned to him. He didn't have to wait a year. He couldn't. He needed a partner right then and there."

Rafe sucked in a breath. "Wait, wait, wait! Luke is your brother?"

"Yes," Diadem said, proudly thrusting out his chest. "Luke is my brother, my *full-blooded* brother. He was made to protect Baylor, and so am I."

"How can you know that?" Rafe asked.

Diadem plunked onto the couch next to Haven in an exasperated heap. "Now we have to explain to him how angels are born."

"No, you don't," Rafe said, shaking his head. "You really don't."

"Actually, we do. Let's go," Haven said, getting to her feet and moving to the door.

"But I don't *want* to know how angels are born," Rafe said. "Aren't we supposed to stay here?"

Hurrying past the boys, Haven opened the door and scooted through it. "Are you coming?" she called over her shoulder.

Diadem grinned. "It's all right, Rafe. Her room is next door. Come on. Don't you want to know why I'm *sure* I'm Baylor's new guardian?"

"Not really," Rafe said, getting to his feet and shuffling out into the hallway after Diadem and Haven. When he caught a glimpse of Haven's room through the doorway, the sight of it left him feeling gobsmacked.

It had the same marvelous vaulted ceilings as Diadem's

room, but the similarities ended there. A sumptuous bed and chair rested underneath a large window, and every other inch of wall space was devoted to huge, arched, mahogany bookcases bulging with the written word. A hand-carved staircase spiraled up to a balcony level which accommodated four more walls of bookcases and a reading area with a desk.

"I knew you liked to read," Rafe said, stepping into Haven's room and motioning to the books surrounding him, "but I never imagined anything like this. Who put all these bookcases in here for you?"

"No one. We actually have replicas of our rooms from Araboth. Every angel in training down here does," Haven said. "The Sakal thinks it keeps us from getting too homesick."

Rafe nodded. Madri Fey had done the same thing in Cliff House for the Ryder-Knight students, and he had to admit, it did help a bit.

"Where do you keep your clothes? I don't see any closets in here," Diadem said, looking around Haven's room.

Smiling mysteriously, Haven pulled a book halfway out from a bookcase next to her. To Rafe's surprise, the bookcase swung open revealing a large walk-in closet behind it.

"This room is something else," Diadem said, sprawling on the end of Haven's bed, "but I suppose it's to be expected when nine out of thirteen of your parents are dominion angels, who eat, sleep, and drink words."

Rafe's eyebrows shot up in surprise. "You have *thirteen* parents?"

"I do, but the number is different for each angel," Haven said. "We all have at least eleven parents. It's not like on Earth where you only have two. That's what I wanted to show you." Haven strode across the floor and pulled a book from the shelf. "This is a fiction book from the angelic library, so we can enter the story together. It's called *The Life and Adventures of Caleb Guardian*. I want you to see the birth of Caleb at the beginning of this book. It's an accurate portrayal of an angelic birth."

Scowling, Rafe said, "I thought angels were created by Go—"

"Yes, of course we are," Diadem interrupted, "but we don't use that word here. We don't use any of the proper names for our Creator. Angels only refer to the place our Creator lives. That's why we say Araboth."

"That way we can never dishonor our Creator, even accidently. Honestly, I would think they would let you remember important things like that," Haven said, with her hands on her hips.

Cheeks burning, Rafe lowered his gaze to the floor. "So would I."

"Not to worry," Diadem said. "You've got Haven and me to help you now."

"That's right, and we won't let you down," Haven said, placing the book on the floor next to her. "Open, please."

Shuddering, the book grew to twelve feet in height and flew open. "Welcome," said the book in a pleasant voice. "Please state your name."

"I am Haven Guardian, and I am here with Diadem Guardian and—"

"Rafe Ryder," Rafe said. He had no wish to be called Raphael Guardian another time today. Scratch that. He had no wish to be called Raphael Guardian *ever* again.

"Please choose your characters and step inside my pages."

"No characters today, thank you," Haven said. "We wish to enter the book as a group for observational purposes only."

"Very well. Will you start at the beginning?" the book asked.

"Yes, please."

"Very well. Please enter."

Haven stepped through the gigantic pages of the book and disappeared.

"Let's go," Diadem said to Rafe, following Haven into the story.

Edging closer to the book, Rafe paused. He'd never given a thought to having angelic parents, let alone eleven or more of them. He had a mother and father on Earth, and he loved them beyond all reason. Just thinking about stepping into the pages of the book felt like he was betraying them.

As Rafe continued to hesitate, Diadem's hand snaked through the pages, circled Rafe's wrist and yanked.

Caught off balance by the sudden jerk, Rafe toppled into the book and onto a gleaming white floor in a large circular room surrounded by ivory arches. An intricately carved white chair with wings sprouting from its back stood alone in the center of the room.

"Thanks a lot," Rafe said, getting to his feet and adjusting his uniform. "Where are we now?"

"In the Palace of Araboth in the Creation Room. Look. Here come the new parents-to-be," Diadem said as twelve beautiful angels filed into the room.

"The angels you see are going to help create a new guardian for a boy who has not yet been born, but the process of creation we're witnessing is the same for all types of angels," Haven said, sounding very wise. "These particular angels have been summoned because they possess certain characteristics, qualities and abilities that the new guardian will need to protect, love, encourage, and understand his or her charge."

"That's right and each angelic parent is told beforehand

which quality or qualities they are expected to pass on to their child," Diadem said.

"Like what," Rafe asked.

"Oh, you know, things like strength, power, wisdom, courage, determination, compassion, loyalty, perseverance, focus, dedication, athletic ability, musical ability, *et cetera*," Haven said, darting a look at Rafe as she rattled off characteristics.

Rafe watched as a male angel took a seat in the chair. Forming a circle and joining hands, the other eleven angels faced outward, away from the angel in the center.

"The angel in the chair is known as the primary parent," Haven whispered. "He or she is called the Elkevah and is appointed by Araboth. The Elkevah coordinates the other parents' participation and involvement in the child's life, making sure each parent has an equal presence."

Rafe nodded. That did made sense. Having so many parents *must* get confusing.

All at once, regal music filled the chamber, and a feeling of tranquility settled over Rafe. Following Haven and Diadem's gazes, he noticed a brilliant quivering orb of light inching into the room along the ceiling line. When it reached the Elkevah seated in the chair, the orb rained down a strange, sparkling light until the angel could no longer be seen.

"Beings of love and light, let us create together my unique one," said a voice from the light.

Closing their eyes and bowing their heads, the angels' faces and hands began to glisten.

"What's happening?" Rafe whispered.

"It's amazing, isn't it," Haven murmured. "Araboth is joining with all of them to create the new angel. You'll need to cover your eyes; the light gets much brighter."

Shielding his eyes with his hand, Rafe watched as the glistening enveloped all the angelic beings, growing brighter and brighter. As the light intensified and embraced the room, so did the feeling of love—blissful, unbounded, unconditional, infinite love. A love that defied explanation with human words. All Rafe knew was the love in the room felt absolutely extraordinary and beyond anything he'd ever experienced on Earth.

As the radiance grew blinding, Haven, Diadem, and Rafe had no choice but to cover their faces with their arms as best they could to block out some of the light.

Just as Rafe thought he could no longer bear such brilliance, a soft breath blew down upon the occupants of the creation room, and the blinding light dimmed. The orb of light ascended, hovering near the ceiling for a few moments before speaking. "The gift of life has been granted. Go forth with my blessings, dear ones."

As Rafe's eyes once again became accustomed to normal light, he saw a tiny new angel lying in the arms of the Elkevah, swaddled in a blanket of twinkling light.

"Come meet Caleb Guardian," murmured the seated angel, gazing into the face of the newborn.

Eager to meet their new son, the angels gathered around the Elkevah and sang a song of rejoicing for the gift that they had just received. One by one, they took turns cradling the infant in their arms and whispering blessings of their own to the sweet babe.

"There it is. That's it," Haven said, linking arms with Rafe and Diadem and stepping out of the book into her room. "That's how angels are born. The child is then nurtured and loved in Araboth until he or she is sent to Mystfira to learn their craft and fulfill their destiny."

Rafe collapsed onto the chair next to Haven's bed. Still in

awe of what he had witnessed, he pointed at Diadem. "How many parents do you have?"

"Fourteen, but that's nothing. Haven and I know an archangel in Araboth who has sixty-four parents," Diadem said.

"But how many parents we have is not the point," Haven said, leaning against her windowsill and wagging her head back and forth. "What's important is *who* your parents are. Guardians are created for one specific individual alone. A full-blooded brother or sister with all the same parents would most likely be created for the same purpose."

"So, if Luke was created to protect Baylor, it more than stands to reason that I was, too," Diadem said, "and I'll be the first guardian in history who knows his charge before going to Earth. Isn't that crazy?"

"No crazier than anything else I've heard since I've been here," Rafe said.

Diadem's spine suddenly straightened, and he pressed a hand to his stomach. "I just thought of something. What if she doesn't like me?"

"Honestly, Diadem. You worry about the dumbest things," Haven said.

"I can't help it," Diadem replied. "They're making us train in these human bodies, remember? It's not my fault. I hate having all these human feelings and emotions. And don't even get me started on having to use a bathroom here. What a complete waste of time!"

Squaring her shoulders, Haven curled her lip and wrinkled her nose. "You are disgusting, Diadem Guardian. I'm going upstairs to read."

Diadem made a face at Haven as she climbed the stairs shaking her head, muttering about boys. "I didn't see that coming.

Although, I *have* heard girls can be complicated. Up one second, down the next."

"I hate to break it to you, but boys can be equally difficult. Better get used to it," Rafe said.

"I bet you flunked your Divine Reassurance and Encouragement class the first time around," Diadem retorted. "You're not very good at it."

Biting his lip to hide his smile, Rafe turned his face to look out the window. *Entirely possible,* he thought.

Diadem walked to the window and drummed his fingers on the ledge. "Look at that sea. It's still boiling. I'd give anything to be in the Palace of Umber Cascades right now so I could see what's going on down there."

"Well, you're not." Haven poked her head over the railing of the balcony. "And since it doesn't look like we'll be going anywhere for quite some time, you might as well come up here and use my desk to finish your report . . . before *you* flunk Divine Reassurance and Encouragement *your* first time around."

Sticking out his tongue, Diadem tipped his head up to greet Haven with crossed eyes.

"Really, Diadem? Really? That is so juvenile," she said, pulling her head back over the railing.

Seeming pleased with her reaction, Diadem chuckled and looked at Rafe with a straight face. "As much as I hate to admit it, the girl makes a fair point."

"About you being juvenile?"

"No, about me finishing my report for Divine Reassurance and Encouragement class. You want to come help me?"

"But we haven't even started that class yet."

"Didn't you look at the syllabus over vacation? It's due the first day of class," Diadem said. "They wanted us to be thinking about reassurance and encouragement over the break. Sadly, I did not."

"Nor did I," Rafe said, "but what are they going to do to me? Flunk me out of a class I passed already."

"Since you don't actually seem to remember anything, you probably should make an effort," Haven called.

"Maybe later," Rafe said, gazing out the window. "If neither of you mind, I think I'd like to sit here and watch the sea for a bit longer."

"Have at it, but call up to us if anything changes."

"You got it," Rafe said.

Leaning his elbow on the arm of Haven's chair, Rafe rested his chin in the palm of his hand, watching the sea continue its rampage. Despite the tumult beneath him, he soon found his eyelids growing heavy, and quite without intending to, he drifted into a deep sleep.

———◆

"Bonggggg!" The jarring, tinny gong of a large bell jerked Rafe from his sleep. Snapping his eyes opened, he saw a baseball-sized purple eye hovering directly in front of his face. *"Aauurgh!"* he shrieked.

At the sound of Rafe's scream, the eye elongated, jumping back several meters in apparent panic. Turning, the eye sailed straight through the closed door at top speed as Haven and Diadem gawked from the balcony.

"What's going on?" Rafe asked.

"The giant bong you just heard was the all-clear bell, but as to why there was a woganot's eye in my room staring at you," Haven said, hurrying down the stairs with Diadem, "I have no idea."

Rafe slumped back in his chair as a sharp rap sounded on Haven's door. "*Uuugh*, George."

"You know a woganot?" Diadem asked in amazement.

Another *whack* caused the door to bulge on its hinges and balloon from the doorframe.

"Better open it before he busts it down," Rafe said.

Looking as if she might have a heart attack, Haven cracked the door open. In front of her stood an imposing woganot, with only one purple eye blinking from his torso. Wrapped around his head, two multifaceted, bulbous eyes twinkled, and the pink tuft of hair in the middle of his face twitched.

"Hello, s-sir," Haven stammered.

"Rafe Ryder is in this room. May I enter?"

"Of course," Haven said, swinging the door wide and stepping aside.

"Come on in, George," Rafe called. "These are my friends, Haven and Diadem."

"I'm pretty sure he knows who we are," Diadem whispered out of the corner of his mouth. "That's kind of his thing, you know?"

Rafe smiled. It did seem like a foolish thing to have slipped his mind.

"Excuse me for a moment." Standing outside Haven's door, George held up a finger. "Three . . . two . . . one," he said.

As soon as George said *one*, a droning noise filled the air in the hallway as eight hundred ninety-nine multi-colored eyes jetted toward the woganot. Hitting their target full-speed they were each absorbed with a loud slurp, restoring the beautiful colored pattern to their owner's body.

"There, that's better," said George, stepping inside the room. "I've come for you, Rafe Ryder."

"Why? Is something wrong?" Rafe asked.

"No. Not any longer," George said, pointing toward the sea.

Pushing up from his chair, Rafe stepped to the window. "I don't believe it," he said as Haven and Diadem rushed to his side.

"Would you look at that!" Diadem said in a shrill voice. "It's back to normal!"

Haven's eyes sparkled with excitement. "Look! The Theoculus has been opened. That means we're going to have the Jarvartan Joining after all."

"That is correct," George said. "Now, if you please, Rafe Ryder. I am to take you to the Presidio to meet with Madri Typhicus."

Having seen what a woganot could do with only one eye at the Brume Theater, Rafe was not about to argue. "Lead the way, George."

Chapter Five

The Jarvartan Joining

Although Rafe didn't have the foggiest notion where they were in the palace, George navigated the hallways as expertly as if he had been holding a map, and within a few minutes, they were standing at the door of the Presidio.

"I will take my leave, Rafe Ryder, and return to my post," the woganot said before lumbering away.

Rafe barely noticed George's departure as he stared at the door, rubbing two fingers over an eyebrow. "Please don't let the whole Sakal be in there waiting for me," he whispered to himself.

"Madri Keva is the only one currently in the Presidio," called George as he rounded the corner of the hallway.

"Thanks," Rafe said, making another note to self. In addition to their exceptional vision, woganots seemed to possess excellent hearing as well.

Turning his attention back to the Presidio's lavish door, Rafe scowled at the embossed gold symbols taunting him from its frame. It was Anfar, the common tongue of angels and fairies. Every angel and fairy living in Mystfira—except him—could read the language. Lifting his fist, he knocked on the door.

"Come in."

As he opened the door, Rafe saw Madri Keva, the scholarly dominion angel, closing a book and rising from a seat around the Presidio's massive round table. She wore her long flaxen hair swept away from her face and pinned at her neck. Her complexion was that of strawberries and cream, and her long, graceful neck reminded Rafe of his own beautiful mother, an elegant dancer. White wings gleaming, Madri Keva beamed a bright smile and scurried toward him in her jubilee robe tipped with turquoise feathers.

"My dear boy," she said, her voice full of compassion, "I know it has been a confusing few weeks for you. How are you holding up?"

Rafe fidgeted with his hands as the madri gazed at him with her deep brown eyes. In addition to being overseers of good, dominion angels were also recorders of history, and he didn't feel the need to have his anger and confusion documented at the moment.

"I'm fine. Really," Rafe insisted, bending his head to look at his palms. "I was told Madri Typhicus wanted to see me?"

"That's correct," Madri Typhicus' voice boomed.

Snapping his head to attention, Rafe darted his eyes around the room, but he could see no one other than Madri Keva.

"Look to the wall," she whispered.

Following the madri's instruction, Rafe canvassed the circular wall of the Presidio. To his utter disbelief, he located Madri Typhicus *in* one of the twelve floor-to-ceiling landscapes depicted on the wall. He was strolling out of a house in the jarvartan village of Truvian. Sporting his wings and jubilee robes, Madri Typhicus sauntered forward with his scepter extended.

"Presidio," he said from inside the picture.

Leaning backward in disbelief, Rafe saw the madri's hand and scepter leave the painting and enter the Presidio. With a slight twist of his scepter, Typhicus parted the thick border of flowers barring access to the landscapes and stepped into the room with them. "Sorry to be late," he said.

Astounded, Rafe opened and closed his mouth a few times without speaking. The madri had just walked out of a painting on the Presidio wall. *Sure, the Sakal called them 'living landscapes,' but come on!*

"My, but it's been an unusual day," Typhicus said.

"You're telling me," Rafe said, finding his voice. "You . . . you live in that picture?"

"No, of course not. I live in Truvian with the rest of the Sakal."

"But—but you came out of that picture."

"I did. The living landscapes make it easy for the members of the Sakal to get where we wish to go while we are convened in the Presidio."

"I don't understand. You don't live in your palaces?"

"We have rooms in the palaces, of course, but we prefer our house in Truvian. Isn't that so, Madri Keva?"

The dominion madri smiled and nodded at Typhicus while Rafe peered doubtfully at the house in the landscape.

"There can't be enough room for the entire Sakal to live there."

"It's much larger than it seems," Madri Keva said, casting a sentimental look at the picture on the wall. "As you know, looks can be deceiving, particularly here in Mystfira."

"*Ahem,*" Typhicus said, clearing his throat. "I hate to be rude and change the subject, but we don't have much time before we need to be at the Jarvartan Joining, so if you don't mind, I'd like to address a more pressing issue."

Typhicus took a step closer to Rafe. "You'll be happy to know, the Sakal and I believe we've caught the dark spirit responsible for opening yesterday's time tuck. Early this morning a band of carrions found the dark spirit Yaltabolt and a few of his nastier companions in the Desert Ring. I don't know if you noticed, but after we escorted them to the entrance of the underworld beneath the Sea of Umber, they decided to put up quite a fight. Nonetheless, they are finally back where they belong."

"It was kind of hard not to notice with the alarm going off and all," Rafe said. "So, who is Yaltabolt?"

"Yaltabolt is a conversation for another day, when we have more time," Typhicus said.

"So, the Ryder-Knight students don't have to be confined to Cliff House anymore?" Rafe said, feeling breathless.

"That is correct, and since the Sakal has been summoned to Araboth tomorrow to discuss the recent unfortunate events we've been experiencing here, all of our students will be having a free day in Truvian," Typhicus said.

"Under gargoyle supervision, of course," Madri Keva added.

Letting his head fall back and looking heavenward, Rafe let out a huge breath of relief. "They'll be happy to hear that. Can I go tell them now?"

"I don't think you understand," Madri Keva said. "You're attending the Jarvartan Joining with us."

Rafe's jaw went slack. "Why would I do that? I'm an unaware angel. I don't need a jarvartan."

"The primary reason would be that Araboth has commanded it," Typhicus said, "but the secondary reason is that you are once again *aware* that you are an angel. You will be safer here in Mystfira with a friend to call upon."

"We were going to tell you this morning when Madri Typhicus and I taught you the art of angelic transporting," Madri Keva said, "but we were dealing with a much larger problem at that time."

Looking preoccupied, Madri Typhicus placed a hand in the pocket of his jubilee robe, fumbling for something. "Here it is," he said, pulling a silver-tipped writing quill from his pocket. "This is the feather that I took from your wing yesterday. It's been fashioned into a quill pen, and it will be used in tonight's ceremony at the Rocker."

"The Rocker?" Rafe said. "Haven and Diadem said the Jarvartan Joining could not take place unless the Theoculus was opened. It's not being held there?"

"The joining takes place in the Rocker, but your confusion is justified," the madri said. "You cannot recall all the things you once knew about Mystfira, so let me refresh your memory. No one may enter or exit Mystfira without passing through the Theoculus, and the Theoculus had to be opened to receive our guests."

"Guests?" Rafe asked, growing more confused.

"The parents of each angel receiving a jarvartan this evening will be attending the ceremony as well as the families of all the jarvartans that will be joined," Madri Typhicus replied.

Rafe looked at the floor and scowled as stony silence filled the room.

"Is there something wrong?" Madri Typhicus asked.

"Will . . . will the ones that made me be there?" Rafe asked, lifting his head and glowering at madrikim.

"Your angelic parents?" Typhicus said. "I'm certain they will."

Raising her eyebrows, Madri Keva offered Rafe a questioning glance. When he didn't respond, she said, "Would you like to meet them? I would be happy to arrange it for you."

"No, no." Rafe shook his head at Madri Keva until he felt lightheaded.

"But—"

"I don't *ever* want to meet them," Rafe snarled. "They are *not* my *real* parents."

Madri Keva's mouth fell open. She could not have looked more surprised if Rafe had reached over and slapped her across her face. Tilting her head down, she frowned. "Well then. That's the end of it," she said.

Madri Typhicus extended his scepter toward Rafe. "I don't mean to rush you, my boy, but we must leave for the joining now. You will need to attend in your angelic body."

"I'm really getting tired of this," Rafe said, pressing his lips together until they formed a white slash on his face.

"I'm sorry, but you must attend in your angelic form," Madri Typhicus said.

"I didn't mind changing the first time you told me I was an angel, but when you changed me yesterday, it was awful. I didn't feel like an angel at all."

"I know, I know," Madri Keva soothed, her voice full of understanding. "Human emotions are dreadfully hard to navigate, but you will be permitted to feel the way you did the first time whenever you stand in the Valley of Shadows."

"What does that mean?" Rafe asked.

"We simply don't have time to explain all these things right now. We must get to the joining," Madri Typhicus said.

Feeling defeated and knowing there was no sense in arguing, Rafe reached out to touch Madri Typhicus' scepter. This time as Rafe sprouted his huge silver-tipped white wings, the change felt almost familiar, and to his delight, he appeared to be wearing more clothes than he had on yesterday.

Hallelujah!

Swathed in a white robe with silver feathers, Rafe brushed his hand over the arm of the velvet robe, startled at how natural the material felt to his touch and how ordinary it felt to have a set of wings once again. He was about to mention these things to

Madri Typhicus and Madri Keva when his eyes fell on the mailbox of the house in the painting. He read, 'Layhish Taylah,' the Lion and the Lamb.

What? Gasping and biting down a smile, Rafe felt his insides vibrating. He had just read the Anfarian writing on the mailbox and translated it into English.

Spinning on his heels, he rushed to the door of the Presidio and flung it open. He could also read the gold words carved into the door there. "It says, 'Live inside hope—the gateway to all possibilities.' I can't believe it! I can read Anfar!" he exclaimed.

"Do you remember anything else? Do you know what to do with the quill pen?" Madri Keva asked.

"I carry this into the ceremony with me," Rafe said, surprised to find he knew the answer to her question. "And I remember . . . I remember . . . not all angels get jarvartans. Only the angels who are charged with some type of protective duty get them."

"That's right," Madri Keva said, pressing her hands together and bringing them to her smiling lips in excitement. "Seraphim, cherubim, dominions, and virtues have no need for a jarvartan."

"I should remind you about your wings," said Madri Typhicus. "You will be arriving at the Jarvartan Joining Ceremony as a mature angel, so the outside of your wings are white except for the silver tip of a guardian while the inside of your wings are dark grey. Do not act shocked or surprised when you see the other angels. Remember, most of them are still very young, so their wings will be all one color—silver, green, gold, royal blue, orange, or purple."

Rafe nodded, grateful for the reminder.

"Excellent. Do you remember how to transport yourself from place to place then?" Typhicus asked.

Rafe searched the air about him with his eyes as if looking for a clue. "No," he said. "I don't."

"What are we going to do, Typhicus? He'll be too drained to enjoy the ceremony if we transport him, and it will take too long for us to fly to the Rocker with him."

"Not to worry, Keva," Madri Typhicus calmly. "This one time, we'll allow him an alternative route."

Typhicus turned toward the circular wall of the Presidio and parted the border of flowers with his scepter to clear a path to the landscape depicting the twelfth Ring of Ice. "Show me the Rocker," he said.

In a scramble of crystals and whites, the landscape contorted and writhed until another picture began to form. The top of the landscape took shape first, and Rafe could see the twelve different moons of Mystfira, each blazing to life inside the frame with their own unique colors: pale blue, rosy pink, silver, green, red, purple, gold, turquoise, orange, royal blue, yellow, and, at last, the dazzling moon striated with each of the other eleven hues.

The bottom of the landscape came into focus next, and there sat the Adomis stadium fashioned from a radiant blue diamond of unimaginable size nestled between two overlapping intersecting spheres, one of burning fire and the other of frigid ice.

Rafe felt his heart skip a beat. The Rocker. He *recognized* the stadium . . . the splendid arena where the angels performed their sacred duty to humankind. In fact, although he had never set foot in the place since he'd arrived in Mystfira, he remembered being there many times.

"Show me the floor of the Rocker," Madri Typhicus said.

As the landscape morphed again, vivid memories of the Rocker and Adomis rushed through Rafe's mind. Seven times a year specially chosen angels and dark spirits competed against each other in Adomis trials for a chance to unleash miracles or disasters onto the Earth.

Spadroons and bucklers fought to deliver the slightest touch of their swords to the opponents on the Rocker's pitch, earning arrows for their team with each tap. On the sidelines, a team archer with psychic abilities fired the arrows toward a randomly lit target, similar to a bullseye, a hundred meters away. If, and only if, the arrow traveled through a circle that was lit at the time, a point would be awarded. Each point for the angels equaled a miracle for the Earthly realm if the angelic team won the trial, and conversely, each point for the dark spirits spelled a disaster for the Earthly realm if the dark spirits emerged victorious.

The trickiest part of Adomis was the unpredictability of the stadium floor. It changed for each trial and was usually quite dangerous and challenging. The trials occurring on the head of a pin, a field of mines, and a buzz saw had been particularly exciting to watch and placed untold demands on the angels and dark spirits proving themselves in the arena that day.

A flash of memory leapt into Rafe's mind just before the stadium floor came into focus. "The floor will be blue marble," he murmured. "It's always blue marble for the joining."

Madri Keva smiled at him. "You remember?"

"Yes," Rafe said, stepping toward the Presidio wall, and gaping in awe at the new picture. The blue marble floors he'd predicted glinted back at him.

Next to the interior walls on one side of the stadium stood hundreds of beginner angels, each stepping onto a colorful tile of moonlight situated slightly above the blue marble floor. On the other side of the arena, mounting their own pieces of moonlight stood the jarvartans, waiting for the joining to begin.

Stationed on either end of the arena, Rafe noted the druri boxes—the unbreakable glass boxes that whizzed around the arena providing an up-close view of the Adomis trials for a special group of angels and dark spirits known as the Board of Adjudicators. Once a team emerged victorious, the dark spirits or the angels on the Board of Adjudicators decided which miracles or disasters would eventually befall Earth.

Today, a gargantuan parchment scroll, suspended in midair next to an inkpot of stardust, looped down over one druri box, and ten members of the Sakal congregated next to the druri box at the other end of the stadium.

The corners of Rafe's lips tugged into a smile. "I think I *almost* remember this."

"That's excellent," Madri Typhicus said.

"Don't try to force it," Madri Keva cautioned. "Let the memories come if they wish to."

Closing his eyes, Rafe listened to the burbling of thousands of excited angels and jarvartans in the stadium stands. A slight breeze wafted out of the living landscape, and Rafe sniffed the air like a dog catching a scent. A concoction of different food aromas caused his mouth to water.

Refreshments in the Rocker?

Rafe's eyes snapped open. "Why do I smell food? Angels from Araboth don't have to eat," he said.

"You are correct," Typhicus replied. "They don't *have* to eat, but every angel visiting Mystfira is once again required to experience human emotions while they are here. I'm sure you can understand their nostalgia for the treats they had in Mystfira as children—hence why we have it available for them."

Chewing his bottom lip, Rafe cleared his throat to get rid of the lump forming there and scanned the floor of the arena again.

He understood all too well what the madri meant. Even in his angelic form, he'd give anything to taste his mother's tea biscuit cake again.

"Look," he said, hoping to change the subject by pointing to a crowd of children in the picture. "Haven and Diadem are over there."

"Your eyes are just as sharp as ever," Madri Keva replied. "Would you like to stand with them for the joining?"

"Yes, please."

"Then you shall." Madri Typhicus passed Rafe the quill pen and turned his attention to the painting. "Show me an empty area in the arena next to Haven Guardian and Diadem Guardian."

The living landscape quickly obliged, organizing itself into a new view of the arena floor.

"Madri Keva will go first. Please follow her. Mind you, I'll be right behind you, so step lively," instructed Madri Typhicus.

Following Madri Keva's lead, Rafe trudged through the open flower border. He held his breath, expecting to feel a painful flattening as he went through the landscape, but as he stepped through the picture and onto the marble floor of the Rocker next to Haven and Diadem, he was pleasantly surprised to have felt nothing at all.

"By the twelve moons of Mystfira! Is that you, Rafe?" Haven asked, eyeballs bulging. "You look ... ho—holder. I mean ... older."

"I'm pretty sure she was about to say hot," Diadem said, staring at Rafe too.

"I was not!" Haven said, needling Diadem with her elbow and blushing.

"Why ever not?" Madri Keva asked. "He's a very handsome angel."

A mortified tingling swept up the back of Rafe's neck. "Okay, we're done here."

"Indeed," Madri Typhicus said in a droll tone, "and as fascinated as I am with this conversation, it is, thankfully, time for the ceremony to commence. Madri Keva, please take your place in the druri box. Rafe, please step onto that silver tile of moonlight next to your friends."

Turning his back to them, Madri Typhicus strolled to the middle of the arena floor with his scepter raised skyward. The few remaining angels and jarvartans who had not yet found their places scurried onto their moonbeams, and a hush fell over the stadium.

"Welcome, one. Welcome, all. Welcome to the Jarvartan Joining Ceremony," Madri Typhicus said, lowering his scepter. "Let us begin. Those angels who are about to be joined, hold forth your quills."

Raising his arm, Rafe held his quill aloft with the other angels. Madri Typhicus tapped his scepter on the floor and Rafe felt the sliver-tipped quill being tugged from his fingertips.

A cheer rose from the crowd as a colorful snowstorm of feathers swooshed into the air, whirling madly around the arena. Madri Typhicus tapped his scepter once again, and the flurry of feathers swarmed to the center of the stadium floor. There, floating down to sit at the madri's feet, the quill pens became a gargantuan haystack of plumes.

Madri Typhicus tipped his head heavenward. "We await the decisions of Araboth," he called.

A rush of wind blew into the stadium, followed by tiny pulsing and quivering scratches of shimmering light which showered the arena from all directions. Darting about to the *oohs* and *aahs* of the crowd, the tiny dashes of light arranged themselves into one long beam over the stack of quills. Then, remarkably, something within the light beam teased the feathers into the air, where they floated.

Flinging both his arms skyward, Madri Typhicus shouted, "It is done! Let us begin!"

A tile of moonlight, balancing a jarvartan boy, shot forward until it reached the glowing column of light. Dismounting the moonlight, the boy placed his arm into the beam of light, and a quill floated down, down, down, until it landed in his open palm.

Withdrawing the feathered pen from the light, the jarvartan released it into the air with a flick of his wrist. Soaring over to the giant roll of parchment, the quill enlarged and dipped itself into the inkpot beside it. Then, in beautiful handwriting and sparkling lettering, the quill wrote:

Mordecai Jarvartan joins with Alspeth Carrion

The moment Alspeth's name was written, her orange tile of moonlight accelerated, carrying her to the middle of the arena to face her new partner. With a glowing smile and bright glossy eyes, Alspeth stepped off her moonbeam. Laying a hand over her heart, she looked at Mordecai expectantly.

Taking one knee before Alspeth, Mordecai placed a fist over his own heart. "I am the one Araboth has chosen for you. I pledge you my life, my devotion, and my loyalty. I will be your faithful friend and trusted ally until Araboth doth choose to part us."

Reaching for Mordecai's fist, Alspeth pulled him to his feet. "May that day never come," she said.

The stadium went wild with applause as Alspeth and Mordecai resumed their places on tiles of moonlight. Waving to the crowd, they flew into a vacant seating section in the stands.

"I've got goose bumps," Diadem said.

"Me too, but if we're going in alphabetical order, it's going to take forever before my name is called," Haven whispered.

"It doesn't. You never know when your name will be called. That's the fun of it," Rafe said, clapping a hand over his mouth in surprise.

"How did you know that?" Haven said. "Do you remember your first joining?"

"Not really," replied Rafe. "Believe me, I'm as surprised as you are about what just came out of my mouth."

Diadem chuckled. "Since we have a couple of final exams coming up, Haven and I volunteer to be your study partners. You know, just in case you accidently remember any of the questions from the last time you took those exams."

"*Shhhhh,* you two," Haven said, shifting impatiently about on her tile.

The children watched jarvartan after jarvartan zoom to the center of the stadium on their moonlit tiles.

Jedidiah Jarvartan joins with Ariyeh Power

Alivia Jarvartan joins with Crystal Archangel

Delilah Jarvartan joins with Shar Guardian

Gideon Jarvartan joins with Jokim Guardian

Jonah Jarvartan joins with Malachi Guardian

Naomi Jarvartan joins with Elias Power

Kara Jarvartan joins with Thaddeus Throne

Declan Jarvartan joins with Obadiah Principality

Reuben Jarvartan joins with Ellabel Archangel

Elijah Jarvartan joins with Nehemiah Principality

Micah Jarvartan joins with Owena Throne

Samuel Jarvartan joins with Levi Power

The list of jarvartans and angels grew longer and longer on the scroll, and still their names had not been called.

"They must have called a hundred names already. Why haven't they called one of us yet," Diadem asked.

"Relax, we're still only half way through," Haven said. "Here comes the next jarvartan."

A dark-haired young man wearing a traditional jarvartan outfit of trousers, cuffed leather boots, and billowy-sleeved shirt rode out to the shaft of light containing the quills.

"He looks older than the other jarvartans. He must have had a partner before and lost him," Haven said.

Narrowing his eyes, Rafe squinted and brought the jarvartan into sharp focus. "That's Thomas. That's your brother's old jarvartan."

"Maybe you're next, Diadem," Haven whispered.

"That would be fine with me," Diadem said, watching Thomas's tile stop at the sparkling beam of light. "Luke always said Thomas was one of the best jarvartans out there."

Reaching into the sparkling shaft, a quill floated down into Thomas's palm. Withdrawing his hand from the light, Thomas tossed the quill pen toward the scroll. Enlarging, the quill dipped itself into the stardust and wrote:

Thomas Jarvartan joins with Raphael Guardian
FOR THE SECOND TIME

"What?" Diadem gasped. "I thought for sure it would be me."

The color drained from Rafe's face, and his breath stalled.

"Rafe, is that you?" Haven asked. "Are you Raphael Guardian?"

"So they tell me," Rafe murmured.

Fragments of memories skipped in and out of his brain. In his mind's eye, he saw himself standing with Thomas in

The Coach and the Footman, walking the red jasper streets of Truvian, and sitting together in The Wind and Wings Tavern. Long before Thomas had been assigned to Luke, Thomas had been *his* jarvartan.

As Rafe's two worlds collided, the silver square of moonlight shot him forward to the center of the arena. Placing his hand over his heart as required, Rafe stepped off the moonlit tile.

With an earnest smile, Thomas knelt before Rafe with his fist over his own heart. "I am the one Araboth has chosen for you. Once again, I pledge you my life, my devotion, and my loyalty. I will be your faithful friend and trusted ally until Araboth doth choose to part us."

"May that day never come," Rafe said, feeling a conflicted strain growing in his throat. He reached for Thomas' fist and pulled the jarvartan to his feet.

Why did things in Mystfira have to keep getting more and more complicated?

Unrestrained cheering and whistling echoed through the stadium as the spectators rose to their feet, celebrating the unusual joining of an angel and his jarvartan for the second time with a standing ovation.

Plastering a smile on his face, Rafe mounted his tile of moonlight and waved to the crowd, as did Thomas, while they traveled to the reserved seating section to observe the rest of the ceremony.

Finding some unoccupied seats in the stands, Thomas put a hand on Rafe's shoulder. "It is good to be back at your side again, friend."

Pinching his bottom lip between two fingers, Rafe drew in a deep breath, and slowly released it. "I'm sorry," he said to Thomas.

"I wish I could say the same, but I can't recall any more than fragments of our time together. I don't *really* remember you."

Thomas smiled. "That is not necessary. I remember you, and that is enough."

Chapter Six
The Valley of Shadows

Leaning his elbow on an out of the way table in the House of Dew, Rafe drummed his fingers on his cheek and looked at the jungle canopy above him. The trees, plants, and flowers forming the comfortable tables, chairs, and benches in the fairy eatery also provided a secluded place to meet, especially this early in the morning.

"There you are, mister. You sure didn't make it easy to find you," Blake said, sliding into a chair across from Rafe and eyeing the food and drink on the table. "Aww, you got me an Angel Slipper and some winrups? *I love you!*"

"Whoa!" Rafe said, pushing the plate of winrups toward Blake. "Don't get crazy."

"Sorry, you know how much I love these things."

Rafe nodded. He certainly did. Both he and Blake loved eating winrups. The treats looked like rocks, but in reality tasted like sweet, sticky buns, and the Angel Slipper sitting on the table waiting for Blake was a frosty caramel and almond concoction his friend was wild about.

"I wasn't sure you'd remember me poking my head into your room last night and asking you to meet me here this morning."

Blake stretched and yawned. "It's a miracle I did," he said, grabbing a winrup. "I hardly slept last night."

"Me either. I spent the second night in a row dreaming about the servants' bells ringing off the wall in the basement of Cliff House. Why couldn't you sleep?"

"My sister's sleepwalking again."

"Baylor sleepwalks?" Rafe asked, watching Blake slurp down his Angel Slipper.

"Wiping his lips with the back of his hand, Blake's expression grew serious. "Yeah. She used to do it a lot when we were little. I thought she'd pretty much outgrown it, but since we got here, she's started up again."

"Why?"

"I couldn't tell you," Blake said with a shake of his head, "but Grams and Gramps always thought it had something to do with stress and anxiety because it started right after our parents went missing."

Resting his elbow on the table and cupping his chin in his hand, Rafe thought about the everyday panic he felt being separated from his own parents. He couldn't imagine how difficult it must have been for the twins, losing their parents when they were so young. Their parents' disappearance had never made sense to his family. How did two well-respected university professors go missing in the middle of their busy day and not leave a single clue?

Leaning back against the bench, Rafe folded his arms over his chest. "It must have been really tough for the pair of you."

"Not really . . . at least for me," Blake replied. "We were only two when it happened. I'm not sure why Baylor took it so much harder than I did, except Grams says she's a sensitive soul, and things seem to affect her more deeply than most other people."

Rafe nodded, mentally kicking himself for feeling sorry for himself all the time.

"Bay's had a bad time of it," Blake continued. "When we

were little kids, she actually thought she could hear our parents calling out to her at night, and then she'd get up and search Cliff House for them."

"In her sleep?"

"Yeah," said Blake. "Anyway, that brings me back to what I was going to tell you. She thinks she can hear Lady Jane calling out to her too. Last night, she came into my room and mumbled something to me about getting rid of the painting in the library, then she went outside and sat by the friendship stump on the lawn and talked to the carving of Lady Jane."

"What?"

"I know. Can you see the dark circles under my eyes?" Blake said, sounding weary. "I don't know what stressed her out yesterday. We both had a flipping fantastic day."

Rafe lifted his eyebrows, staring at Blake. The Sea of Umber had been heaving like the inside of a volcano yesterday, and the Ryder-Knight students had been locked up against their will inside Cliff House, but the twins had a "flipping fantastic" day?

"You should have been there. It was sick!" Blake said, waving his winrup in the air. "Madri Fey changed the ballroom into a humongous fairy water park for us. Oh, and after the water park, Madri Fey conjured up some magic carpet clouds. They weren't like magic carpets at all, though; they were like soft, little feathered nests. And the ballroom floor became this cool aerial view of Mystfira. She let us fly over the twelve rings of Mystfira for hours. It was epic!"

"Let me get this straight," said Rafe, a sour smile forming and then fading from his lips. "You were at a fairy water park in the ballroom all day?"

Blake blinked. "Yeah," he said, his eyebrows bent with confusion.

"None of you looked out a window or went outside *all day?*"

"Nope. Madri Fey got us out of bed wicked early and herded us into her waterpark."

"*Humph.* So, you have no idea what *really* happened yesterday?"

"I thought I did, but maybe I don't." Blake drew in a sharp breath. "Wait! Did the madrikim find Sully? Is he all right? Spit it out."

"No, it's not that."

Pushing up his sleeves, Rafe spent the next quarter of an hour explaining yesterday's events to Blake. To his complete surprise, Blake seemed far more interested in the Jarvartan Joining than he did about Yaltabolt and the trouble beneath the Sea of Umber.

"Aren't you just Mr. Popularity?" Blake said, leaning across the table and glowering at Rafe. "Whose side are you on, anyway? Ours or *theirs*?"

"Don't be a git, Blake. You know whose side I'm on. I *need* to get back to Earth, and it needs to happen sooner rather than later."

"Well, that's going to be awfully hard now that *Thomas* is in your life."

"What are you talking about?"

"Everyone knows the older students in angelic training go to classes with jarvartans," Blake replied. "I didn't know it was because they were *joined* at the hip with you guys, though."

"It's not like that, especially with Thomas and me."

"Really? Why?"

"Because unlike me, Thomas remembers all of his training, and since he's an experienced jarvartan, he's been asked to teach the younger jarvartan students in Truvian."

"I'll take your word for it, but I really, really need to be *sure* your first loyalty will always be to me and Baylor since you're supposed to be helping us look for a way home."

Rafe rested his forearms on the table and snorted impatiently. "Not only am I helping you look for a way home, mate. I've found one."

"Get out of town!"

"It's true. Did you see that giant ring filled with clouds in the Brume Theater the day before yesterday?"

Blake nodded.

"Poppe and Potts told me it's a fairy portal. Every Halloween when the curtain is thin enough, the fairies are allowed to visit Earth for one night. All we need to do is figure out a way to slip through it in October."

Blake's eyes gleamed. "Baylor's gotten really, really good at using fairy magic," he said. "She might be able to disguise us long enough so we can all go through, but that's still almost six months away."

"The upside is we've got plenty of time to prepare, and who knows, if we keep our ears open, we might find another way home before that."

"Like you said, the sooner the better," Blake said. "I'd like to get home before they find another reason to lock us up in Cliff House."

Rafe chuckled. "To be honest, it really didn't sound like you had it all that bad yesterday."

"Okay, maybe we didn't," Blake said, "but just so you know, I have no intention of being held hostage again for any reason."

"I hear you," Rafe said.

Blake folded his hands on the table and leaned closer to Rafe. "So, I have some news too. A few days after you and Baylor came back from the Well of Wisdom, Bay came into my room in the middle of the night. I asked her if she was okay, and when she mumbled nonsense, I got up to look at her eyes, and sure enough she was sleepwalking. When she left my room, I followed her to make sure she didn't hurt herself."

"Why didn't you try to wake her up?"

"Have you ever tried to wake a sleepwalker? It's no picnic," Blake said, rolling his eyes into the back of his head. "When we've had to wake her, she gets really scared. Trust me, it's easier just to follow her."

"Where did she go?"

"She went to the basement and took one of the old servants' tunnels out to the tower overlooking the cliffs. It's a doggone good thing I got up to follow her because that tunnel comes out on a rock ledge."

"Even here in Mystfira?"

"Yes, and she walked right out onto it. Long story short, I kept her from falling off the edge and got her back to bed."

"Does she remember?"

"That's the dickens of it, she never does," Blake said, waving his hand back and forth. "But listen to this, a few days later, I went back through the tunnel and checked out the ledge again. You won't believe it, but I found a way we can get into Truvian anytime we want—without being seen."

"That's brilliant. Why didn't you say something to me sooner?"

"I dunno." Blake shrugged. "It was after you told me you were an angel, and I guess I wasn't sure if you'd rat me out or not."

"You should know better—"

Rafe cut off his sentence as an enchanting young fairy approached their table. "Sir, would you like another Dewdrop?" she asked.

"I didn't order a Dewdrop, but maybe my friend would like another Angel Slipper," Rafe said.

The fairy held up a finger. "One moment, sir. I'll be right with you," she said, flitting past Rafe and Blake.

Stopping at a tiny opening in the jungle behind them, the fairy repeated her original question.

"Yes. I'd love one," came the answer.

Leaning out of his booth, Rafe twisted his head around to see Oliver Harper tucked into a tiny alcove behind them at a table for one.

"I didn't know there was a table back there," Blake said, getting to his feet and peering around the edge of his booth. "You found a sweet little place to hide."

Oliver flushed. "I'm not hiding. I'm drawing," he said, turning his sketchpad to face Rafe and Blake. An unusual fairy flower dangling from the canopy above Oliver's secluded table peeked out from the page.

"Breakfast is on me, guys," Blake said, placing two tiny gold nuggets on the table beside him, and tossing another nugget onto Oliver's table.

Rafe coughed. "Don't you mean breakfast is on Baylor?" he said, knowing full well the Parrot Wind had left a small fortune of gold nuggets on Baylor's windowsill in honor of her bravery after she and Rafe kept the Well of Wisdom from being opened.

"That's right. What he said," Blake said, catching Rafe's shirtsleeve between his fingers. "We got to skidoo on out of here now. See ya, Oliver. Bye."

Dragging Rafe by the shirtsleeve, Blake ducked out of The House of Dew and onto the golden sidewalk of Dressage Street.

"What is the matter with you?" Rafe asked.

"You do know Oliver probably overheard *every* word we said."

"So? Eventually we'll have to tell all the Ryder-Knight students about the escape plan."

"That's not it. I don't care if he knows about that. Oliver heard us talking about the servants' tunnels. No one can know Cliff House has secret passageways. I'm serious. When we get back to Earth, Gram and Gramps will have my hide, and maybe other parts of me as well," Blake grumbled. "If we have to, Bay and I will buy his silence with her gold."

"I'd say you're off to a good start then, but I think you're borrowing trouble. Oliver really did seem to be into that drawing of his. He probably wasn't even listening to us."

"Highly unlikely, but I like your optimism," Blake said, jabbing a finger in the air. "Now I gotta jet."

"Where are you going?"

"The Treasure Trove. Bay talked Seamus into revamping it, and I got roped into helping sort out that wasteland he calls a shop."

"How did that happen?"

"Remember when Baylor and Leopold were recuperating, and Seamus came to visit them every day?"

"Yes, but he wasn't the only one. Madri Isabo stopped by every day, too, and still does."

"Madri Isabo wasn't coming just to be friendly, though. She was helping Baylor learn how to get a handle on her psychic abilities."

"Really? Is it helping?"

"I don't know. Bay won't talk about it with me anymore. She says it's because I don't understand, and I've made one too many wisecracks about her psychic abilities."

"If it makes you feel any better, I don't understand how Baylor does what she does either, and supposedly I'm an angel."

"Anyway," Blake said, glancing at the sidewalk and evading

Rafe's gaze. "I think you know Bay doesn't have a lot of friends, and even though the other Ryder-Knight students have been a little bit nicer to her lately, they still call her the Sorceress behind her back, and she knows it. It's nice for her to finally have a real friend, even if he's not a human friend."

"Now, wait a minute. I'm her friend," Rafe protested, suddenly feeling guilty.

"Yeah, yeah. You know what I mean."

"I'm not sure I do. What am I missing? I thought you didn't like Seamus. You said he was a right old grump."

A smile surfaced on Blake's lips. "I did not. I said he was a *cantankerous, miserable, mean old grump.* Geez Louise! Do you ever listen?"

"Apparently not closely enough," Rafe replied with a lopsided curl of his lip. "Seamus is cantankerous—I'll give you that."

"Bay says he's only like that because he's lonely and doesn't have a family. I kind of believe her. Did I tell you Seamus has been so worried about her that he enchanted the little ring he gave her at Christmas time? I don't think I did," Blake said, answering his own question. "He told her if she were ever in trouble again, all she had to do was twist the ring on her pinky finger, say his name, and he'd be there in flash to help her."

Surprised, Rafe shuffled back a step. "He did?"

"He did, and anyone who wants to help me watch out for my sister is okay in my book," Blake said, stepping into Dressage Street. "If you don't want to be put to work, I'd advise you to get while the gettin's good."

Having nothing better to do for next couple of hours, Rafe decided to follow Blake.

He actually enjoyed Seamus's shop. The leprechaun's collection of valuables, oddities, and curiosities were parallel to none in Truvian, but locating a specific item in his shop was always a hit-or-miss affair, even for Seamus.

It was highly doubtful anyone in the twelve rings of Mystfira would dispute the fact The Treasure Trove was in desperate need of a makeover, especially the lackluster display window. The royal purple drape, meant to block the interior of the shop from public view, sported only a sad little hand-lettered sign: YOU WANT IT? I GOT IT.

"Hey," Blake said as he crossed Dressage Street with Rafe, "I meant to ask you if you took my sword from the library desk the night of the time tuck?"

"No, and no offense meant, but I'd hardly call that sorry piece of metal a sword."

"*Huh,*" said Blake. "I went back to get it in the morning, and it wasn't there. I asked everyone, and no one will cop to taking it."

"Don't look at me. I've got my own swords," Rafe said, "but if I were you, I'd ask Poppe and Potts. You know how they like to *borrow* things."

"Those sticky-fingered little boogers."

"They're probably pretending to be pirates in one of the leprechaun tunnels as we speak," said Rafe, opening the door to The Treasure Trove.

"Whoa! Check this out," Blake said, peering into the shop.

To Rafe's shock, everything in the shop had changed. Three and a half walls of floor-to-ceiling shelving of immaculate and well-organized items greeted the boys. Instead of long, glass display counters strewn haphazardly about the room, three and a half counters sat underneath the shelving. Jewelry, musical items, antiques, toys, housewares, magical items, and outdoor supplies from a myriad of galaxies had each been assigned their own particular spot.

In the middle of the shop stood Seamus and Baylor, closing a fourth glass display case of rare magical powders and potions while another leprechaun looked on.

"Dat's dat," Seamus said, wiping his hands on his red breeches. "Say 'ello ta me friend, Lochlan MacNamara, boys. 'E was kind enough ta 'elp Baylor and me wid da changes ta me shop, which is more dan I can say fer da two of ya muzzy muppets."

"In my defense, I kind of thought this was gonna be an all-day thing," Blake said.

"Oh, please," Baylor replied, rolling her eyes heavenward. "We're in Mystfira. Seamus has a shillelagh, and I know fairy magic. It was *never* going to be an all-day thing."

Baylor walked to shop's window and pulled back the purple drapery. "Now for the finishing touch." Pulling a tiny grain of fairy dust from her pocket, she crushed it between her fingertips and sprinkled it over the display area, chanting:

"Make The Treasure Trove's window a giant collage
To bring in the people from the street of Dressage."

Whirling off the shelves, items flew into the shop's display window and suspended themselves in a symmetrical pattern. Looking pleased, Baylor continued her charm:

"So this window will look totally dope,
Move this display like a kaleidoscope."

Holding her breath, Baylor waited. Thirty seconds later the items reorganized themselves into another eye-catching pattern and continued to periodically cycle through new arrangements.

"There," Baylor said. "Now, you have one of the most interesting windows on Dressage Street, Seamus."

"Ya 'ave da best ideas. I tank ya, Baylor Wingate. Now let's take a look at dat fiddle ya were so fascinated wid earlier."

"And my work here is done," Blake said, holding his hands out on either side of his body in satisfaction. "Let's go, Rafe."

"No, wait. I want to show you what Seamus found," said Baylor.

Seamus waddled toward Baylor carrying a violin and bow. "Do ya play da fiddle, love?"

"I do," Baylor said, eyes sparkling as she took the instrument from Seamus, "but this isn't just any fiddle. This is a Stradivarius violin."

With a look of awe, Baylor slowly spun the stringed instrument around in her hand. "See how red the wood is, and just look at the purfling and edging on the scroll of this violin. It's a true masterpiece."

"You're speaking Greek to me," Blake said.

"How about this, then," Baylor said, narrowing her eyes at her brother. "Seamus's great-great-great-grandfather bought this from the most famous violin maker in history, Antonio Stradivari in the village of Cremona, Italy in 1715."

"Are you having a laugh, or is that right?" Rafe said, walking to Baylor's side to examine the instrument with her.

"What's the big deal, you two? It's *just* an old violin," said Blake.

"A really rare old violin which has unique tonal qualities from centuries of aging and mineral treatments," Baylor said. "I promise, if I played it for you, even *you* would be able to hear the difference."

"I seriously doubt that," Blake replied.

"Let's play a duet ta see den. I'll get me fiddle," Seamus said, scurrying behind one of the counters.

A moment later, a lively Celtic tune rang through the air as Seamus walked around the glass case playing his own fiddle. Springing to a shelf beside him, Lochlan plucked an Irish flute from it and added an airy rasp to Seamus's melody.

Biting her lip, Baylor smiled, listening. She looked happier than Rafe had seen her look in a long, long time. Positioning the violin beneath her chin, she placed her bow on the strings and proceeded to weave another song into Seamus's Celtic tune. It only took Rafe a few moments to recognize the song as Mason Williams's "Classical Gas", one of his mother's favorite songs.

In Baylor's hands, the sound of the Stradivarius bewitched them all. Baylor had already been a violin virtuoso, but the fairy xant she had captured had elevated her musical ability beyond anything possible on Earth—and for all Rafe knew, perhaps even the heavens.

Apparently curious about the marvelous music coming from Seamus's shop, several more leprechauns wandered into the store.

"Get da bodhrán behind ya, Magnus," shouted Seamus to one of them.

With an ear-to-ear grin, a young leprechaun grabbed a frame drum from the shelf and added a complex drum pattern to the music.

Tickled by the musical mashup, Blake locked arms with Rafe and jigged him around the floor until the group finished playing.

"Yer quite good," Seamus said, giving Baylor an admiring look. "I've never 'eard anyone play like dat until now, and I've 'eard a lot of angels playin' in me day."

"He's right," Rafe said. "That was absolutely incredible."

Baylor's cheeks colored as she smiled demurely. Flustered by the praise, she dropped her chin, letting her long dark hair fall across her face like a shield. Peering up through her long lashes at Rafe, she hurriedly thrust the violin back into Seamus's hands and disappeared out the door of The Treasure Trove.

"What did ya do?" Seamus said, glaring at Rafe.

"Me?" Rafe asked, giving Blake a look of confusion.

"Nobody did anything wrong. The girl has trouble owning her own awesomeness sometimes, that's all," Blake said, starting toward the door. "I'll go talk to her."

Before Blake could take a step, The Treasure Trove pitched violently, causing items to fly from the shelves and onto the floors. Outside a low growling quickly grew into a savage howl.

"It's the angels' call to the Valley of Shadows," Blake said, widening his stance to keep his balance.

"We know dat, ya eejit!" Seamus exclaimed, bounding to the door and holding it open. "Anyone dat doesn't want ta get knocked in der noggins by fallin' objects, needs ta get out of 'ere now."

Covering their heads with their hands, the occupants of the stores bolted through the door and joined a crowd of people out on Dressage Street waiting for the call to end.

A faint glowing outline of a muscular body shimmered next to Rafe, and a moment later a winged Madri Typhicus appeared wearing a red and brown battle skirt. Leather arm bracers covered his forearms, and two scabbards containing swords crisscrossed his back along with a heavy shield. Never before could Rafe remember having seen Madri Typhicus look so dangerous and intimidating.

"I must take you to the valley," he said to Rafe.

"Who says?"

Madri Typhicus glowered. "Who do you think might have commanded such a thing? It was certainly not my idea."

"Fine," Rafe bristled. "But if I have to go, then I want to fly there myself."

"That would require my scepter, and I do not carry it to the Valley of Shadows," Typhicus said. "This conversation is at an end."

Grasping Rafe firmly around the waist, Madri Typhicus leapt into air. Swift and sure, his great white wings sliced through the sky carrying them both aloft. As their elevation grew, Mystfira's landscape materialized below, and Rafe saw twelve glowing concentric circles of various colors.

Air shivering around him, Rafe heard what sounded like an invisible broom brushing the sky as hundreds and hundreds of other angels joined the madri's flight pattern.

Soon Typhicus banked north, and Rafe caught his first glimpse of the Valley of Shadows, a long, vast, deep fissure gouged into the fifth Ring of Rock and stretching all the way to the twelfth Ring of Ice. Fiery reds, oranges, and golden yellows striated the two towering rock cliffs forming the jagged walls of the narrow canyon. Etched into the valley floor beneath them, two separate ribbons of blue and red liquid snaked their way along its length.

Spiraling up from the bottom of the chasm, enormous pillars of rock with small flat tops beckoned the angels from the sky. Rafe watched as the angels each chose a pillar and landed on them with solid *thuds*.

Dipping lower, Madri Typhicus winged his way toward an empty pillar between Haven and Diadem. Touching down with Rafe, Madri Typhicus pointed to the valley floor, which had to be at least two and a half kilometers below them. "I cannot stay here on this pillar with you. You *must* assume your angelic body, or it is very likely you will die in the Valley of Shadows today."

Doing a double take on the madri's face, Rafe's body tensed. "Are you mad? No one has shown me how to do that yet. I—I—you know I can't do that," he whispered.

"I have been commanded to leave you here today. As an angel and as your ... madri, it is the most difficult thing I've ever been asked to do. We both must have faith today, Raphael," Typhicus said, placing a hand on Rafe's shoulder. "Everything is possible when an angel joins with the divine mind of Araboth. Remember that."

Giving Rafe's arm a reassuring squeeze, the madri stepped off the edge of the stone pillar and took to the sky. While his strong wings carried him away, Haven and Diadem exchanged looks of disbelief.

A gust of wind swept into the valley and a sudden burst of panic hit Rafe's core as he absorbed the seriousness of his situation.

"We aren't permitted to go to a pillar occupied by another angel, or Diadem and I would come over to help you," Haven called as the wind buffeted the stone columns. "You have to remember how to change into your angelic body. Do you hear me? You *have* to!"

"Believe me, I'd love to," Rafe said, raising his voice over the wind. "I just don't know how."

"Yes, you do. It's just like we do in Celestial Meditation class," Diadem shouted.

"Really?" Rafe bellowed. "I don't recall class being quite this windy."

Hearing a crack of thunder, Rafe spun around to see black clouds entering the valley. As the winds grew stronger, Rafe had no choice but to lower his body to the ground and cling to a stone outcropping on his pillar.

Tucking her silver wings tightly against her back, Haven crouched at the edge of her pillar and called to Rafe. "Listen to me. Calm down and concentrate. Think about the shape you use to anchor yourself to the divine mind of Araboth in class. What is it?"

"The vesica piscis."

"Good. That's good. Make your connection to the divine. *Power, love, strength,* and *intention.* Say it with me, Rafe," she cried.

Rafe closed his eyes as another bit of whipping wind stung his face. "I can't," he said through gritted teeth. "I'm too angry."

"That's okay," Haven shouted. "Use your anger to make yourself stronger. Focus on your connection to the divine, and say the words. *Power, love, strength,* and *intention. Power, love, strength,* and *intention.*"

Bowing his head, Rafe raised an arm to shield his face from the thorny bite of the wind. Not knowing what else to do, he added his voice to Haven's, wholly concentrating on each word as he said it.

"*Power, love, strength,* and *intention. Power, love, strength,* and *intention. Power, love, strength,* and *intention.*" Repeating the words for the ninth time, Rafe felt a strange peace filling his body.

Raising his head, he faced the wind with a knowing smile forming on his lips. There was no more panic. He could feel his body changing. More than that, he could feel his mind transforming as it connected to the undiluted love, power, and pure consciousness of Araboth.

With one hand on the rock outcropping and the other resting on the ground, Rafe easily pulled himself up to one knee as large white wings tipped in silver sprouted from his strong muscular back. Clad in his battle garb, complete with both his swords and shield, he felt, at long last, whole again.

Fully aware of each one of his angelic talents and capabilities, Raphael Guardian stood. "Thomas," he bellowed into the wind.

"Don't do that," Diadem yelled, fighting to stay upright against the wind. "We don't call our jarvartans unless we need them."

Leaning his body into the harsh pulsating wind, Rafe's feet lifted from the ground, and he hung suspended in the air with his arms out on either side of his body. Eyes closed, he smiled, reveling in the familiar feeling.

Thomas materialized next to Rafe. "I see you are required to participate in angelic training exercises once again."

"Hello, old friend," Rafe said without opening his eyes. "I've missed you."

"Indeed, and I you. You do not look as though you need my help. Why have you summoned me?"

"It's the first call to the Valley of Shadows after the Jarvartan Joining."

"*Ahh,*" Thomas said.

"And you know what that means."

"I do."

"I can hear it coming. Are you ready?"

"Always."

The next moment a whirling vortex of air rushed into the valley, and an eerie howl pummeled Rafe's eardrums. Snapping his eyes open and setting his feet back on solid ground, he saw sheets of water pouring from massive clouds ahead of him.

"Call your jarvartans," Rafe shouted to Diadem and Haven.

"No," Diadem shrieked. "It's just water."

Rafe could not fault Diadem for his confidence. Today, no rains of fire, iron, salt, or wax accompanied by toxic fumes would fall, and it would not snow either. *Thank the heavens!*

Snow in Mystfira was the worst! Standing against the glass-like shards of glesh and thick tarry silch would require more help than a novice jarvartan would be able to provide to his angelic friends. But clearly, Diadem was not fully aware of just how powerful *regular* water could be under the right circumstances, nor could the young angel comprehend what was about to happen. Within minutes, Rafe and the other angels would stand against a flood of astronomic proportions, and the beginner students would not be prepared for it.

"Look beneath you. The Blue Wind River and the Blood River are both rising," Rafe bellowed.

"The water won't reach us," Diadem roared back.

"You could not be more wrong," Thomas shouted. "Call your jarvartans while there is still time!"

Glancing over at Rafe and Thomas with uncertainty written on her brow, Haven adjusted her feet into a wide stance, and fought to stand against the wind. Turning her head back to the task before her, she set her jaw and screamed, "Yohanna!"

Giving in to the prodding, Diadem shouted, "Noah!"

Thomas cupped his hands around Rafe's ear. "With or without their jarvartans, they will be swept away," he said.

"Maybe not. Stay back here with them and do not come to me unless I call for you," Rafe shouted, leaping onto an empty pillar in front of him.

Positioning himself on his new perch, Rafe faced the approaching maelstrom, and the air around him filled with chilling supernatural wails. As the winds grew stronger and stronger, the beginner students dotting the pillars ahead of him struggled to remain on their feet.

Rafe couldn't help but flash back to his first disastrous attempt to stand against wind, storm, and flood. None of the beginner students or their jarvartans had returned unscathed from the valley that day; each of them had to be found and rescued. All had arrived in the angelic infirmary bruised, broken, and wounded.

Now directly overhead, the storm's colossal grey clouds unleashed a deluge. The rivers, which only a few minutes ago had been fifteen hundred meters or more below the pillars, surged and a purple foamy slough swallowed Rafe's ankles.

The water grew muddier as it surged up to his thighs. Glancing downward, Rafe saw the last warning sign, small twigs, sticks, leaves, and pebbles percolating around his legs. Hearing a ferocious roar, he lifted his head, spotting exactly what he expected to see, a churning stew of water, rocks, trees, and branches blasting toward him.

Knocked from their columns, the beginner students ahead of Rafe screamed, twisting helplessly in the seething mix.

Scanning the tumultuous scene, Rafe saw a large tree torn from the valley floor, bouncing and shivering toward him with several waterlogged beginner students clinging to it. The tree's root end was so heavy that the tree floated upright in the water. As it bobbed closer, Rafe recognized Malachi, the most athletic of all the beginner students, clinging to one of the branches.

Lifting his arms toward the tree, Rafe willed the wave to bring it toward him. Divine Interventions and Intercessions had been one of his better subjects, and the heavy swell of water had no choice but to obey his command. The tree rocketed toward him. Rooting himself to his pillar, Rafe clamped his arms around its enormous trunk.

He heard Haven and Diadem coughing and gagging as the swift cold water continued past him, crashing over the pillars behind him. He needed to act fast.

"I'm going to turn this tree!" Rafe shouted to three angels clutching the tree's branches in a desperate attempt to stay afloat. "Get onto the trunk of it, and don't let go no matter what!"

Forcing the tree to its side, Rafe held it lengthwise at rib level. The water churned around his makeshift dam, funneling the majority of the twisting current away from the pillars Haven and Diadem stood upon.

Turning his head enough for Thomas to hear him, Rafe shouted, "Do they stand?"

"They stand," Thomas bellowed.

As bits of debris, large and small, began to lodge against the tree Rafe held, Malachi shouted, "You can't hold all this weight by yourself."

"I will hold it!" Rafe roared. "Stay put."

Winds chugging and pulsating, the storm persisted as Rafe knew it would. Minutes became hours, but he held tight, calling to Thomas only when a great weariness had settled over his numb body.

"There you are," Rafe said, when he felt Thomas' back pressed against his own. "How are they doing back there?"

"Much better than we did our first time."

"Good." Readjusting his grip on the tree, Rafe bowed his head against the relentless wind and rain and settled into his new position. With Thomas shoring him up, he could stand like this all night, if need be.

Several more hours passed until Rafe felt the wind and rain abate. He lifted his head to look around. He had been tricked by temporary lulls in storms in the past, and he knew better than to abandon his stand until he was sure the storm had ended.

Everything looked clear, but he waited for the floodwaters to recede before calling to the angelic students clinging to the tree.

Balancing on the tree trunk and spreading their soggy wings like birds after a bath, the battered angels shook themselves dry. Then with a nod and a salute to thank Rafe, they flung themselves into the sky.

Dropping the tree, Rafe turned and caught his first glimpse of Haven and Diadem since the deluge began. A deep gash bloodied Haven's arm, and Diadem's side had been slashed open. "They're hurt!" he exclaimed.

"Their wounds are minor," Thomas said. "Their jarvartans should be able to heal them. You must go now. It is time for you to leave the valley."

"I am not leaving until I know Haven and Diadem are going to be okay."

"Somehow I knew you would say that," Thomas said, shaking his head. "I will go help the young jarvartans with their first healings."

As Thomas turned away, Rafe caught his arm. "You don't need to hurry. I'd like to stay here for as long as I can."

Thomas' eyes registered understanding. "Because you are free from human emotions here."

"Yes, and I know who I am here. I know my purpose. I feel like my old self again," Rafe said.

"Your old self? Have you regained your memories then?"

"Not really, but I remember my skills and some of my classes . . . but mostly I remember you."

Thomas gave Rafe a warm smile. "I am grateful for that."

"I wouldn't get too excited about it, if I were you," Rafe said. "Who knows what I'll remember tomorrow.

Chapter Seven

Whereabouts Unknown

The instant Rafe's feet thudded onto the back porch of Cliff House, his body returned to its human form, and a sudden bone-crushing fatigue washed over him. As he walked toward the back door, Rafe felt beads of sweat popping out on his brow. Without warning, his vision blurred, tilting his world sideways. Head throbbing, he staggered a few more steps and collapsed onto the floor of the porch.

Rolling onto his back, Rafe looked at the sky, which, for some strange reason, was spinning like a pinwheel above him. Something was definitely wrong, but he had no idea what. Burying his eyes in the crook of his arm, he groaned.

Hearing the commotion, Leopold, who had been patrolling the backyard when Rafe arrived, bounced up the porch steps to bestow doggie resuscitation in the form of sloppy, wet chin licks.

"Not now, Leo," Rafe said, nudging the dog away from his face with his free hand.

Sprawling on the porch at Rafe's side, Leopold laid his muzzle on Rafe's chest and whined.

"My feelings exactly," Rafe mumbled, placing his arm around the dog's neck.

Feeling too sick and weary to move, he lie on the porch floor until a faint fluttering rustled the air around his body. Pulling his elbow away from his eyes, Rafe slowly brought into focus a pair of unnaturally green eyes, short curly black hair strewn with tiny drops of light, and a delicate upturned nose. "Madri Fey?" he croaked in a weak voice.

"Hello, my dear."

Rafe blinked and tried to reply, but the madri placed a finger to his lips to stop him from speaking. "*Shhh*. You're home now. Let's get you up to your room."

Shooing Leopold away, she waved her glowing yellow scepter over Rafe and chanted:

> "*Tuck this boy into his bed*
> *Let him rest his weary head.*"

Before he could blink again, Rafe found himself nestled snugly between the sheets and blankets of his own comfortable mattress. Madri Fey stood by his side, her green eyes dripping with sympathy.

"I'm sorry I wasn't here when you got back. I could have prevented this."

"Clearing his dry throat, Rafe whispered, "H-how?"

"You could have touched the tip of my scepter to return to your human form instead of having your angelic body automatically make the shift. Do not worry, my dear. Soon you will be able to transform and transport to your heart's content. Your human body will eventually make these changes with few, if any, side effects, but it takes time," said the madri. "Poor boy, you must feel dreadful."

That was the understatement of the century. Dreadful didn't begin to cover it. When he had been transported to Diadem's room yesterday, the shift had left him feeling drained, but it had been a piece of cake compared to the way he felt at this moment.

The madri perched on the edge of his bed and placed a cool wet cloth on Rafe's forehead. "I'm afraid you're going to have to sleep this off."

Rafe brought a finger to his wrist and tapped it.

"You want to know the time, my dear? It's three fifty-five in the afternoon."

"N-no." Rafe tapped his wrist again.

"Oh," the madri said, finally understanding Rafe's gesture. "How long will it take to recover?"

Rafe gave a faint nod.

"I'd say eight to twelve hours," she said, patting Rafe's hand. "Now then, it's all hands on deck to bring back the injured students and jarvartans from the Valley of Shadows, so I'll check on you tomorrow. Just close your eyes and rest."

No problem. Rafe's eyes flickered shut.

———————

The sound of servants' bells ringing stirred Rafe awake enough to glance at the clock on his bedside table. *Midnight.* Why did he keep hearing those blasted bells every night? Struggling against the profound fatigue shrouding his body and mind, he tried to rouse himself to a more conscious state, but it was useless. Surrendering to the exhaustion, Rafe drifted back into a deep sleep.

Hours later he woke with a start. Rubbing his face, he sat up and dangled his feet over the edge of his bed. Except for the hunger pangs stabbing his midsection, he actually felt quite well.

Stretching, he glanced at his bedside table and stopped mid-yawn. *4:00 a.m.?* If the clock next to him was to be believed, he'd slept for twelve hours. *Twelve hours!* No wonder he was famished. Spokes wouldn't be open this early, but he could raid the kitchen downstairs since Madri Fey kept it magically stocked with the Ryder-Knight students' favorite snacks.

Still dressed in yesterday's school uniform, Rafe padded down the hall to the spiral staircase and wound his way to the palatial entrance foyer below. To his surprise, the library door stood ajar, spilling a sliver of yellow light into the foyer.

Who else could be up at this hour?

With footsteps as light as a cat, Rafe crept to the door and peeked inside. His eyes widened at the sight of a fully dressed Baylor haphazardly winding sheets of plastic around the painting the boys had carried into the library a few days ago.

Hands propping up his chin, Blake sat slumped over the library desk wearing a T-shirt, pajama pants, and a dejected expression.

"Hey, guys. What is going on in here?" Rafe asked, sticking his head into the room and throwing Blake a quizzical look.

"Isn't it obvious?" Blake said, motioning for Rafe to come in.

Stumbling over to the desk with a glassy-eyed stare, Baylor muttered an incoherent sentence and took the last roll of packing plastic from the desktop.

Taking a few steps toward Baylor, Rafe waved a hand in front of her face. There was no response. "Is she . . . sleepwalking?" he asked as Baylor floundered her way back over to the painting.

"Ding, ding, ding!" Blake said. "She's been up for almost an hour now. First, she looked for Leo and couldn't find him. Then, she went outside and tried to push the tree stump over, and when she figured out she couldn't do that, she went up to the attic, grabbed six rolls of packing plastic and came back down here to wrap up that painting."

"Why?"

"I don't know. She doesn't seem to like it at all. My best guess is she wants to pack it up and put it upstairs in the attic. Anyway, fingers crossed," Blake said, folding both of his middle fingers over his index fingers and shaking them at Rafe. "When she figures out she can't move it on her own, she'll wake up."

Rafe loped behind the library desk and stood next to Blake. "I don't know," he said. "Something tells me if your sister really wants to move that painting, she'll find a way to do it."

"And how would she do that?" Blake said, swiveling his chair to stare at Rafe. "Are you giving her powerlifting lessons I don't know about?"

"She could use fairy magic."

"Nope, that's impossible because I'm always thinking ahead," Blake said, tapping his temple with his forefinger. "Before we go to bed at night, I make Bay give me all the grains of fairy dust she has in her pockets, so she can't bippity-boppity-boo in her sleep."

"But she could bippity-boppity-boo if she had a wand, couldn't she?"

"Well, yeah . . . I suppose, but Baylor doesn't have a wand. Madri Fey would never allow it."

Rafe scratched the back of his head. "Then what's that long pointy thing she's holding in her hand right now?"

"Bumbleball," Baylor chirped.

Blake swung his head to look at his sister just as a small orb of yellow light flew out of the tip of the wand she held. The ball shot past Blake's head and missed clipping his ear off by the narrowest of margins.

Diving for cover under the desk, the boys listened as the angry projectile ricocheted around the room, striking lamps and papers from the desktop, and flinging books and knickknacks from the library shelves. After a few minutes, the bumbleball fizzled out with a furious pop.

Grasping the edge of the desk with their fingertips, Rafe and Blake peeped their eyes up over the top of the desk to survey the damage. The library was a disaster.

Unfazed by the chaos and still in a trancelike state, Baylor faced the painting. Flicking her wand at it, she muttered a chant:

> *"So I am not filled*
> *With more doom and gloom,*
>
> *Take this dumb painting*
> *To the attic room."*

A cloud of smoke swirled around the painting, and it disappeared with a hiss and a poof.

"Poof," Blake said in a high-pitched voice, his eyes as big as saucers.

A mysterious Mona Lisa smile appeared on Baylor's lips.

"Poof? Poof?" Rafe said, swapping incredulous looks with Blake. "Look, I don't want to tell you how to handle your sister, but I think you'd better go over there and get that wand out of her hand before something else goes poof."

"No *duh*, Sherlock. Just give me a second. You're not the one who almost had his ear lopped off."

Rolling his eyes, Rafe pulled himself to a standing position and strode to Baylor's side. "Bay, can I see your wand?" he said. "Bay, please, can you look at me?"

A moment or two passed before Baylor seemed to comprehend what had been asked of her, but finally she lifted her chin to gaze at Rafe still wearing the glazed expression he'd seen on her face when he entered the library.

"Hey there, Bay. Hi." Smiling, Rafe slowly reached for her wrist and held it in his hand. "May I take a turn with the wand now? Please?"

Gazing at Rafe with a distant expression, Baylor opened her palm and relinquished the wand. Then she shuffled a few steps away to pick up a book from the floor.

"Okay, Braveheart," Rafe said, turning to Blake who was still cowering behind the desk. "You can come out now. I've got the wand. Do you have any idea where she got this thing?"

"No. None. I've been with her the whole time," Blake said, emerging from cover. "I mean, I lost sight of her once or twice when we were in the passageway from the attic to the library, but only for a few seconds."

"Long enough for her to pick something up off the steps in there?"

Blake watched his sister wandering toward the library door. "I don't know. Maybe," he said. "Look, I'll figure this out, but I don't have time right now. I need to get her back up to her room before she wakes up, and then I need to come back down here and clean up this mess. Otherwise, she's going to totally freak when I tell her what she did."

Rafe stuck the fairy wand into his back pocket and retrieved a fallen lamp from the floor. "You stay with her. I'll clean this up," he said, setting the lamp back on the desk.

"You will? Seriously?" Relief flooded Blake's face. "I don't know if anyone's ever told you this before, but you're a *real* angel!"

Rafe curled his lip. "Ha. Ha. Very funny. Now get out of here before I decide to use Bay's new wand on you."

"Okay, I'm out," Blake said, clomping over to his sister. Putting a gentle hand around her waist, he guided her out of the library.

"Not wanting to risk having to explain why the library looked like a disaster area to any more early morning risers, Rafe closed the door and locked it behind the twins.

Working at a brisk pace, it took Rafe over thirty minutes to put the library right again. Glancing at the clock on the library desk, he saw that he still had enough time to take a shower, change his clothes, and arrive for breakfast at Spokes the moment it opened.

The thought of food made Rafe's stomach gurgle in anticipation. "I know, I know. I don't need any reminders," he mumbled. "Just one more thing to do."

Stepping to one of the library shelves, Rafe turned the figure of an ancient-looking gold bird to the left, and the panel in the bookcase creaked open. He slid his fingers along the inside wall of the passageway and flicked on a light. Stepping inside, he closed the bookcase door behind him.

With his eyes glued to the staircase, he retraced the twins' footsteps, looking for a clue. When he reached the second-floor landing, the stairway forked. Choosing the left stairway, Rafe switched off the light to the staircase below him and switched on the one that illuminated the next set of stairs.

Out of the corner of his eye, he caught the glint of something sparkling on the bottom step of the other staircase and sucked in a surprised breath. Since his blackout experience in the xant caves, he'd know that sparkly substance anywhere. Xant dust.

Approaching the glittery flecks with caution, Rafe crouched beside the step. In the midst of the gleaming powder, a bare spot formed a clear outline of the small fairy wand he had in his back pocket. Carefully, he brushed the xant dust into his hand and pocketed it. He didn't want to chance the stuff being accidently scuffed up into the air.

On the way back to his room, Rafe contemplated what might have happened. It was clear that Baylor found the fairy wand in the passageway when she was sleepwalking, and the only fairies who came to Cliff House on a regular basis were Poppe and Potts . . . and Madri Fey, but the madri didn't use a wand. She used her scepter. No. The wand *had* to belong to either Poppe or Potts, and if Blake had been concerned about Oliver finding out about the passageways and tunnels in Cliff House, Rafe was pretty sure Blake was going to have a conniption fit when he found out Poppe and Potts knew about them too.

———

Ravenous, Rafe tucked into his breakfast at Spokes with a vengeance. He was on his third plate of food when Haven and Diadem slid into seats across from him with their breakfasts.

"Are your ears burning? *Everyone* is talking about you," Haven said, leaning across the table and touching his arm.

Rafe paused with his fork halfway to his mouth. "Me? What for?"

"What for?" Diadem said. "What for? Let me tell you what for. Because for the first time in the history of Mystfira, according to Madri Typhicus, a few of us beginner students actually made it through our first stand against a flood without being swept away."

"That's right," Haven said with a satisfied smile. "Thanks to you, Malachi, Rufus, Jericho, Diadem and I are eating breakfast in Spokes this morning, instead of the angelic infirmary. Don't tell me you haven't noticed all the looks you've been getting from the upper classmen?"

Suddenly feeling self-conscious, Rafe glanced around Spokes. He'd been alone when he arrived at Spokes, but now it buzzed with activity. The other Ryder-Knight students had arrived and were filling their plates at the sumptuous round buffet on the outer circular wall of Spokes. Half of the angelic students were eating, but the other half had congregated in small groups, whispering, pointing, and staring at him.

"Great," Rafe said, suppressing an urge to bury his head in his hands.

"Never mind them," Haven said. "You need to tell me how in the seven heavens you stayed perfectly still and floated in that wind after you changed into your angelic body yesterday? I was fighting to stay on my feet, and you looked like you were enjoying yourself."

Rafe tore his eyes away from the students ogling him and brought his attention back to Haven and Diadem. "I promise you, it's not hard, especially after you've taken Divine Interventions and Intercessions . . . and Universal Anemology."

"Universal Anemology?" Diadem asked.

"The study of the movement of the winds in all the universes."

Haven's eyes widened. "I cannot wait. I hope one day I'll be as good as you."

"As soon as you take those classes, trust me, Haven, the way you study, you'll be far better than I am."

Depositing her plate onto the table beside Rafe, Deidre slid into the seat next to him. "What in the world is going on here? Everyone in this room is talking about you."

Splotches of red spotted Rafe's face. "So I've heard," he said, pushing the food around his plate as the rest of the Ryder-Knight students filled in the vacant seats around him.

"We need details," Deidre said.

Rafe shook his head. He had no intention of telling anyone what had happened in the valley, but, unfortunately for him, a beaming Haven and Diadem were only too happy to share the particulars of Rafe's stand in the valley with the other students.

"Very impressive," Parker murmured, tucking her long blonde hair behind one of her ears and gazing at Rafe. "You sound like a real-life Hercules."

Parker's adoring gaze did not escape Blake and Baylor. Rafe noticed Blake hiding a grin behind the heel of his hand and winking at his sister.

"I don't mean to be rude and change the subject, but has anyone seen Tahj this morning," Ebon asked, looking around the table at the other Ryder-Knight students. "Anyone?"

Baylor wrinkled her brow as the other Ryder-Knight students shook their heads. "You know, I couldn't find Leopold this morning either, and he never misses a meal."

"Maybe Tahj took Leo for a walk," Blake said.

Ebon shook his head. "Tahj would never do something like that without informing me first. He's a creature of habit, as am I, and Tahj and I meet in the Butterfly Conservatory each morning at precisely 7:15 a.m. to walk over here to Spokes together."

"You know what, guys? I'm done with breakfast. I'll go find them," Rafe said, rising from his chair.

"No. You can't!" Deidre protested. "You're not done talking to us yet. Somebody else can go check on them."

"I'll go," said Oliver, springing to his feet. "I have to go back to the house anyway. I forgot my art eraser."

His escape plan thwarted, Rafe jammed himself back down into his chair with a sigh as a group of older and very curious angelic students flocked around him. Crossing and uncrossing his arms and legs, he endured another fifteen minutes of questions and adulations before the trumpet sounded, signaling the beginning of classes.

Scrambling to his feet, Rafe scooted into the palace corridor. Zigging and zagging through the teaming hallways, he hurried toward his Fairies 101 class.

"Stop right there, Rafe Ryder. I want to talk to you," called an unpleasant voice from behind him.

Lowering his brow and coming to a halt, Rafe turned to see Yediyah Principality, a tall, burly, chestnut-blond angel belonging to the fourth-year angelic class, pushing through the crowd toward him. Rafe knew Yediyah because they shared the same expert swordsmanship class.

"You think you're pretty special now, don't you? Well, I'm here to tell you, you're not!" snarled Yediyah, catching up to Rafe and hovering over him with a piercing black stare.

As murmurs and whispers filled the hallway, Yediyah trained his eyes on the admiring horde following Rafe through the hallway. "He is not *the* chosen one. Up here, he is only *one* of the chosen. Stop following him around!"

Baffled by Yediyah's hostility, Rafe pursed his lips and exhaled slowly as the burly angel's flinty glare returned to him.

"What's the matter, Ryder? Are you having trouble understanding what I just said?" Yediyah asked. "Let me break it down for you using smaller words then. *You. Are. No. Big. Deal.*"

Feeling his pulse increase, Rafe scowled at Yediyah but remained silent, which seemed to agitate Yediyah even more.

"Every advanced student is capable of doing what you did in the valley yesterday," Yediyah sneered.

"Really?" Rafe said, unable to contain his indignation for another second. "Then why are all the beginner students in the infirmary right now, except for the five I saved?"

Shooting daggers at Rafe, Yediyah's eyes twitched and his face fiercened. "We are forbidden to stand on a pillar with another angel. We couldn't save them."

"You're telling me an advanced student, such as yourself, couldn't figure out a way to rescue even one beginner student without bringing them onto your pillar?" Rafe narrowed his eyes and stared back at Yediyah without blinking. "You don't have much of an imagination, do you?"

"You know, Rafe Ryder, someone up here needs to take you down a peg or two," Yediyah roared, cracking his knuckles in anticipation.

"That's it! I've had it with you, whoever you are," Deidre bellowed, slamming the textbook she carried to the floor and storming toward Yediyah with her finger pointed. "The Ryder-Knight students are *my* people—not *your* people, and you will never talk to them like that again! Do you understand me? You will respect them, or you'll be answering to me!" she fumed, backing Yediyah up against the wall without so much as a touch of her finger. "Am I making myself clear?"

"Perfectly. Now let me make myself clear," Yediyah said, grabbing Deidre's finger and twisting it until she yelped in pain. With a satisfied smirk, he used his other hand to shove the girl to the floor.

"You just made a big mistake!" Deidre shrilled, bouncing back up like a bedspring. With a ferocious snarl, she flew at Yediyah's face, grabbing him by his nose.

Striding to Deidre's side, Blake seized his cousin around her waist and swung her away from Yediyah. "As you can see, our kitty has claws. It's best not to provoke her."

"She's insane!" Yediyah screeched, cradling his nose in his hands.

"No, she's perfectly sane," Ebon assured. "Just feral at times."

Baylor sighed. "Yes. We're hoping she'll outgrow it at some point."

"Well, I say you got exactly what you deserved, roughing up a girl like that," Blake said. "Serves you right."

"My nose is bleeding!"

"You're lucky I didn't break it," Deidre shrieked, thrashing about and trying to extricate herself from Blake's grip to go after Yediyah again. "I swear if you ever so much as mutter Rafe Ryder's name in the future, or the names of any of my other Ryder-Knight classmates, I will have my cousin turn you into a toad!"

Pressing a hand to her forehead, Baylor winced as if in pain.

A rapid clattering of heels echoed through the corridor and the crowd of angelic students shrank away from the quarrelling parties, allowing Rafe to spot an unhappy-looking Madri Ronan and Madri Avalon steaming toward them with Haven at their side.

"Madrikim! That girl just attacked me!" Yediyah said, holding his dripping nose with one hand and stabbing a finger at Deidre with the other.

"After you put your hands on me first!" Deidre shouted. "I was defending myself!"

"Do not add lying to your list of sins, Yediyah," Madri Ronan chastised in a stern tone. "Haven Guardian came to find us when she saw you push Deidre to the ground."

Still holding his nose, Yediyah lifted his chin and thrust out his chest. "She backed me up against a wall with her finger in my face. She *made* me lose my temper. This was *her* doing."

Madri Avalon locked eyes with Yediyah. "You have the audacity to blame someone else for *your* inability to control yourself? This is very serious, Yediyah. Angels who cannot regulate their emotions are rarely in control of their powers. You will need to report to your principality master immediately."

"Absolutely not!" Madri Ronan bellowed.

Looking hopeful, Yediyah turned to face Madri Ronan.

Madri Ronan's eyes narrowed and tightened as he stared at Yediyah. "I will not wait for Madri Uriah to deal with him. You are not on Earth, young man. You will *not* get away with this type of behavior here. Bullying and violence are strictly forbidden. Because you have chosen not to follow the rules, you will do your schoolwork in a classroom by yourself for the period of one month. In addition, you will no longer be allowed to participate in any group or school activities, nor will you speak or have contact with any other student during that time period."

Yediyah glowered at Deidre. "That's not fair. What about her? *She* started it."

"That is not true," Haven said with an emphatic shake of her head. "Yediyah started it by threatening to take Rafe Ryder down a peg or two. Deidre was simply defending her friend, and she used only her words to do so. You can ask anyone standing in this hallway."

"That will not be necessary. We believe you," Madri Avalon said, flinging the small train of her rose-pink gown behind her as she turned to leave.

"If I'm going to be punished, *she* needs to be punished, too," Yediyah shouted.

"If you'd kept your hands off me, I never would have touched you," Deidre shrieked.

"I believe that to be truth," said Madri Avalon. "The girl will not be punished for defending herself against your bullying, Yediyah. However, if this should ever happen again, Miss Dunn, we may take a different stance."

"Thank you, madri," Blake said, still keeping his arm tightly wound around Deidre's waist. "That's very decent of you. I'm positive this will not happen again. Isn't that right, Deidre?"

"That's right," Deidre said. "Unless, of course, some other nincompoop up here decides to put their hands on me."

"Come with us, Yediyah," Madri Ronan said. "We will escort you to your new classroom."

"I want to talk to my madri. This is not over," Yediyah growled, glaring at Deidre.

"Talk to your madri all you wish. It will change nothing," Madri Avalon said, taking Yediyah by the arm and leading him away.

Raising his arms above his head, Madri Ronan clapped his hands to get everybody's attention. "Off to classes with the rest of you." Certain that his command would be obeyed, Madri Ronan turned and stalked down the hallway with his crimson robe flapping briskly about his ankles.

"You can let go of me now," Deidre said, trying to pry Blake's hand from around her waist.

"Are you out of battle-maiden mode yet?"

"Yes. Now let go of me."

Blake released his grip on Deidre's waist. "You need to learn when to back down, Deidre! I blame your parents for this behavior. They never should have let you play a Valkyrie in last year's Summer Stock Theater."

Leaning against the wall, Deidre pulled up a sagging knee sock and tucked her blouse back into her skirt. "I'll have you know, I was excellent in that role."

"She was," Baylor said, bobbing her head in agreement. "She really, really was."

Rafe stooped to retrieve Deidre's textbook from the floor.

Handing the book to her, he said, "I appreciate you standing up for me, but I can take care of myself."

Chin held high, Deidre smoothed back her hair before turning away from Rafe. "Never said you couldn't, and you're welcome," she called over her shoulder.

Baylor bit her lip and giggled. "You have found favor with the Queen, peasant. Next time, just bow and be grateful for her intervention."

"Time for class, you guys. Walk this way, like me and Deidre." Placing his hand on his hip, Blake traveled along behind Deidre swishing his hips side-to-side in the same exaggerated manner as his cousin.

By the time Rafe took his seat at the table next to Baylor and Blake in the classroom, he was in a much better mood, thanks to Blake's comedic imitation of his cousin's stroll down the hallway.

With the whole class finally seated, Madri Fey touched the tip of her scepter and snapped her finger. The classroom lights flickered on and off, and the children quieted.

"Good morning, class. Welcome to your Fairies 101 class. Giggling, Madri Fey laid her scepter on the desk at the front of the classroom and seated herself behind it, surveying the students.

"You'll find the word *fairy* encompasses a large assortment of magical creatures. Today, I would like to talk about some of the peskier varieties of fairies, starting with goblins and gnomes. These fairies are known for their unpleasant temperament and their greed. As coincidence would have it," she said, her face growing serious, "I am also known for my unpleasant disposition when people skip my classes. Would anyone care to tell me where Tahj and Oliver are?"

Before anyone could answer the madri's question, the door

at the back of the classroom burst open, and a little fairy hurried toward Madri Fey with a worried pout.

"Zola, my dear, what is it?" Madri Fey asked, leaning over so the diminutive fairy could whisper in her ear.

"What?" Madri Fey sprang to her feet, bouncing a curled knuckle against her lip. "Are you sure their beds were not slept in?"

"Yes, madri."

"And nobody has seen them since yesterday?"

"All right," said the madri, reaching for her scepter. "Thank you, my dear. Go back to the forest and wait at the Tree of Tuatha. I'll be there shortly."

Zola flitted down the aisle toward the door, where Oliver nearly knocked the tiny girl over when he burst through the classroom door with his chest heaving as if he'd just finished running a marathon.

"You're late, young man, but I'll have to deal with you later," Madri Fey said. "I must attend to an emergency in the Fairy Forest."

"No. Please, madri, wait," Oliver blurted, bending forward and resting his hands on his knees. "Tahj is missing. I can't find him or Leopold. All sorts of stuff's knocked over in Tahj's room like someone had a fight."

The Ryder-Knight students' eyes went round as they gaped at each other, alarm etched in their faces.

"Are you sure?" Madri Fey asked.

"Yes. I checked the whole house. That's why I'm late."

A flush crept into the madri's cheeks. "Two of my fairies are missing as well."

Rafe straightened in his chair. "Poppe and Potts?"

"How did you know?" the madri asked. "Have you seen them?"

"No, but I found one of their wands in the library this morning," Rafe said. "I'll bet they were playing a game at Cliff House last night."

"A game?" Madri Fey's eyes twitched. "Did you see them there?"

"No. It's just a hunch," said Rafe, "but they're always trying to get us to play make-believe with them, and they love pretending to be pirates. I could definitely see them getting carried away and kidnapping Tahj and Leopold as part of their game."

"I don't know," the madri replied. "That seems extreme . . . even for Poppe and Potts. They are very mischievous and can even be naughty at times, but they've never broken their bedtime curfew, or, to my knowledge, abducted anyone."

"There's something else," Blake said. "My sword went missing from the library a couple of days ago, and none of the Ryder-Knight students took it."

Madri Fey's expression turned stony. "I suppose your explanation is within the realm of possibility. Very well," she said with a sigh. "The investigation will begin at Cliff House. You're all dismissed."

Deidre raised her hand. "Madri? May I just make a teeny, tiny, little comment?"

"You may," said the madri.

"If we didn't live in the dark ages up here and you allowed us to use our cellphones, no one would have to search for Tahj—or Sully, our friend that went missing in that time tuck, for that matter. We could call them and ask them where they were and who they were with."

Rafe and the other students stared at Deidre. The girl made a fair point.

"That's right," Parker said. "If you made our cellphones

work everywhere with your magic, we could keep track of each other."

"That's a *great* idea," Audra chimed.

Ebon stroked his chin. "I must concur with the ladies. Given the myriad of dangers we face up here, we should have a way to quickly ascertain each other's whereabouts."

"*Ooooo.* Can the angelic students have cellphones too?" Diadem said.

Haven perked up in her chair. "We should. Since people on Earth use them all the time, phones should be part of our human experience up here."

"Enough," the madri snapped. "Why do you Ryder-Knight students have cellphones? You are far too young to own that sort of technology."

"Oh, please. I had my first cellphone when I was eight," Oliver said. "That's what happens when you go away to a boarding school. Our parents need some way to keep track of us, so they buy us phones and expect us to answer them."

Lost in thought, the madri rubbed her forehead. Finally, she spoke. "Normally I would consult with the other members of the Sakal before making a decision like this, but for safety purposes, I'm inclined to grant this request to the Ryder-Knight students immediately—but only to the Ryder-Knight students."

Haven and Diadem traded sour looks as Deidre clapped her hands lightly and rapidly in excitement. "Yay!"

"Wicked!" Blake said, grinning at Baylor and Rafe.

"Mind you," the madri warned, "you students will only be allowed to speak to each other on your phones. No Book of faces, Snappy chats, Birdy tweets, or Instant pictures. You may only speak with one another. That is all."

"Got it. No social media," Blake said. "We can live with that."

Ebon regarded the madri with a thoughtful expression. "I think you may want to also consider allowing us to use the camera feature on our phones," he said. "Then, if we should see something suspicious or out of the ordinary, we would be able provide the Sakal with photographic evidence."

Madri Fey frowned but nodded. "I will allow it."

"Uh, madri?" Oliver said, swishing a finger at her. "I'm more of a texting kind of guy, so it would be fabulous if we could text too."

Madri Fey's frown deepened.

"Or not," Oliver said, tilting his eyes downward.

"Ryder-Knight students, please close your eyes and concentrate on your cellphones," the madri said. The crystal on the end of her ivory scepter glowed hot yellow as she chanted:

"So, I am not forced to hear one more moan,
Bring back to life all their cellular phones.

May their batteries ne'er die or go weak,
Letting the children take pictures and speak."

When Rafe opened his eyes, his mobile phone sat on the table in front of him. He snatched it up and tucked it into his pocket. There were only three people he wished to speak with on the phone and none of them were sitting in Madri Fey's classroom at the moment.

Chapter Eight

Not Sully

L ed by Madri Fey, the angels, woganots, gargoyles, and fairies combed Cliff House for the missing. Except for tangled bed sheets and blankets and an overturned bedside table and lamp, no clues to Tahj's disappearance could be found in his room.

Next, every nook and cranny of The Palace of Angels and Truvian Village were scoured for Tahj, Leopold, Poppe, and Potts, but once again, no trace could be found. As hours melted away, the madrikim extended their search further into the rings of Mystfira.

Each day, after classes ended, the angelic students also joined the search—all except for Rafe. Madri Typhicus would not allow it. Rafe had no choice but to grudgingly accept the mandate.

"You may attend angelic classes, but I do not think it wise to aggravate your fellow Ryder-Knight students by allowing you to search for your missing friends while their existence is strictly restricted to the grounds of Cliff House," he'd explained.

Losing yet another friend and being confined to Cliff House disturbed and dismayed the Ryder-Knight students. Their spirits spiraled downward along with the weather, Rafe's included. If they'd been able to escape to the grounds outside their new prison, their incarceration might have been a bit more tolerable. But two weeks of salt and wax drizzle, followed by another week of fire and iron rains accompanied by noxious gases, had made outdoor time impossible.

Without Madri Fey to help the Ryder-Knight students escape their captivity, tempers flared. Squabbles between the children erupted over just about anything.

Oliver commandeered the library for his art studio and flew off the handle when he discovered Baylor had removed the painting he loved so much. He demanded she move it back, and with great reluctance, Baylor complied.

A few minutes later, after Oliver set up his canvas and easel, he discovered he didn't have enough Cerulean blue paint to begin his own painting, and another meltdown ensued.

Hoping to defuse some of the tension in the house, Rafe offered to go into the jarvartan village at lunchtime to get the paint Oliver needed from Celestial Paints, Pigments, Polishes, and Plasters and anything else the other students might want him to bring back from the village.

Shortly after noon, armed with a long shopping list, a tote bag, and some gold nuggets, Rafe began his trek around Dressage Street, the wide, circular main street of Truvian. The buildings here reminded Rafe of a medieval English village, except for the gleaming gold sidewalks and polished, red jasper streets. The shops' signs featured signs lettered in Anfar and, since the arrival of the Ryder-Knight students, English.

First, Rafe stopped at Sweet Dreams, the fairy shop that featured candy and sweet treats galore, to purchase a container of Above and Beyond ice cream. Blake and Baylor were crazy about the secret fairy spice swirled into the frozen goodie. Fairy ice cream never melted, so he didn't need to worry about having a soupy mess by the time he made it back to Cliff House.

A few moments later, Rafe stood in front of Celestial Paints, Pigments, Polishes, and Plasters. Splashed across the shop's front door, a beautiful painting depicting a shimmering nighttime scene from the Fairy Forest greeted the shop's customers.

A bell jingled as Rafe opened the door and entered the spacious, neat-as-a-pin shop. Floor to ceiling aisles overflowed with art supplies and every type of paint imaginable.

Overwhelmed and confused, Rafe scratched his neck and gawked at the sheer volume of materials available. How did artists find anything in stores like this? *What a nightmare!*

Wandering the aisles, Rafe came upon a lanky middle-aged jarvartan man stacking cans of paint onto a shelf.

"Welcome, friend," the man said, gazing at Rafe with wide violet eyes. "I have not seen you here before. I am Vincent. May I help you?"

Breathing a sigh of relief, Rafe pulled the list from his pocket and consulted it. "Yes, please. I'm looking for Cerulean blue paint."

"An excellent choice of color," Vincent said. "Would you like that in an acrylic, watercolor, oil, gouache, pastel, tempera, or polymer paint? I also have it in fluorescent and glitter paints, as well as beeswax."

Rafe scowled. "I don't really know. Is that important?"

"Let me see if I can help you narrow it down," Vincent said. "Would you like it in a tin, tube, pan, pot, bottle, stick, block, or can?"

"Uhhh. I don't know that, either."

"Let us start with this, then," Vincent said with a perplexed frown. "What do you need the paint for?"

"I don't need the paint," Rafe said. "It's for my friend, Oliver Harper."

"Oliver, the little artist from Earth? Say no more. He is one of my best customers, and if I am not mistaken, he is working with oil on canvas right now. He has not been by in quite some time, though. Good heavens! He is not the student that went missing with that dog, is he?"

"No. No," Rafe said, "but the other Ryder-Knight students have to stay in Cliff House until Tahj is found."

"I see. Poor things," Vincent said, walking down the second aisle and retrieving a bottle from one of the shelves. "They must be terribly fidgety by now."

"Stir-crazy is more like it." Rafe glanced down at the list in his hand as he followed Vincent. "Some of the girls want me to get them nail polish. Do you know which store in Truvian carries nail polish?"

"I certainly do." Vincent turned to Rafe with a faint smile. "For Deidre and Parker, I imagine."

Rafe raised a questioning brow. "You know them?"

"I sell them makeup and nail polish on a regular basis,

"You sell makeup and nail polish here?" Rafe asked, astonishment creasing his brow. "Really? In a paint store?"

"Of course," Vincent replied. "I sell paints, pigments, polishes, and plasters for any type of canvas. Although, in my humble opinion, those young girls' faces are not canvases that require any type of enhancements. They are beautiful just the way they are."

Rafe nodded in agreement. *Especially Parker.*

Delighted to cross two things off his list from one store, Rafe placed the items in his tote bag before stepping out onto golden sidewalk and setting out for Second Sight Opticals across the street.

A giant magnifying glass—surrounded by mirrors, lenses, binoculars, telescopes, and periscopes—twirled in the front display window of the store. Compared to Celestial Paints, Pigments, Polishes, and Plasters, this shop seemed rather small.

Stepping into the store, Rafe admired several large, round prisms dangling from the ceiling. They lit the room with dazzling rainbow colors.

The next item on Rafe's list was for Ebon, who had set up a telescope in one of the towers on the grounds of Cliff House and wanted a more powerful lens to stargaze. Fortunately, Ebon had had the foresight to write the exact make and model of the lens he wished to purchase on a slip of paper for Rafe.

While the shopkeeper, Lydia, a sturdy leprechaun woman with round cherry cheeks, retrieved the desired lens from a storage room, Rafe occupied himself looking about the store, taking care to fold his arms across his chest and not to touch any breakable items.

A small shiny black telescope rested on a tripod in the middle of the shop, facing an empty wall. That was strange. *Who angles a telescope to look at a wall?*

Squinting, Rafe stooped to peer through the scope. His breath caught in his throat, and he straightened. Staggering backward, he caught his balance before crashing into a stack of telescopes on the floor behind him.

"Easy does it there, diddly doo," Lydia said. "Are you okay?"

"Yes . . . I mean, no! I can see *through* that wall and into The Coach and Footman next door with this *thing*!" Rafe exclaimed, pointing at the telescope.

Lydia sauntered to the side of the small black object. "Well, of course you can, and that *thing* is called a soriscope. Not only does it let you see great distances, it allows you to see through solid objects."

"*Through?*" Rafe croaked.

"Absolutely." Lydia smiled and flicked a dial to a different setting on the soriscope. "Tell me what you see now?"

Rafe peeked through the scope again and gasped. "Is that a waiter in the Wind and Wings Tavern? That's got to be at least three stores away from here."

"I know. Isn't it fabulous?"

Rafe quirked an eyebrow. "What about other people's privacy?"

"What about it?" Lydia bristled, planting a hand on her hip. "I don't use it to spy on unsuspecting people."

"But isn't that what *I* just did?"

"Of course not! I've gotten permission from all the storeowners around here to look into their establishments for soriscope demonstration purposes. My goodness, you ask a lot of questions."

"Sorry."

Leaning toward Rafe in a confidential manner, Lydia said, "I think the only question you should be asking yourself right now is why you haven't already purchased one." She paused for a moment, her large blue eyes giving Rafe the hard sell. "They're an absolutely indispensible item to have on hand here in Mystfira. Why, I just sold one to an angelic student named Yediyah so he could watch this month's Adomis trial from the Palace of Angels."

Rafe's face tightened. "But, but," he stammered. "The Rocker's in the twelfth ring near Baeldavar."

"I know," Lydia said with a lopsided grin.

"You can see that far with a soriscope?"

"Yes, of course."

Rafe chewed his bottom lip. If he had the ability to see vast distances and through solid objects, then he could help look for Tahj and Leo from Cliff House, and the Sakal couldn't stop him. Maybe he could earn the money by working in Truvian after classes. Seamus was always looking for someone to do odd jobs at his shop.

"How much is it?" Rafe asked.

"Only ten gold nuggets."

Rafe's expression dulled. "I'm not going to be able to buy it for a while, then. I can't afford it. All I can afford today is the lens for my friend's telescope."

"You can't afford it? You can't afford it?" Lydia sounded appalled. "The way I see it—you can't afford *not* to take this opportunity."

"I wish I could buy it from you now, but I really don't have the money."

"Not necessarily," Lydia said with a sly wink. "I could let you take the soriscope for one gold nugget today and another nugget, say, every other week or so? I'll even throw in a free lesson on how to use it today. What do you say?"

Rafe blinked. "Sold."

An hour later, with his new soriscope shoved into his back pocket, Rafe emerged from Second Sight Opticals still marveling at how the soriscope could be collapsed into such a neat pocket-sized item.

Slinging his tote bag over his shoulder, he headed for the towering crescent-shaped ivory structure a short distance away. He couldn't wait to get back to Cliff House to show the twins his new treasure, but he still had to stop at the library for Audra.

Racing up the steps, Rafe skidded into the colossal library. The breath-taking chandelier ceiling composed of millions and millions of bits of glowing glass and beads was reflected in the glass floor beneath his feet.

Ignoring the assortment of colored lampposts denoting the various sections of the library, Rafe clapped his hands together. "Traditional Library," he said.

The emptiness around Rafe disappeared and he found himself standing in a more familiar library lined with massive bookshelves storing books, magazines, and papers of every type. Hurrying to the library counter, Rafe greeted the jarvartan librarians, Prentiss and Zane, working side-by-side in their brown tweed jackets.

"Sorry to bother you. I'm running errands for the other Ryder-Knight students stuck in Cliff House, and Audra wanted me to check out a few books for her," said Rafe, patting the tote bag at his side.

"Bless that child," Zane said, trying to tame his unruly white hair with a stroke of his hand. "Prentiss and I have missed her. What is she after today?"

Rafe pulled his list from his pocket and read, "*Gulliver's Travels* by Jonathan Swift, *Jane Eyre* by Charlotte Bronte, and *A Wrinkle in Time* by Madeleine L'Engle."

"The way that girl reads, those books will not keep her busy for very long," Prentiss said, eyebrows waggling.

"That's true," Rafe agreed.

"I will get them," Zane said, stepping away from the library counter.

"Oh, and could you add a history book about the royal House of Windsor for me?" Rafe asked.

Looking at Rafe in genuine surprise, Zane stopped in his tracks. "The current British royal family on Earth? You must be very homesick."

"I am. All the Ryder-Knight students are, but this book is not for me. It's for George."

"The woganot guarding the door between Cliff House and the palace?" Prentiss asked.

"Yes. He wants to know more about their royal highnesses, and I've run out of things to tell him," said Rafe.

"All right, but the book is going on your library card, and you will be responsible for it," Zane said, disappearing into the book stacks.

"The British royal family seems like such an odd topic of conversation for a woganot," Prentiss said.

"It all started after I mentioned that I liked the name George because there's a little prince in my country with that name, and George, the woganot, has been asking about the royal family nonstop ever since."

Prentiss tilted his head back and boomed out a laugh. "That explains it, then."

"It does? Really?"

"Of course," Prentiss said. "On your Earth and here in the heavens as well, many people share the same name, but not woganots. In all eternity, George will be the only woganot who will ever carry that name. It only stands to reason he would be interested in a namesake, especially if the little lad on Earth is a prince."

"I get it now," Rafe said with a grin.

At that moment, the library floor heaved underneath his feet, and the massive building shuddered. Reaching for the counter to steady himself as the tremoring continued, Rafe heard the moan of the wind outside escalate to the telltale wail of the call to the Valley of Shadows. "No, no, no. Not now," Rafe moaned.

"Go," Prentiss said. "Leave your things with me, and do not worry. I will see the items get to Cliff House for you."

———➤

With another stand in the valley behind him, Rafe winged his way through the heavens. Reflecting the twelve moons of Mystfira, a multitude of stars, resplendent and intense, provided a dazzling spectacle. As much as Rafe wanted to see the twinkling lemon-yellow and white stars of Earth's skies again, flying through the dark night sky awash in vividly colored moons and stars sent chills of excitement racing up and down his spine.

Touching down on the back porch of Cliff House, Rafe's body returned to human shape with no unfortunate side effects. After three weeks of daily practice with Haven and Diadem, transforming between his angelic body and his human body seemed almost natural to him now.

He patted his trousers' back pocket. Good. The soriscope was still there. He couldn't wait to use it to help search for Tahj and Leo, but that would have to wait until tomorrow. Tonight's stand had been challenging. He hated fire as passionately as Blake and Baylor hated snakes, but he knew that's what he'd be facing the moment he soared into the valley and saw a tree and a gadaboot plant dotting each of the pillars.

After all the angels had assumed their positions, a crackling wild fire flamed to life in the valley below, igniting the dry grasses and trees there. Soon Rafe and the others realized that the copious, thick, black smoke was not the only thing rising. Carrying a blazing inferno, the entire floor of the valley beneath them ascended to meet their pillars.

Surrounded by a sea of flames, Rafe called Thomas, and together they spent ten hours protecting the tree and gadaboot plant from the fire. Holding back the smoke and flame wouldn't have been such a monumental task if Thomas had been able to help him, but the little red-blossomed gadaboot plant made that impossible. Every time Thomas thought he'd convinced the little plant to stay in one place, it panicked, pulled up its boot-shaped roots and tried to flee the pillar. Thomas had spent all his time trying to corral the little rascal so it didn't accidently set itself on fire.

Rafe found himself chuckling. It was funny now, but it hadn't been at the time. Pattering through the kitchen and dining room to the grand entrance hall, he heard the mahogany grandfather clock strike three as he passed the library door.

The faint jangling of a bell sounded inside the library. Oddly enough, it sounded exactly like the servants' bells Rafe had heard in his dreams a few weeks ago. Glancing toward the closed door, he noticed a smidgen of light seeping out from underneath it.

Was the jangling from the new bell system Blake's grandparents had installed? Hadn't Blake said the bells not only rang on the board in the basement, but also now rang in the kitchen, the butterfly conservatory, his grandparents' bedroom, his grandmother's sewing room, and *the library*?

Unable to contain his curiosity, Rafe scurried to the door and pressed his ear to it. The bells were no longer sounding, and he heard no voices coming from inside the room either. Turning the handle, Rafe gave a small push and the door creaked open.

He held his breath in shock as his eyes took in the wreckage before him. The library's devastation couldn't have been more complete if Baylor had conjured up and blasted off ten bumbleballs.

The desk had been upended, bookshelves split and broken, books scattered and torn. Papers, brushes, and palette knives peppered the floor along with Oliver's slashed canvas and broken wooden easel. Tubes and cans of paint had been opened and hurled about every surface of the room.

Crouching in the door's entrance, Rafe examined several sets of barefoot prints in the paint on the floor. Whomever the footprints belonged to had been slipping and sliding all over the place.

Rafe stood and turned out the overhead light. The desk lamp, overturned in the corner, cast a ghostly glow over the room. As far as Rafe was concerned, the light could stay on indefinitely. He wasn't going to wade through all the broken debris and paint just to shut it off, and he most certainly wasn't going to volunteer to clean the aftermath of this mess up either. *Nope. No way.*

It was safe to assume a sleepwalking Baylor had something to do with the library's devastation, and as far as Rafe was concerned, Blake was on his own this morning. Rafe needed a shower to rid the stench of smoke from his body, and then he was going to get some sleep.

Removing his shoes, he tiptoed up the stairs and down the wide hallway to his room. His shower took longer than normal because he had to wash his hair three times before it stopped reeking of smoke.

Dressed in clean pajamas, Rafe picked up his uniform trousers from the bathroom floor and removed the soriscope. Padding through the sitting room to his bedroom, he assembled the soriscope to its proper size and placed it on the bedside table next to him. Clicking off the lamp, he curled up in his bed and contemplated his new ability to join in the search for his missing friends.

Rafe had just closed his eyes when he heard a frenzied clawing noise coming from the inside of the wall near the bottom of his bed. Bolting upright, he clicked the lamp back on and crawled to the end of his mattress to investigate. As he peeked over the edge, a small body wearing jeans and a blouse smeared with paint unexpectedly smashed through his wall and onto the wooden floor, producing a dull *thud.*

As if it were a small door, the sheetrock of his wall stood open at the bottom of his bed. "Baylor?" he asked, staring at the girl on his floor.

Slamming the sheetrock shut, Baylor scrambling to her feet and shot out of Rafe's bedroom door and into his sitting room. He heard her lock the door to the hallway before racing back to his bedroom and locking that door too.

"How did you get in here?" Rafe demanded.

Baylor held her trembling hands out in warning. "*Shh, shh, shh,*" she whispered in a frantic tone. "He'll hear you. If he hears you, he'll come for us."

Her dark brown eyes welled with tears as she slumped against Rafe's bedroom door and crumpled to the floor like an old rag doll.

"What are you talking about? Who will come for us?" he asked in a softer voice.

"Sully," she whispered.

Sully? Sully had been missing since the time tuck at the Brume Theater, and Baylor knew it. What on earth was wrong with the girl? She certainly wasn't sleepwalking. She seemed too awake and alert for that.

Drawing her knees up to her chest, Baylor covered her mouth with both hands to muffle convulsive sobs. Her long dark hair hid a portion of her face, but Rafe could see a pink flush creeping into her cheeks. In all his life, he had never seen Baylor cry like this and for a moment her pain almost felt as if it were his own.

Leaping out of bed, Rafe legged it to Baylor's side and sat down beside her. "Bay," he said, leaning his shoulder against hers. "What's the matter? Talk to me."

"I know it sounds crazy," she whispered through soft hiccupping breaths, "but Sully was in my room, except *not* Sully. His eyes were a weird purple color, and his teeth were all sharp and funny-colored."

Rafe ran a hand through his hair as a wave of helplessness washed over him. "Do you know what I think?" he said gently. "I think maybe you were having a bad dream."

Dabbing her eyes with the cuff of her blouse, Baylor lifted her head to look at Rafe. "No, I wasn't," she said with a sniffle. "I haven't even been to bed tonight. Blake and I were down in the tower with Ebon helping him with his telescopes until we saw you get home from the valley."

Brows tightening, Rafe chewed the inside of his cheek, thinking of the disaster in the library. It seemed much more likely Baylor had wrecked the library and taken the secret passageway out to one of the towers on the cliffs like she'd done in the past. She'd probably woken up in the tower, and Blake had convinced her they'd spent the evening there with Ebon. After Blake had gotten Baylor back to bed, he'd probably gone back out to the tower to do damage control with Ebon. Whatever happened, Blake was the only one who would be able to calm Baylor down.

Getting to his feet, Rafe found a pair of jeans and an old shirt on top of a pile of dirty clothes in the corner. "Turn around and face the door, Bay. I'm going to get dressed."

"You can't go out there," she said as Rafe yanked off his pajama top and tugged on a shirt.

"Turn around."

Baylor turned and faced Rafe's bedroom door. "Listen to me," she said in an agitated whisper. "After we got here and heard you taking a shower, we went to my room so I could get a sweater because I was freezing. When I was closing the wardrobe door, Blake and I heard someone coming up the steps of the secret passageway behind it."

"But no one knows about that passageway except us," Rafe said, jamming a leg into his jeans.

"I know, and since we heard the shower water running in your bathroom, we knew it wasn't you, so Blake made me hide behind the secret panel in my room."

Rafe recalled the narrow cupboard hidden behind an intricately scrolled wooden panel beside her fireplace. It led into Blake's room and opened by his fireplace in the same way. "You can still fit into that cupboard?" he asked, pulling the jeans over his hips and buttoning them.

"Barely, and that's not the point," Baylor said, her voice dripping with impatience. "Can I please turn back around?"

"Go ahead."

Whirling back around, Baylor continued her story, her words rushing out in a terrified torrent. "I left the panel open a crack so I could see. When the wardrobe swung off the wall, out popped Sully . . . but *not really* Sully. I don't know how else to explain it. I don't think Blake noticed because he was just so excited to see him again. Sully rushed toward Blake, and they gave each other this big bear hug, and then—suddenly, Blake just disappeared right in front of my eyes. I screamed. Sully heard me and pulled me out of the panel and tried to hug me, too. I fought him off, but I really only got away because Simon was flying around outside my window and saw what was happening. He broke through the glass and flew at Sully's eyes—but Sully grabbed him, and Simon melted away too."

"You mean Sion?"

"Whatever," Baylor paused, wiping her nose on her sleeve.

"And then?" Rafe prompted.

"And then before Sully could grab me again, I squeezed through the panel into Blake's room and locked myself in his closet. A few minutes later, I heard Blake's door open, and I peeked through the keyhole of the closet. It was Sully . . . but *not* Sully. I didn't want him to find me, so I used the secret door in the back of Blake's closet to get into Grams' sewing room. It took me a minute to find the latch in the dark, but I finally got the door open and came through it."

"You certainly did."

Rocking on his heels with his thumbs in his pockets, Rafe pretended to study the floor. He was sure Baylor had been having a nightmare, or sleepwalking, or perhaps even both. Blake said she never remembered sleepwalking, but maybe Rafe could help jog her memory this time.

"The paint on your clothes, Bay? Where did it come from?"

Baylor looked down at her blouse and jeans, examining them with genuine surprise. "I don't know. It might have happened when Sully tried to hug me."

Rafe flopped down on his bed. Jogging her memory wasn't going to work. He needed to find a new approach, but even more than that, he *needed* to find Blake. Reaching for the soriscope on his bedside table, he said, "This thing is called a soriscope. It's like a telescope, but better because it sees through things. We can see outside this room without leaving it."

"Really?"

"Really and truly," Rafe answered. "I got it from Second Sight Opticals yesterday."

Wiping the last tears from her face with the back of her hands, Baylor watched as Rafe whirled and twisted the dials and gauges on the soriscope. When he was certain he had the right setting, he pointed the scope at the bedroom wall facing the hallway and peeked through the eyepiece. The hallway was empty.

Rising, Rafe offered Baylor the soriscope. "There's no one in the hallway right now. Have a look for yourself."

Pushing to her feet, Baylor took the scope. She trained it on the wall and looked through the finder just as Rafe had done.

"Oh, my gosh!" she gasped. "You *can* see through the walls. Check and see if Sully is still in Blake's room."

Retrieving the scope from Baylor, Rafe focused the soriscope on the wall beside his bed and scanned Blake's room. It was also empty.

Clicking a dial on the side of the soriscope, Rafe enabled the scope to see through two walls at a time so he could view Baylor's room.

Sucking in a breath, Rafe's heart quickened and skipped a beat as he surveyed the room. Baylor's bed was perfectly made, and it had not been slept in. Her wardrobe, which hid the entrance to the secret passageway to the ballroom, had been swung off the wall and stood open. Fragments of shattered glass lay scattered over her bedroom floor. The windowpane had been smashed—just as she said—and puddles of paint stained her floorboards!

"What? What did you see?" Baylor asked. "Is Sully in Blake's room?"

"No, he's not . . . but then I changed the scope so I could look in your room. The passageway to the ballroom is open, and your window is broken."

"I told you that already," she whispered.

Rafe's jaw tightened and a vein popped out on his neck. *She had, and he hadn't believed her.* Remembering the destruction he'd seen in the library and still holding the soriscope, Rafe sprinted to unlock his doors and raced toward Oliver's room.

Baylor broke into a run to catch up to him, and as he raised his fist to knock on the door, she blocked his hand with hers. "No," she whispered. "What if Sully is in there? Look with your scope thingy first."

Nodding, Rafe flicked the dial on the side of the soriscope to the setting he needed and leveled it at Oliver's door. As he scanned the room, a tranquil forest mural materialized on three of the walls. The fourth wall featured Oliver's many sketches, diagrams and paintings. Oliver's bed had not been made, and his room looked messy, in an artistic sort of way, but no one was inside.

Lowering the scope, Rafe tried the door handle. Finding it unlocked, he scurried over to look out the window. He didn't see anyone walking around the grounds of Cliff House beneath him, but there did seem to be a dim light coming from one of the towers near the cliffs.

Rafe hoisted the soriscope again and looked at the lighted tower. "Bay," he said, "I see Ebon sitting at a desk made out of a plank."

Baylor covered her mouth with her hand. "Oh, thank goodness! Is he okay?"

"He's got his head cupped in his chin, and he's leaning against his elbow. I think he's sleeping."

Exchanging looks of relief, they stepped out of Oliver's room and Rafe handed the soriscope to Baylor. "We need to check on Audra, Parker, and Deidre, but I don't feel right looking into their bedrooms. You do it."

Baylor nodded and tiptoed down the hallway to Deidre's room. Lifting the soriscope and puckering her brow, she peered through the eyepiece. "Deidre's not in her room."

"What about Parker?" Rafe asked, heart galloping. He tilted the end of the soriscope in the direction of Parker's room with Baylor still looking through it.

With a sharp inhalation, Baylor bleated, "She's not in there, either."

Baylor moved down the hallway to investigate Audra's room

as Rafe stared at Parker's door. Flinging it open, he burst into Parker's room. Rafe's scalp prickled and his stomach quivered. *No. Not Parker.*

Baylor's breathless voice sounded from behind him. "There's paint all over Audra's floor, and she and Pebbles are gone just like everyone else."

Rafe knew Audra never let her cat leave the room without her. She was too afraid Pebbles would get lost someplace in the mammoth house and never be found.

Rafe, . . . look over there," Baylor said, pointing to the floor next to Parker's bed. "There's paint on Parker's floor, too."

"It's downstairs, too. Come on, I'll show you," Rafe said, grabbing Baylor by the hand and dragging her to the top of the spiral staircase.

"Wait, no!" she protested. "What if not-Sully is down there?"

"I'll check. Stay here."

Rafe raced halfway down the steps and peeked over the stair railing. The grand entrance hall stood empty. He tripped down a few more steps and trained the soriscope at the library door. It was empty too.

He motioned for Baylor to join him, and she reluctantly tip-toed down the steps to stand next to him. "Where are we going?" she whispered.

"The library," Rafe said as they crept down the stairs.

Keeping watch over their shoulders as they passed through the grand entrance hall, Rafe and Baylor edged toward the library. When they reached the door, Rafe opened it and shooed Baylor under his arm before following her inside and clicking the door shut.

The overturned desk lamp cast a flickering pool of dim light. Locking the door, Rafe snapped on the small overhead chandelier.

Baylor surveyed the devastation surrounding her with great alarm. "What happened in here?"

Grasping her arms with a gentle grip, Rafe turned Baylor to face him. "Are you sure you don't know?"

"I know what you're thinking, but I didn't do this," Baylor said. "Blake and I were with Ebon in the tower all night. Blake was helping Ebon build another telescope while I looked through the other telescope and recorded my observations. I promise you, Blake and I didn't leave the tower until we saw you come home."

Releasing the grip on one of her arms, Rafe scratched his jaw. "I'm just trying to figure out what happened here."

Baylor pulled her cellphone from her back pocket. "Well, you could start by believing me. I'm telling you the truth. Call Ebon and ask him yourself."

"That's brilliant, Bay!" Rafe said, squeezing her arm in his excitement. "Do you have everyone's numbers? If they have their phones with them, we can find out where they are."

"*Uh-huh,*" she said, nodding her head as she punched up her contact list and pressed a number.

Bzzzt. Bzzzt. Bzzzt.

"It's ringing in here. Whose number is that?" Rafe asked, snapping his head around. "Ebon's?"

Bzzzt. Bzzzt. Bzzzt.

"It's Blake's . . . but it can't be!" Baylor said, her voice cracking in panic. "I saw his phone in his back pocket when Sully hugged him."

Bzzzt. Bzzzt. Bzzzt.

"Why is it vibrating instead of ringing?" Rafe asked, honing in on an area near the painting.

"Because Audra called Blake while we were in the tower, and

Ebon asked him to silence it," Baylor replied. "Shoot, it just went to voicemail."

"Ring him again. I'll try to find it."

Baylor tapped the face of her phone again, and Blake's cell-phone pulsated to life once more. Laying his soriscope atop an open book on the floor next to Baylor, Rafe skidded through the wet paint to reach the picture. He pulled scattered art supplies, books, and papers away from the painting until the floor around it was empty, but he could not see the phone. Getting down on his hands and knees, he peeked behind the painting. *Still nothing.*

"I don't get it. It sounds like it's vibrating right in front of the painting," Baylor said. "Why can't we see it?"

"I don't know. Give it one more go."

Baylor pressed the number again.

Bzzzt. Bzzzt. Bzzzt.

Rafe stooped next to the painting and placed his ear nearly against it. The vibration seemed to be coming from inside the painting. Placing his hand on the canvas, he felt the painting quiver beneath his fingertips.

Lifting his head, Rafe's body stiffened as his gaze met Baylor's. The sound of his heartbeat thrashed in his ears as he tried to think of a way to tell her what he suspected. *Best to come right out with it.*

"I think Blake's phone is *inside* the painting," Rafe blurted.

A strangled cry escaped Baylor's lips, and the phone she held slipped from her grasp and fell to the floor with a dull *clunk*.

Chapter Nine

The Brushstroke of Time

"Seamus," Baylor rasped, twisting the silver ring on her pinky finger.

Waving his shillelagh, the pudgy little leprechaun materialized, clad in a maroon tartan nightshirt and nightcap.

"What is ailin' ya, lass? Ya look as pale as da dead."

Lifting a trembling finger, Baylor pointed behind Seamus.

Wheeling around, the leprechaun caught sight of Rafe and the devastated library. "Ya scoundrel!" he said, shaking his shillelagh at Rafe. "Ya'll pay fer dis!"

"I didn't do it," Rafe said, holding his hands up in surrender. "We found the room like this."

Setting his jaw, Seamus raised his chin and crossed his arms. "Likely story."

"I'm telling you the truth."

Seamus's eyes suddenly narrowed and froze on the painting behind Rafe. "Janey Mack! Janey Mack! Janey Mack!" the leprechaun exclaimed, sounding horrified. "Where'd ya get dat ting?"

"It was a gift from the fairies on Feadh-Ree," Baylor muttered.

"That's right," Rafe said, picking his way over the paint and jumbled wreckage on the library floor to get back to where Baylor and Seamus stood. "We found it when we got back from the Brume. It was sitting with the rest of the thank-you gifts the fairies left us for performing at the theater."

"I guarantee ya 'twas not a gift from da fairies," Seamus said. "Dat paintin' is called *Da Brushstroke of Time*. 'Tis one of da most cursed tings in da 'eavens and every livin' ting in Mystfira is charged wid immediately returnin' it ta its proper place in da Keep of Time should we find it."

"I knew it was bad," Baylor whispered. "I could *feel* it."

"Er more of yer friends missin'?"

"Yes, everyone except Ebon," Rafe replied.

"I called you because we just heard Blake's phone ringing inside of that painting," Baylor said.

Turning to face Baylor, Seamus shoulders drooped, and he stared down at his hands. "Den 'tis a safe bet yer broder's in der wid da rest of yer missin' friends."

Crouching in front of Seamus, Baylor gazed into the leprechaun's eyes. "How is that even possible?"

"A dark spirit, by da name of Nauk, was imprisoned in dat paintin' and den banished ta a dungeon in da Keep of Time years ago."

"But I saw who took Blake and Sion. It wasn't a dark spirit. It was Sully . . . except his eyes were purple, and his teeth were all jagged and funny-colored."

"I doubt what ya saw was yer Sully. 'Twas more likely Nauk usin' yer friend's body."

Baylor pressed a hand to her chest and drew in a sharp breath. "Are you saying . . . Sully is . . . dead?" she asked in hoarse whisper.

"I don't know, poppet. I cannot say," Seamus said, giving the top of Baylor's head a comforting pat.

Rafe's lips twitched. "No, Sully *has* to be okay. Even if that painting somehow came through the time tuck, swallowed Sully, and bounced around a couple of different times, it landed on the grounds of Cliff House—which is protected by the Blue Star. No harm can come to us here."

"Dat is true," Seamus said, brightening, "but what I don't understand is da time tuck 'appened nearly four weeks ago now. Why did Nauk wait all dis time ta take da rest of ya?"

"Who knows," Rafe said. "Maybe he couldn't get out of the attic."

"What er ya talkin' about? Da paintin's not been down 'ere da whole time?"

"No. It was only in the library for three days before Baylor put it up in the attic," Rafe said.

"I, *umm,* didn't like it, so I wrapped it in plastic and stored it in the attic until yesterday morning," Baylor said, failing to mention to Seamus she'd been sleepwalking at the time.

Seamus puckered his forehead. "Den da stories I 'eard told about da paintin' er true. If da paintin' is covered or wrapped, da dark spirit cannot escape from it, but when da paintin' is uncovered Nauk can leave da frame fer a few 'ours every day, between midnight and tree-tirty in da mornin'. What time is it?" he asked, darting an anxious eye toward the painting.

Baylor snatched her cellphone from the floor and glanced at the screen. "It's four a.m."

"Den we're safe fer now."

Biting his lip, Rafe shook his head from side to side. "I should have known something was off. I heard servants' bells ringing in my room all three nights the painting was down here in the library, but I thought I was dreaming. I should have gotten up and checked the passageways. And you know what else?" he said. "When I got home from the valley this morning, I heard them again as I was passing the library to go upstairs."

"You heard the servants' bells?" Baylor said, springing to her feet and locking eyes with Rafe. "Oh, my gosh. That's right. Your room used to be my gram's sewing room, and they ring in the library, too."

Rafe felt a thickness growing in his throat as he silently berated himself. *I am a guardian angel. How could I be so stupid? How could I let this happen?*

"Why did ya 'ave ta take da paintin' out of da attic?" Seamus asked, tugging at Baylor's sleeve.

"It wasn't my idea," Baylor said, wringing her hands. "Oliver threw a fit and made me put it back in the library yesterday."

"If there is a way to get into that painting, there has to be a way to get out of it," Rafe said.

"Da only way inta dat paintin' is ta be taken der by Nauk. Da canvas serves as a prison fer da creature. 'Tis a wall we cannot cross."

Wall? Rafe's head bobbed up.

"Maybe we can't cross it, but we can see through it," he said, grabbing the soriscope from the book on the floor next to Baylor. "If Nauk took the other Ryder-Knight students into the painting, we should be able to see them with this."

Training the scope on the picture, Rafe spied a cavernous room with walls painted in a warm linen tone, the perfect backdrop for the colorful, macabre abstract paintings hanging on them.

In the front of the room, seated behind an immense artist's easel, Rafe saw a creature, a three-dimensional blob of colors, shapes, patterns, and textures—as abstract and bizarre as any of the paintings on the walls around it. Whorls of muted reds, violets, and purples mixed with odd shades of greens and blues shrouded the ghastly body.

The creature's hair, if the swirling whirlpool of colors could be described as hair, rose in a thick, crooked plume before cleaving in the middle and surging down to graze the top of a protruding forehead curved into two arches like the letter *M*. Two black-purple eyes tucked into the top of the humps of the letter stared at the canvas with a fierce glint.

The facial features, fluid, misshapen, distorted, and wrinkled could not be described with mere words, although Rafe thought he could make out what served as the creature's mouth, a dark splotch echoing the m-shape of his forehead and filled with rows of jagged multi-colored teeth. Below the mouth, he saw what seemed like a chin with a long triangle of light violet hair sagging from the center of it.

A gold paintbrush dangled from the creature's long grotesque fingertips. Dabbing the paintbrush into a deep magenta color in the middle of his body, the creature loaded his brush and skewed the paint over the canvas.

"I see him. I see Nauk," Rafe whispered, "and he doesn't look like any dark spirit I've ever seen before."

"Do you see Blake?" Baylor asked.

"Not yet, but the room's really big. I'm still looking."

Exploring the back of the vast room with his soriscope, Rafe spied hundreds of colorful life-like sculptures encased in an exquisite crystalline veneer. Scanning the sculptures, Rafe could see a gargoyle, several onks, a rumbrumie, fairies, goblins, selkies, even a hellhound dog, and most every other creature known to Mystfira.

As Rafe continued to survey the sculptures, he caught sight of a stunning girl with long sunrise-gold hair, porcelain skin, ocean-blue eyes, and a dazzling smile.

He couldn't breathe. A hollowness filled his chest. *Parker! What did Nauk do to you?*

Skipping the soriscope from sculpture to sculpture, Rafe found the others: Oliver, Sully, Leopold, Pebbles, Sion, Blake, Tahj, Audra, Deidre, Poppe, and Potts, all frozen in expressive, artistic poses.

"I found them."

"Are they okay?" Baylor asked, pressing a hand to her throat.

"Hold on," Rafe said, turning a gauge on the side of the soriscope, and directing it toward Blake's chest cavity. To his immense relief, he could see Blake's heart beating rhythmically. Quickly, he checked the other Ryder-Knight students as well.

"They're *all* alive!" Rafe exclaimed. "Their hearts are beating, but Nauk has made them into some sort of living sculptures encased in glass or ice. I can't tell which."

"What?" Baylor said. "Show me."

Giving Baylor the soriscope, Rafe helped her locate her brother and Leopold. As he stepped away from her, he saw Baylor cringe. He didn't need to ask; he knew she'd just seen Nauk.

"He's repulsive," Baylor said, taking the scope away from her eye and handing it to Seamus.

"True," Rafe replied.

"So . . . how do we get them out of there?" Baylor asked.

Seamus lowered the soriscope. "I don't know if ya can," he said.

"That's it," Rafe said. "I'm going to go get George."

"Dat woganot? I don't recommend dat, especially if ya ever want ta see yer friends alive again. Apparently, ya didn't notice, but yer friends er da only ones in der wid der 'earts beatin'. Da rest of dose creatures are *kuuuuchh*," Seamus said, drawing two fingers across his throat.

"Are you kidding? That's even more reason for me to call George," Rafe argued.

"What part of 'every livin' ting in Mystfira is charged wid *immediately* returnin' da paintin' ta its proper place in da Keep of Time' did ya not understand? If da paintin' is removed from Cliff House, yer broder and yer friends will die like da rest of da creatures in dat paintin', and no matter da consequences, da woganot must remove da paintin' from dis house, and so must yer Sakal. Dey er commanded ta do so by Araboth."

White-knuckled, Baylor wrung her hands together. "But you're a living creature of Mystfira, too, Seamus."

"Dat I am."

"Please, please don't tell anyone. Don't let anything happen to them. Please," Baylor pleaded.

"I'm willin' ta pretend like none of dis ever 'appened, and I'll even 'elp ya try ta get dem out of dat paintin', but ya'll both owe me a favor in da future."

"Done," Baylor said, shooting Rafe a don't-you-dare-say-otherwise look.

"Perfect," said Seamus. "Den while I put dat paintin' back in da attic and go about puttin' tings right in dis house again so no one can guess what 'appened, collect da one friend ya 'ave left, and go ta me shop and wait fer me der. I tink I know someone who can 'elp us."

"But, Seamus, how are Ebon and I going to get there? It's not like we can walk out the front door beside Rafe."

"I'll use me magic to transport ya."

"You can't," Baylor said. "Not without the Sakal finding out. Yesterday, Madri Isabo told me that the Sakal would be tracking major magic like transporting and transforming from now on."

"That's not good," Rafe said. "Seamus used magic to transport here. Eventually, they'll discover he was here and question him."

Seamus waved Rafe's concern away with his hand. "Den I'll tell dem dat ya summoned me, but when I got 'ere, not one of ya could be found."

"Okay, but that still doesn't solve the first problem. Baylor and Ebon are forbidden to leave this house, and every exit is guarded. They can't get out."

Baylor hung her head, and Rafe could see her fighting back fresh tears. His throat tightened. It physically hurt him to see her so upset, but there was nothing he could do.

Except . . .

Rafe's heart jerked in his chest as he recollected something Blake had said to him a few weeks ago in The House of Dew. "Wait a minute," he said, breaking into a grin. "There *is* a way to get the three of us off the grounds of Cliff House and into the Truvian Ring without being seen."

Baylor lifted her chin to look at Rafe. "Go on," she said, with the faintest hint of a smile forming on her lips. "I'm listening."

Chapter Ten

Mai

Unlocking the door of The Treasure Trove with the key Seamus had given her, Baylor trooped inside with Rafe and Ebon. "We're here," she said."

""Tis about time," Seamus replied, waddling out from a backroom of the shop now dressed in his elaborate red and gold jacket and breeches. "What took ya so long?"

"*Uhh, umm . . .* I had to change my clothes," Baylor said. "Sorry, Seamus."

Rafe was glad they were all still invisible so Ebon couldn't see how far he'd rolled his eyes up into the back of his head. Baylor's wardrobe change hadn't been the issue. She'd changed her clothes in a quick little jiffy.

No. Getting Ebon to The Treasure Trove had been the real problem. First, they had trouble convincing the boy genius that he had to go into Truvian with them, and right after they'd gotten over that hurdle, they'd discovered Ebon's stubbornness was superseded only by his fear of heights, which seemed rather ridiculous to Rafe since they'd just retrieved Ebon from one of the towers overlooking the cliffs.

There had been a shorter more direct way to ascend the cliffs, but Ebon's fear prevented them from taking it. Getting Ebon over the cliffs by the light of day would have been difficult, but asking him to tackle the jagged rocks and footholds lit only by the twelve moons of Mystfira had been a monumental task.

Seamus tapped his shillelagh on the floor, and the children became visible again.

Ebon materialized, pacing the floor near the display window with his hands clasped behind his back. "Forgive my aporetic skepticism—"

"Don't apologize fer yer skin bein' a different color den mine, lad," snapped Seamus. "Ya need ta be proud of who ya er. Dat's 'ow it works up 'ere in da 'eavens."

"Aporetic skepticism has nothing to do with the color of my skin. Aporetic is an adjective that describes my current state of perplexity as I'm trying to comprehend how you plan to facilitate our friends' liberation from the painting."

"Oh, yer perplexed, er ya?" said Seamus irritably. "Dat makes two of us, den, because I could 'ave sworn ya were talkin' about da pores in yer skin."

Ebon smacked his face into the palm of his hand and groaned.

Half-snorting and half-coughing into the crook of his arm, Rafe did his best to hide his laughter. Tahj usually translated Ebon's obscure words and covered Ebon's tendency to overuse long words in conversations, or, as Tahj liked to refer to it, "Ebon's sesquipedalian loquaciousness," for the Ryder-Knight students. Without Tahj, communicating with Ebon was challenging.

"Blake and I talked to you about this last night, Ebon. Remember?" Baylor prodded. "You and Tahj both have amazing minds, but most people don't have the vocabulary that the two of you do. You have to try to make it easier for us like Tahj does."

"I'll try, but surely you know what the word skepticism means."

"Dat wasn't da word we were stuck on, ya melter."

"Seamus, be nice," Baylor said.

"What? 'E's meltin' me brain wid all dose long words of 'is!"

The Treasure Trove's display window rattled in its frame as a hazy column of air spun down from the early morning sky, landing on Dressage Street in front of the leprechaun's shop.

"Good," Seamus said, the tension in his shoulders visibly easing. "Mai is 'ere."

"Is that May with a *y* or Mae with an *e*," Ebon asked.

"'Tis Mai with an *i*, and what does dat matter ta ya anyway? All ya need ta know is 'er name is Mai, she's a wind gypsy, and she might know 'ow ta get yer friends out of dat paintin'."

At that moment, the whirlwind in the street blew the door open with a loud *bang*, and every eye in The Treasure Trove turned toward the street outside. A large metal shopping cart filled with white garbage bags bounced out of the pirouetting haze and onto the red jasper street followed by two spindly legs covered by thick twisted stockings, a torso covered with a threadbare plaid skirt and layers of ratty sweaters, and a head topped with unkempt, wild grey hair.

"Harriet?" Baylor said, sprinting toward the open door.

Rafe and Ebon traded confounded looks with each other. *Homeless Harriet Hobbs from the corn maze was a wind gypsy?*

"What is she doing here?" Ebon asked.

"Mai's me art expert friend. If der's a way ta get anyone out of dat paintin', she'll know about it."

The wheels of the shopping cart squeaked over the threshold of The Treasure Trove, followed by the grungy old woman. Removing her hands from the bar of her cart, she threw open her arms.

"Children! How good to see you again!" she exclaimed.

"Mrs. Hobbs," Baylor said, rushing into the woman's arms for an embrace.

Without thinking, Rafe sped into the old woman's arms for a hug as well.

"I'm just Mai in the heavens, my dears. Goodness me, but you two give the most wonderful hugs," she said, dropping a kiss on the top of each of their heads.

Rafe drew back from Mai, a flush creeping across his cheeks and traveling to the tip of his ears. He'd run into the arms of an old woman like a small child. *Well, that was embarrassing. Why on earth had he done that?*

"I don't know if I'll ever get used to all these different names. Harriet is Mai, Simon is Sion, Rafe is Raphael. Do you have another name I should know about, Seamus?" Baylor asked.

"I like ta keep tings simple. Wherever I go, me name is Seamus O'Shanahan."

Mai ogled her new surroundings for a moment. "I love what you've done with the place, Seamus, but I don't see any chairs. I'd love to take a load off these old ankles."

Seamus tapped his shillelagh on the floor, and a soft cushy armchair appeared next to Mai.

"That's perfect," Mai said, tumbling backwards into the chair. "What can I do for you, my friend?"

"'Tis a delicate matter, and I'll need ta 'ave yer promise dat ya'll keep what I'm about ta tell ya a secret."

"Are you being a naughty leprechaun again, Seamus?"

"I suppose ya could say dat, but dis time 'tis fer a good reason. Da lives of dese children and der friends er in danger. I need ta save dem, so I'll need yer promise."

"To save the children? Of course, you have my word. I promise I won't tell a soul," Mai said, pretending to zip her lips shut. "But, I'll need a favor in return."

"I expected dat. Dat's 'ow promises work best," said Seamus

before launching into the story of the other missing children and ending with his discovery of *The Brushstroke of Time* in the library of Cliff House early that morning. "And dat's why I need ya, Mai. I need ya ta tell me everyting ya know about dat paintin' and da dark spirit, Nauk, who lives inside it."

"Who said anything about Nauk being a dark spirit?" Mai asked.

"Dat's what I 'eard."

"Well," Mai said, leaning forward. "That's not the case at all. Let me tell you the story." Springing to her feet, Mai rummaged around in her shopping cart and pulled out a book. "Here it is. I borrowed this book from the angelic library some time ago. Oh, dear," she said, making a face as she opened it. "It's overdue."

"Yer sure ta be scolded fer dat by dose jarvartan librarians."

"Don't I know it," Mai said, placing the book on the floor and giving it a pat. Swelling to one hundred times its size, the book transformed itself into a large movie screen.

Seamus tapped his shillelagh on the floor, and four little stools appeared. "Will ya do da voices fer me, Mai?" Seamus asked, motioning for the children to take a seat. "I love it when ya pretend ta be each character."

"Absolutely. It's the only way I know how to tell a story." Folding her hands under her chin in excitement, Mai waited for everyone to sit down on their stools.

"Many, many years ago before the stars were born in the heavens, there lived a beautiful seraph named Naukiel, who preferred to be called Nauk."

An image of a gorgeous angel materialized in a palace filled with stupendous architecture, drawings, paintings, and sculptures.

"There never lived a more clever, imaginative, talented artist.

Nauk was loved by all the heavens, but most particularly by the seventh heaven of Araboth.

"One day, as the seraph soared through the skies of Araboth, he viewed his work from afar, and suddenly his contributions seemed quite meager and unremarkable to him.

"'Certainly, an angel with my gifts and talents should be able to produce more exceptional pieces of art than these,' he thought.

"And so began Nauk's quest. He explored all the universes known to angels, hoping to discover something to spark his angelic creativity to new heights. Unfortunately, Nauk's search for inspiration consumed him . . . so much so, that he dared to travel to the underworld without the protection of a carrion."

"What was dat eejit tinking?" Seamus squawked in horror. "Only da carrions know 'ow ta control da dark spirits."

A smoky, cluttered, chaotic room materialized on the screen. The walls, splashed with paint, looked as if they had been used to clean the artist's paintbrushes. A hulking figure standing at an easel with his back to the screen skimmed paint across the canvas.

"Blinded by ambition, Nauk met with the most famous dark artist of the underworld."

On the screen, the figure turned, revealing a pale, ugly, tattooed face with cold black eyes.

"Yaltabolt?" Seamus murmured, teetering on the edge of his stool.

"That's right, and as an artist himself, Nauk should have known to leave the moment he set eyes on Yaltabolt's studio—for to look into an artist's studio is to look into their mind, but he did not. He stayed to talk to the wicked creature, and Yaltabolt told him of the tapestries being woven at the mysterious citadel, known as the Keep of Time, behind the walls of the Castle of Reckoning.

"Something stirred inside Nauk's mind when he heard mention of the Castle of Reckoning. Long ago, he'd learned of the castle during his training at The Red Beryl Palace. He even remembered that it was hidden in the Valley of Waterfalls and presided over by three dominion angels—Clariel, Emmiel, and Mortiel—but he failed to see how the tapestries would be of any value to him or Yaltabolt."

"Excuse me," Ebon interrupted, "but the three dominion angels you just mentioned bring to mind The Fates, the three mythological sisters who control the life and destiny of everyone on Earth. The ancient Greeks believed Clotho spins the thread of life, Lachesis draws lots to see how long a life will be and measures it out, and Atropos cuts the thread of life."

"Poppycock and twaddle!" Mai said with a snort. "That ancient Greek legend didn't get one thing right. Clariel, Emmiel, and Mortiel simply keep an artistic record of what goes on with each little human on Earth in their heavenly tapestries, and they most certainly *do not* control the fate of the people there."

"Wait. I thought dominion angels record *in writing* what humans say and do," Rafe said.

"They do. Fitting words together is an art form for dominion angels, but one which does not capture the beauty and purpose of the *grand* design. The heavenly tapestries of the dominion angels, however, do," Mai said, "and they are a wonder to behold."

"Are you purporting that we as humans are masters of our own fate?" Ebon asked.

"Oh, my dear. I'm not purporting anything . . . not today, anyway," Mai said, fixing her gaze on Ebon. "I'm simply saying you humans are primarily the masters of your own destiny, and with the exception of your birth and death and a few odds and ends in between, there is really very little out of your control. Your decisions, choices, and actions determine your fate."

Ebon shifted on his stool and crossed his arms. "Interesting. Then using your logic, being transported to Mystfira against my will would be classified under the category of 'a few odds and ends in between' as would my superior intellect and allergy to cats."

"Dat's it! Dis is a story, not a discussion," Seamus shouted. "Shut yer gobs, all of ya! She was just gettin' ta da good part where Yaltabolt was tellin' Nauk about da Keep of Time." Holding his hands out in a "please-continue" gesture, Seamus nodded at Mai.

"'The Keep of Time is a place where the air is spun into the white thread of life and sewn into to the great tapestries of earthly time,' Mai cackled in an evil voice, pretending to be Yaltabolt. 'A place where billions of magical brushes dip themselves into the vat of time before decorating each and every thread of the tapestry being worked. No artist has ever painted with time itself before. Just think of it. With time in our skilled hands, we could create supernatural masterpieces the likes of which have never been seen in this world or any other.'

"As soon as Yaltabolt produced pictures of the gorgeous tapestries kept behind the walls of the Castle of Reckoning, Nauk knew he had to go to the Keep of Time. If he could paint with the colors of time itself, he could finally produce a piece of art worthy of the seventh heaven of Araboth.

"It took Nauk and Yaltabolt a long time to learn how to get past the many safeguards shielding the Castle of Reckoning, but learn they did, and after many months, the two of them made it through the castle's defenses and into the Keep of Time."

A stone staircase in the Keep of Time appeared on the screen in front of them.

"'How will we get the paint? They're not just going to give it to us,' Nauk asked Yaltabolt as they ascended the stairs together.

"'Leave that to me. I told you I have the perfect plan. You just need to distract the dominion angels for me.'

"'You promised you wouldn't harm them.'

"'And I'll keep that promise. No harm shall come to them,' Yaltabolt whispered as they arrived at a door at the top of the keep.

"Yaltabolt cracked open the door, and Nauk peeked into the room where the angels worked."

A great room of prodigious size, formed of whitewashed stone, materialized on the screen.

"Nauk had expected to see a gargantuan loom, but instead he glimpsed a monumental canvas of thin translucent fabric stretched across the room. Hovering at different points along the canvas, billions of needles with blunt points poked in and out of the tapestry at their own pace and of their own accord.

"Nauk's heart quickened when he noticed the colossal black pot in the corner of the room with billions of paint brushes floating over it. As each stitch was completed, a brush would dip itself into the vat, swish through the air to the tapestry, and dab color on it.

"Sweeping the room with his eyes, Nauk spotted Clariel sitting at her spinning wheel, garbed in her white velvet jubilee robe with turquoise feather edging. He could scarcely believe what his eyes beheld. Clariel was, indeed, spinning the sparkling thread of life from the very air around her.

"Emmiel stood nearby measuring the thread Clariel had spun, and, according to what she saw on a massive book in front of her, she clipped strands from the wheel to certain lengths and threaded them through new needles. Scooting over to a particular place in the tapestry, Emmiel placed the first few stitches until the needle leapt from her hand to stitch for itself.

"Circling the canvas in a perpetual loop, the last dominion angel, Mortiel, oversaw the whole project. She moved to and fro making sure the threads were secured in the back of the tapestry when their lengths ran out. Occasionally, a needle would stop, and Mortiel would have to take a quick stitch or two until the needle moved on its own again.

"'Fear not, dear ones. We mean you no harm. We are artists ourselves. My name is Naukiel, and this one is called Yaltabolt.'

"Mortiel scowled. 'My name is Mortiel, Clariel is at the wheel, and Emmiel is threading. I have heard of you, Naukiel, but even if you were here without a dark spirit, I could not permit you to remain. Go, now, before we are forced to remove you.'

"'We have permission from Araboth to be here to observe and to learn,' Yaltabolt lied. 'How else would I have crossed your water barriers?'"

On the movie screen, Rafe watched Mortiel stare at Nauk and Yaltabolt like a boxer sizing up her opponents.

"'Pray tell us,' Nauk said, walking around to the front of the tapestry with his hands behind his back, 'why are there so many needles and brushes, and why are they not guided by your hands at all times?'

"'We guide the needles until the Earthly souls start directing their own lives, and after that we interfere only for events out of their control, but the Earthly souls decide on all the shades of their lives. We have nothing to do with the vat of time or the brushes," Mortiel said in a gruff tone. 'Please go now.'

"'But the paint on this tapestry is so unique,' Nauk said, continuing his stroll around the tapestry. 'These colors are different from every angle. I've never seen anything like it before.'

"'Yes, yes,' Yaltabolt said. 'The paint is the most amazing I've ever seen as well. Say, I see the vat has a ladder reaching all the way to the top over there. Do you use it to stir the paint?'

"'I already told you we have nothing to do with the paint or those brushes. The queen of the castle alone is charged with their care,' Mortiel replied.

"'Please,' Naukiel said, 'if we could just have one glimpse of the colors of time, we'll go and leave you in peace.'

"'You will leave immediately after that and promise never to return?' Mortiel asked.

"'Absolutely,' Nauk replied.

"'Then look and go.'

"Nauk felt a thrill of euphoria. Soon, he would be in possession of the essence of time itself, and what a masterpiece he would create with it! How grateful he was that the Keep of Time was located in Mystfira so he could feel this wonderful human emotion again!

"Beckoning for Yaltabolt to follow him, Naukiel and Yaltabolt approached the gigantic black pot with awe. Together they scaled the ladder and peered into the vat. Swirling and billowing, ribbons of intense colors churned about inside of it, snaking every which way. Unlike most paints, the colors of time smelled fresh and sweet.

"'Exquisite,' Nauk murmured, 'but how are we going to get some?'

"'Take four more steps up the ladder, turn your body toward Mortiel, and call out a question to her. She'll be paying attention to you, and I'll do the rest,' Yaltabolt whispered.

"Excited and smiling, Nauk climbed four more rungs on the ladder. He had the perfect question in mind. 'Mortiel, could you please tell me what makes the paint smell—what—nooooo!' Naukiel screamed as Yaltabolt's arms seized his legs.

"With an almighty heave, Yaltabolt sent the seraph somersaulting backwards into the enormous vat.

"Pushing, pulling, and kneading Naukiel's body in every direction, the blazing colors enveloped him. He held his breath as his head slipped under the surface. It felt strange, almost as if he had melted into the colors themselves.

"Kicking hard, Nauk shot to the top of the vat and caught the lip of the rim and sloshed himself up and over the edge. He tried to grasp the ladder with hands and feet, but for some reason, his paint-soddened limbs slipped right through the rungs. It wasn't until he had splashed to the floor below that Nauk realized he was no longer an angel, but instead, just a writhing, thick puddle of swirling colors.

"Kneeling over Nauk, Yaltabolt conjured a large flask. 'Looks like time is finally on your side, friend, and every other part of you as well,' he said with an evil smirk.

"An accomplished magician of arcane magic, the dominion named Clariel swung into action. Leaping up from her spinning wheel, she pulled a handful of fairy dust from the pocket of her jubilee robe and ran to Nauk's side. Crushing the grains in her fist, she threw the dust across the squirming puddle on the floor and onto Yaltabolt, saying:

'Carrions take Yaltabolt
For his sight doth me revolt.'

"Thank goodness, carrions always arrive on the scene in the same moment they are summoned, and they snatched Yaltabolt away before the wicked creature had time to dip his flask into the paint.

"Then, with Yaltabolt out of the way, the angels set about trying to save Nauk's life. Clariel grabbed a paintbrush from the air on its way back to the vat after painting a stitch on the tapestry. Using another fairy spell, she loaded the paint, which had once been Nauk, into the brush and hurled him into a magical canvas to protect him until she and the other dominions could consult with Araboth.

"Nauk didn't know it, but when he was thrown through the unusual canvas, his new image had been captured on the surface. Flecks of silver and gold from the fairy dust Clariel had thrown and tiny bits of the threads of life accentuated the purples, greens, and blues of the new piece of art.

"The seventh heaven of Araboth, taking pity on the dear naïve angel, proclaimed the picture *The Brushstroke of Time* and charged that no heavenly hand or hand of the underworld may ever harm the painting or the creature inside of it. Although the painting was a masterpiece fit for the heavens, it would never be displayed. Araboth decreed that it was to hang in a dungeon in the Keep of Time as a warning that good should never consort with evil."

The movie screen went dark. With a snap of Mai's fingers, the screen disappeared, and the book shrank to a readable size again.

"That's one of the saddest stories, I've ever heard," Baylor said as Mai retrieved the book from the floor.

"I think so, too," Mai said, "but my story has not quite ended yet. Yaltabolt was not content to leave things there. Years later, after he heard that Nauk was still alive and preserved as a heavenly masterpiece in the Keep of Time, he escaped the underworld and plotted to steal the painting. If he could get his hands on *The*

Brushstroke of Time, he'd have unlimited access to the paint on Nauk's body.

"As you know by now, Yaltabolt was successful, and once he acquired the painting, he left the underworld with his stolen prize. He ferried the painting from place to place to avoid capture and eventually became Nauk's only friend.

"Using dark magic, Yaltabolt made it possible for Nauk to leave the painting for a few short hours a day, but in order for Nauk's new body not to dry out and die, Nauk needed to inhabit other creatures' bodies. One day when they were hiding in the heavens, Yaltabolt brought Nauk a rumbrumie and encased him in ice so Nauk could paint.

"You see, in the heavens, if an artist needs a person to sit or stand completely still for a portrait, they will often wrap a subject in ice and put them into a state of hibernation, like bears on your Earth."

"Da creatures in dat paintin' er not sleepin', Mai," Seamus said. "Dey er done fer."

"Naukiel does not know that. His brain has been muddled by time. He doesn't mean any harm. When Nauk comes out of the painting to find subjects to serve as his models and uses the ice technique to keep them from moving, he has no idea he is stilling his subject forever."

"Oh, I see. He doesn't mean any harm, so that makes it okay," Rafe said, voice dripping with sarcasm.

"Mai, do you think Yaltabolt was responsible for pushing the painting through the time tuck?" Baylor asked.

Mai nodded. "I am certain of it."

"But why?" Baylor asked

"One does hear whispers in the wind," Mai said. "My guess is it may have something to do with Yaltabolt's brother."

"Who's his brother?" Rafe asked.

"Vexxon."

Seamus threw his hands in the air. "Dat figures! Da fiend probably offered Yaltabolt a place at 'is side when 'e conquers der planet, and Yaltabolt agreed ta 'elp em get rid of da Ryder-Knight students once and fer all."

"Do you mean to tell us that if we had all been captured and impounded inside that painting, and the angels found *The Brushstroke of Time* in our library, they wouldn't have tried to set us free?" Ebon asked.

"I don't know. Who can say?" Mai said with a shrug. "All I know is that every living thing in the heavens has been instructed by the seventh heaven of Araboth to return the painting to the Keep of Time with no questions asked."

"But you aren't going to do that, are you, Mai?" Baylor asked, sliding to the edge of her stool.

Mai winked. "No worries, sweet girl. Seamus made me promise not to tell, and a wind gypsy never breaks a promise."

Standing, Ebon crossed his arms across his chest. "Does anyone else see the irony in this situation?"

"What is 'e prattlin' on about now? Who is Irony?"

"Irony is a thing, not a person," replied Baylor. "It's when something happens the opposite of the way you'd expect it to."

Seamus pressed a fist to his mouth and puffed out his cheeks.

No doubt to keep himself from saying something rude in front of Mai, Rafe thought.

"That's exactly right," Ebon said, "such as an angel in possession of the Blue Star bringing us to the heavens to protect us, and the dark spirits using another angel to destroy us instead of doing it themselves."

"Yer words make me brain puddin', boy, and I'm not sure I like ya much at all. But just da same, I don't want ta see any of ya cark it up 'ere. I tink yer parents would like ta see ya again."

"Cark it?" Baylor asked.

"Die," whispered Rafe.

Seamus turned to speak to Mai. "If ya known of a way ta get da children out of dat paintin', ya need ta tell me now."

"Where there's a will, there is always a way, but I'm not sure you're going to like it," Mai replied. "It involves a dangerous quest, and to make matters worse, you'll have to free Nauk before you can rescue the children."

"Yer right. I don't like it. Is dat da only way?"

"I'm afraid so."

"Den tell me what I need ta do."

"Oh, dear," Mai said with a sigh. "I guess I haven't made myself clear. Neither you, nor Rafe, can free Nauk. That task belongs to Baylor and Ebon alone."

"Are you sure that's wise?" Ebon asked. "Given the parlous state of this situation."

Throwing her hands up in the air in an I-give-up gesture, Baylor shook her head at Ebon.

"What I meant to say," said Ebon, "is given the inherent danger and risks of this situation, Baylor and I don't seem to be the logical choices for a task such as this."

"I agree," Rafe said. "Araboth said no heavenly hand could harm Nauk, but you just said we had to free Nauk. So why can't Seamus and I help them?"

"Because at the end of day," Mai said, "the body Nauk functions in now must be destroyed, and Baylor and Ebon are the only ones who can do that since they do not have *heavenly hands*. You and Seamus can go with your friends and act to protect and advise them, but neither of you may do anything else. Do you understand?"

Looking sullen, Rafe and Seamus both nodded.

"Good. Now then, Baylor and Ebon will have to collect two things before they can go into the painting to free everyone. The items can be found at the Castle of Reckoning. Once you've gotten through the castle's defenses, one of you must go to the Keep of Time where you will need to persuade one of the keepers there to spin you a length of rope made from the thread of life, and the other one must go to the queen's house where they will consult with the chemist in order to learn how to create a solvent to dissolve the paint on Nauk's body."

"The queen of the castle has her own chemist? That's impressive," Ebon said.

"That's not the impressive part," Mai replied. "The impressive part is . . . the queen of the castle *is* the chemist."

"And after we do that?" Baylor said.

"Then you'll go back to Cliff House and summon me. I'll tell you the rest when we get to the attic."

"Why can't you tell us now?" asked Rafe.

"It seems dreadfully silly for me to waste my breath unless you prove successful," Mai said. "I'll be needing that favor now, Seamus. Would you be a dear and fetch me a winrup from The House of Dew before I leave?"

"Aw, Mai," Seamus said, scuffing the floor. "Right now?"

"Yes, please."

"Fine."

As Seamus padded over to the door, Rafe remembered something Madri Typhicus had said. "Mai? Were you the one who gave the Parrot Wind a note for me in Luke's handwriting that said: *Listen to the wind. For it brings you wisdom*?"

Mai giggled. "Guilty, and if I may just toot my own horn for a moment, I have to say I'm excellent at forging other people's handwriting."

"I'd say so," Rafe said. "It really did look like all the others Luke wrote, but why did you do it?"

"Why did I give you the note?" Mai asked. "I should think it was obvious. You were in need of a little help. The Parrot Wind had been trying to tell you about your friend Gerand for such a long time, and you weren't listening closely enough."

"I was listening, but you know how bad the Parrot Wind is with names. It would have been more helpful if you sent a note that actually said, 'Gerand Rial is an unaware dark spirit.' How was I supposed to know the wind meant Gerand Rial when it kept saying Danger Real or Danger Liar?"

"*Hmmm.* I don't know, Reef Derry. How could you or Gate Winblank or B. W. Ekal Etagin possibly have pieced that together sooner than you did?" Mai asked.

Rafe dropped his gaze to the floor of The Treasure Trove. He felt his face growing hot and red. He knew her question required no answer, it was meant as a statement, and she was right, he should have figured out Rand was a dark spirit way sooner than he had.

"Oh, my dear," Mai said, catching sight of the little silver ring on Baylor's finger. "Did Seamus give that ring to you?"

"Yes," Baylor said, giving Mai a curious look. "How did you know?"

"Because it looks very much like the protection rings Seamus gave to his wife and daughter. He must be very fond of you."

"Seamus has a wife and daughter?" Baylor asked, eyes wide.

"*Had* a wife and daughter. He's never been quite the same since they passed. His daughter Róisín was a beautiful girl of thirteen years with lovely dark hair and eyes; he called her his little rose. I think you must remind him of her."

Rafe, Baylor, and Ebon stared at Mai in mutual shock.

"You see," Mai said. "Seamus, Róisín, and Teagan, his wife, were famous musicians. They lived over in the Ring of Rocks. Oh, you should have seen the house Seamus built for them there. He used only the most magnificent stones, crisscrossed with deep grains of color and frosted with crystals and lichen. It was gorgeous. Nothing was too good for his girls."

"I can't believe it," Baylor squeaked.

"Believe it. And they led such a very happy life together. There wasn't an instrument that they couldn't play between them. During the day, they would mine gold with the other leprechauns, and at night they would travel the heavens together as *The O'Shanahan Family* to entertain us all.

"Unfortunately, one day, enticed by ten large pots of gold, Seamus accepted an invitation to play in Baeldavar. It was there his family met Vexxon, who asked them to come back to the underworld in a month to play at his father's birthday party."

"Oh no," Baylor whispered.

Mai nodded with a sad expression on her face. "After their concert in Baeldavar had ended that evening, Seamus had no intention of ever going back to the underworld again, no matter how much money he was offered. But he lied to Vexxon and told him that *The O'Shanahan Family* would be happy to accept the engagement."

"That can't have been received well," Ebon said.

"Indeed not. Vexxon was outraged when *The O'Shanahan Family* did not show up in the underworld for his father's birthday party, and he went to the Ring of Rocks to exact his revenge. He meant to punish Seamus in the worst possible way, and he did.

Seamus had gone into the tunnels earlier than usual the day it happened. Teagan and Róisín had not yet risen, and Vexxon dispatched them to Araboth while they slept in their own beds."

"But how did Seamus know it was Vexxon and not someone else?" Rafe asked.

Baylor rubbed the red *V* burned into her own wrist. "Because he marked them," she gasped.

"That's right and when Seamus came home to discover his precious girls had breathed their last breath, he went wild with grief. He's never been back to that house since. He's tried everything possible to be reunited with his family. He even went to the Castle of Reckoning, hoping to find a way to turn back time. But when he didn't succeed, he moved into Truvian and started The Treasure Trove."

"How long have his girls been gone?" Baylor asked.

"At least twenty-five of your Earth years," Mai replied.

"Poor Seamus," Baylor whispered, biting her lip and looking at Rafe.

"I guess that explains why he's got such a soft spot for you, Bay."

"Please, you mustn't tell him I told you," Mai said. "He doesn't think I know."

"Don't worry, Mai. We won't," Baylor said. "I promise."

The bell over the door tinkled as Seamus opened it. "I got yer winrup, Mai. Tanks fer 'elpin' us."

"You're quite welcome." Mai pulled a handkerchief from the sleeve of her sweater and folded the winrup neatly into it. Rising from her easy chair, she ambled back over to her shopping cart and dropped the winrup into it. "Oh, and Seamus, you're going to need to get help from two of the Upons when you go to the Castle of Reckoning. You'll need Cinderella as well as Goldilocks this time.

Seamus did a double take. "Who told ya I've been der before?"

"Who knows? I hear so many things in the wind."

Gripping the handle of her shopping cart, Mai pushed the cart over to where Seamus stood. Stooping low, she cupped her hands around her mouth and whispered something into his ear.

"Janey Mack! Ya got ta be kiddin' me? What did ya do dat fer, Mai?"

Mai whispered to Seamus one more time and for a little longer this time.

"Of course, I'll take care of it fer ya, I promise, but 'twill 'ave ta wait."

"Thank you. Goodbye for now, Seamus," Mai said, walking her hands up her legs to help her straighten up again. Turning, she smiled and waved to the children. "Goodbye, children. I wish you every success, and please be sure to give Lady Jane my love the next time you see her."

Chapter Eleven

Trespassing in Truvian

"So, Seamus . . . you've been to the Castle of Reckoning once before?" Rafe asked.

"Maybe," the leprechaun said, raising his voice. "What's it ta ya?"

"I'm just glad we're going with someone who has firsthand experience. That's all," said Rafe. "You'll know how to get around the castle's defenses and into the keep."

"I did at one time, but dat was long ago, and tings change."

"Still," said Rafe, leaning forward, "you have some experience, and that's better than none."

"Do we have a plan of action?" Ebon asked.

"We'll travel ta da Valley of Waterfalls, and grab da Upons, Goldilocks and Cinderella. Den we'll get up ta da Castle of Reckonin'. Once we're der, ya'll go ta da queen's house ta learn 'ow ta make whatever dat stuff was dat Mai was goin' on about," Seamus said, pointing to Ebon.

"It's called paint solvent," Ebon said.

"Yeah, dat, and da rest of us will go ta da Keep of Time. When we get past da barriers der, ya'll get da tread of life. Den we'll meet back up, get ta Cliff House, and call Mai."

"Okay, we're in the third ring now, and the Valley of Waterfalls is in the eighth ring. We've got to get through the Fairy Forest, the Ring of Rocks, the Weeping Woods and Mukrot to get there," Baylor said, counting on her fingers. "That's a long way from here."

"'Tis," Seamus agreed.

"And just who are these Upons we're supposed to get help from?" Rafe asked.

"Der a race of people too dangerous ta stay on yer Earth. Ya may know of dem because dey er written about in yer storybooks."

"Wait," Baylor said, crinkling her brow. "Are you saying Cinderella and Goldilocks are the same storybook characters we grew up hearing about?"

"'Tis exactly what I'm saying, child. Der Upons. If a tale in yer world starts out wid da words 'Once *upon* a time,' ya can be sure da fairies changed da real version of da story, so as not ta scare all da little children on yer planet."

"You can't be serious, Seamus. How could Cinderella possibly be dangerous?" Baylor said.

"She doesn't go by dat name up 'ere. She goes by da name of Blaise, and she commands da power of fire. Da little pyromaniac burned 'er stepmudder's house down twenty-nine times before she married 'er prince."

"And Goldilocks?" Rafe asked.

"*Ahhh*, Goldie! Dat girl is da finest lock pick in any universe. She'll be able ta get us inta da Castle of Reckoning, but I'll 'ave ta get 'er out of da tower dey keep 'er in first."

"They keep her in a tower?" Ebon asked.

"Dey 'ave ta. Da little wench pinches anyting dat isn't nailed down."

Taking a deep breath, Baylor fanned herself with her hand.

"What?" Seamus asked.

"Nothing. Just sounds like we've got our work cut out for us," she replied.

"We do, but just be glad we don't 'ave to use 'Ansel and Gretel fer anyting. Dose little cannibals er da worst. What dey did ta dat witch was barbaric!"

"Where do these Upons live?" Ebon asked.

"Dey live in da Valley of Waterfalls."

"I don't understand how we're going to get all these people together and do everything Mai told us to do without getting caught," Baylor said.

Seamus tottered toward the door in the back of his shop. "Leave dat ta me. We'll go da same way I did last time. I'll get me map."

Baylor and Ebon followed Seamus into his room, but Rafe lingered in the doorframe, sizing up Seamus's living quarters.

Two small pieces of Brandire wood sat in a stone fireplace, taking the chill from the room. Popular in Mystfira as a heat source, Brandire wood gave off heat only when needed and only when one was a safe distance from it. The wood was never consumed by fire, so it was passed down from generation to generation in most families.

In one corner of the room, Rafe spied a small wooden table and chairs. Angled into another corner of the room was a low bed, wide enough to sleep an army. It sported a cozy blue-and-white quilt, puffy pillows, and a tattered old teddy bear. Rafe guessed the bear probably used to belong to Seamus's beloved daughter, Róisín.

Throwing open a huge trunk at the bottom of the bed, Seamus sifted through the objects inside. "Da safest way ta get ya der is ta use da leprechaun tunnels," he said. "I've got a map in me chest 'ere somewhere. 'Tis a bit old, but so am I, and I'm still useful."

"How long will it take to get to the Valley of Waterfalls?" Rafe asked.

"I'm tinking two weeks if we don't run inta any troubles."

"Two weeks? That's way too long," Baylor said. "There has to be another way."

"If I can't use me magic ta transport ya places, den der's not."

"Maybe there is," Rafe said, crossing his arms and leaning against the doorframe. "I think I know another way, but it's in the Presidio. The day of the Jarvartan Joining, I was there with Madri Typhicus and Madri Keva. They knew I didn't know how to transport yet, and if they had to fly to the Rocker with me, they said we wouldn't be on time, so they took me through the living landscapes right to very spot they wanted to go."

"That's amazing," Baylor said.

"But illogical for us to even consider," Ebon replied. "The palace is guarded by gargoyles and a woganot."

Rafe smiled. "We don't have to sneak into the palace to get to the Presidio. All we have to do is sneak into Madri Typhicus' house in Truvian, and we can enter the Presidio using his scepter."

"Madri Typhicus has a house in Truvian?" Baylor asked. "I thought the members of the Sakal lived in their palaces."

"They each have a room in their palaces, but they keep a house together in Truvian as well," Rafe said. "Madri Keva said they prefer to stay in their house."

"Well, there is an Adomis trial scheduled for tonight, and Madri Typhicus is a spadroon," Ebon said. "Maybe he won't take his scepter with him."

"As Blake would say, 'you need to slow your roll' and think about this," Baylor said. "Let's say Madri Typhicus does leave his scepter at his house tonight. When he comes home after the Adomis trial, he is most certainly going to notice his scepter is missing, and he probably has a way to track it. It will lead him right to us."

"We're not going to steal it. We're only going to borrow it," Rafe said. "We'll use it to get where we need to go and then Seamus can put the scepter back and meet us in the Valley of Waterfalls."

"But how do we know if the scepter will even be there?" Baylor asked. "What if the madri dresses for Adomis in the palace?"

"A few days ago, I overheard Madri Typhicus telling the other members of the Sakal there was a mandatory meeting at their house in Truvian right before they go to Adomis tonight. Madri Typhicus will more than likely dress there and leave his scepter there as well. He has to," Rafe said.

Shaking a finger at Rafe, Seamus said, "Normally, I disapprove of earwiggin'. Dat is, unless I'm da one doin' it, but I'll let it go dis time."

"Five members of the Sakal participate in the Adomis trials," Rafe said, "and if even *one* of them leaves their scepter in their house in Truvian tonight, we'll be able to get into the Presidio."

"Hmmm," Seamus said, tapping his chin. "Truvian will be a ghost town dis evenin' and so will dat palace. If we can find one of der scepters, yer idea might work."

"Let's say we procure the scepter and use it get to the Valley of Waterfalls," Ebon said. "And, let's even speculate that we get into the Castle of Reckoning and are in possession of all the items we require to save our friends. If Seamus puts the scepter back, we've lost our only expeditious and untraceable way to get back here to the third ring."

"And won't people be suspicious if you close your shop and disappear at the same time we do, Seamus?" Baylor asked.

"I'll get someone ta watch me shop while I'm gone. I go ta da Valley of Waterfalls every couple of weeks ta collect giant snail slime fer da dark spirits in Mystfira because dey pay me dear fer it. Everybody knows dat. No one will miss old Seamus, and if we er fortunate enough ta get everyting Mai told us ta get, I'll tink of a way ta get us home quick-like, even if I 'ave ta turn ya inta baskets and fill ya wid snail slime. Now stay back 'ere in dis room, and keep quiet until it's time ta go."

"I guess that'll be all right," Baylor said, looking at Ebon and Rafe. "None of us really slept last night."

"Nod off, den. Da bed's plenty big enough fer all of ya. I'll come fetch ya when 'tis time ta go."

—————●

After three cups of strong tea and an amber-flavored celestial spear, Rafe finally cleared away the blur of exhaustion, which had settled over him the moment he lay down to sleep.

"Sorry," he said, emerging from the back room. "I guess yesterday's stand in the Valley of Shadows took way more out of me than I thought it did."

"Dat's okay, Tinker Bell. Just step lively from now on," Seamus said. "Time ta go."

"And tonight, the part of wisecracking Blake Wingate will be played by Seamus O'Shanahan," muttered Rafe.

"What er ya whisperin' about over der?"

"It's nothing, Seamus," Baylor said, stepping toward Ebon and Rafe with three grains of fairy dust. "Ready?" she asked.

When the boys nodded, Baylor crushed the grains between her fingers and sprinkled the dust over all three of them, chanting:

> *"As we travel up and down Dressage Street,*
> *Make us invisible to all we meet."*

Seamus cloaked himself using his magic, and the four of them stepped out of The Treasure Trove. The little group walked in the gloaming until two rows of whitewashed stone houses straddled the red jasper street.

"Dis is it," Seamus said, stopping in front of a narrow two-story house that said Layhish Taylah in Anfar on the door. "Da lion and da lamb."

"How are we going to get inside, Seamus? Your friend Goldilocks isn't here yet," Baylor whispered.

"We don't need Goldilocks. Teft and 'ome invasion is not someting da Sakal ever worry about. Nobody in der right mind would dream of enterin' der abode uninvited, let alone traipsin' around inside it."

"Not even a dark spirit?" Ebon asked.

"Especially not a dark spirit. Dey can't touch a scepter widout gettin' paralyzed," Seamus said, twisting the door handle and pushing the door open. "Get in. Hurry!"

"Whoa," Rafe whispered as he entered the spacious entrance hallway under an elegant, yet understated, crystal chandelier. At the far end of the hall sat a dignified, broad, polished oak staircase.

"Impossible. The dimensions of this house from the outside seem far too inadequate to accommodate such spaciousness," Ebon said.

"Yeah, well . . . nothing is ever how it seems up here, is it?" Baylor replied, examining an antique-looking, carved console table and mirror in the hallway.

Seamus snapped the door shut behind the children. "Now don't go touchin' anyting, except fer dat scepter when we find it," he warned.

In a haze of wonder, Rafe looked at the splendid rooms on

each side of the gracious entrance hallway, which was decorated with the colors of the sand and sea of Earth. Nothing seemed grandiose in the rooms on either side of him, except perhaps the grand piano in the sitting room—Madri Roanin's, no doubt.

The dining room's soft blue-and-cream color palette and gleaming gold accents set the tranquil tone of the room. Its round table, not as ostentatious as the one in the Presidio, sat on a pale blue decorative rug in front of a large fireplace.

As Rafe's eyes scanned the room, he found them drawn like a magnet to the painting of two caramel-haired boys hanging above the hearth. The portrait captured the young boys' sense of wonder and glee as they leaned out a window trying to catch flowers from the once-a-year floral rain in Mystfira.

Baylor noticed Rafe staring at the painting and scooted over to stand next to him. "They're adorable. Who do you think they are?"

"I don't know," Rafe said with a shrug. "Hey, Seamus? Did the madrikim ever have any children of their own?"

"Don't know. Don't care," replied the leprechaun. "Dat's not what we're 'ere fer."

Remembering their mission, Rafe pried his eyes away from the painting and walked to the bottom of the staircase. Placing his hand on the first carved newel, he said, "Seamus, you and Ebon take the first floor, and Bay and I will look upstairs."

"Fine, but no dawdlin'. Be quick about it," snapped Seamus.

"Got it. Let's go, Bay."

Baylor scrambled up the stairs beside Rafe to the second floor. The hallway there was an open balcony overlooking the entrance hall below and held in place by colonnades of richly carved oak.

Rafe counted the doors he saw on the floor. "We need to

find Madri Typhicus' room, and we've got twelve rooms to check. Maybe we should split up."

Baylor shook her head. "Look at the transom windows above each door. They're different colors like the different colored robes the madrikim wear. I don't think we need to check every room."

"This one is rose pink, so it should be Madri Avalon's room," Baylor said, cracking open the first door with a rose-pink transom above it.

Peeking over Baylor's shoulder, Rafe knew she was right. Decorated with shades of rose and burgundy red, an intricate white lace duvet covered the large bed. It looked as lovely and feminine as the madri herself.

"That will save some time," Rafe said, looking around the hallway. "So, where's the room with the multi-colored transom then?"

"Over there, across the way, but there are two of them," Baylor said, turning a corner of the balcony hallway and walking toward the rooms.

"That's strange," Rafe said, following her. "Why does Madri Typhicus have two rooms?"

"I don't know. I'll take the first one; you take the other one?"

"Sounds like a plan."

Baylor disappeared into the first room as Rafe pushed open the door to the second bedroom. Pictures, murals, swords, and other paraphernalia from the Rocker covered the four walls, conveying a serious teenage attitude and a certain fascination with the Adomis trials. The floorboards were coated with stripes of purple, turquoise, orange, pale blue, gold, silver, rose pink, emerald green, crimson, and royal blue. Even the matching bunk beds, desks, and chests of drawers made a colorful and bold statement.

It was a safe bet the room belonged to the two caramel-haired boys in the painting downstairs, both of whom had obviously matured since the time the portrait had been painted.

Dropping to his knees, Rafe looked under the bunk bed, but all he found there was a stray boot sock. Next, he checked the closet and found a few striped cloaks and another large collection of Adomis swords.

Maybe he hadn't found Madri Typhicus' scepter, but he'd discovered something else rather interesting: the madrikim were obviously parents to at least two children. For all Rafe knew, he and the other Ryder-Knight students might even be attending classes with their children now. He'd have to remember to ask Haven and Diadem the next time he saw them.

Rafe took one last look around the room, and with no scepter in sight, he clicked the door shut.

"Well," Baylor said, stepping out into the hallway. "That was Madri Typhicus' room, but I couldn't find his scepter. How about you?"

"Nothing, but it's got to be in this house someplace," Rafe said. "Let's go back downstairs and see if Seamus and Ebon found anything before we search any more rooms up here."

Descending the staircase, Rafe and Baylor saw Ebon standing in the entrance hall, resting an elbow on an arm folded across his chest and tapping his chin.

"You didn't find anything?" Rafe asked.

"No, I checked the dining room, library, study, and music room," Ebon replied as Seamus tottered into view.

"And I checked da parlor, da kitchen, da larder, and da pantry. Hmmm. Now, if I were a scepter, where would I be?" Seamus mused, scratching his chin. "I don't tink I'd be left out in plain sight."

"Wait a minute," Baylor said, glancing over the railing of the staircase. She tripped down the steps and stood in the center of the hall. "Most houses usually have a closet under their stairway, and there is more than enough room for one to be hidden behind one of these panels of woodwork."

Stalking past the others, Ebon knocked on the paneling with his knuckles. Locating a hollow sound, he pushed on the panel, and it opened easily. "Et voilà," Ebon whispered, pulling Madri Typhicus' multi-colored scepter from its interior. "How clever of you, Baylor. What was your first clue?"

"I'm not clever. It's just that my bedroom in Cliff House has raised white oak paneling like this, and there's a small cubbyhole next to the fireplace behind one of the panels there."

And a much larger secret door located behind her wardrobe, thought Rafe.

Striding to Ebon's side, Rafe surveyed the cupboard under the stairs. To one side there were steps leading downward, and on the other was a large framework of pegs holding four other scepters tipped with crystals of gold, crimson, royal blue, and silver. "I can't believe the madrikim would leave their scepters in an unlocked house in a closet under the stairs," he sputtered.

"But 'twas a secret closet," Seamus said.

"Not secret enough," Baylor said.

"Dey've never 'ad ta worry about someone swipin' der scepters before now. Only anoder angel can wield dem, and until tanight der's never been an angel born stupid enough ta even try such a ting."

"Stupid is such an ugly word," Rafe said. "I prefer desperate."

"Dat, too."

"Let's just get this over with as quickly as possible. How do we use the scepter to get into the Presidio?" Baylor asked.

Taking the scepter from Ebon, Rafe said, "Hopefully by

copying what I saw the madri do, but first we need to go outside. Are we still invisible?"

Baylor nodded and scooted through the entrance hall to open the door for the others.

Emerging from the house last and closing the door behind him, Rafe walked into the street and extended his scepter in front of him the way he'd seen the madri do.

"Presidio," he said in an authoritative tone.

Chapter Twelve

Leprechaun Gallery: Number 5697

A tingling sensation flowed down Rafe's arm, and a sliver of murky mist appeared before the little group. Expanding rapidly, the haze transformed into a shimmering doorway, and Rafe could see into the depths of the Presidio, the magnificent round meeting room of the Sakal. Light from the twelve moons of Mystfira streamed through the windows at the top of the cathedral ceiling, each shaft of moonlight hitting and highlighting one of the twelve concentric circles carved into the polished top of the massive round table.

He'd done it!

Twisting his scepter in the same way Madri Typhicus had on the day of the Jarvartan Joining, Rafe parted the thick border of flowers barring access to the room. "Step into the room," he said to the others.

Gaping in awe, Seamus shuffled into the Presidio followed by Ebon and Baylor. Once they were safely inside, Rafe stepped into the room with them, and, although he didn't see the gateway close behind him, he could feel it.

"So, dis is where all da important decisions er made. Never believed I'd ever 'ave a chance ta see dis place."

"Now what?" Baylor said.

Rafe closed the flower border to Typhicus' house and parted the flowers in front of the landscape depicting the Valley of Waterfalls. "Where do you want us to wait for you, Seamus?"

Seamus dug into his pocket, pulled out a map and consulted it. "In Leprechaun Gallery 5697. 'Tis abandoned, and ya'll be safe der."

"How will you get out of the Presidio and back to the Sakal's house, Seamus?" Baylor asked.

"Don't ya worry about me. I'll 'ave dis ting back where it belongs before me deodorant wears off. Den I'll go get da two Upons we need and meet ya in da gallery. Don't ya dare go movin' from der until I get back ta ya."

"Perhaps you know of a place less barren and a little more temperate than a leprechaun gallery," Ebon said.

"I do, but yer not goin' be stayin' der."

Ebon cleared his throat. "I see."

"Show me leprechaun gallery: Number 5697," Rafe said, pointing the scepter at the living landscape.

The lush green valley of waterfalls disappeared, and the wall flashed to blackness—silent, dark, and deep.

"Der she is," Seamus said. "Just like I remembered."

"But I don't see anything," Baylor said, staring at the pitch-black landscape.

"Dat's only because ya don't 'ave leprechaun eyes." Tapping his shillelagh, three blankets, a lantern, a basket of food, and a small piece of Brandire wood materialized next to Baylor and Ebon. "Ya'll be warm and fed until I get back ta ya."

"*Umm*, Seamus. How long are you planning on leaving us in there?" Baylor asked, grabbing the blankets and lantern from the floor.

"Don't worry, lass. I'll be quick about it, only a few hours."

Looking conflicted, Ebon rubbed the middle of his forehead, but after a few moments, he tucked the Brandire wood under an arm and reached down and grabbed the basket. "I'm ready," he said.

"Let's to our purpose, den," Seamus replied.

In a wave of shuffles and scuffles, Baylor and Ebon crossed into the darkness. With the lantern now silvering the gallery walls, Rafe could make out a cobwebbed room containing a low dusty table and a few chairs. Draped in shadows and angling off in every direction, arched passages honeycombed the walls there.

Rafe could tell by looking at the stone on the walls, floors, and ceiling of the gallery that it had been abandoned, as Seamus said. The leprechauns, who still mined for gold on a daily basis in Mystfira, only surfaced their underground tunnels and rooms with stone after an area had been depleted of its supply of gold.

"Seamus, I need you to hold the scepter with me," Rafe said. "I have to keep my hand on it until the last second or the portal will close."

Laying his shillelagh on the floor, Seamus secured the end of the scepter with both hands and Rafe plunged into landscape so as not to leave any bits of himself behind in the Presidio.

"Made it," Rafe said, skidding across some of the small loose stones littering the floor.

Ebon placed the basket of food on the small table. "I don't know why Seamus bothered to give us food. The miasmic stench of this place leaves me with no appetite whatsoever," he grumbled.

Rafe didn't have the slightest idea what miasmic meant, but he was familiar with the word stench, and Ebon was right. The place did smell foul. In fact, if happiness were to choose a good place to go to die, this place would have to be high on the list of possible contenders.

"Well, it's not like we have to stay here long," Baylor said, trying to sound cheerful. She placed the lantern on the table and passed blankets to Rafe and Ebon. "It really is drafty in here, though. Let's wrap up in these until the Brandire wood warms things up."

Cloaking himself with the blanket, Ebon thumped down into one of the low chairs and sighed. "I wish I had a book."

"What book would you like?" Baylor asked.

"Celestial Chemistry," Ebon said. "I should really be brushing up on solvents before I meet the queen."

Taking a grain of fairy dust from her pocket, Baylor crushed it and said:

"Appear now a book of Celestial Chemistry
For Ebon Lavey must learn academically."

A large book appeared on the table in front of a delighted Ebon. "Thank you," he exclaimed.

"How do you do that, Bay?" Rafe asked.

"Do what? Fairy magic?"

"No. How do you come up with those rhymes off the top of your head like that?"

"I don't know," she giggled, wrapping her blanket around her shoulders. "It's a gift, I guess."

"One I don't have," Rafe said. "I can barely rhyme 'cat' with 'hat.'"

Appearing distracted, Baylor sniffed the air about her. Rising, she walked toward one of the many arched tunnel openings in the gallery.

Rafe's breathing accelerated. He knew the expression on Baylor's face. The girl could sniff out trouble like a bloodhound. Striding to her side, he waited.

Don't say it. Don't say it, he thought.

"What is that smell?"

She said it.

"Look," Baylor whispered, pointing toward the tunnel in front of her. Vague shadows flickered and flitted against the tunnel wall. "Something's moving out there."

"In low light, human vision degrades. It can lead to the perception of movement where there is none," Ebon said, not bothering to glance up from his chemistry book.

"That's not it. There's a light coming from somewhere in that tunnel," Baylor said.

Rafe edged closer to the opening of the tunnel. In the distance, long shadows shivered on the cave walls. Baylor was right. Someone or something was out there.

"Is Seamus back already," Ebon asked, coming up behind the pair holding the lantern.

"You both stay here. I'll go check," Rafe said, grabbing the lantern from Ebon.

Baylor squared her shoulders. "I'm going with you."

"I'll accompany you as well," Ebon said, "There is strength in numbers, or so they say."

"Fine, but stay behind me."

Entering the arched stone tunnel, they crept forward as the cave floor sloped downward. With each step they took, the smell of smoke grew stronger. Reaching a bend in the cave, Rafe stuck his head around the corner and spied a good-sized hissing fire, spitting showers of red-orange sparks and tendrils of thick grey smoke into the air.

Narrowing his eyes, Rafe scrutinized the new section of tunnel. "Someone built a fire, but they're gone now," he whispered, stepping around the corner.

"That does seem rather peculiar, especially since I've read that leprechauns prefer Brandire wood for their heating needs," Ebon said, coming around the corner with Baylor.

Chewing a fingernail, Baylor walked around the fire, watching it leap and crackle with its tongues of red, orange, yellow, and blue flames darting about the burning embers. Shuffling back a step, she clasped her hands over her mouth and gasped.

"Bay?" Rafe said.

Flying to the edge of the fire, Baylor latched onto a shoe lying there and hauled with all her might. To Rafe's utter astonishment the entire fire slid across the floor as a unit as Baylor yanked on it.

Releasing her grip on the shoe, Baylor dove into her pocket for another grain of fairy dust. Crushing it she chanted:

"Unmask the magic so I can see . . .
Beneath that fire, please let it be."

The blazing fire with its stabs of autumn-colored tongues licking away the darkness of the tunnel, suddenly rose and hung in the air like a limp dishcloth, radiating shimmering heat waves and a white-hot mass of sparks.

Underneath the fire, curled on his side and cradling his abdomen was an unconscious boy. His face pale and distressed, the boy labored to breathe. The smell of stale cigarettes stung Rafe's nostrils with the unmistakable smell of a human dark spirit. Rafe would know that face anywhere, even with its new, hollowed-out cheeks and dark circles under the eyes. It was Rand!

Kneeling by his side, Baylor pressed her hands to her forehead in horror. "Rand? Can you hear me?" she whispered, laying a light hand on his shoulder. "I'm going to help you."

"Baylor!" Rafe barked. "Don't you dare! You leave him be!"

"I concur," Ebon said. "Although I did not witness it, I heard Rand nearly killed you."

Baylor winced as if their words stung her sensibilities. "He's finding it hard to breathe, and just look at his arm and side . . . and leg. He's all torn up, and he's bleeding really badly."

Crouching beside Baylor, Rafe inspected a multitude of jagged wounds running the length of Rand's right side. "I don't care. You are *not* going to help him," he said, gripping Baylor by the elbow and forcing her to rise.

"What's wrong with you?" Baylor said, wrenching her elbow away from Rafe. "You're an angel, for crying out loud! Why don't you try acting like one?"

Planting his feet wide, Rafe placed his hands on his hips. "Right now, it's my job to protect you and Ebon, not some dark spirit who tried to kill us. But that's not even the point, Bay. If you help him, it will sap your strength like it did last time, and we need you. Either you want to save him, or you want to save your friends and relatives. It's as simple as that."

"I can do both," Baylor said, fumbling in her pocket for another grain of fairy dust.

Rafe lunged for her hand, but not in time to prevent her from crushing the grain between her fingers. Throwing it toward Rafe and Ebon, she chanted:

> "Still you stand, you may not move
> Until Rand's health I do improve."

Rafe's legs, feet, and arms instantly stiffened, and he found himself frozen dead in his tracks. All he could move were his eyes and mouth. "I cannot believe you just did that," he fumed.

"Nor can I," Ebon said.

"I'm sorry, but I'm not going to let either one of you stop me from helping Rand. Madri Isabo has been giving me lessons. I can heal him without hurting myself."

Kneeling beside Rand again, Baylor rubbed her hands.

Pressing her palms together, she brought them to her lips and blew into them.

"This is a mistake," Rafe said.

"And it's mine to make," Baylor replied.

"Clearly you are ignoring the 'good should never consort with evil' moral of the story in The Brushstroke of Time," Ebon said.

"I'm not consorting with evil," Baylor whispered. "I'm healing it."

A pathetic whimper escaped Rand as Baylor placed one hand on his injured side and the other over his heart. As she bowed her head, Baylor's hands began to glow golden yellow. The golden light grew, circling Rand's body like a cocoon. The boy's face, distorted by pain, gradually grew peaceful.

"Rand?" Baylor whispered. "Rand? Rand, you need to wake up now. Please, Rand."

Rand's body jerked. Rolling onto his back, he opened his eyes and stared into Baylor's face.

"There you are," she said, removing her hands.

"I heard you calling for me," he whispered.

"That's right, I was."

Reaching for his right side, Rand ran his fingers along his arm. "I dreamed I was all busted up and dying."

"You weren't dreaming. I healed you," Baylor said. "What happened?"

"I don't suppose you'd believe I got pushed off a cliff by a giant snail?" Rand replied, licking his dry, cracked lips.

"I wouldn't," Rafe said. "I don't believe anything you say."

"If Rand is capable of even an ounce of verisimilitude, what he said could be accurate. Perhaps he was collecting snail slime for his friends in the underworld," Ebon said.

Turning onto his previously injured side, Rand propped himself up on an elbow and peered around Baylor. "I see you have company. Why are the two of them frozen in place like that?"

"We had a disagreement on whether or not I should heal you," Baylor said with a faint smile. "I won."

Groaning, Rand pushed himself more or less upright against the hard stone of the tunnel. "Why did you help me?" he asked Baylor, searching her eyes. "After what I did to you and Rafe . . . and Leopold. Why?"

Baylor shrugged. "I guess because you were my friend a lot longer than you've been my enemy, and because in all the time I've known you . . . you never once called me the Sorceress."

"Because he never called you the Sorceress? Are you insane? That is the stupidest thing I've ever heard," Rafe raged. "He doesn't deserve to be healed by you or anyone else."

"He's right about that," Rand said. "I'd like to tell you I'm sorry for what happened, Bay, but I'm a dark spirit, so I can't. I say what I say. I do what I do. I am what I am."

"You can't even apologize to her after she healed you? You are so lucky I can't move right now," Rafe shouted. "I've never wanted to thrash someone this much in my whole life."

"Ignore him," Baylor said. "But just the same, Rand, I've told you before—we all have choices. You can be whoever you want to be. Being a dark spirit is not an excuse."

"A cat can never be a dog, Baylor, and no matter how much you'd like one to be the other, it doesn't happen."

Baylor shook her head. "I've met cats who act like dogs and dogs who act like cats. You have choices."

"Maybe in your world you do, but not in mine," Rand replied. Pushing to his feet, he came face to face with the crackling fire suspended in midair. "What's my fire blanket doing up there?"

"A fire blanket? So that's what that thing is," Baylor said. "I'd say it's just *hanging* around."

A wan smile played on Rand's lips. "Your jokes haven't gotten any better since we were kids."

"At least I'm consistent," Baylor replied. "So, here's a little tip for when you decide to use that blanket of yours again. Make sure you're all the way under it. Your foot was sticking out from underneath it."

"I guess I'm lucky it was this time. Thank you, Baylor."

Rafe found himself wishing Baylor had also had the foresight to strike him deaf, dumb, and blind. If he had to witness any more of the ridiculous verbal exchange going on between Baylor and Rand, he was pretty sure, despite being cemented in place and unable to move, he'd retch up the contents of his stomach.

"I'm going to go now, and I'd appreciate it if you could give me a head start before unfreezing that one," Rand said, pointing to Rafe as he pivoted to leave.

Still guarding his side, Rand shuffled down the tunnel. "Keep the blanket, Bay," he called over his shoulder. "If you handle it by the bottom, it won't burn you, and you can fold it up as small as a handkerchief to put in your pocket. I promise it will come in handy while you're out here."

"Take it with you! She doesn't want it!" Rafe bellowed at Rand.

Crossing her arms, Baylor turned to face Rafe. "Oh, but I do," she said coolly. "I really, really do."

Chapter Thirteen

Firefall

Baylor seated herself at the low table in the gallery. With a sigh, she folded her arms on the table and cushioned her head on top of them.

"Does your head hurt?" Rafe asked.

"A little."

"Good," he said. "Maybe next time you'll listen to me, then."

Baylor lifted her head from her arms. "I don't like being ordered around."

"That is not what I did."

"That is exactly what you did," Baylor said, scowling at Rafe. "You told me not to help Rand. You wanted me to walk away and let him die."

Rafe dragged a hand through his hair. When Baylor put it that way, it really did make him sound like an awful person.

"Did it ever once occur to you that Rand might come back with a few of his friends to help finish us off. Then none of us Ryder-Knight students will ever be going home again. I was only trying to protect us."

"Fair point," Ebon interjected.

Whipping her arms away from the table, Baylor straightened, glaring at both boys. "He won't."

"You don't know that," Rafe said.

"I *do* know that!" Slamming her elbows on the table, Baylor buried her face in her hands. "Do you have any idea how hard it is to keep believing in yourself when nobody else will? I know you don't understand the things I can do, and you know what? Most of the time, I don't understand it myself . . . but can't you at least try to respect it?" Lifting her face from her hands, Baylor turned toward Rafe. "There are angels up here who can do the sorts of things I do."

"I know, but—"

"No 'but's. Isabo has been coming to Cliff House and working with me every day. She is teaching me to trust myself and to trust my instincts. That's all I did today. Rand is not going to hurt us. He is not coming back, and he won't be telling his friends about us either. I *know* he won't."

Scraping a hand over his face, Rafe pinched his lips together in frustration. He'd never make Baylor see that saving Rand had potentially put them all in danger. It was pointless to argue with her.

At that moment, Rafe heard faint voices echoing from another tunnel feeding into the gallery. Scraping her chair back from the table, Baylor stumbled to Rafe's side looking as if she expected an I-told-you-so to spring from his lips.

She let out a breath of relief when Seamus burst through the tunnel with two beautiful, buttercup-blonde women trailing behind him in bell-shaped ball gowns.

Shrinking behind Rafe to hide her peasant blouse and jeans, Baylor murmured, "Nobody said anything about this being a dressy occasion."

"Der dey er. Dese er da children I've been tellin' ya about," Seamus said to the women at his side.

Lifting the skirt of her pink satin gown trimmed with pink tulle, crystal beads, and glass pearls, the taller woman minced into the gallery. Clasping her hands to her chest, she declared,

"Oh, aren't you just the most adorable children I've seen in all my life!"

"They could be pigs, and I'd still love them," the shorter woman, replied, trotting into the room and standing next to her friend. Smoothing her golden silk brocade gown with one hand, she twirled a blonde curl with a finger of the other hand. "They're the ones responsible for Seamus getting me out of that dreadful tower I'm stuck in day in and day out, so they're my heroes."

"Why, I never! I come to visit you every single day, Goldie," said the pink-gowned lady, her large brown eyes growing even larger as she stared at her friend.

"Only because your husband makes you come sew with me every day to tire your fingers and keep your hands from being idle."

"Well, I should say it's a good thing he does, or you'd have no friends at all, Goldie P. Locket," the woman retorted. "Speaking of sewing, don't you think that pale-green silk chiffon trimmed with velvet we're working on would look fetching on that beautiful little girl over there. And just look at those boys standing in front of her. Why they're handsome enough to be princes themselves!"

"Yes, I suppose they are," Goldie replied, "but I think the blue silk organza would have suited the girl better . . . you know, the one you burned to a crisp the other day when you were in a mood."

"Certainly, that would have looked lovely on her as well," the lady replied, ignoring her friend's jab, "but with her coloring, she could also pull off any shade of red. Oh, my goodness. I know—the rose taffeta we started a few days ago. That would be perfect for her."

"Enough of yer goin' on about dresses. Dat is not what we're about 'ere. We've got ta get up ta da Castle of Reckonin'."

"How rude of you, Seamus! You haven't even introduced us to the children yet." Grabbing the skirt of her pink gown, the woman dipped into a deep curtsy. "I'm Blaise Charming, and this is my friend, Goldie P. Locket."

Unsure of what to do next, Rafe executed a stiff bow. "Pleased to meet you," he said. "I'm Rafe Ryder, and these are my friends, Baylor Wingate and Ebon Lavey."

"Okay, dat's enough of dat stuff. We've got ta get ta da cliffs," Seamus said. "Ladies, after ya."

"*Oooh,* I can't wait for this adventure to begin," Blaise said, looping her arm through Goldie's and strolling out into the leprechaun tunnel ahead of Seamus. "Let's get back to the boat."

"Boat?" Baylor asked.

"Dat's right. We're goin' fer a boat ride. Off with ya, lass," Seamus said, tapping his shillelagh on Baylor's backside to get her moving.

Scampering into the stone passageway with Baylor and Ebon, Rafe saw Blaise and Goldie clambering into a wide, flat-bottomed boat docked in a flooded section of the tunnel.

"In wid ya," Seamus commanded.

Climbing into the boat, Rafe extended a helping hand to Baylor, Ebon, and Seamus as they entered the bobbing vessel.

"We had such a pleasant ride on our way here," Blaise said, looking over her shoulder at the children seated in the row behind her. "The boat didn't rock at all."

"Ya may feel a bump or two dis time," Seamus warned. "We're takin' a shortcut ta da waterfalls. Better 'old on."

Just as Seamus finished his warning, Rafe heard the sound of rushing water. The boat rose, tilting at an odd angle and, without warning, lurched backwards.

"Oh, dear," Blaise gasped, grasping the bench she sat upon

to steady herself. "We don't seem to be facing the right way for this ride at all."

Before Rafe had a chance to prepare himself, the boat pitched off the edge of some unseen precipice behind them and plunged downward accompanied by the visceral screams of the boat's frightened occupants. Serpentine curves whipped the boat backwards and forwards. One moment they faced one direction, and the next moment, another. Careening around one last hairpin curve, the boat plummeted again, landing with a massive splash in a cavern of calm water.

Taking a deep breath, Rafe tried to collect what remained of his wits as he looked ahead. Spilling over an opening in the cave, a sheet of water raged in front of the boat. Not knowing whether they were near the top or the bottom of a waterfall, Rafe braced for another nosedive, but it did not come.

Instead, the water parted by itself, and the boat sailed out into the middle of a large mirror-surfaced lake flanked on both sides by soaring mountain peaks and towering rock faces.

Rafe had never seen anything like it. Hundreds of waterfalls gushed down over the sheer, vertical cliff walls, culminating in frothy cauldrons of foam at their bases. The spectacular natural beauty felt powerful, raw, and magnificent.

Ashen-faced, Ebon gulped in big breaths of the fresh crisp air, appearing quite oblivious to the immense beauty surrounding him. Baylor patted him on the back as she would a small child, whispering words of reassurance and encouragement.

"Why, I never! A little warning would have been nice," Blaise sputtered, trying to coax her hair back into place as the boat slid up to a small dock in a tranquil meadow strewn with a sea of wildflowers and decorative grasses.

"Thanks, Seamus. That's always good fun," Goldie said,

stepping out of the boat and onto a path at edge of the meadow. "So now we're off to the Cliffs of Wisdom?"

"Dat's right."

"Cliffs?" Ebon asked in a feeble voice as Rafe and Baylor scrambled out of the boat to help Ebon get his feet back on dry land.

"Over there," Goldie said, pointing to another set of imposing rock walls on the other side of the meadow.

Ebon's eyes bulged and his nostrils flared in panic. "How do you expect me to climb that? Those cliffs must be two thousand meters in height, and they're nearly perpendicular!"

"Now, now," Goldie soothed. "Don't work yourself into a dither. There's an entrance to the cave under a waterfall over there, and it leads to a set of stairs. Of course, it will take about three hours to climb, but you're young. You'll do fine."

"Oh, good heavens! Why is this the first time I'm hearing that mandatory physical activity on a mountain is required? You do know I'm wearing glass slippers, don't you?" Blaise asked, her face clouding with disapproval.

"Janey Mack! Stop yer bleatin', and pluck up some courage, people. Now, let's get on wid it," Seamus said, stepping onto the path beside Goldie.

Throwing a haughty look at Seamus's back, Blaise proceeded down the path after the leprechaun and her friend.

Rubbing an eyebrow with his finger, Ebon darted an apprehensive gaze at Rafe and Baylor. "I cannot say I'm looking forward to this trip with unbridled enthusiasm, but if we want to see our friends again, I suppose we should follow them."

Rafe clapped his hand on Ebon's shoulder. "Well done, you. That's the spirit."

As they rambled down the meadow path behind Seamus

and the Upons, several little gadaboot plants uprooted themselves and walked along beside the children.

"Aren't they sweet?" Baylor asked. "I just love gadaboot plants, but now I wish I'd paid more attention in Madri Ezekiel's Flora and Fauna of Mystfira classes. There are so many other beautiful flowers in this meadow, and I can't identify a single one of them."

"Perhaps I can be of assistance. Which plants are you curious about?" Ebon asked.

"The yellow ones here and those blue ones just over there."

"The yellow ones are called cuppyducks, and the blue ones are jelligents."

Rafe bit his lip to hide a smile. Flora and Fauna of Mystfira had been one of Baylor's favorite classes. He was positive she knew the names of the flowers she was asking about by heart, but focusing Ebon on the plants would keep him from thinking about the daunting cliffs ahead of them.

Joining in the pretense, Rafe feigned interest in Ebon's jabbering about plants as they walked along the path together for the next twenty boring minutes. Deep in his description of a purple flowered plant, known as moodispanks, Rafe grabbed Ebon's arm to keep him from running into Seamus and the Upons who had stopped abruptly on the path ahead of them.

"We're here," Goldie said. "These are the legendary Cliffs of Wisdom."

Above them, steaming hot, fiery, red-orange water poured over the face of the cliff like hot lava, yet when it flowed into the white terraced pools beneath it, the water was a gorgeous shade of bluish-green.

"It's so beautiful," Baylor murmured.

"It is quite lovely," Ebon agreed. "I'm not sure why the water is two different colors, but I believe those step-like geological formations where the water is pooling are called travertine terraces. It usually happens near hot springs, though. It's actually very interesting. When scalding water forms carbonic acid and flows through porous limestone, it dissolves it and forms calcium carbonate. Those blindingly white deposits are a type of limestone known as travertine."

"I've never heard of travertine before," Rafe said.

"Of course, you have. It was used to build the Colosseum in Rome."

"Seamus? I'm with the kid on this one. I don't understand what's wrong with that waterfall," Goldie said, twirling a bedraggled curl. "It didn't look like that the last time we were here."

"Dey decided ta step up security after we got by da troll dat guarded da steps. Dey replaced da troll wid a dragon. 'Tis a firefall now."

"Just make us invisible, and we'll scurry right past him like we did the troll," Goldie said.

"About dat . . . I can't use me magic 'ere anymore."

"Where exactly is *here*?" Blaise asked. "*Here* in this meadow, or *here* in the Valley of Waterfalls?"

"I can transport meself ta da valley fer snail slime and conjure baskets, but dat's all da magic I'm allowed since Goldie and me broke inta da castle last time."

"Then I'll use mine. I used fairy magic when we were in the leprechaun gallery," Baylor said.

"Ya can't. 'Twon't work out 'ere. No one can use magic 'ere anymore."

"I feel faint," Blaise said, fanning herself with her hands.

Rushing behind her friend, Goldie caught Blaise as she slumped backwards in a fake diva swoon.

"Now we're in a fine pickle, Seamus," Goldie said. "Pity you didn't think to mention you couldn't use your magic when you asked us to join your little adventure."

"Now don't go gettin' yer knickers in a knot. 'Tis only one little dragon," Seamus said.

Snapping out of her fake swoon, Blaise cleared her throat and said, "I am an expert when it comes to fire, Seamus, and the amount of flame it would take to light up that waterfall like magma has to come from more than one little dragon."

"I'm tellin' ya! 'Tis just one dragon."

Goldie crouched in front of Seamus, looking deep into his leprechaun eyes. "And how many heads does this dragon have?"

"Oh . . . dat? Four," Seamus replied, dropping his gaze to the ground.

Blaise waved toward the firefall. "I can easily get by a four-headed, fire-breathing dragon because I'm immune to flame, but my concern is for Goldie and these precious children. What's your plan for getting everyone else around that thing?"

Remaining silent, Seamus blinked innocently.

"You little stinker!" Goldie said, jumping to her feet. "You don't have one, do you?"

"I tought we would discuss it when da time came."

"The time has come," Blaise said, twirling her index fingers at the group as if she were stirring a pot. "Discuss."

Scratching his temple, Rafe tilted his head skyward to look at the cliffs. "Maybe I can change to my angelic body and fly you up there one at a time."

"Ya can't do dat. Ya'd lead da Sakal right ta us as soon as ya made da change ta yer angelic body, and beside dat, der's a force field around da Cliffs of Wisdom. Da only entrance is behind dat firefall."

"So . . . let me get this straight," Rafe said. "We have to *slay* a four-headed, fire-breathing dragon before we can get to the staircase behind the falls over there?"

"Oh, no," Blaise said. "No, no, no, no, no! Out of the question. We are not killing or maiming that dragon. He or she is a living creature who has just as much right to live as we do."

"I don't know 'ow else we're gonna do it, Blaise" Seamus said. "We don't 'ave time ta tame dat beast."

"I don't care. You're not killing it. I won't allow it!" Blaise said, stamping her foot for emphasis.

"Yer against killin' a dragon?"

"I most certainly am. I may burn enchanted buildings down now and then, but never with any living creature trapped inside them. I have a conscience!"

"Then that just leaves distracting it, tricking it, or trapping it," Rafe said.

"And that will be difficult because the heads of a four-headed dragon face in four different directions—north, south, east and west," Goldie said. "You will have to come up with at least three distractions in order for us to sneak by it. One for the head that sees us straight on, one for the head that sees the side view, and one for the head guarding the cave."

"Does this dragon have the ability to speak, like Smaug in Tolkien's book *The Hobbit*?" Ebon asked. "Perhaps we can reason with it."

Seamus snorted. "Dat dragon does not speak or ta my knowledge understand language as we know it."

"Then it can't be bribed or reasoned with. I guess, we'll have to wait until the dragon falls asleep, then," Rafe said.

"Dat won't work eider. One 'ead sleeps at a time, so der is always at least tree 'eads ta worry about."

"This just keeps getting better and better," Rafe said, shaking his head.

"How about treasure? Don't dragons like shiny gold things?" Baylor said.

From a pouch at his side, Seamus pulled one gold coin. "I tink da only treasure he's guardin' is da steps ta da Castle of Reckonin', but we can see if dis piece of gold strikes 'is fancy."

"That's not going to do the trick. Empty your pockets, Seamus," Goldie said.

Clenching his jaw, Seamus's eyes looked as though they might leap from his head as he glared at Goldie.

"I'm the one that sewed those enchanted pockets into your breeches, and I know you always keep a pot of gold in them. If gold is to be the distraction, we'll need the whole pot," said Goldie.

"What? Da whole pot?"

Blaise crossed her arms and stared at both Goldie and Seamus. "How do you expect little old *me* to carry a pot of gold to the banks of that firefall?" she asked.

"Right, right," Seamus said, looking indignant on Blaise's behalf. "'Ow can ya expect 'er ta do such a ting?"

"I expect you to because you're the only one that can, princess," Goldie said, "but first, you'll need to go down there and learn just how far out that dragon is willing to come from underneath the waterfall. Then, once we've determined how close the rest of us can come without getting hurt, Seamus will empty his pockets."

"Fine. It's fortunate for all you that I had the foresight to get this dress fireproofed," Blaise said, tossing her head and stomping away from the rest of the group.

"Is she going to be all right by herself?" Baylor said, watching

Blaise trudge toward the white-terraced pools of blue-green below the falls.

"She'll be fine. I promise, she's not as delicate as you might think," Goldie said.

Arriving on the bank next to the firefall, Blaise cupped her hands around her mouth and bawled, "Yoo-hoo! Yoo-hoo! Mr. Dragon! Come out, come out, wherever you are!"

Gnashing, razor-sharp yellow teeth set into a black-gummed snout exploded out from behind the curtain of scalding water.

"Hello there, handsome. Fancy meeting you here," Blaise said, smiling sweetly.

As Blaise spoke more of the massive russet and copper scaled head slithered forward. The dragon's monstrous green eyes, with pupils slit vertically like a cat's, glinted a warning at Blaise. An instant later the dragon spewed a jet of flame at Blaise, completely engulfing her.

Even though Blaise had claimed to be fireproof, Rafe could not believe his eyes when the flame subsided. The princess stood completely unscathed.

"Whew! Somebody has dragon breath today," Blaise said, fanning the odor away from her nose with a hand.

The dragon roared and sprang out from under the falls entirely. Rafe could hear the flint clicking in the back of its four throats, and heat blistered the air as two heads of the magnificent beast let loose with another torrent of flames."

"Stop that right now, or I'll be forced to retaliate," Blaise shouted.

Unfurling its titanic wings, all four dragon heads gave thunderous screams and the same two heads unleashed another volley of flames at Blaise.

Unable to watch anymore, Baylor buried her head in her

hands, but Ebon continued scrutinizing the situation. "The dragon's heads only travel in 180-degree arcs in the direction they are facing," he observed. "They only overlap their flames in the corners."

"Blaise!" Rafe shouted. "You need to stay out of the corners."

Paying no heed to the advice, Blaise walked backward, red-hot flames enveloping her, luring the dragon further and further from the waterfall.

Blaise raised both hands, and flames ignited in each palm. She moved her hands together, swirling them through the air until two gargantuan balls of fire formed. A smile danced on her ruby red lips as she sent the fireballs sailing toward the two fire-snorting dragon heads.

The enormous fireballs quickly found their target, smacking both dragon heads squarely on their long snouts. Flailing its front claws, the dragon reared back, heads shrieking in what sounded like irritation and astonishment.

"That's right, boys," Blaise shouted. "Momma's packing heat, too. You better start minding your manners around me."

Enraged the dragon clawed further out into the white-terraced pool area until Rafe heard the distinct metal against metal clank of a chain reaching the end of its tether. The forward-facing dragon head sent out another long plume of flame, but Blaise was far enough away that it only set fire to a patch of grass in front of her.

"That's as far as it can go," Blaise yelled. "You can come down here now."

Walking toward Blaise, Rafe noticed Baylor eyeing the patch of smoldering grass at Blaise's feet.

"Take 'old of dis. Don't let go," Seamus said, giving Rafe the edge of his pocket and walking a few feet away. With the pocket stretched to capacity, out popped a pot of gold as big as the leprechaun himself.

"I'm going to have to see if I can get one of those secret pockets sewn into my trousers, too," Rafe said.

"As am I," said Ebon.

Baylor giggled. "You think so? What would you carry around with you, Rafe? A grand piano?"

"And a bench," Rafe deadpanned.

"You can't be serious?" Blaise said, traipsing over to the pot and trying to lift it from the ground. "I cannot carry this thing."

"Maybe there is an easier way. What if we tried to sneak past the dragon underneath a fire blanket?" Baylor asked.

"What part of 'I can't use me magic 'ere' did ya not understand," Seamus groused.

Fishing into her pocket, Baylor pulled out the fire blanket she had folded and placed there earlier. "I think only one or two of us can fit under this thing at a time," she said.

"Where'd ya get dat ting, child?"

"I, *umm*, we came across it while we were waiting for you in the gallery."

Oh sure, Bay. Just leave out the part about there being a dark spirit underneath it at the time we discovered it, Rafe thought.

"Me and ya will be 'aving a serious little talk later, lass, but right now, dat idea is all we got."

Unfolding the fire blanket, Seamus tried to hand it to Blaise who shook her head and hid her hands behind her back.

"Blaise, dear. It's worth a try," Goldie said. "If you distract the dragon's heads while we crawl along under the blanket, we just might be able to make it through the waterfall, and then, of course, we'll need to creep high enough up the staircase so that the last dragon head can't see us."

"And ya can bring da blanket forward and back until we're all over der and safe."

"Am I the only one who sees the flaw in this plan?" Blaise asked. "Dragons usually recognize their own fire, or every Tom, Dick, and dark spirit could sneak by them using one of those things. They'll shoot their flames at that blanket. I guarantee it, and while their fire won't destroy the blanket, it will incinerate anyone beneath it, except me."

"There is only one way to find out for sure," Goldie said, tearing a piece of trim from the bottom of her gold silk brocade gown and handing it to Blaise. "If this doesn't burn up, we'll be safe."

Tipping her neck back in exasperation, Blaise slumped her shoulders. *"Aauugh,"* she cried, grabbing the fragment of cloth from Goldie's hand and tucking it into a belt at her waist. "Fine, but I'm not crawling on my hands and knees like a dog."

"You have to," Goldie said. "Otherwise how else will we know if the children will be safe?"

"Never again, Goldie P. Locket and Seamus O'Shanahan, will I ever agree to one of your stupid adventures!" Blaise sputtered, grabbing the blanket from Seamus and cloaking herself with it.

Inching along the ground, Blaise crawled within striking range of the dragon, and the first head promptly blasted her. Flinging off the blanket, Blaise looked at the remains of the smoking fragment of cloth at her waist. She stomped back to the group dragging the blanket behind her. "I told you it was not going to work."

"Then I guess we have to try the pot of gold plan," Rafe said.

"We?" Blaise asked. "By we, I think you mean me—alone—and without any help from the rest of you."

"Are you done with the histrionics, princess?" Goldie asked.

Clasping her hands at her waist, Blaise took a deep breath. "I think so," she replied.

"Good. Now let's all of us help make this thing light enough for Blaise to lift," Goldie said, scooping gold from the pot and placing the coins in her pockets.

"What er ya doin'? Put dat gold on da ground, not in yer pockets, Goldie!"

"Oh, sorry," Goldie said. "Force of habit. How much do you think you can lift, Blaise?"

"Maybe a quarter of the pot?"

Rafe had never imagined in his wildest dreams on Earth that he'd ever be rummaging through a leprechaun's pot of gold. If he wasn't so preoccupied with saving his friends, taking the gold out of Seamus's pot would have been good fun, but he couldn't stop thinking how high the stakes were if they failed to get past the dragon.

When three-quarters of the gold had been removed from the pot, everyone stopped scooping out coins, and Seamus nodded at Blaise. Flexing the muscles in her slender arms, she stooped to lift it. The pot only came off the ground a few inches, but it was just enough for her to stagger two steps away from the group.

"You go, girl!" Goldie said. "You've got this!"

Stumping away and stopping every few steps, Blaise kept putting down the pot to catch her breath and massage the sore muscles of her lower back. The task was clearly exhausting the princess, but she carried on like a champ with the group cheering her on from the sideline.

This time, Blaise approached the dragon at a different angle, so only the first head of the dragon could see her. At present, the dragon's flames could easily reach her, but the creature did not strike.

Instead, the dragon's enormous green eyes watched Blaise, glowing with a mixture of wariness and curiosity while plumes of white smoke puffed from its nostrils.

"It seems to be working," Goldie said.

Blaise inched the pot closer and closer until it sat almost right under the dragon's nose. "Good boy," she said, stepping away from the pot. "I'm just going to leave this right here with you. Look at all this nice lovely gold, and it's all yours."

The great head of the dragon loomed over the pot of glittering gold as he allowed Blaise to walk away without breathing fire at her. After she was a safe distance away, he brought his nostrils close to the pot, sniffing it suspiciously. Then he devoured it in one gulp.

"Janey Mack! 'E ate it! 'E ate it! 'E ate me pot of gold!" Seamus screeched, stamping his feet and trampling the grass around him in rage.

A light breeze flitted through the meadow. "Ha—ha—ha!" came a voice from on high. "Ha—ha—ha!"

"STOP DAT!" Seamus shrieked into the wind.

Baylor gazed into the air as the wind wafted through her hair. "Parrot, you can't tell anyone where we are, no matter who asks. This is so important. Promise me, please?"

"I promise—ise—ise."

"What good does that do, Baylor? It doesn't matter who knows we're here now. We're not going to be able to get past that dragon," Rafe said with a rising sense of panic.

Baylor sank to the ground. "Don't say that. There has to be a way."

"I'm sorry, love. I wish I 'ad me magic," Seamus said, plopping to the ground beside Baylor. "If I did, we'd get yer friends back, and I'd get me gold back, too. Den I'd teach dat dragon a lesson. I'd do just like Ludd and Llefyelys did ta dose two dragons in dat old Celtic legend me mam used ta tell me."

"I am unfamiliar with the story of which you speak," Ebon said. "How did Ludd and Llefyelys defeat their dragons?"

"Dey dug a pit and filled it wid mead. Da dragons drank it all and got so buckled, dey vomited, and passed out. Den dey bound da dragons and imprisoned dem in a stone chest underground."

"Lovely," Blaise said sarcastically. "At least they didn't kill the poor things."

The Parrot Wind picked up again, this time ruffling Rafe's hair and smacking three little zorts into his cheek. Brushing the worms away from his face, he watched as a fourth zort wiggled past his nose.

"Wait a minute," Rafe said, snatching the zort out of the air. "Your story just gave me an idea. How many stomachs does that dragon over there have?"

"It 'as four 'eads, but one of everyting else," Seamus said, eyeing Rafe's hand. "Why?"

"Poppe and Potts told me that zorts are poisonous and can make you really sick. How many zorts do you suppose it would take to make a dragon sick to its stomach?"

"*Hmmm,*" Seamus said. "I'm guessin' five 'undred er so."

"Then, if it's okay with Blaise here, we could ask the Parrot Wind to collect them for us."

"Yes—es—es! I go—o—o!" the wind said, zipping away.

"No, I'm against it," Blaise said, shaking her head. "Zorts are living creatures, too. They shouldn't have to die to induce vomiting in a dragon."

"True," Goldie said, "but they don't die. They wiggle away like nothing ever happened."

"How do you know?" asked Blaise.

Goldie wrinkled her nose. "A dreadful personal experience."

"Excellent. Then we can use the zorts," Rafe said, his hope growing. "I was thinking we could mix them in with some of the gold Seamus has left, and Blaise could carry it down to the dragon in the fire blanket. If he eats the bundle and gets sick, we should be able to run by the dragon heads while they're busy throwing up."

"I don't want ta lose more of me gold."

"I'll give you some of mine then, Seamus," Blaise replied. "Gold is a small price to pay, especially if no one dies, and for the record, I'm willing to go along with this plan with one small caveat—we can't use the fire blanket to carry the gold down there. It will make the dragon testy, and he might flame off and burn up the poor little worms."

Goldie nodded her affirmation. "I agree. We'll have to use one of your petticoats instead."

"Absolutely not!" Blaise snapped. "If we're using a petticoat, Goldie P. Locket, it will be yours."

"No can do, my friend. Mine's not fireproof."

"You—you," Blaise said, clenching her jaw and glaring at her friend. "You are truly testing the limits of my patience today!"

"Sorry about that," Goldie replied, "but you never leave your castle wearing less than four petticoats, so you have nothing to worry about. Your dress will still look perfectly poofy with one less petticoat underneath it."

Muttering something about needing to find new friends, Blaise slipped behind a nearby tree and came back holding a pink silk petticoat with layer after layer of ruffles and ribbons.

Rafe felt the breeze tickle the back of his neck, and the next moment, the Parrot Wind rained down zorts upon the group.

Goldie grabbed the petticoat from Blaze's hand, tied it off at the waist, and spread it out on the ground in a circle. Pulling out a needle and thread from one of her pockets, she said, "Bring the zorts to me. I'm going to baste them into the first tier of ruffles in this petticoat."

"Don't hurt them," Blaise said.

"I won't, I promise. It's just to keep them corralled until we can get the gold into the petticoat and down to the dragon."

Rafe snatched a handful of the tiny, sticky, squirming worms and brought them over for Goldie to tuck into the ruffled pocket she was sewing into Blaise's petticoat.

Every now and then, on his way back over to Goldie with a bunch of zorts, Rafe glanced over at the dragon who seemed to be following the small group's leaping and bounding about the field with a great deal of curiosity.

Capturing zorts wasn't hard; the Parrot Wind had certainly found enough of them. Soon the ruffle pocket lay full, wriggling like a snake on the ground. Placing the gold into Blaise's petticoat for her, Rafe took care not to squish the worms.

After rearranging some of the gold, the sack finally met Blaise's approval, and she hefted it over her delicate shoulder and trudged off to meet the dragon.

This time the creature's first head let her approach without so much as a puff of smoke or a click of flint in the back of his throat.

"Here you go, handsome!" Blaise said, placing the makeshift sack on the ground. "I've brought you some more yum yums." Digging into her pockets, she sprinkled some pieces of glittering gold over the top of the sack.

The princess had only taken a few steps away when the dragon gulped down the sack of gold, ignited the flint in its throat, and surrounded Blaise in flame.

As the flames subsided, she whirled around and pointed her finger at the dragon's snout. "That was wrong on so many different levels, but I can assure you, you will regret having done that and *very, very soon.*" Having said her piece, Blaise marched back to join the others.

"Okay, everybody," Goldie said, taking charge. "After the dragon starts feeling the effects of the zorts, I'm going to be sprinting across this meadow to the cave opening under the waterfall, so follow me as fast as you can. Blaise and Seamus will bring up the rear."

"How long will this take?" Rafe asked.

"That largely depends on whether we've got ourselves a dragon with a cast iron stomach or not," Goldie said.

The dragon's russet-and-copper-scaled heads shimmered in the light as Rafe stared at the dragon, waiting.

Then, without warning, the dragon farted. The fourth head, situated over the tail, appeared startled at the choice its body had just made for it and meandered down to have a peek at the situation.

"Was that a little root-toot I just heard?" Baylor asked.

"Yes," Blaise said. "That was definitely a trompette de la rumpette."

Rafe smirked. *Leave it to a princess to make farting sound fashionable.*

A moment later, the first head coughed, and a bit of green saliva dripped from the side of its mouth. Looking confused and unable to balance, the dragon staggered, flapping its wings. The second head belched, choked, and retched, fouling the air in the meadow with an especially putrid odor. Then, the third head followed suit, followed by the fourth.

"There it is; all four dragon heads are barfing," Goldie screamed. "Go! Go! Go!"

Chapter Fourteen

The Castle of Reckoning

Surrounded by iridescent shades of blue and turquoise, the group barreled to the white travertine staircase tucked into the corner of the cave. Climbing the steps with Seamus and Blaise behind him and the rest of the group ahead, Rafe heard a howling sound and had the pleasure of witnessing double trouble being catapulted against the cave wall by the fourth dragon head and tail end, along with a few pieces of gold and some zorts, all of whom wiggled away, just as Goldie had predicted.

"I'm tellin' ya! Someday we're comin' back fer dat gold down der, Blaise."

"Yes, yes," she said, scrunching her nose at the dreadful smell emanating from the cave beneath her, "but not anytime soon."

The little group hurried up the stairs until they were out of reach of the dragon. When they slowed their pace, Rafe was able to admire the surreal beauty of the cave. Light poured in from somewhere above them, shimmering and dancing against the colorful blues and greens of the walls. Flight after flight of stairs twisted upward, the view from each step more breathtaking than the last.

A full two hours and forty-eight minutes later, after taking several breaks for Blaise to whine and rest, Seamus called for the group to stop.

"Did you find it?" Goldie asked, leaning against one of the gorgeous walls of the staircase and looking back at the leprechaun.

Seamus brushed a bit of debris from a step in front of him and dug a small hexagonal-shaped cylinder from the pouch attached to his belt. "I tink so. Let's see if da key still fits."

Guiding the cylinder into a crevice in the floor, Seamus pushed, and a portion of the wall next to him swung open revealing a hidden entrance to yet another leprechaun tunnel. Compared to the cave they stood in, the leprechaun tunnel looked like a boring hollowed-out piece of rock, lined with drab grey stones.

"Oh, thank heavens!" Blaise said, bulleting into the tunnel. "There'd better be a chair in here."

Seamus produced a basket of food and drinks from one of his enchanted pockets and placed it on the step where Rafe stood before waddling into the tunnel and grabbing a grappling hook attached to a long, coiled rope hanging from a peg at the entrance. Taking a match from his pocket, he struck it and lit two torches on the wall.

"Take one of dese torches and get Blaise and da children ta da gallery, Goldie." he said, looping the rope over his shoulder. "I'm gonna lay a false trail and get a gander at da Castle of Reckonin' from da ledge. I need ta see if anyting changed."

"I'll go with you," Rafe said.

"Suit yerself, but stay behind me."

Baylor paused as she passed Rafe on her way to the tunnel's entrance. "Be careful," she whispered.

"How about I start taking your advice, when you start taking mine?" Rafe asked.

Baylor's brow puckered. "Fine by me."

Immediately regretting how harsh his words sounded, he decided to try downplaying his snarky retort with humor. "Don't worry, I'll be careful. I'm only following a leprechaun who can't use his magic in the Valley of the Waterfalls out onto the ledge of a cliff. What could possibly go wrong?"

Turning away from Rafe, Baylor shrugged as if she could not possibly care less, and walked on by him.

Stooping, Rafe grabbed the picnic basket from his step and handed it to Goldie as she passed by him. Seamus had tottered out of view, and although Rafe wanted to charge up the stairs after the leprechaun, his burning thighs had a slower pace in mind.

When Rafe reached the end of the stairway, he saw Seamus standing out on a small lip of rock framed by the dwindling light of day and the twelve moons rising. The straying fingers of moonbeams brushed muted shades of purple, green, silver, turquoise, pink, red, orange, yellow, gold, and blue on the narrow promontory as the moons began their blaze to life in the night-time sky over Mystfira.

Rafe's jaw dropped as he stepped out onto the ledge behind Seamus. The Castle of Reckoning far beneath them could only be described as formidable. Encased within two vast defensive curtain walls and a massive moat, stood an enormous quadrangular stone keep with four projecting turrets soaring from each of its corners.

Crenellated stone parapets defended by battalions of archers sat at the top of both the defensive ramparts and the keep itself. To make matters worse, the ground around the castle and its towering keep was flat and clear, giving the archers a perfect shot if anyone dared approach.

Seamus secured the grappling hook to a wall of stone on the ledge and threw the rope over the side.

"You cannot be serious, Seamus. We will never get over that moat or those walls, let alone get past those archers."

"Now don't go brownin' yer trousers, boy. We ern't goin' *over* anyting. I told ya I was laying out a false trail, didn't I?" Seamus said, starting back down the stairs. "We're not getting' inta da castle from out der."

"Okay. How then?"

"We're goin' underground. Me and da seven dwarfs dug some leprechaun tunnels some years ago, but dey don't remember doin' it. I made sure of dat."

"The seven dwarfs as in *Snow White and the Seven Dwarfs*? They helped you build tunnels?"

"Dat's what I said, wasn't it? Der good boys and fine miners, and dey could of stayed on in yer world, but dey couldn't bring demselves ta leave der little ice princess, Snow White."

"Were you here looking for gold?"

"Let's just say I was lookin' fer a long-lost treasure."

Rafe pressed his lips together. Seamus had to be referring to his wife and daughter. In that moment, it seemed if anyone could understand how important family was to Rafe, it just might be Seamus O'Shanahan.

"Hold on a minute, will you?" he said. "I don't know if Baylor ever told you about my father on Earth. He's very sick. I've been afraid he might die before I find a way to get back home to him—but if we find a way to change time while we're in that castle, maybe I can save him."

Seamus cast an uncharacteristic glance of sympathy over his shoulder at Rafe as he continued to clump down the stairs. "I'm sorry, boy. What's done is done. Time cannot be changed, in dat castle keep or anywhere else."

"You're sure about that?"

"I am. Da past cannot be changed, but da future is yers ta shape. Right now, what ya need ta do is focus on savin' yer friends."

Hanging his head, Rafe exhaled heavily. As much as he hated to admit it, the leprechaun was right. His tendency to spiral into melancholy over his father and his obsession to get back to Earth would make Rafe useless in the present. He really did need to focus on getting his friends out of that painting. Whispering himself away from the edge of gloom, he trailed after Seamus until they reached the gallery.

Seamus knocked on the thick wooden door. "We're back," he called in a gruff tone.

The door swung opened into a warm and cozy chamber lit by the pale, yellow glow of lamps. Unlike the gallery they had been in earlier in the day, this room only had the one entrance. Along the backside of the chamber sat four bunk beds with large chests on the floor beneath them. Blaise and Ebon stood smoothing fresh sheets and blankets onto them.

"Good," Goldie said, closing the door behind them. "You're just in time. We're ready to eat. Baylor and I just finished setting the table."

Glancing to the other side of the room, Rafe beheld a sturdy table surrounded by eight chairs. Covered with a gold cloth, the table was laid end to end with a superb feast. Every type of fruit imaginable adorned the table, along with cheeses, finger sandwiches, breads, jams, jellies, pickles, and relishes. Juices to drink and cakes for dessert rounded out the small banquet.

"You brought *all* my favorites from Earth," Blaise said. "Cucumber with mint butter, smoked salmon with dill butter, ham and cheese, chicken salad with shredded coconut, egg salad and caper, tomato and avocado, and watercress."

"I told ya I would. 'Twas part of da deal."

"Bless your little heart," Blaise said, beaming at Seamus.

Seating himself at the head of the table, Seamus motioned

for the others to gather around. Sitting at the table, Rafe soon discovered he was hungrier than he had imagined possible, and he filled his plate full as the food was passed around.

"We'll eat and den we'll get a few 'ours of sleep before da quest begins," Seamus said.

"Since the sheets and blankets smell freshly laundered, I've no problem with that plan," Ebon said.

"Good. Let's talk about da rules tamorrow, den. Ya must all use yer quiet voices, and der is ta be no pushin', no shovin', and no bitin', and I'm especially talkin' ta ya over der, Miss Goldie."

"I was having a panic attack. I couldn't help it," Goldie retorted, opening her eyes wide and fluttering her eyelashes.

"Goldie Phyllis Locket, you bit Seamus?" Blaise said, looking aghast. "How unlady like of you!"

"You try listening to nearly eight billion ticking clocks while you're trying to pick a lock. It's disconcerting, to say the least."

"First ting in da mornin', I'll mark da passageways ta get Ebon over der ta da queen's place wid a white *X*."

"I'm going alone?"

"Absolutely not," Blaise said. "I'm going with you. You need someone steeped in royal protocol who can help you make a good impression on the queen."

"Are you sure that's wise?" Ebon asked. "I don't mean to offend you, but I can say with some degree of certainty that merging chemicals with flame is often disastrous."

"Relax, young man. I'm perfectly capable of controlling myself, particularly in front of another royal. You have my word."

Ebon took a bite of the chicken salad sandwich in his hand, not seeming a bit comforted by Blaise's reassurance.

"Thanks for getting me out of that tower for a while, Seamus. I'd say the six of us make a great team," Goldie said.

"Team?" Blaise said. "I believe I'm the one who single-handedly dealt with a four-headed, fire-breathing dragon."

"That's true, and you were magnificent," Baylor said, nudging Rafe's leg under the table with her foot.

"Ohhhh," Rafe said, dropping a piece of cheese that was halfway to his mouth. "Yes. Strong work out there today."

"Thank you," Blaise purred.

"And our bargain still holds, Seamus? I don't have to go back to the tower right away?" Goldie asked.

"Yer free ta knock yerself out stealin' til da powers dat be catch up wid ya."

"Excellent. I propose a toast, then. To freedom and a successful quest," Goldie said, holding her glass high.

Clinking their glasses of juice together, the little group continued to feast.

Full and relaxed after the meal, Rafe struggled to keep his eyes open as he helped Baylor and Goldie pack up the leftovers in the basket. He wasn't the only one suffering from the fatigue of the day. Ebon, Blaise, and Seamus had already collapsed onto three of the lower bunks.

Goldie locked the door to the gallery while Rafe and Baylor clattered onto two of the top bunks and pulled the blankets over them.

"Are you done being mad at me?" Baylor whispered to Rafe.

"I was never mad at you," he said softly. "I was just worried about you. There's a difference."

"Really? Because I wasn't even sure if we were still on the same side anymore," Baylor replied in a hushed tone as Goldie snuffed out the lanterns and sank into the last bottom bunk.

Exhaling through pursed lips as silently as he could, Rafe was glad Baylor couldn't see the sheepish expression growing on his face. He could almost hear Lady Jane whispering in his ear, "Anger is like throwing hot coals with your bare hands, my darling boy. It's only too late that you realize you've harmed yourself in addition to another."

"That's on me," he murmured. "I'm sorry, Bay. I may not agree with everything you do or say, but I'm always going to be on your side."

"*Awww,* dat's sweet," Seamus barked from the bunk beneath Rafe. "Now, shut yer gobs, and go ta sleep."

As he huddled under his blanket, sleep came almost before Rafe closed his eyes, but morning came just as quickly.

The day arrived with Seamus thumping his shillelagh on the bunks to rouse the children from bed. Fighting back yawns, Rafe groaned and dropped to the floor next to Ebon and Baylor who were still rubbing sleep from their eyes.

Looking fresh and lovely, Blaise and Goldie sat at the table, sipping tea. Rafe could not imagine how they'd been able to touch themselves up so thoroughly without using any type of magic.

"Look alive, ya sorry lot," said the leprechaun.

"Believe me, I'm trying to," Baylor said. "When do we leave?"

"As soon as ya get some tea and Irish pancakes inta yer bellies," replied Seamus, herding the children toward the table and the two smiling Upons waiting for them there.

"How is the tea hot?" Rafe asked, sitting down to one of the three steaming cups on the table.

"Luckily for us, Seamus is a very clever leprechaun," Goldie said. "He enchanted the food before he packed it, so none of it will spoil. What is meant to be cold stays cold, and what is meant to be hot stays hot."

Blaise pushed her chair away from the table and stood. "Did you finish marking the route to the queen's house for us, Seamus?"

"I did. Da passageways er marked with a white *X*. Now ya must remember what I told ya. Ya'll come up under a suit of armor in da entryway. Pull da cord in da 'allway and wait ta be announced ta da queen."

"How can we be sure the queen will help us?" Ebon asked, taking a bite of his pancake.

"Charming is not simply my last name, young man. It's an art I'm well versed in," Blaise replied. "Rest assured, she *will* help us."

"When ya've got da formula fer da paint solvent, and we've got da tread we're supposed ta get, we'll meet back 'ere in da gallery. Understood?"

Goldie snapped a salute. "Aye, aye, captain! We're ready when you are."

"Good," Seamus said. "One more minute. Eat fast."

Stuffing the rest of his pancake in his mouth, Rafe got to his feet.

Baylor giggled. "You look like a squirrel that's stuffed one too many acorns in his cheeks." Taking one last bite of her pancake and one last sip of tea, Baylor rose and made her way to the door of the gallery.

"This is going to be so much fun," Blaise said, clapping her hands excitedly. "*Andiamo*, everyone! That means 'let's go' in Italian."

"Blaise, will ya stop wid da Italian lessons and take one of dese lanterns like Goldie?" Seamus said, shooing the group out of the gallery and shutting the door.

Baylor nervously twisted a loop of hair around her finger as she entered the murky depths of the arched stone tunnel.

"Are you ready?" Rafe whispered to her.

"I think so, as long as we don't run into any more dragons," Baylor said with a faint smile.

Seamus marched the group through seven winding passageways containing a maze of other tunnels branching off in all directions before finally stopping at one marked with a white X.

"Dis is where we split up. Mind da trail I've marked fer ya, and ya'll be all right."

"Why do these tunnels run in such mysterious and perplexing directions? Was this design premeditated?" Ebon asked.

"Why is dat important?" Seamus bellowed.

"Let's ask Seamus about that after we've completed our assignment," Blaise said, directing Ebon into the marked passageway. "You needn't worry about a thing, Seamus. I've got this under control."

Lantern swinging, Rafe watched as Blaise and Ebon disappeared down the dark-as-a-crypt shaft and out of sight.

"Right. She's got dis under control until she decides ta stop and give da mice Italian lessons," Seamus muttered. "*Andiamo,* da rest of ya."

Seamus struck off down the tunnel with Goldie, but Baylor stood still, staring at the white X on the wall next to her.

"Bay?" Rafe whispered. "Is something wrong?"

"What?" Baylor said, dragging her eyes away from the X to meet Rafe's gaze. "No. Nothing. Let's do this."

"Come on, you two," Goldie called. "No dawdling."

Twisting and turning, Rafe and Baylor followed Seamus and Goldie through one leprechaun tunnel after another until they reached a rounded stone chamber housing the gaping maws of twenty-two dark and foreboding subterranean passages.

"Which one is ours?" Rafe asked as the leprechaun paused to lift his lantern higher.

"None of dem. Da entrance ta da keep is just up der." Seamus pointed to a rickety ladder strapped to some protruding rocks above them. "Goldie, go first, and den wait fer da children ta climb up ta ya."

Goldie did as she was told, and Rafe and Baylor scrambled up the ladder after her to find themselves standing in yet another arched passageway. As they traveled along the new stone tunnel, however, the ceiling shrank lower and lower until Seamus was the only one able to stand fully upright.

Traveling along in their new hunched-over positions, the group soon arrived at a dead-end.

"This can't be right," Rafe said. "Are we lost?"

Goldie chuckled. "Nope. There's a trapdoor right above us."

"Dat's right, and I can't use me magic ta open it. Slide da bolt, Goldie, and put yer back inta it."

Goldie fumbled over her head, and Rafe heard the scrape of a bolt being pulled back. Leaving her lamp on the floor next to Seamus, Goldie positioned herself under the trap door, straining to open it. The door groaned but did not budge.

"A little help, handsome," Goldie said, turning her head to smile at Rafe. "The floor tiles in this keep are heavy."

Standing next to Goldie, Rafe tensed his back muscles against the door, and with one great heave, they pushed it open. Shimmering gold light streamed into the tunnel around them, and Rafe shut his eyes against the brightness.

"Well done! Dat's it!"

Seamus and Goldie extinguished their lanterns, and Seamus dropped them into his enchanted pocket. Holding the door aloft, Rafe straightened and waited for the others to scramble through the opening.

"It's the same room as before," Goldie said, climbing into the room with Baylor.

"Da Orchard Room?" Seamus chuckled as Goldie and

Baylor pulled him into the room. "Dat means dey didn't discover me trapdoor."

Rafe's jaw dropped as he climbed through the opening and joined the others. "Room?" he said. "I don't think so. It feels more like a small country in here."

While Seamus and Goldie wrestled the marble floor tile back into place, Rafe and Baylor gaped at spectacular opulence surrounding them. Hundreds and hundreds of mottled green Corinthian columns sprung from the creamy marble floor and soared heavenward to support the magnificent, vaulted ceiling panels above them. Gold chandeliers shaped like suns hung from landscapes painted on the panels directly above a sea of dark green marble in the middle of the floor.

"It's gorgeous," Baylor murmured. "Oliver would love this."

"How big is this place?" Rafe asked.

Goldie tilted her eyes upward in thought. "In Earth measurements? I'd say a little over a square mile, or 2.60 square kilometers, wouldn't you, Seamus?"

"I don't know. 'Tis a good long walk, dat's fer sure," the leprechaun, said, scuffing over to a stupendous golden door in the wall next to him.

Fashioned from pure gold, the door was inlaid with five large circles, which surrounded a central, raised dial fashioned in the shape of a sun.

Wowed by the door, Rafe drifted past Seamus to examine it more closely. The first and largest ring of the embossed circle held intricate carvings denoting ancient civilizations on Earth. The second ring contained a myriad of animal symbols carved into it, and the third consisted of symbols related to ancient transportation. The smaller fourth ring held the English alphabet, and fifth ring contained the numbers one to ten.

Squinting, Rafe studied the raised dial. Twenty small holes sat at the tip of each beam radiating from the sun.

"The keyhole is different this time," Goldie said to Seamus.

"That's a lock?" Rafe asked. "I don't know anything about locks, but this one looks hard to pick."

"You're right about that. This one is impossible to pick. Even if you find the key, it's a puzzle lock, and the statistical probability of my finding the right combination is staggeringly low. I guess we have no choice but to do this the hard way again."

Seamus waddled over to check the lettering on a gilded wall plaque next to the door. "We're in luck. Da instructions er da same as before."

Moving to Seamus's side, Baylor read out loud from the plaque.

"To leave tHis space:
Go above and go beyond
To a place wHeRe knowledge dawns."

"Well, that's as clear as mud," Rafe said.

"Relax, you two. It took Seamus months, but he figured out how to solve that riddle." Turning, Goldie quirked an eyebrow at Seamus and smiled. "Which one of them is climbing this time?"

"I tink it will 'ave ta be 'im," Seamus said, pointing to Rafe with his shillelagh.

"*Huh?*" Baylor said in a mystified tone. "What is he supposed to do? Shimmy up one of these columns?"

"No. It'll be much easier than that. He's only got to climb a tree," Goldie replied.

"Say what now?" Rafe asked.

"You've got to climb a tree," Goldie said, enunciating her words very slowly for Rafe. "I assume you've done that before?"

Rafe gave Goldie a mock smile. "Yes, I've done that before, and I understood what you said the first time, but there are no trees in this room."

"Oh, but there will be," Goldie said, sashaying past Rafe.

"Get a wiggle on, ya sorry lot," Seamus said, striking off. "We're in da *W* section and we got ta walk down ta da letter *R*."

"I'm glad they seem to know what they're doing because I'm totally confused," Baylor whispered to Rafe as they plodded along behind Seamus and Goldie.

"You aren't the only one," he replied.

The group walked along in silence for several long minutes until Seamus spotted the letter *R* on a nearby column. "Dis is it," he said, making a right turn and heading for the dark green marble tiles. At the edge of the green tiles, Seamus squatted and looked down.

Hurrying to the leprechaun's side, Goldie stooped to scope out the green floor as well.

Swapping bewildered looks, Baylor and Rafe scurried toward Seamus and Goldie. Nearing the pair, Rafe's brow furrowed as he realized the green marble floor tiles were not really floor tiles at all. The greenery stretching out before them actually contained a minuscule diorama of a strange and fantastic orchard. No wonder Seamus and Goldie had stopped. They would have crushed the tiny trees had they charged ahead.

Reaching the miniature orchard, Rafe surveyed it with great interest. On Earth, orchards typically grew only one kind of fruit, but this orchard was altogether different and quite extraordinary.

Different types of fruit and nut trees grew right next to each other, side-by-side. Apples, plums, peaches, pears, bananas, cherries, oranges, lemons, olives, coconuts, mangoes, walnuts, chestnuts, and almonds. Every fruit- and nut-bearing tree Rafe had ever seen on Earth and still more he did not recognize. One particularly eccentric-looking tree teamed with cucumber-like clusters of fruit.

Stranger still, the trees in the diorama spanned different stages and seasons. Bending on one knee next to Seamus, Rafe peered more closely at the tiny orchard.

He spotted a few new trees just sprouting their first leaf buds and still others bursting with blossoms of every color. Many trees appeared leafy green and in their prime, some heavily laden with fruit and others bearing no fruit at all. Sprinkled among the healthy young and middle-aged trees stood ancient trees, nearly leafless, gnarled and withering. However, every tree in this mystifying orchard appeared beautiful in its own right.

"There must be billions of them," Rafe murmured.

"You're quite right," Goldie said. "Billions. Every tree in this orchard represents a life on Earth. Seamus and I don't have trees in there, but each of you do."

"We do?" Baylor said. "How do we know which one is ours?"

"Because yer name is on it, of course," Seamus said.

"Okay, but these trees can't possibly be the ones you need me to climb," Rafe said.

"*Au contraire,* my dear," Goldie replied.

"But, how am I going to—"

Grabbing Rafe's index finger, Seamus brought the startled boy's hand down onto the edge of the greenery.

Without warning, Rafe found himself lying on his back in a grassy lane of the orchard, which, for some inexplicable reason, was now full sized. Tracing the contours of the dark brown angular trunks and branches above him with his eyes, he smelled the loveliest sweet scents of all kinds of blossoms mixing together and wafting over him.

"Ooof," Baylor said, materializing next to Rafe and sprawled on her back as well.

Seamus and Goldie appeared a few moments later.

Pushing himself off the ground, Rafe brushed the grass off his trousers. "You know, Seamus, I would really appreciate it if you could learn to be a little less handsy. I could have done that myself."

"Don't be givin' out stink ta me, boy. I won't 'ave it!" Seamus said.

Muttering under his breath, Rafe gave Baylor and Goldie each a hand, helping them to their feet.

"Let's see where we are," Goldie said, dashing over to the nearest tree. "The name on this one is Alexander Rzewski. We're not that far away, but I think we'll need to go through the trees here and down a row to find the Ryder family name."

"Why can't I just climb one of the other trees in this row?" Rafe asked.

"You can . . . if you enjoy being electrocuted," Goldie said. "I don't recommend it though. My hair has never quite been the same since I touched Ernestine Patricia's tree."

"The trees *shock* you?" Rafe asked as Seamus struck off between the trees to the next row. "Why?"

"As near as we can figure, it's a protection mechanism," Goldie said, taking Baylor by the hand and following the leprechaun.

"If I can't touch the trees, how do you expect me to climb one of them?" Rafe asked, falling into stride with Goldie and Baylor.

"You can touch the tree that belongs to you or a member of your family. It's simple, really; although, it did take us quite a long time to figure it out."

"Would you please tell me why I have to climb a tree at all?" Rafe asked.

"I would have thought Seamus had already explained this to you," Goldie said, huffing out a breath. "You did notice the wheels of circles in the door back there with the symbols, letters, and numbers on them, didn't you?"

"Of course."

"Well, at the top of every great tree, there is a quiet place where you will see and hear things which will tell us the correct settings or sequences to dial into those circles. You'll also be physically handed a key for the center lock of the door."

"So that's what all this 'go above and go beyond' nonsense is about. Wait a minute." Rafe wrinkled his brow and straightened his back. "You said that you and Seamus don't have trees in this orchard, which means you would have had to get someone from Earth to make the climb for you. Who was it?"

Goldie gave a full-throated chuckle. "We enlisted the help of a delightful little chap who climbed his grandmother's tree for us."

"Does this chap have a name?" Baylor asked.

"Prince William Arthur Phillip Louis Mountbatten-Windsor."

"WHAT?" Rafe shrieked. "Seamus asked Prince William to come up here and climb a tree in the Keep of Time for him? Unbelievable! What is everyone's obsession with the British royal family up here?"

"Oh for pity's sake, child. There's no obsession. Her Majesty Queen Elizabeth simply had the grandest, tallest tree up here. If knowledge was going to dawn, we guessed it would be at the top of that tree, and we were right."

"I'm positive I'm not related to the Queen, so climbing Her Majesty's tree is out of the question," Rafe said as they caught up to Seamus.

"No one's askin' ya ta," the leprechaun said in a peevish tone. "I tink it will work if ya climb da tallest tree we find in yer family."

"You *think*?"

"Dat's right, I *tink*. We won't know fer sure until ya try."

"Nothing is ever for sure in the Keep of Time, but that's the fun of an adventure like this," Goldie said.

That's the fun of it? That's the fun of it? Rafe calmed himself with a few deep breaths. For Goldie, this was only a fun excursion outside of the tower she lived in, but to his friends, this adventure meant life or death.

"How in the world did you convince Prince William to come up here and climb that tree for you, Seamus?" Baylor asked.

"What young person in der right mind says no ta a leprechaun standin' at da end of der bed in da middle of da night and invitin' dem ta go on an adventure?"

"Honestly, knowing what I know now, no young person in their right mind should ever say *yes* to a leprechaun for *any* reason," said Rafe.

"No need to be so prickly," Goldie chastised. "The little prince had fun. He thought he was dreaming."

"What did he see up in the treetop?" Baylor asked.

A wide smile spread across Goldie's face. "Something marvelous! Two ancient Egyptians in a chariot being pulled across the sky by a huge lion who went by the name of Clawde."

"How did Prince William know the lion's name?"

"There was a tag with 'Clawde' written on it dangling from the lion's collar. One of the fellows riding in the chariot beat on a drum, and the other one held a fistful of spears. Anyway, to make a long story short, the chariot stopped, the lion roared, and the prince was handed one of the spears, the tip of which we discovered later fit perfectly in the keyhole of the door to the next room."

"I get it," Baylor said. "So, you set the first ring to the Egyptian civilization, the second to a lion, and the third to a chariot, but how did you know what letter and number to use?"

"That's where it got complicated, but eventually, we figured out the last two wheels needed a *series* of letters and numbers. When we spelled out the letters c-l-a-w-d-e and figured out the number of beats in the drummer's different rhythms, the door opened right up."

Overhead, an aged tree with the name Zephaniah White Ryder carved into its trunk unexpectedly stirred and shivered, startling the group. The tree's barren serpentine branches, stark against the striking colors of the vaulted ceiling overhead, relinquished its frail grip on its last remnant of foliage. The withered yellow leaf waltzed with the colors of the ceiling for a few moments before fluttering to the ground in slow noiseless circles.

"Don't move," Seamus said, stretching his arms out to corral the children behind him. "Stand perfectly still."

Shaking convulsively, the tree disappeared with a spectacular crack into a gaping hole which had suddenly opened in the ground.

"What happened?" Rafe gasped as he watched the orchard floor repair itself and seal over. "It's as if the tree was never there."

"Watch," Seamus said.

A small sprig of green pushed up from the soil where the tree had once stood.

"A new tree?" Rafe asked, giving Seamus a puzzled look.

"Dat's right. It came from da roots of da old one. Go and see what da name on dat bark is. Me old eyes can't make it out, and whatever ya do, make sure ya don't touch it. 'Tis small, to be sure, but it can still give ya one almighty shock."

"Let me do it," Baylor said. Striding to the plant, she stooped beside it and read the tiny lettering on it, "Zephora Diana Ryder."

"We've found yer people," Seamus said, nodding at Rafe. "Now we'll look fer yer tree."

"And while we're doing that, is there anything else you'd care to tell us about this orchard?" Rafe asked.

"I know an interesting tidbit of information," Goldie replied. "Apparently the trees decide what fruit they bear and how much."

"Actually, I meant information like the trees electrocuting you or giant holes opening up in the ground next to us," Rafe said.

"I don't appreciate ya trowin' out da smart aleck remarks," Seamus said.

Goldie sighed. "I suppose there is one more thing we should warn you about," she said. "While you're up in the treetops, you have to make sure you don't read any of the leaves on the trees. You'll go blind."

"Tanks fer nothin'," Seamus squawked. "I was gonna wait ta tell em dat when we decided what tree he was gonna climb."

"Might as well fess up now," Goldie said with a shrug.

Baylor's mouth dropped open. "Please don't tell me you know this because you blinded the future King of England?"

"Pish! He was having fun right up until that point, and it was only temporary," Goldie said.

"How long?" Baylor asked.

"I can't remember exactly, but I'm guessing it was twenty minutes to half an hour." Goldie stooped to pick up a leaf from the ground and handed it to Baylor. "Here, look at this. Don't worry—the leaves on the ground are safe to read."

Baylor twirled the leaf in her hand. "One side of this leaf says 'Zeke Ryder' and the other side says, 'Burns himself on a frying pan while his mother cooks dinner.'"

"The leaves describe events that have already happened in your lives; then they discolor and fall from the tree," Goldie said.

"Let me get this straight," said Rafe. "The trees know what our future will be, and it's written on the leaves up there."

"No, no, no. The prince told us most of the leaves are blank in the treetops, but on his way back down the tree, he saw, 'The Queen goes for a horseback ride at Windsor Castle' as it was being written on one of her leaves. Your choices and decisions determine what is written on the leaves of your tree."

"Maybe," Rafe said, thinking of his own experiences. "Or maybe what's written on the leaves up there is due to the choices and decisions someone else makes for you."

Goldie raised an eyebrow. "I'd say that sort of thing must be logically expected when you're young and have parents or guardians."

Jerking his eyes from Goldie, Rafe felt a sour tang building in his mouth. He didn't feel like arguing with her. He was old enough to make his own decisions, thank you very much, and his parents should have allowed him to do that.

As Rafe brooded and the group walked on, Baylor skipped ahead and skimmed the tree trunks, looking for names. "Rafe," she called a few minutes later. "I think I found your tree. This one says: *Richard Arthur Fredrick Edward Ryder.*"

Seamus snickered and touched a pinky finger to his chin in a *la-di-da* manner. "Should I bow, yer royal 'ighness?"

Goldie wrinkled her brow. "You said your name was Rafe Ryder when we met. Are you a prince of Earth, too?" she asked.

"No, definitely not."

"Then why do you have four names?"

"My father's name is Richard as was my grandfather's before him. My dad wanted that to be my name, too, but my mother wanted to call me Rafe, and eventually she came up with a clever way for them to both get what they wanted. Rafe is an acronym for my real name, which is why I have so many."

"Richard Arthur Fredrick Edward. R-a-f-e," Goldie said as they reached Rafe's tree. "How terribly clever! Your mother's ingenuity is to be admired."

Standing bold and proud, a stocky young tree with reddish-grey bark stood in full glorious bloom. Gorgeous pinkish-white flowers exhaled a faint delicious scent, enticing Rafe to come closer. Etched into the trunk in graceful calligraphy, Rafe studied his name.

"I could stay here all day," Baylor murmured, closing her eyes and inhaling the fragrance.

"What kind of tree is it?" Rafe asked.

"'Tis an apple tree," Seamus replied. "I don't know what kind of apple if dat's what yer askin'."

"It's a sturdy enough little tree, but it isn't very tall yet," Goldie mused. "What about that grand old apple tree a little further down the row? Why, that one has to be at least twelve feet in circumference, and it towers over all the other trees in this row!"

"Of course, dat's it! If 'e is related ta dat person, dat's da one 'e will climb."

"Let's go see," Goldie said, lifting the skirts of her gown and scampering toward it.

"Wait," Rafe said to the others, plodding over to a large peach tree standing next to his. He smoothed his hand over the name written in the reddish-brown bark there. Many of the tree's broad flat leaves were green, but some had begun to yellow and drop from the tree. Most of the tree's branches appeared healthy with velvety salmon-yellow fruit dangling from them, but a few branches seemed to be shrinking and withering. His eyes misting, Rafe dropped into the leaves under the tree and began to read.

"It's his father's tree," Baylor murmured.

"Give da lad a minute, den, but don't let em stay der long. I'm goin' ta go catch up wid Goldie," Seamus whispered to Baylor.

Biting her bottom lip, Baylor nodded. A flush crept into her face as she strode to Rafe's side and knelt down beside him.

"This one says he practiced the piano for a few minutes, and this other one says that my mother made him his favorite meal." Rafe glanced at Baylor through misty eyes.

"What's his favorite meal," Baylor asked.

"Shepherd's pie."

Wrapping her arms around Rafe's shoulders, Baylor rested her cheek against his head.

"I want to go home, Bay."

"I know you do. Me too."

"All things considered, I think his tree looks pretty healthy, don't you?"

"I do," Baylor said, releasing her hold on his shoulders and gazing into Rafe's eyes. "I really do."

Rubbing his hands over his splotchy face, Rafe sprang to his feet. "Where are Seamus and Goldie?"

"They're waiting for us under that big apple tree over there."

Rafe took one last look at his father's tree. "We should go then."

As Rafe and Baylor marched out into the grassy lane, Goldie shouted, "Do you know a Catherine Jane Ryder?"

A lopsided grin appeared on Rafe's face. *Of course, a tree as splendid as that one would be hers.* "It's my grandmother," he called back.

"Catherine?" Baylor asked.

"Yeah. That's Lady Jane's first name."

"I had no idea. I've never heard anyone call her Catherine before."

"That's because no one ever does," said Rafe. "Honestly, if I wasn't her grandchild, I'm sure I'd never have known that was her first name either."

Breaking into a jog, Rafe and Baylor closed the distance between themselves and the marvelous old tree. In the bark of the tree's stout rugged trunk and framed by a rounded knot was inscribed the name Catherine Jane Ryder.

Tipping his head back, Rafe surveyed the tree. Lovely, thick, vigorous leaves overhead knit themselves into a canopy of dense green foliage. The tree's massive branches and limbs arched both skyward and downward toward the ground, holding luscious deep dark-red fruit. Just like Lady Jane herself, the tree radiated grandeur and majesty.

Chapter Fifteen

Above and Beyond

"I don't suppose I can change bodies and use my wings to get up there," Rafe said.

"I told ya once before. Not unless ya want ta call every angel in Mystfira ta dis location," Seamus replied. "Yer teachers er most likely monitorin' any student changin' der form now in an effort ta find ya."

Wrinkling his forehead, Rafe studied the tree. It was a long way up to the first branch, and the trunk was so large he'd never get a good grip on it using his calves and thighs.

"I can give ya a leg up," Seamus said, dropping his shillelagh and interlacing his fingers to make a boosting step.

"Thanks, but let me try something else first. Clear a path," Rafe said, motioning the others away from tree trunk.

Backing up, Rafe ran toward the tree at top speed. Planting the ball of his foot against the trunk, he catapulted upward and managed to get a handgrip on the lowest branch. Biceps straining, he pulled himself up until both his forearms rested on the branch. Grunting, he hauled the rest of his body up and swung his legs around the branch.

"Der ya go," Seamus said.

"That's the hard part, kiddo," Goldie said. "The rest of the climb will be a piece of cake. Just look at all the branches you've got to choose from."

Rafe gazed down at them. "How far do I have to go?"

"Just get yer 'ead above dat canopy of leaves, and ya'll see."

Swinging himself from branch to branch like a wiry monkey, Rafe scrambled up the tree.

"My heavens, that boy's good at this tree-climbing thing," Goldie observed from the ground.

Climbing steadily, Rafe soon reached the crown of the tree. Poking his head above the leafy canopy, he gazed at the strange orchard beneath him. It stretched on and on, but only a few other trees equaled the height and magnificence of his grandmother's. It felt rather surreal to be sitting in the arms of such a commanding tower of a tree, but at the same time, it felt familiar, almost as if Lady Jane were with him and giving him one of her warm hugs.

A faint slapping noise caught Rafe's attention, and he turned his head to investigate. To his utter amazement, he spotted a single, blood-red, square sail billowing in the distance. Underneath the sail, a sleek, high-bowed ship with a menacing dragon's head rowed into view.

The ship's oars slashed through the air in unison, but there was not a single oarsman to be seen sitting on any of the twenty-odd rowing benches. Save for one lone man under the mast, the ship was empty.

As the longboat flew toward him, Rafe felt goosebumps rising on his arms. He finally understood what he'd learned at secondary school in England about the sight of Norse warships striking fear into the hearts of medieval settlements that were pillaged and plundered by the Vikings of old.

"Oarsmen, let it run!" shouted the man. The oars lifted, and the ship glided to a smooth stop beside Rafe.

Written in bold red letters on the side of the longboat were the words: *Flessor B. Dounnaheffstup.*

You've got to be kidding! Rafe thought, staring at the lettering. *What a name to have to remember to spell!*

No matter. He'd use one the mnemonic techniques his mother had taught him and make a few silly sentences out of each letter he needed to remember.

With his eyes fixed on the side of the boat, Rafe's mind quickly worked out the sentences. They were a bit gross, but honestly, that just made them easier for him to remember.

F̲lies l̲ove e̲ating s̲ticky s̲yrup o̲n r̲ats. B̲ut. D̲onuts o̲n U̲ncle N̲ick's n̲ose a̲re h̲ardly e̲ver f̲ine f̲ood s̲erved t̲o u̲ppity p̲eople.

Rafe turned his attention to the ship's deck and the blond bearded man in a long tunic and blue cloak standing there under the mast. He had probably been a handsome fellow earlier in life, but no longer. His face, littered with battle scars and weathered by long exposure to sun, air, and sea, reminded Rafe of a scraped-up leather shoe.

"Hello, sir," Rafe called.

Ignoring him, the man stared straight ahead and sang in a crisp, clear voice the same odd words over and over again. "I tame my trials with this lullaby, so I don't die."

"Hello?"

The warrior turned his head, and his gaze settled on Rafe. "Sing it," he demanded.

Rafe's brow furrowed. "Sorry?"

"Sing my song with me."

"Maybe next time, but today I am actually looking for a key to the door below, and I was told I might get it up here."

The man frowned. Thumping to the edge of the ship, he pulled a sword from a scabbard at his side and jabbed the sharp blade at Rafe's throat. "You will have the keys that you need *after* you sing my song with me."

Astonished to find a sword almost nipped into his neck, Rafe tried to blink away his disbelief. "Since you put it that way," he said, "a sing-along sounds ace. Let's do it."

"I'll sing it first, and then you sing it with me."

Eyes wide, Rafe watched as the Viking pulled a pitch pipe from his belt. *"Hmmm,"* hummed the Viking, imitating the note from his pitch pipe. "I tame my trials with this lullaby, so I don't die."

"I tame my trials with this lullaby, so I don't die," Rafe sang after the warrior.

"You'll need to remember that," the Viking said, lowering his sword. Bending over, he lifted an exquisite silver tiara, dripping with glittering diamonds and lustrous, white, pear-shaped pearls, from the deck of his ship. "For you," he said, offering the tiara to Rafe.

"*Umm,* thanks," Rafe said, taking the sparkling object. "But what about the key?"

"You have been given all you need."

"Okay, but—"

"Oarsmen!" the Viking shouted to the phantom rowers. "Ready, row!"

Thrusting forward, the warship slid away from Rafe and disappeared into thin air.

Jamming the tiara on his head, Rafe abandoned the two branches he'd wedged himself between and began his descent from the treetop, trying to stick to the same path he'd used to climb up.

Nearing the bottom of the tree, Rafe saw three gaping faces gawking back up at him. His cheeks grew hot as he realized they were all staring at the tiara he'd donned for the climb down. Humiliated, Rafe diverted his gaze to a branch below him just as writing magically appeared on it, and without thinking he read it. It said, "Lady Jane kicks the wall of the tree in frustration."

Wondering what the wall of a tree was and why Lady Jane would be kicking it, he tried to read the words again, but as he did, his vision dimmed, growing darker and darker until he could see nothing at all. Janey Mack! He was blind!

Rafe brought a hand to his eyes. Losing his eyesight shocked him, but he took comfort in the fact that his eyes were at least still in their sockets.

"I can't see," he shouted.

"Der ya've gone and done it now! I told ya not ta read any of da leaves up der!" Seamus scolded.

"Yeah, yeah, yeah," Rafe said, wondering what to do next.

"Was it worth it? What's your grandmother doing?" Baylor asked.

"Apparently she's kicking the wall of a tree in frustration. Whatever that means, and I didn't read it on purpose, Bay. It just happened."

"I'd be kickin' a tree meself right now, but I don't want ta get electrified," Seamus snapped.

"You're all right. You're almost at the bottom branch," Baylor said. "I'll tell you where to put your feet, and then when you reach it, you can drop down here to us. Okay?"

"Fine."

Listening to Baylor's directions, Rafe inched his way to the bottom branch.

"Better throw your tiara down here, princess, so you don't poke out an eye when you jump out of that tree," Goldie said.

"Ha. Ha. Very funny," Rafe said in the most sarcastic voice he could muster. "Someone catch it." Removing the tiara, he let it fall straight underneath him.

"Got it," Baylor said. "Now you."

Dropping over the side of the branch, Rafe dangled from the branch feet first. His hands slipped from the branch, and the next thing he knew, he was splayed out on the ground like a Christmas turkey.

"Are you hurt?" Baylor asked, helping Rafe to his feet.

"Other than losing my eyesight and what's left of my pride, I'm just ducky."

"Good. Let's go back ta da door den," Seamus said.

"Here, take my arm," Baylor said, giving Rafe her elbow to grasp. "I'll guide you until you can see again."

"So, what happened up there?" Goldie asked as the group retraced their steps through the orchard.

"A Viking warship with a dragon on its prow and an invisible crew rowed up to me. There was one man I could see, a warrior, commanding the ship. He had a pitch pipe and made me sing a song with him at sword point. After that, he gave me that lovely tiara I threw down to you, and he told me I had all I needed to open the door."

"A Viking with a pitch pipe? Do you remember the pitch he gave you?" Baylor asked.

"Who knows? I don't have perfect pitch like you do, Bay," Rafe replied.

"But you have perfectly good relative pitch," she argued. "You must have some idea."

"Dat's really not important now," Seamus said. "Da important ting is we got most of da answers we were lookin' fer."

"True," Goldie said. "It's obvious the first circle in the door will be a Viking, the second a dragon, and the third a ship, but what about numbers and letters? Did you see any while you were up there?"

"There was a name on the side of the ship. It was called the *Flessor B. Dounnaheffstup*."

"Dat's a stupid name fer a ship," Seamus said.

"Maybe it's an old Viking family name," Baylor said.

"Whatever it is, it *has* to be the combination of letters we need to spin into the door. What about the numbers? Did you hear any drum beats?" Goldie asked.

"All I heard was that song the Viking kept singing over and over again. Like I said, he even made me sing it with him."

"Then it must be important," Baylor said.

"Did da song 'ave any numbers in it?" Seamus asked.

"No numbers, but the words were 'I tame my trials with this lullaby, so I don't die.'"

"Sing us da tune," Seamus said.

Scowling, Rafe obliged, singing the song in a quiet voice.

"Maybe it's the number of steps between each musical note," Baylor said.

"No way! That's too complicated," Goldie said. "It should be simple enough for anyone to figure out. The last time we were up here, we only had to count the number of drumbeats Prince William heard."

Rafe felt Baylor halt in her tracks. "Why did we stop?"

"We're at the end of the orchard."

"And?"

"And we've all got to step out at the same time so we resume our original size together," Goldie said, taking hold of Rafe's other arm. "I guarantee giant feet and tiny people don't mix well."

"Someone better count so I know when to step then."

"On three. One . . . two . . . three," Goldie counted.

As he took a step forward, Rafe heard Baylor's exclamation of surprise, but he didn't feel any different himself.

"Back ta normal. Dat's a relief," Seamus said.

"Speak for yourself," Rafe replied. "I'm still blind."

"Stop yer complainin'. Yer not stuck inside a paintin', and yer not dead."

Rafe opened his mouth to deliver a sarcastic reply, but realizing the leprechaun had a fair point, he shut it again.

The group moseyed along in silence for another five minutes before stopping again.

"We're at the door. Can you see anything yet?" Baylor asked.

"Not yet, but it was pitch black, and now it's like my eyes are closed against really strong sunlight," Rafe said, letting his hand drop away from Baylor's elbow.

"Hopefully, it won't be too much longer," she said.

"Is dat tiara da key, Goldie?"

"I think, yes. There are twenty upright pearl spikes and twenty little holes in the locking mechanism," Goldie said.

Rafe heard a clinking noise and the scrape of stone as something was turned.

"What's happening," he asked Baylor.

"Goldie fit the tiara into the lock, and now she and Seamus are setting the circles to the right places on the door," Baylor whispered.

"Rafe, spell the letters you saw on the side of that ship to me," Goldie asked. "There are only small letters on this dial so disregard any capital letters you may have seen."

Recalling his silly sentences, Rafe rattled off the spelling. "F-l-e-s-s-o-r-b-d-o-u-n-n-a-h-e-f-f-s-t-u-p."

After much whirring and more stone-on-stone scraping, Goldie said, "There. That's it for our letters, but now we need to figure out what the numbers are."

"Maybe it's got someting ta do wid dat song's rhydem" Seamus said.

"The songs rhythm?" Goldie said. "I don't think so, or there would have been drum beats like the last time."

Maybe it has to do with the number of syllables in the words," Baylor said. "I tame my tri-als with this lull-a-by, so I don't die. There are ten syllables before the rest in the song and four syllables after it."

"Not only that, there are ten notes before the rest and four notes after the rest," Rafe said. "That has to be it."

"Yes, yes," Goldie said breathlessly. "We only used two numbers last time as well. Let's dial in ten and four, Seamus."

Wispy tendrils of light trickled into Rafe's vision as he heard stone grating against stone again, followed by the sound of several metallic locks being pulled back, one after another.

Standing beside him, Baylor gasped. "It worked! The lock with the tiara in it just vanished, and now the circles are disappearing one by one into the doorframe."

"What's in the next room?" Rafe asked

"It's a cave," Baylor whispered.

"I don't like this at all," Goldie said. "Last time, the room after the orchard was a jungle, not a cave."

"Don't fret. Dey probably just changed da rooms leadin' ta da staircase fer security purposes after we broke in," Seamus said, his voice fading away from Rafe. "We'll get it figured out. We always do."

"I suppose. On the plus side, though, it's much smaller than the Orchard Room," Goldie said, her voice fading away, too.

"Come on. We need to follow them," Baylor said, taking Rafe's hand. As she dragged him into the cavern after her, Rafe heard a harsh grinding followed by a thud of something very heavy. Startled, Baylor pulled her hand from his.

"What was that?" he asked.

"The door we just came through. It's gone!" Baylor cried. "It's part of the cave wall now."

"Don't fret, lass. Dat's da way it works up 'ere in da keep. One door closes and anoder door stands ready—waitin' fer ya ta find a way ta open it."

"He's right," Goldie said. "Look over there, you two . . . up that little slope. There's an alcove with a door tucked into it."

Rafe pinched his eyebrows together in a pained expression. "I'm sorry, but telling a blind guy to *'look over there'* is just bloody insensitive."

"I apologize, kiddo. I forgot," Goldie said, trying to strangle a giggle. "In the spirit of full disclosure, I suppose I should mention there's a plaque hanging over the alcove, which says: *Dismal's Deluge.*"

"'Tis probably da name of dis room den."

"It fits," Baylor murmured. "A creepy name for a creepy place."

"I don't like it in 'ere. Get over der, and see if ya can get dat door open, speedy-like, Goldie."

"Will do, but if you want me to be quick, I'll need an extra hand to hold my picks."

"I remember da drill from last time. Get goin'. I'm right behind ya," Seamus said.

Rafe heard the sound of feet sloshing through puddles. Placing his hand behind him, he shuffled back a few steps, searching for the cave wall. His fingertips touched something hard, damp, and cold.

"Bay? Is there a lot of water in here?"

"There are puddles everywhere, but I think I can guide us around them," she said.

Ka-kunk! Another heavy thud reverberated through the cave.

"Seamus! Goldie! Noooo!" Baylor screamed. "Rafe, the cave wall in the alcove just snapped shut behind them! They're trapped inside!"

Whipping his head side-to-side, Rafe strained to focus. He heard Baylor splashing through puddles ahead of him and assumed she had gone to the place she'd last seen Seamus and Goldie, but he needed her to be his eyes.

"My vision is coming back," he said, "but everything is foggy, like I'm looking through a really cloudy piece of glass. Please come back here and tell me what you see around us."

"It's just a cave with a low ceiling, a dirt floor, and four stone walls," Baylor said, her voice on the edge of hysteria.

"But there's light in here, I can see it. Where's it coming from?"

Rafe heard Baylor's ragged breathing calm as she walked back toward him. "There are lanterns tucked inside of small recesses in each of the walls. I think they're sitting behind druri glass."

"Okay, good. Now what is that dripping sound I hear?"

"Dripping? I don't hear—wait," she said, her voice moving away from him again. "How could I miss those monstrosities?"

"What? Talk to me."

"Sticking out of the wall below each one of the lamps is a ginormous stone crocodile head, and there's water dripping out of their mouths," Baylor said, walking back toward Rafe.

"Take me over to one," he said, holding out a hand to her.

Placing her trembling hand in his, Baylor led Rafe to one of the walls and positioned his hand on top of a massive crocodile head.

Sliding his fingers over the figure, Rafe felt the features of the stone carving, large plated scales; a long, slender snout; and two rows of wet, jagged, conical teeth. Squinting, he made out the color of gray-green. "Is it painted?"

"You can see that?" Baylor asked.

"Somewhat. Things are still a little fuzzy, but my eyesight is getting better by the second," Rafe said, moving his fingers to the wall beside the glowing lantern. "We should check around to see if there's a switch or a pressure plate that will move one of these heads. Maybe there's a way out behind one of them."

"I can feel something carved into the wall on this side. I think there's some sort of writing here," said Baylor, "but it's too caked with dirt to read."

Feeling his way around the crocodile head, Rafe made his way over to Baylor. Standing behind her, he squinched his eyes and watched her hazy figure brushing filth from the wall.

"Here it is," she said, blowing grit from the letters. "It's a rhyming verse. It says:

> 'Too high or too low,
> Nothing but woe.'"

As he squinted at the area over Baylor's shoulder, the writing on the wall suddenly flashed into sharp focus.

"It sure does! I can see!" Delirious with happiness, Rafe surprised Baylor by wrapping his arms around her waist and lifting her off the ground. "I can see! I can see!"

"Awesome," she said. "Now put me down, and tell me you *see* a way out of this place."

Crashing back to reality, Rafe planted Baylor's feet back on the dirt floor and released his hold. Frowning, he paced the drab cave, probing it with his eyes. "Not yet, but we'll find one. Let's check out the other crocodiles."

"All right," Baylor said, rubbing her forehead, "but . . . just for the record, I'm not wild about the 'nothing but woe' ending to that verse."

"Neither am I," Rafe said, striding over to the next crocodile. Scrubbing the wall beside it with the side of his fist, he wiped away several layers of dirt. "There's more writing here. It says:

'Stop tHe RisiNg wateRs' suRge,
OR you will quickly be submeRged.'"

Baylor's faced blanched. "Rafe, . . . the crocodile."

The occasional drip of water from the crocodile's mouth had transformed to a steady trickle.

"You don't think—"

"No, no. I don't," Rafe said, shaking his head from side to side.

Shooof! Powerful torrents of water ripped into the small cavern from the mouths of each crocodile, nearly knocking Rafe and Baylor off their feet.

"But then again, I could be wrong."

"You think?" Baylor said, holding her posture rigid against the cold water spilling into the room.

Righting himself, Rafe waded through the calf-deep water to the next crocodile head and pawed at the dirt on the wall beside it. "I guess we know how the dirt got into this lettering now. How about you go see if there is any more writing by that last crocodile over there, Bay?"

"Sure. Why not?" Baylor shrugged. "It's not like I have anything else to do while I wait around to drown or die of hypothermia," she said, slogging through the muddy water to reach the far wall.

Of course, Baylor's remark had been sarcastic, but with

hundreds of gallons of frigid water flowing into the cave every second, it was hard not to share her sentiment.

Stripping off another layer of dirt, Rafe glimpsed a faint outline of letters in the wall as the water reached his waist. "I've got this one! It says:

'Use tHe RigHt key,
ANd you will be fRee.'"

"That doesn't help at all," Baylor said. "Even if we had the *right* key, the door is behind the rock of that alcove now. There is no way we can get to it."

Rafe clenched his jaw, and his lips tightened into a rigid line as the water splashed about his waist. They needed to find a key . . . and not just *a* key, the *right* key. *Think, Ryder, think!*

The cave walls had been bare and relatively smooth except for the lanterns and the crocodile heads. There wasn't even a place to hide a key in here.

Unless . . .

"What if the keys were inside the crocodile's throats?" he said, thinking out loud.

"If they were, I doubt they're there anymore," Baylor replied.

The force of the water spewing into the room had been powerful; the keys would have certainly have been dislodged and were probably sitting in the middle of the floor someplace.

The water continued its surge, burying the lanterns, but from behind the safety of the druri glass, they burned on. The eerie glow beneath the surface produced strange, flickering shadows on the cave walls.

"There's more writing over here," Baylor said. "I can't see it, but I can feel it."

Swinging around, Rafe spied the back of Baylor's shivering

shoulders across the room. The water now covered most of her body, and he could hear her teeth chattering as she worked her fingertips beneath the water, tracing the shapes of the letters. "I've got the first line," she said with excitement. "It says, '*There is only one remedy*'."

"While you do that, I'll see if I can find anything on the floor of the cave." Taking a breath, Rafe pushed under the freezing water. With the four lanterns piercing through the murkiness of the water, he scoured the bottom of the cave, swiveling his head back and forth as he swam.

Out of the corner of his eye, Rafe caught the glint of two small, flat gold objects jutting out from the muck. He swam to them and plucked first one then the other from the bottom. Then, he shot to the surface for air. Once there, he was stunned to find the bone-numbing water had risen over his head, and he now had to tread water.

"I've almost got it," Baylor panted, not bothering to ask Rafe if he'd found anything. Taking a deep breath, she disappeared beneath the water.

Breath hitching from the cold, Rafe raised one of the shiny rectangular objects over his head to examine it. Two sides of the piece were flat, one side had a knob protruding from it, and the last side, a hole punched into it.

Great. He needed a key, but he'd found a couple of puzzle pieces instead. Still, if a tiara could be a key, then so could puzzle pieces. There had to be a place for it in the cave, but where? Maybe Baylor knew.

Rafe glanced about the surface of the water. Too much time had ticked by; she should have surfaced by now. His own legs and arms ached from the crippling cold of the water, and Baylor was much smaller than he was. She was in trouble! He could feel it!

Stuffing the puzzle pieces into one of his pockets, Rafe swam to the spot where he'd last seen Baylor. Dragging as much air as he could into his lungs, he sank beneath the water.

There in a shimmering shaft of light from one of the lanterns, he spotted Baylor locked in a half-hearted struggle to surface. Particles of ice raced up and down his spine as he cut through the water with frantic strokes, reaching her in mere moments. Knotting his arm around her waist, he kicked for the surface, pushing her up ahead of him.

When he surfaced beside her, he'd never in his life been so relieved to hear someone coughing and gasping for air. "It's okay. Breathe," he said. "You're all right now. Breathe."

"The k-k-key," she sputtered back at him. "It's th-the Viking's lull-aby! The writing said:

'THERE is only one Remedy
You must stRike tHe RigHt melody!'"

"That's the key?"

"W-what else could th-that m-m-mean?"

Very little air remained in the cave for them to breathe, so Rafe prayed she was right. "I tame my trials with this lullaby, so I don't die," he sang.

He waited, fixing his eyes on a spot in the wall beside him. In a matter of moments, the water covered it.

"D-did it w-work?" Baylor asked.

"No, the water's still rising."

"*T-t-too high or t-too low* ... it has to be s-sung in th-the right k-key," Baylor croaked.

"Bay, I told you I don't know what key the Viking sang it in."

As the water raced higher, Rafe had to tilt his head back in order to breathe and so did Baylor. A small pocket of air was all that separated the water from the cave's ceiling. Very soon now, there would be no air left to breathe, and there was nothing Rafe or anyone else could do about it.

Why couldn't the Viking have just told him what key the song was in instead of using a pitch pipe? How was he supposed to guess without perfect pitch? He wished Baylor could have climbed the tree instead of him. She would have known! That stupid Viking and his stupid, stupid, stupid ship!

Rafe blinked. *The Viking ship! That was it!*

"Bay! It's the name on the Viking ship. *Flessor*! F-lesser. F minor! That has to be the key the song was in!"

"G-g-good. W-what note did he s-s-start the song on?"

"B. Dounnaheffsup. B-down-a-half-step. Bay, the song start-ed on a B flat!"

"So th-that w-w-would be B flat, B flat, C, D flat, E flat, b-back down to C, A flat, B flat, B flat, B flat," she said through chattering teeth. "Th-then A flat, B flat, B flat, B flat. Rafe, you've got to t-try to s-sing it again in th-the r-r-right k-key."

The tiniest sliver of air remained between them and the ceiling of the cave. "Okay, but you've got to be my pitch pipe, Bay. Give me that B flat."

"*Ahhhhh,*" Baylor sang out the note.

Taking the perfectly pitched B flat, Rafe sang as the water gurgled over his throat, "I tame my trials with this lullaby, so I don't die."

Pressing their lips to the top of the cave, Baylor and Rafe took one last breath of precious air before the water swallowed every last inch of the cave.

Reaching for Rafe's hand, Baylor squeezed it tightly. With her long hair fanning out around her in slow motion like a mer-maid, she gazed at him, smiling a sweet, sad, goodbye smile.

So, this is how it ends, he thought, smiling back at her. *I'm sorry, Bay. I'm so sorry I couldn't save us.*

Chapter Sixteen

The Enigma Room

Hearing a faint underwater gurgling noise, Rafe twisted his head to see a mixture of water and dirt spinning into spiral vortices beneath each one of the crocodiles' mouths. *Whirlpools? Yes!* The water was draining from the cave!

Rafe scrambled for the surface, tugging Baylor with him. Gasping in a breath, he faced her. "Bay, it worked!" he exclaimed. "The water is going down!"

A wan smile worked hard to form on Baylor's blue lips. The tiny silver water droplets dusting her eyelashes quavered as she shivered beside him.

He felt the cold gnawing at him as well, but never before had he ever seen Baylor look so pale and exhausted. "Put your hands on my shoulders," he said.

"N-n-no. I'm o-k-kay," she said through clattering teeth.

Gripping her wrists, Rafe pulled her closer and placed her hands on his shoulders. "Just until you can touch the ground."

Without further protest, Baylor rested her forehead against Rafe's chest and waited. It was a little warmer for both of them huddled together like this, and he could keep them both afloat.

The water level declined steadily, going down even faster than it had rolled into the room.

When the water had fallen to Rafe's waist level, the alcove door snapped open on the rise above them. Seamus stood in the doorway gaping at the flooded cave and the drenched children.

"Janey Mack!" he said. "What 'appened ta ya?"

"Dismal's Deluge," Rafe replied, tucking Baylor under his arm and wading toward the leprechaun. "The room flooded with ice-cold water, and we nearly drowned."

"Is she all right?"

"She's freezing."

"Get 'er over 'ere! Goldie's almost got da door open, and we'll warm ya both up in da next room."

Rafe slogged up the incline with Baylor. Quick as thought, Seamus produced a blanket from his enchanted pocket and flung it around their shoulders. "Er ya still wid us, lass?" he said, gazing into Baylor's eyes.

"Th-th-thanks, b-but I'd rather have a hot t-t-tub, if you've got one of th-th-those on you."

Seamus chuckled. "Not dis time, lass, but next time we come, I'll make sure ta bring one wid me," he said.

Entering the alcove with Baylor, Rafe saw Goldie on her knees in front of a massive, rusted iron door. With a final creak, click, and whir of her picks, the lock tumbled open. "There! That took forever, but we're in," she said, turning around to face them. "Good heavens! What happened to the two of you?"

"Da room flooded on dem. We need ta get inta da next room and warm dem up."

Turning back to the door, Goldie nudged it open and peered inside. "Drat it all! It's another room we've never seen. We're going to need both your lanterns, Seamus. It's pitch-black inside."

Seamus pulled two lanterns from his pocket and handed one to Goldie. "Be careful den, and make sure der's actually a floor under yer feet before steppin' inside."

Biting her bottom lip, Goldie stuck the lantern through the door and swung it around. Drawing in an awestruck breath, she bolted into the room. "There's a floor underneath me all right, and it's made of gold! In fact, the whole room is!" she exclaimed.

Rafe steered Baylor into the room, and Seamus followed.

"Yer fire blanket, lass. Is it still in yer pocket?" Seamus asked as the door sealed shut and disappeared behind them.

Her fingertips a ghastly shade of blue, Baylor reached into the pocket of her jeans. After several moments of fumbling, she slid it out and gave it to Seamus before sinking to the floor in exhaustion.

Kneeling beside her, Rafe slipped the blanket Seamus had given them over her shoulders and tucked it around her.

"Poor thing," Goldie said, putting down her lantern and scurrying to Seamus's side. "I'll help you open the fire blanket."

"Stay right still, love. I'm goin' ta take dat regular blanket and give it ta Rafe. Den Goldie and I er goin' ta put dis blanket over ya."

"No, you're not," Rafe said. "You are not putting that thing over Baylor."

"Don't ya be givin' me yer lip, boy! What is wrong wid dat 'ead of yers? Do ya 'ave no circulation ta yer brain?"

"Baylor's human, and that fire blanket is a tool made and used by dark spirits. It could be dangerous," Rafe argued.

"Let me explain someting ta ya. A tool is a ting, and tings don't decide if dey want ta be used fer a good purpose or a bad one—dat's up ta da people usin' dem. I don't care if da devil 'imself owned dis fire blanket; it will dry 'er clothes and make 'er warm in less den a minute."

"He's telling the truth," Goldie said. "She'll be safe."

"D-d-do it," Baylor chattered, handing the regular blanket Rafe had tucked around her to Goldie, who tossed it around Rafe's shoulders.

Shaking out the fire blanket, Seamus gently positioned it

over the head of the shivering girl. The fire quivered and sparked as Baylor shuddered beneath it, but after a few moments, the fire stopped moving.

"How did you know what the blanket could do?" Rafe asked Seamus.

"I've sold a few in me time . . . ta dark spirits livin' in Mystfira. Dey er used fer many purposes, but da number one reason dey like dese blankets is because dey despise water. Dey use dese blankets ta dry demselves if dey get wet," Seamus said, pulling a large thermos from his pocket.

The leprechaun poured a cup of hot tea and handed it to Rafe. "Sit by da fire wid Goldie, and drink dis while I check on da patient."

Lifting the corner of the fire, Seamus peered under it. "'Ow er ya feelin', love?"

"Wonderful," came Baylor's muffled voice. "Toasty warm."

"Do ya want to stay under fer anoder minute?"

"No thanks, I'm good. I'll come out now."

Goldie and Seamus peeled back the edges of the fire and held it as Baylor crawled out. The warmth of the fire blanket had caused her skin to flush pink and had brought the sparkle back into her dark eyes.

"Your turn," she said to Rafe.

"I'd rather not," he said.

"But your clothes are still sopping wet."

"Please, they're dampish at best."

"Suit yourself," Baylor said, flicking her gaze upwards in exasperation.

Rafe glanced around the dimly lit rectangular room. "I don't see any doors in here. I thought you said when one door closes, another one appears waiting to be opened, Seamus?"

"I did, and dat's da way 'tis always worked . . . until dis room."

Shadows from Baylor's fire blanket flickered on the gold brick walls, casting bizarre shapes against them. Other than the shiny gold bricks, the room was without ornament of any kind.

Fishing into his pocket, Rafe produced the golden puzzle pieces he'd found on the floor of Dismal's Deluge. "Maybe these fit into a place on one of the walls in here, and then the door we need will appear."

"We can only hope it's as easy as that," Goldie said. Plucking one of the lamps from the floor by the fire blanket, she walked to the nearest wall and held it aloft. Even in the dim lamplight, the lustrous sheen of gold dazzled. "Oh, my! Seamus, these aren't just bricks, they're real bars of gold!"

The leprechaun trotted to the wall, stuck out his tongue, and licked the bricks. "Right ya er," he said. "'Tis pure gold."

Baylor clapped her hand to her mouth and grimaced. "Did he just lick that wall?" she whispered.

"Yes," Rafe said, nodding his head. "Yes, he did."

"What er da pair of ya waitin' fer? An invitation? Start lookin' around," Seamus called over his shoulder.

"Leave the fire blanket where it is, though," said Goldie. "It helps with the lighting situation in here."

Rafe picked up the lantern next to him. "Pick a wall, Bay."

"And what am I looking for? A place for your puzzle pieces?"

"That, or some writing, or a loose brick that will shift when you touch it. Anything out of the ordinary."

"Like that light up there in the middle of the ceiling?" she asked.

Tipping his head back, Rafe spied a black-domed lighting fixture recessed into the gold of the ceiling. "Just like that," he said. "There must be a way to turn that on. Let's look for a switch."

Hours later, the little group of four had twice accomplished a fruitless and frustrating search of the room. As they began their third sweep of the room, Baylor balked.

"I've got to take a break for a minute. This is driving me crazy." Walking to the center of the room, Baylor collapsed next to the fire blanket, staring at the dancing tongues of flames blazing from it.

"I'm with her," Goldie said, following Baylor.

Seamus tromped over to the fire dragging his shillelagh behind him. "What er we missin'?"

"I don't know," Rafe said, joining the others. "You pressed, kicked, and knocked on every brick in here with that shillelagh of yours."

"I don't think we're missing anything," Baylor said. "Other than the light in the ceiling, the walls in this room are blank. No carving, writing, or missing pieces to be seen on a single brick."

"Why have a light in this room at all if there is no way to turn it on?" Goldie said.

"*Hmmm.*" Rafe brought a finger to his lip and tapped it. "What if it *is* on? I don't know about lights up here in Mystfira, but there are some types of light we can't see on Earth."

"What?" Seamus asked. "'Ow do ya know dat?"

"When I was younger, my parents took me to an amusement park. One of the rides took us into this pitch-black tunnel, but I saw things glowing in the dark all around us. Even the white shirt I wore had a weird shine to it. It kind of freaked me out until my father explained the tunnel was lit by black lights."

"Black lights? I still don't know what yer talkin' about," Seamus grumbled.

"I do," Baylor said, smiling at Rafe. "Black lights use ultraviolet light which the human eye can't see, but certain substances will glow under that type of light."

"So, it's possible a room can look dark and yet be filled with this invisible light you're talking about?" Goldie asked.

"Exactly," said Rafe.

"What are we waiting for then? This room may be made of gold, but I want out," Goldie said, lifting the corners of the fire blanket and folding it over and over until it was small enough for Baylor to slip back into her pocket. "Now, the lanterns," she said blowing out the first one.

A small circle of light flickered around the last lamp in Seamus's hand. "May da deep tings of darkness in dis room be revealed to us," he whispered, almost like a prayer, before extinguishing the flame.

Darkness, as thick as tar and deeper than the darkest night, shrouded the room, and as quickly as the darkness descended, luminous white symbols sprang to life on some of the bricks.

"Well, I'll be jiggered," said the leprechaun. "'Tis Elder Fuvarg."

"I don't care how dark it is in here, Seamus. There is no need to be rude," Goldie said, emphasizing her words with a stamp of her foot.

"I am not soundin' off rude. Dose twenty-four symbols er da runic alphabet used by da ancient Norsemen and Celts. Da first six letters spell out *Fuvarg*. Dat's 'ow da language got its name."

"Again with the Vikings?" Rafe said. "I'm over Vikings."

"I don't think you're saying the name of the language correctly," said Goldie. "How do you spell it?"

"'Tis two words. Elder: E-l-d-e-r. Fuvarg: F-u-t-h-a-r-k."

"Well, it's certainly not spelled the way you're pronouncing it," Goldie said.

"Dat's 'ow ya say it if yer a leprechaun!" Seamus said with a scowl.

"Who uses this language nowadays?" Baylor asked.

"I don't tink anyone speaks it anymore, but every leprechaun, fairy, and angel in Mystfira is taught 'ow ta read it."

"Why would the heavens require you to know an obsolete language?" Goldie asked.

Rafe tilted his head down and frowned. He must have known Elder Futhark at one time, he was sure of it, or he wouldn't have been sent to Earth as an unaware angel. Haven had mentioned that when they became upperclassmen they'd be required to learn every language on Earth and be fluent in all of them, even the ones which no longer existed, or else they would fail their training. But why would the leprechauns and fairies learn the language?

"I'm wondering the same thing as Goldie," Rafe said.

"'Tis a simple way fer us fairies ta communicate wid one anoder. Ya see, in most alphabets, da letters er just letters and 'ave no meanin' on der own, but each rune letter symbolizes someting in da natural world ta us."

"Then you're going to need to translate the runes for us," Goldie said.

"'Tis not dat simple as it depends on if we're usin' da fairy meanin' fer da symbols or da old Vikin' meanin's. Dey er two different tings."

"These runes aren't raised," came Baylor's voice from across the room.

Rafe could see her shadow passing in front of the gleaming runes ahead of him. "Baylor Wingate, you shouldn't be taking off by yourself. Anything could happen in here."

"The bricks feel smooth. You wouldn't even know these symbols were here if they hadn't begun to glow," Baylor said, ignoring Rafe's admonition.

Putting his arms out in front of him, Rafe stumbled toward her voice. "Hold on, Bay. We need to stick together in case something happens. Where are you now?"

"I'm standing over by the *X* rune."

The *X*. He'd seen Baylor staring at the *X* Seamus had used to mark the path for Blaise and Ebon this morning.

"Stop touching things until we get over to you," Rafe said.

"So, what does the *X* mean, Seamus?" Baylor asked.

"Ta da Vikin's, it means a gift, and ta da fairies it means a place where tings come togeder and make sense."

"This is the rune we need to look at, then!" Baylor exclaimed. "I know it is. I can feel it."

"You know what else *X* means on Earth?" Rafe asked, stumbling to Baylor's side with Seamus right beside him. "It means beware. Danger. Don't touch it . . . as in a skull and crossbones."

"I'll do it," Seamus said. His stubby little fingers tripped across the surface of the gold brick. "I don't feel a notch chiseled inta it, and I can't get it ta move."

"Let's check the other runes," Goldie said, moving to the next symbol on the wall.

The glow from the *X* rune next to Baylor gave off enough light for Rafe to see her pressing her cheek to the brick beside the symbol. Even in the dark, he could see the disappointment on her face.

"I was sure it was this one," she said, tracing her finger over the *X*. "So much for trusting my instincts."

All at once, a loud clang and the *chuggachuggachugga* of chains lowering sounded over their heads. Jumping away from the wall, Rafe pulled Baylor along with him as four glittering cracks appeared and the ceiling began to descend.

"What is dat?" shrieked Seamus.

"Baylor traced the X with her finger, and that piece of ceiling above us started moving down," Rafe said.

Rafe heard Goldie and Seamus bustling toward them as the ceiling came to rest several feet from the floor. A jumble of glowing gold pieces sat in a pile on the middle of it.

Inspecting the gleaming contents of the ceiling-now-turned-table, Rafe realized straightaway what it held. "They're puzzle pieces, like the ones I found in Dismal's Deluge, except these glow," he said.

"Puzzle pieces?" Goldie said. "Call me crazy, but I was really hoping for a door."

"Janey Mack! If I wanted ta play wid puzzles, I would 'ave stayed in me shop," said Seamus.

"Obviously, we need to put it together to leave this room," said Baylor.

Rafe sighed and shook his head. "It's not going to be easy. The pieces are all one color, and we don't have a picture, so we don't really know what we're trying to accomplish here."

"Since I was banished to that tower, I've put together more than my fair share of puzzles," Goldie said. "Let's find the four corner pieces first and sort out the flat border pieces next. If we each tackle a small cluster of pieces, it won't be so overwhelming."

"One of the pieces I found in Dismal's Deluge is a corner piece," Rafe said, digging into his pocket. When he laid both puzzle pieces on the table, they lit up like the other ones.

Grabbing the two puzzle pieces Rafe had just placed on the table, Baylor snapped them together. Two squares of dazzling green lit up the furthest corner of the room. Seamus waddled over to the green squares and squatted.

"What happened? What is that?" Goldie asked.

"Grass," said Seamus. "Dis must be an enigma room."

"I've heard of them," Goldie said. "Three-dimensional puzzle rooms. After you put the puzzle together, you can go inside the picture and enjoy it."

"Yeah, because being inside a picture has worked out so well for everyone else we know," Rafe said, bristling at the thought.

Leaning over the table, Goldie rummaged around in the puzzle pieces, looking for another match. "There's got to be a door in here, someplace, and I mean to find it."

Usually Rafe found puzzles tedious, but this one was different. With everyone in their group collaborating and shuffling the gold fragments around as needed, the puzzle quickly fell into place, and a picturesque scene formed piece by piece.

Soon a stone bridge arching over tranquil water and grassy banks materialized. Then a bridge leading to a gorgeous wall carpeted with wild climbing roses formed.

Inside the room, it began to feel to Rafe like a beautiful summer day in England, and as the delicate perfume of the roses swirled around him, he found himself smiling.

Continuing to snap piece after piece of the puzzle together, Rafe had almost given up hope of finding a door when he tapped an odd-shaped piece into place. To his delight, a door appeared in the wall at the end of the bridge.

Laughing, Goldie high-fived him. "A few more pieces to that bridge and we can walk over to that door. Let's go, people!"

A few minutes later, Baylor and Rafe placed the last pieces into the puzzle, and the table and puzzle abruptly disappeared, leaving their group in the idyllic setting. Rafe savored the cool breeze on his face and the sound of birds singing. It felt almost a shame to leave a place like this, but leave they must.

Skedaddling across the bridge, Goldie stopped at the door

and examined it as the others made their way over to where she stood. "I can open this," she exclaimed, taking her lock picks from her pocket.

Walking across the bridge, Rafe's feeling of peace disappeared, and a spasm of tension hit his chest as Goldie worked her magic on the lock. What new horrors or mysteries waited for them on the other side of that door?

Holding his breath, Rafe waited.

Chapter Seventeen
The Thread of Life

The lock quickly gave way to Goldie's prodding. Turning the knob, she pushed the door open, revealing a narrow stone staircase leading upwards.

"Dat's it. Da stairway ta da keep!" Seamus cried. "We've made it!"

"Oh, thank the good heavens!" said Goldie.

Rafe released his breath. "Who's going first?"

"Dat would be me," said Seamus starting up the stairs, "and since I know da keepers, I tink 'tis best if ya let me do da talkin'."

"That's fine with me, as long as you make sure we leave with what we came for," Baylor said as Seamus started climbing the stairs.

The short flight of stairs led to another door, and Seamus paused on the landing, waiting for the others to catch up with him. Turning the handle of the door, Seamus barged into the room with his little entourage.

The great room looked exactly as it had in the book Mai had shown them. It was all there—the whitewashed stone with colorful tapestries gracing the walls, the monumental canvas in the middle of the room with billions of needles working their way in and out of it, and whizzing brushes dabbing the canvas and then darting back to the colossal vat of time in the corner.

Glancing up from her spinning wheel, Clariel said, "It seems the leprechaun is back again, and he's brought a few more of his friends this time."

"So it appears," Emmiel said, looking up from the massive book in front of her.

Turquoise feathers swishing on the bottom of her white velvet jubilee robe, Mortiel strode out behind the canvas and over to face Seamus. "Leprechaun," she said with her hands on her hips. "I understand you've suffered a terrible loss, and we sympathize with you, but as I told you before, time cannot be undone even in this keep."

"I didn't come about me girls dis time. I know dey er lost ta me until it is me time ta join dem." Seamus's nose reddened. "I came because of da children wid me. Dey er in desperate need of yer assistance."

Mortiel sighed. "We cannot change time for them either. You know that."

"But we don't need you to change time for us," Baylor said, taking a step toward the angel. "Hi. My name's Baylor. Please, I just need some thread to fashion into a rope to save my brother and our friends. They're in *The Brushstroke of Time* with Naukiel."

Drawing in a short, horrified breath, Emmiel covered her mouth with one hand.

"If you know the whereabouts of that painting, you must return it to the keep," Mortiel said, narrowing her eyes.

"I'm sorry. I can't do that. I won't. My brother, my cousin, and my friends will die if I do that."

"Not ta mention a dog and a cat," Seamus said.

"We will not help you, and you *will* return the painting immediately," Mortiel said.

"No, I won't," Baylor said, shaking her head from side to side.

"You dare defy me?" Mortiel said, raising her voice.

"Now, ta be technical, da girl is not defyin' ya," Seamus said, thrusting out his chest. "She is perfectly willin' ta tell ya where ya can locate da paintin' right after she gets 'er family and friends out of it."

"Stay out of this, leprechaun," Mortiel warned.

"I can't very well stand by and let ya bully da child. She knows what she needs, and she asked ya fer it nicely."

"Mortiel," said Emmiel, thrusting her arm in the air and pointing to a tapestry on the wall above Baylor's head. "The prophecy. These may be two of the eleven from Earth."

Following Emmiel's finger, Rafe turned to look at the wall above the door. Leering down from the tapestry were eleven costumed Ryder-Knight students, arms crossed and their faces full of serious attitude.

"My goodness," Goldie said. "That seems like a rather stern pose for a group of children."

"What are we doing up there?" Rafe whispered to Baylor. "We look like we're ready to take names and kick butt."

"Who knows, but that's not all of us. Mikiko and Neil are missing," Baylor replied.

"Because since the Brume Theater, it's like they never came to Mystfira in the first place," Rafe murmured.

"Do you know anything about the Ryder-Knight students and a prophecy, Seamus?" Baylor asked.

"Dis is da first I've 'eard about it," said the leprechaun, staring up at the picture. "I tink dey should tell us what dey er talkin' about."

Mortiel wrinkled her nose in disgust. "If you are unaware of the prophecy, we certainly will not be the ones to tell you," she snarled.

"Suit yerself. I plan ta find out one way or anoder."

"It is them! I'm sure of it," Clariel said, glancing back and forth between the faces in the tapestry and Baylor and Rafe. Springing from her spinning wheel, she scurried to Mortiel's side. "If they are truly the champions of the heavens, we should help them."

"Champions of the heavens?" Rafe scowled. "I guarantee we're not the champions of anything."

"Maybe not at this moment in time, but if the prophecy is true, you will be someday," Clariel replied. "I'll get you the thread."

"You will not!" Mortiel exclaimed. "We will follow the rules and instructions we have been given by Araboth. That is my final word on the matter."

A lurching shudder shook the floor and a swirling nebula of blues, reds, and greens descended from the ceiling. The strange mist settled in a corner of the room, and as the colors dissipated, three shadowy figures slid into sharp focus.

A serene and dignified elderly woman, her hair pulled into an intricate chignon and her dress a rich blue cashmere gown, stood before them with Blaise and Ebon at her side. A whorl of diamonds and sapphires crowned her beautiful, soft, white hair.

"Your majesty," said the dominion angels together, dipping their heads in respect.

"Thank goodness, you're all safe," Blaise said. "This is our new friend, Queen Yosoy. We've had such a lovely time with her today."

"Thank you. That's very sweet of you to say," the queen said, her smoky grey eyes sweeping over the room and coming to rest on Baylor and Rafe. "And unless I'm mistaken, Mortiel, I still rule here, and I have the final word on what happens in my castle, not you."

"Your majesty," Mortiel said with a cool stare. "No disrespect intended, but Araboth's commandment regarding the painting is very clear. We are to secure—"

"I alone will answer to Araboth. You will make the girl the rope she seeks."

Mortiel drew her lips into a tight line and nodded. "If that is what you wish and command."

"It is," said Queen Yosoy. "The thread is to be braided together with nine other threads of life. The child will need an exceptionally strong rope."

"How long must the thread be?" Clariel asked, rushing to her spinning wheel.

Biting her lip, Baylor hesitated. "I—I don't know."

"I guess it depends on what standard of measurement you're using these days, Clariel. I'd say 60 meters, 197 feet, or 248 fairy bobbins," the queen replied without hesitation.

Nodding, Clariel rushed to her stool and lifted the spindle to spin the new thread.

"Thank you, your majesty," Baylor said. "I wasn't sure. I don't know what the rope is to be used for yet."

The queen smiled, revealing two rows of dainty white teeth. "It is my pleasure to help you. The rope will be instrumental in your rescue attempt."

"Thank you again . . . very much," Baylor murmured.

"As my friend, Baylor, indicated, the purpose of the rope hasn't been fully explained to us," Ebon said, "but you seem to know a great deal about it. Would you please enlighten us?"

"It would be my honor," the queen replied. "No one may enter the painting unless brought there by Nauk, and as you know, it usually doesn't end well for the poor creatures he chooses to bring into his domain. Your brother and his friends are so very fortunate to be under the protection of the Blue Star, or there would be no chance to save them."

Clasping her hands at her waist in a regal manner, the queen continued. "The rope spun from the thread of life will allow you to enter the painting to reason with Nauk and perhaps save your friends. It will also afford Blaise the opportunity to melt the ice around your friends and bring them out of their hibernation."

"Reason with him?" Rafe said. "I've seen him, and he doesn't seem like a very reasonable fellow."

"'Tis true," Seamus said. "Not all da man's teacups er sittin' in 'is cupboard."

"Perhaps you're right, but if anyone can persuade Nauk to leave the painting, I think it will be this child," said the queen, turning her gaze toward Baylor. "Can you not feel how she radiates warmth and light. I do believe Nauk will respond to that."

"Maybe if she stayed out from underneath fire blankets, she wouldn't have that problem," Rafe said.

Returning the queen's smile, Baylor rewarded Rafe with a surreptitious kick to his ankle.

Clariel rose from her spinning wheel, holding a long, coiled rope. "It is ready," she said.

"Well done, dominions." The queen held out her hand, and Clariel brought the shimmering silver rope to her.

"May I loop this over your head and shoulder," the queen asked.

"Please," Baylor said, lifting her arm to make the queen's job easier.

"There. Now both you and Ebon have what you need to succeed, and in addition to that, you also have my deepest admiration. Your commitment to your family and friends is truly commendable."

"Yer queenliness," Seamus said, bowing low before the queen. "Tank ya fer all yer 'elp. May I ask ya fer one small favor, and if ya could find it widin yerself ta grant it, I'd be ferever grateful ta ya."

"You may," the queen replied.

"Would ya please allow us ta leave by da front gate? I can't use me magic 'ere, and 'tis a long way back wid dis group of scallywags."

"Also, there's the matter of the vat of paint solvent I made, ma'am," Ebon said. "It's much too large for us to carry."

"Indeed it is," the queen said. "Tell me where your group is going, and I'll see that you get there immediately along with the vat."

Shooting Mortiel a withering look, Seamus said. "Er ya sure dat's wise? I tink der may be some loose lips and tattlin' tongues in dis room."

Wide-eyed with amusement, the queen threw back her head and gave a long hearty laugh. "Whisper it to me, then, leprechaun," she said, leaning over far enough for Seamus to be able to whisper into her ear.

Seamus cupped his hands around his mouth and spoke into the queen's ear in a hushed tone.

"Have no fear. It will be done, leprechaun." Drawing herself up, the queen smiled and snapped her fingers. Glistening droplets of color showered from the ceiling. Mixing, bouncing and glowing, the walls and floor surrounding Rafe became planes of thick shadow, and his mind blurred.

Feeling dizzy, he widened his stance to maintain his balance. A moment later, when he could focus again, Rafe found himself standing in the attic room of Cliff House with everyone except the queen and dominion angels.

Next to Ebon, rocked a noxious-smelling vat of chemicals in a cradle-like contraption on wheels. Situated on the surface of the lip of the vat sat a small iron ring with a length of rope attached. A dozen skunks couldn't have produced a more putrid stink.

Baylor covered her nose and mouth with one hand and tried to push the smell away from her nose with her other. *"Auuuck,"* she said, "That smells absolutely vile."

"You'll get used to it," Blaise assured. "You won't smell a thing in a minute or two."

"Right, because by then, the lining of our nose will be destroyed," Rafe said, making a face. "Did you really need to make so much of that stuff, Ebon?"

"The queen assured me we would need this much."

Seamus ran to an attic window, cracked it open enough to stick his head out and took some deep breaths. Goldie followed him and stuck her head out to breathe as well.

"Seamus, Goldie, come back here right now. What if someone spots you?" Baylor said.

Goldie took a deep breath of fresh air and savored it before returning to the center of the room with the others.

"I need ta call Mai." Seamus drew his head back into the attic and threw open the window as wide as it would go.

"That's not a good idea," Rafe said. "It smells like a chemical plant in here."

"Mai's got ta get inta da attic, and we don't want 'er ta use da front door."

"But, Seamus, someone is bound to investigate the stench, and we haven't got anyone out of that painting yet," Baylor said.

"Speaking of the painting, where is it?" Rafe asked, looking around the attic.

"'Tis in dat big box over der against da wall."

The attic window quivered as a cool wind nudged its way inside the room. Outside, the sky darkened, and an earsplitting crack of thunder exploded overhead.

"A storm coming," Blaise said. "Fingers crossed for fire rain."

Seamus scanned the sky. A greyish mass funneled downward from one of the dark clouds, churning like boiling water.

"She's 'ere," Seamus said, stepping back from the window.

The swirling whirlwind spilled into the room, and Mai emerged from the cloud with her shopping cart, whistling a happy tune. "Out you go," she said shooing away the wind she'd arrived on. "Do be a love and shut that window, Seamus."

"We did it," Baylor said. "We got what you told us to get."

"I see," Mai replied.

"What's next?" Baylor asked.

"You're asking me?" Mai said. "You don't have a plan? I should think in the five months you've been gone, one of you might have devised a plan."

"Five months?" Baylor said. "No, Mai. That's not right. We've only been gone for one night."

"Oh, Seamus, really?" Mai said, turning around to waggle her finger at the leprechaun. "You didn't tell them?"

Seamus shrugged. "I don't know why you're singlin' me out. Goldie 'as a mouth, too, and 'twasn't 'er first time der eider."

Mai sighed and turned back to the children. "Time passes differently in the keep. It's a shame your traveling companions didn't mention it to you children before you went."

"Forget the children!" Blaise bellowed. "Goldie Phyllis Locket, you did *not* tell me I would be losing five months of my life. My poor husband probably thinks I deserted him."

"We left him a note," Seamus said sheepishly.

"You left him a note. A note!" Blaise shrilled.

"Will you chill, princess?" Goldie said. "Absence makes the heart grow fonder. Besides, I'm sure your husband and the fire brigade needed a break. In fact, they've probably already sent me a fruit basket to thank me for temporarily taking you off their hands."

"*You . . . you . . .* you are *not* a nice woman . . . and you are not invited to my next ball," Blaise said, crossing her arms and turning away from her friend.

"Oh, don't be like that, Blaise. I'm sorry," Goldie said. "We both have our flaws. That's why we get on so well with each other."

"Oh, now you're throwing my flaws in my face! I'll have you know, I'm a really good person, Goldie P. Locket! I have a code. I only burn broken-down, abandoned buildings or enchanted buildings that rebuild themselves right after they burn."

"I know," Goldie said, lowering her chin in a contrite manner.

"Aside from your obsession with fire, Blaise," Mai said, "It is widely known in the heavens that you have a tender heart and love all people and creatures alike. Surely, you would have given up five months of your life to save the poor innocent beings held captive in that painting."

Leveling her gaze at Mai, Blaise's expression softened. "Of course, I would. Seamus and Goldie should have trusted me with the truth, though."

"I agree," Mai said.

"So, what do you need me to do, Mai?" Blaise asked

"There she is," Goldie said. "That's my girl."

"I'll unwrap da paintin', and we can begin," Seamus said.

"Hold up, now," Mai said. "Nauk can't hear or see anything because he's packed away in the painting, and we need him to stay that way until you've come up with a plan to lure him out, so Ebon can tip the vat of solvent over him."

"But Mai, I thought *you* had a plan and would tell us what to do after you got here," Baylor said.

"Oh, no, dear. That would involve subterfuge, and I don't get involved in things like that," Mai said. "You'll need to come up with a ruse to get him out of the painting all on your own."

"Mai's right," Seamus said. "We don't 'ave da time ta wait fer Nauk ta come out of da paintin' on 'is own between midnight and tree-tirty. We need a ruse."

"I agree." Rafe nodded. "We can't wait and risk being discovered before we've rescued everyone."

"Well, I don't have the slightest idea how we're going to trick him out of that painting," Baylor said. "I hope someone else does."

"If only we knew someone who was capable of such deception," Blaise said, drumming her fingers on her chin. "Oh, wait. We do."

All eyes in the room turned to Seamus and Goldie.

"I'm an amateur compared ta dat one," Seamus said, pointing at Goldie. "She's da criminal genius."

"Don't make a big whoop–de–do about this. At best, I'm a small-time petty thief."

"Don't sell yourself short, my friend," Blaise replied.

Straightening her shoulders, Goldie pushed up her sleeves. "All right, fine. Let's think about this. First off, is Naukiel capable of reasoning?"

"I believe he is," Mai said.

"And who is going into the painting? Ebon or Baylor?"

"The vat is excessively cumbersome, and I don't believe Baylor has substantial-enough body weight to topple it in a timely manner," Ebon said.

Goldie paced the attic floor, hands on her waist. "Then Baylor needs a way to gain Naukiel's attention, his confidence, and trust. More than that, she needs a legit reason to get him to come out of the painting." Goldie snapped her fingers. "I've got it! She needs to pretend to be an accomplished artist studying under the tutelage of a seraph Naukiel would have known about years ago—preferably, one that was almost as good as he was. She'll ask him to step out of the painting and look at her work. The only thing is we really need to stage this attic like it is Baylor's art studio, but without Seamus's magic, I don't know how we'll do that."

"I could arrange to have a few things blown in," Mai said. "I know a certain Alabaster Seraph quite well, as would Naukiel. I'm sure if Naukiel thought Baylor painted as well as Alabaster, he'd be tempted to leave the painting."

Baylor closed her eyes and rubbed her neck as if it were sore. "I'm not much of an actress—that's my cousin's department—but I'll do whatever it takes to get the others out of that painting."

"Good," said Mai, tottering to the window to open it. "Then let's get this show on the road. I'm going to tell the wind what I need. As soon as it arrives, Seamus will very quietly cut open that box, and Baylor will enter the painting."

Chapter Eighteen

Nauk

As they waited for the wind to deliver the items Mai requested, Rafe felt a sinking feeling in his stomach. "I am not letting you go into that painting by yourself," he whispered to Baylor.

"You can't help. No heavenly hand can hurt Nauk."

"I won't harm him, but I can be there to protect you."

"He'll see you, and then what will I do?"

"He won't. There are too many paintings and things to hide behind in there."

"Everyone, stand back," Mai called from the window. "The stuff is here."

A dark cloud blew through the window depositing a desk, a drafting table, lights, inspiration boards, and several little carts on wheels, containing writing utensils, erasers, paints, brushes, canvases, and papers.

"Wow! Oliver would love this set up," Baylor said, as the cloud rushed out and the window thwacked down behind it. "Where did you get it?"

"I borrowed part of Alabaster Seraph's studio," Mai said. "I thought a real artist's studio would help Naukiel believe you're a serious artist."

"I sure hope he doesn't ask me to prove I'm an artist. I can't draw a stick figure," said Baylor.

"Now what?" Seamus asked. "Is it time fer me ta cut open da box?"

"Almost," replied Mai. "First we've got to tie one end of the rope to Alabaster's monstrosity of a desk."

"Why?" Goldie asked.

"So the rope can't be pulled into the frame. The desk is larger and longer than the frame. The last thing we need is for Nauk to have a way out of that painting any time he wants and for us to have no way in to reach Baylor," Mai replied.

"I'm going with her. I'll stay hidden, and if things go wrong. I can get to her quickly," Rafe said.

"I'll go in ta protect da girl. It should be me. I've got magic," Seamus said as Baylor pulled the looped rope from her shoulder and lifted it over her head.

"Oh, let the boy go, Seamus. He's a guardian angel, isn't he?" said Mai, while Blaise and Goldie exchanged dumbfounded looks.

"But 'e can't go in der as an angel. 'Twill call da Sakal right ta us."

"I'll only change to my angelic form if I need to," Rafe assured.

"Let the boy go, Seamus. Time is of the essence, and we can't waste it fighting about silly things."

Seamus glowered at Rafe. "Fine, but ya better keep 'er safe."

"He's a guardian? Why didn't you tell us, Seamus?" Goldie said.

"I wasn't sure ya'd go wid me if I told ya. Ya don't much care fer da angels dat keep puttin' ya back in dat tower of yers."

"You're right about that," Goldie snapped.

"We're wasting time," Mai said. "We need to cut off a piece of rope for Rafe to tie around his waist like a belt. I have scissors in my cart, someplace. I'll get them."

"No need," Blaise said, pointing her index finger toward

the rope. A small flame shot from the end of her finger, striking a small section toward the end of it with laser-like precision. Baylor gasped as the end of the rope she held sizzled apart and dropped to the attic floor.

Blowing her finger out, Blaise retrieved rope. "Here, tie that around your waist nice and tight," she said, handing it to Rafe. "Now I'll take the end of the rope you're holding, Baylor, and tie it to the desk like Mai said."

"What do I do with the other end?" Baylor asked.

"Tie it around your waist for now, my dear," Mai replied. "Remember, the rope is the only way in and out of the painting."

Baylor nodded, securing the other end of the rope to her waist.

"So, here's the plan as I understand it," Mai said, stepping behind the desk. "After Seamus opens the box with the painting, he will hide behind it, and Goldie, Blaise, and I will hide behind the desk over here. Ebon will position himself to the side of the picture frame and stand ready to tip the vat over Naukiel's head when he steps outside of the painting. Then, once Nauk is safely neutralized, I'll transport the poor dear back to Araboth. Blaise will defrost the children, removing them from their current predicament, and, as they say in England, 'Bob's your uncle!'"

Ebon scowled. "It's highly unlikely that everyone in England has an uncle named Bob, so I assume you're using a British colloquialism."

"It means 'you're all set' or 'you've got it made,'" Rafe said. "I'll explain it later. Now is not the time."

"Me box cutter is ready if da rest of ya er," Seamus said.

Mai motioned for the Upons to join her behind the desk, and Seamus quietly sawed away the cardboard from the picture frame.

When the leprechaun finished, Baylor took a deep breath, squared her shoulders, and stepped into the picture. Bouncing a foot, Rafe counted to twenty, giving Baylor a chance to stay well ahead of him, and then he followed her.

Bent over an easel, the grotesquely mottled and misshapen creature's body faced away from both of them. He seemed unaware of anything besides the artwork in front of him.

Darting a look behind her, Baylor eyes met Rafe's. He smiled and gave her the thumbs-up sign as he dodged behind a nearby canvas.

Blowing out a series of short, silent breaths, Baylor shook out her hands in an effort to relax and marched over to plant herself in front of the gruesome creature.

"Hello, there," she said. "I'm Baylor Wingate. I heard a rumor there was a brilliant artist named Naukiel Seraph living inside this painting. By any chance, would that be you?"

The crooked plume of hair at the top of the creature's head bobbed up and down. *"Haaum,"* the creature said in a throaty gurgle.

"It is such a privilege to meet you. My teacher, Alabaster Seraph, wasn't exaggerating when he said you were the greatest artist he had ever known," Baylor said, ogling the artwork around her. "After he told me that, I made it my mission to meet you. I must say, it was quite the ordeal. I had to break into the Keep of Time and persuade the dominion angels to give me this rope, which allows me to enter and exit the painting whenever I want."

"Roooohh," said the creature, sounding surprised.

"Oh, come on!" Baylor said, pointing at something blocked from Rafe's view by the creature's paint-slathered back. "How did this guy get in here?"

Rafe tiptoed over to another painting and ducked behind

for a better vantage point. Blake's ice statue had been moved to the front of the studio and was the model for the artist's current portrait.

"How *did* you do it? How in the seven heavens did you ever get *my* brother to sit still? I've never been able to do that before."

The *M* in the creature's forehead deepened, and his black-purple eyes stared at Baylor. He seemed genuinely puzzled. *"Hemmoonooon,"* came another vocalization.

"Hibernation?" Baylor laughed. "How clever of you! You need to teach me that technique so I can use it in the future when he's being a pain."

Strolling over to Blake's ice sculpture, she leaned against her brother's frozen shoulder. "He's taller with blue eyes, and I have dark brown ones, and you wouldn't know it by looking at us, but we're twinsies."

Another surprised sound sprung from what passed as the creature's lips, and Rafe realized the creature had no ability whatsoever to articulate clearly. How Baylor understood the creature's vocalizations was beyond him.

"That's right. Fraternal twins. Now, I know what you're thinking, he's no more related to me than any other sibling—we just happened to share a womb together—but that's not how either of us feel about it. I don't know what I'd do without him. We're the best of friends."

"Mmmmmmm," purred the creature, motioning for Baylor to sit in a nearby chair.

"Why, yes, thank you. Actually, I'd love to have our portrait painted together. That's very kind of you. Do you mind if we chat while you paint?"

The creature gave a guttural grunt.

"Wonderful," said Baylor. "Did I mention I'm from Earth?"

The *M* in the creature's forehead deepened again, and he gestured to the other ice sculptures behind him.

"Yes, all of us are from Earth. Anyway, back to Blake and me. I guess we were a handful when we were little kids. My grandmother used to say, 'what one of us didn't think of, the other one did.' We were born in Texas. That's in the United States, in case you're wondering . . . at Baylor University hospital. Oh, and here's a fun fact for you. That's how I got my name."

A gnarring sound rolled around in the back of the creature's throat. He seemed to be enjoying Baylor's conversation.

"It's a long story, but I'll shorten it. You see, my mother and father were expecting my brother, but they weren't expecting me. Apparently, I hid behind my brother at every ultrasound, so the doctor never saw me. My parents had a name all picked out for my brother, Blake, but since I was a total surprise, they had no name whatsoever for me. My father thought the name of the hospital sounded kind of cute with Blake's name, so my parents went with it."

"Mmm Umm," Naukiel rumbled.

"Thank you. I didn't care for it when I was younger, but it's growing on me," Baylor said. "I think I mentioned earlier that I'm an artist myself. I usually don't like to toot my own horn, but I'm actually quite accomplished for my age. In fact, I already have a student. Small, blond kid, named Oliver Harper, and just between you and me, I think the kid's got real potential."

The creature mumbled some long drawn out sounds, which sounded unintelligible to Rafe and pointed toward the other ice sculptures behind him.

"No way! Is he in here, too? I was wondering why he wasn't showing up to his lessons. Don't tell me you've been teaching him? I'm the one who wants to take lessons from you."

"*Ooooo,*" the creature said, followed by more incomprehensible gibberish, which Baylor seemed to understand.

"What do you mean he's the only one you ever saw painting at Cliff House?" Baylor placed a hand on her hip. "Obviously, you never made it up here to the attic, then. But no matter, that's where you are now. I brought your painting up to my studio for inspiration." Baylor leaned toward Naukiel. "Confidentially, I have to ask, how did you ever paint such a masterpiece?"

The violet smear of paint serving as the creature's chin hair quivered as he frantically motioned to his body with his gold paint brush, and a deep guttural moaning akin to something one might hear from a walrus stranded on an ice floe issued from his throat.

"An accident?" Baylor said, pretending to be horrified. "You poor thing! I'm so sorry. Still, the rest of the paintings in this room are just as amazing, if not better than *The Brushstroke of Time.* You can't tell me the rest of these paintings were all accidents."

The creature gave another forlorn cry and motioned to his body again.

"No," Baylor said. "I don't believe it. It is *not just* the paint. You're entirely too modest. Say, I don't suppose I could persuade you to come into my studio for a moment? I'm working on something, and I'd love to get another artist's perspective."

"*Aaaah Aaaai,*" the creature said.

"Oh no, you don't have to wait, not as long as we have this rope, that's why I went to the Keep of Time and got it in the first place," Baylor said. "We can go in and out of the painting any time we want."

The creature's face changed, and it uttered another string of vocalizations Rafe could not decipher.

"Is that so? Well, then, you underestimate how I feel about

your artistry," Baylor said. "Since I've gone to such great lengths to see you, I'll tell you what. If you come out and critique the painting I'm working on now, I'll give you a piece of this rope. Then you can come and go from the painting any time you please."

With an enthusiastic wail, the creature stood and gestured at the ice sculptures behind him.

"No, no, no, no," Baylor said, untying the rope from her waist. "You don't need one of their bodies to go out. We'll only stay a minute. You won't dry out."

The creature watched Baylor as she approached him with the rope. "Let me tie this rope around your ankle. There's enough slack in the rope that I can twist it around my wrist, and then we can get out of here."

"*Aaaar*," rasped the creature, showing two rows of jagged, multi-colored teeth.

Rafe hoped '*Aaaar*' meant it was okay to tie the rope around the creature's ankle. Just in case it didn't, he readied himself to leap out of his hiding place to protect Baylor should the need arise. To his relief, the creature remained docile while Baylor attached the rope.

Baylor beamed at the creature as she sprung to her feet. Running her hand a short distance up the rope, she wrapped her wrist in it. "There you go. I have special scissors in my studio that we'll use to snip the rope when we get out there, and you can keep the piece tied around your ankle. Are you ready? Here we go," she said. "Or as the famous Earth artist Michelangelo might have said, '*Andiamo.*' Can you tell I've recently had my first Italian lesson?"

"*Aaaar!*" bawled the creature enthusiastically.

The patterns and colors on the creature's body changed and shifted like a freakish kaleidoscope as it stumbled along behind Baylor to the edge of the picture frame. Slinking up behind the pair, Rafe darted behind a nearby canvas for cover. He had to give Baylor credit; although she'd been a reluctant actress, she'd done a magnificent job charming the creature.

Hesitating at the edge of the frame, the creature studied Baylor's attic art studio. Pointing at the painting on the easel in the attic, the creature groaned out another sentence Rafe didn't understand.

"What artist inspired me as I worked on this painting? *Uuhhh,* why would you ask me that? I should think it would be as clear as day," Baylor said.

The creature made another deep-throated and mysterious articulation, which Baylor once again seemed to comprehend.

"Van Gogh? Because of the intense, turbulent swirling patterns that roll across the surface in waves?" Baylor said with a half-shrug of her shoulder. "I suppose, but I can honestly say I wasn't thinking about his work while I was painting that. My mind was a total blank at the time."

Glancing over her shoulder, Baylor spied Rafe, and he made a shooing motion with his hand to encourage her to get the creature out of the painting. One more step and they could rescue the others.

Baylor strode out of the painting and into the attic. "Come on, now. You're not stuck in there anymore."

The creature took a step forward and seemed genuinely surprised to be standing in the attic with Baylor. *"Aaaar!"* cried the creature.

"Perfect," Baylor said, stepping out of range of the vat's contents. "About this painting on my easel over here."

To Rafe's horror, the creature sauntered out from beneath the vat. *Why hadn't Ebon tipped the solvent?* Tiptoeing to the edge of the frame, Rafe peeked out. Ebon was frantically tugging at the rope attached to the vat, but it had caught on the edge of the picture frame. Rafe instinctively reached up to help but caught sight of Seamus waving him off and mouthing the words, "No 'eavenly 'and. No 'eavenly 'and."

Startled by the sawing noise of the rope on the picture frame behind him, the creature whirled, spotting Ebon, Seamus, Rafe, and the vat of chemicals. Roaring with fury, the creature pawed the air with his arms and headed for the safety inside his frame.

"No, Naukiel, No!" Baylor shouted, tugging at the rope tangled around her wrist to stop him. "We're trying to save you!"

The creature kept going, pulling the desk and Baylor along behind him as Ebon freed the rope.

"Naukiel, stop! You're hurting me," Baylor cried, trying to disentangle the rope from her wrist.

"Get out of the way, Baylor," Ebon yelled as Baylor struggled. "The chemicals will kill you."

"I don't care! Tip it!" Baylor screamed.

"No," Ebon shouted.

"Twelve others will die if you don't! Tip it!"

With his eyebrows knit together in trepidation, Ebon jerked the rope.

Adrenaline surging, Rafe felt his body change into its angelic form in a split-second, faster than it had ever done before. The paint solvent seemed to be spilling in slow motion as Rafe reached Baylor's side and snapped the rope from her wrist with his bare hands.

He whisked her backwards, and Baylor fell to the attic floor as he covered her body with his, shielding her from any solvent that might splash her way. Looking over his shoulder, Rafe saw the solvent cascading over the flailing creature, who screamed as if he were being scalded and fell to the floor writhing in pain.

As the screams subsided to moans, Mai rushed to the angel's side and knelt at the edge of the puddle of solvent. "There, there, dearest Naukiel," she whispered, touching his shoulder. "You are free from the burden of time."

Naukiel lifted his head to look at Mai, grief and shame warring in his expression. Whimpering, he stretched out his hand to her. "I am . . . I am—"

"Free," Mai said, smiling at Naukiel.

"I am . . . I am so truly sorry," he said, his voice catching.

Squirming out of Rafe's grasp, Baylor caught sight of Naukiel's beautiful face. "Oh, thank goodness," she murmured.

Paint solvent dripped from Naukiel's body as he gazed back at Baylor and forced a weak smile. "Thank you," he whispered.

"Would you like me to take you home now?" Mai asked in a soft, sweet voice.

Naukiel nodded and reached for Mai's hand. She helped the angel to his feet and over to her shopping cart. When she made a swirling motion with her wrist, the grey whirlwind swept into the room and snatched them both away.

"Blaise and Goldie," Seamus said. "Get da end of dat rope now. Da boy changed inta an angel. Da Sakal er comin', and da children er still in dat paintin'. We must defrost dem before da angels get 'ere."

He tapped his shillelagh next to the puddle of solvent on the floor, and the puddle disappeared along with the giant vat. Grabbing the other end of the rope, which had been in the solvent, the leprechaun dashed into the painting with Blaise and Goldie hot on his heels.

"Are you all right, Baylor?" Ebon said, voice cracking as he sank to his knees on the floor by the picture frame. "I thought I'd killed you for sure."

"Not a scratch on me, thanks to our angelic friend over here," Baylor said.

"That was an incredibly stupid thing for you to ask Ebon to do," Rafe said. "What if I hadn't been able to save you?"

"But you did," she said, touching her forehead to Rafe's for a brief moment, "and you have my permission to yell at me all you want, as long as you do it after we get everyone out of that painting."

Gasps of surprise popcorned around the room behind him, and Rafe scrambled to his feet. He didn't even have to look to know the Sakal were standing in the attic behind him.

"Raphael, you're safe! Baylor! Ebon!" Madri Keva exclaimed, her eyes glowing with relief. "Thank the seven heavens!"

"Indeed," Madri Typhicus said. "Where have you been, Raphael Guardian, and please tell me it doesn't have anything to do with that painting at your back."

Madri Uriah, the principalities master, squinted at the painting. "Is that—? It is! It's *The Brushstroke of Time*. Madri Typhicus, we must return it to the Castle of Reckoning immediately."

Baylor sprang to her feet and rushed to the painting. With outstretched arms, she faced the Sakal. "You can't take it yet. I won't let you. You'll kill them," she cried.

"*Kee-eeeee-an!*" screamed the red-tailed hawk, suddenly winging his way out of the painting and swooping around the heads of the Sakal. A small piece of the rope made from the thread of life clasped in his talon, the hawk came to rest on the floor next to Baylor, and immediately transformed into his angelic shape.

"Please, madrikim," Sion said. "Stay your obedience to Araboth for but a few more minutes. It will allow the children, the dog, the cat, and the fairies to escape."

"Poppe and Potts are in there, too?" Madri Fey said with a delighted squeal.

"They are," Rafe said.

"You were in that painting, Sion? How is it you are still alive?" Madri Isabo asked. "Every being taken into that painting dies."

"I do not know. How is it that I am alive, Rafe Ryder?" Sion asked, leveling his gaze at Rafe.

"The Blue Star," murmured the archangel Michael.

Rafe nodded. "That's right. Anyone captured and taken into that painting under the protection of the Blue Star stays alive as long as the painting remains here. Sully is in there, too."

"And that's why you can't move it yet," Baylor said, rocking in place. "They'll all die if you do, and my brother is still in there. I'm sure it will only be a few more minutes. Seamus and the Upons are rescuing them now."

"It is true," Sion said. "The leprechaun and two Upons are in there now. One of them melted the ice around me, and the other one gave me this piece of rope so I could escape. They said it is made from the threads of life and would allow me to pass through the canvas."

Madri Estel's hand flew to her throat in astonishment. "You children went to the Keep of Time? I can't believe it."

"Good heavens!" Madri Avalon exclaimed. "That explains why they've been missing for so long."

"How did this painting come into the possession of the Ryder-Knight students?" Madri Typhicus asked.

"We think it was pushed through on the day of the time tuck by Vexxon's brother, Yaltabolt," Rafe said. "We brought it inside, thinking it was a thank-you gift from the fairies because we'd agreed to be part of the entertainment at their Feadh-Ree celebration."

"We did leave the children gifts on their doorstep as is our custom on Feadh-Ree," said Madri Fey. "I sent Poppe and Potts to leave their baskets myself. If the painting popped out of the time tuck next to our baskets, I can see how the children would have made that mistake."

"Sully must have somehow bounced into that painting during the time tuck. It is indeed fortunate for him the painting landed at Cliff House," said Madri Saniel.

Madri Isabo grimaced. "It is my fault," she said. "I was so preoccupied with getting back to the Brume to help the rest of you manage the time tuck, I didn't walk the children to the door of Cliff House."

"Forget placing blame, Isabo. None of this is important," Madri Omega said. "What's important is for me and my carrions to return Naukiel and his painting to the Castle of Reckoning as we have been instructed to do. He is a danger to all the inhabitants of Mystfira."

Ebon strode to Baylor's side and stood with her between the angels and the painting. "I think you may need to procure new instructions, as I am quite sure your old ones are no longer valid," he said. "Naukiel is once again an angel. Baylor and I saved him."

"That's right," Rafe said, "and a wind gypsy named Mai just took him back to Araboth."

The entire Sakal looked stunned.

"Madri Fey, stay with the children. The rest of the Sakal and I are going to pay a visit to Araboth," Typhicus commanded. "We will be back as soon as possible."

Madri Fey tightened her grip on her scepter, and her delicate facial features tightened as the other members of the Sakal disappeared from the attic. "I do hope your friends are able to rescue everyone before their return."

CHAPTER NINETEEN

Reunited

Just as Rafe changed back into his human body, he heard an excited yowl behind him. He twisted around in time to see Leopold leap out of the painting into Baylor's outstretched arms, a piece of rope dangling from his neck. The squeals, tail wagging, nuzzling, and slobbery dog kisses bestowed on the girl made everyone in the room smile.

"Leopold! I missed you so much!" Baylor cried.

Lavishing her attention on the dog, Baylor did not see her brother stumble out of the picture behind her. "Bay?" he said in a quizzical tone.

"Blake!" Jumping to her feet, Baylor flung her arms around her brother's neck and cried.

"You all right, mate?" Rafe said, placing a hand on Blake's shoulder and giving it a shake.

"I dunno. I feel fuzzier than a caterpillar," Blake said, pulling back from Baylor and rubbing his forehead. "What happened? What's this rope on my wrist for?"

Baylor's brow puckered. "You don't know? The rope is what allowed you to escape from the painting."

"No way! I was in a painting?" Blake yelped, his eyes widening. "That one over there?"

"You don't remember?" Baylor asked.

Looking distraught, Blake stared at his sister. "Bay, I think someone slipped me drugs," he said in a high-pitched voice.

"No, no, no," she soothed. "You've just been asleep for a long time."

A jolting caterwaul rung through the attic as Audra's cat, Pebbles, pranced out of the painting. Tail extended straight up in the air, Pebbles trotted over to Baylor, brushing up against her leg.

"Hello, there," Baylor said, smiling down at the cat. "How are you?"

Pebbles rewarded Baylor with a slow feline blink and a purring sound.

Blake rubbed his eyes. "I need coffee."

"Blake . . . you don't drink coffee," said Baylor.

"I don't? Why?" he whined. "Why don't I drink coffee?"

"Because you don't like the taste of it."

"What's wrong with me?" Blake howled. "Everyone drinks coffee."

"That's not true, mate. Not in England," Rafe said. "Most everyone over there enjoys a good cup of tea."

"Yeah? Well, we're not in England." Blake examined his surroundings. "We're in . . . an attic. Bay, why are we in an attic?" he asked in another high-pitched whine.

"Calm down," Baylor said, patting her brother's back. "I'll tell you the whole story."

"A story? Do I like stories?"

"You *love* stories, especially when they're true, and this one is."

Leaving Baylor to explain things to Blake, Rafe stepped closer to *The Brushstroke of Time*. One by one, the other Ryder-Knight students popped from the picture frame, looking befuddled and lethargic.

Oliver seated himself on the floor in front of the easel and gazed with a glazed expression at the painting done by Alabaster

Seraph. Audra raked through a large box full of old newspaper clippings as if she had found a treasure. Sully and Tahj made their way over to an old silver rocking horse in the corner.

"I'm the Lone Ranger," Sully said, mounting the horse. "Tahj, you be Tonto."

"Why? Because I'm from India?" Tahj threw his hands in the air.

"No, because I'm already riding Silver."

"Deidre," Tahj called over to a girl stepping out of the picture frame. "What do you think of Sully asking me to play the role of Tonto? That's typecasting, right?"

Refusing to acknowledge Tahj's question, or even his existence, Deidre dragged herself past the boys, tossed herself over an antique armchair like an old throw blanket, and groaned.

"Okay, Tahj," Sully said, sliding off the silver horse. "If you're going to make such a big deal about it, you can be the Lone Ranger first."

Scrunching his nose and forehead in confusion, Rafe studied Deidre's face. A "normal" Deidre would have stepped out of that picture frame and not only fired off a retort to Tahj's request for backup, but would also have been in someone's face demanding explanations and freely assigning blame for all the inconveniences she felt she had endured.

Rafe scooted to Ebon's side and spoke in a low tone. "I think something is wrong. None of them are acting like themselves."

"Not necessarily. I believe they're in a state of torpor," replied Ebon.

"Translation, please."

"Sorry," Ebon said. "In other words, I believe they're still in a light sleep. I surmise that when their body temperature and metabolic rate return to normal, their sluggishness will subside."

"But Sion, Leopold, and Pebbles were fine when they came out of the picture," said Rafe.

"Yes, but Sion, Leopold, and Pebbles are animals."

"Hey, watch it!" Sion said, overhearing the remark and glaring at Ebon.

Moving closer to the painting once again, Rafe waited for Parker. When she stepped out of the frame, the girl straggled to his side, wearing a feeble smile. Standing on tiptoe, she pulled Rafe's face to hers and planted an awkward kiss on the side of his face.

Rafe's hand flew to his cheek. "I—uh—hello."

"I like you. Do you like me?" she asked, slipping her hand into Rafe's.

Rafe's cheeks flamed red. "Uh—thanks," he said. "Y-yeah. We're friends, aren't we?"

"I'm so glad," she replied, leaning her head on Rafe's shoulder.

A warm glow bubbled up inside Rafe's chest, and at the same time, he felt weak in his knees. He wasn't quite sure if it was the best feeling he'd ever had in his life or the worst until Parker lifted her chin and smiled up at him.

It was the best . . . definitely the best!

He found himself unable to look away from Parker's beautiful eyes until Poppe and Potts fluttered out of the picture frame beside Blaise, Goldie, and Seamus.

"Dat's everyone," said the leprechaun.

Madri Fey gathered Poppe and Potts in her arms, and they buried their faces in her shoulder. "There you are, my darlings. I thought I'd lost you."

"Are you gryan with us?" Poppe asked.

"No, little ones. I am not angry with you. I'm sure I should be, but I'm not," said Madri Fey, kissing the tops of their heads.

"Dat's dat, den. Let's get out of dis attic before da rest of da Sakal gets 'ere."

"That ship has already sailed, leprechaun," Madri Fey said. "They've come and gone."

"Ta where? Araboth?"

"Yes."

"I see. Am I in trouble wid dem?"

"That remains to be seen," said the madri, "but as far as I'm concerned, you helped rescue my little fairies. I'm more than willing to speak on your behalf when the Sakal convenes again."

"Madri Fey," Rafe interjected. "We couldn't have done it without Blaise and Goldie's help either. I really hope you'll put in a good word for them as well."

"Oh, you're so sweet," Blaise said, clasping her hands together over her heart. "Isn't he sweet, Goldie?"

Goldie twisted her lips to the side. "The jury's still out on that."

"What?" Rafe muttered.

"Don't take it personal," Seamus said. "She doesn't much care fer angels because dey er da ones dat keep slappin' 'er back in dat tower of 'ers."

Blaise stepped further into the room, stopping by Rafe and Parker. There, she perused the room full of creatures she had helped save. "We did it, Goldie. We did it," she said with a sniffle. "I haven't been this happy since the prince came looking for me with that glass slipper in his hand. How about you?"

"Are you kidding?" Goldie whispered out of the corner of her mouth. "I got out of that stupid tower, practiced my lock-picking skills, and kept a few pieces of gold Seamus doesn't know about. What more could I want?"

"You're hopeless, Goldie P. Locket. Hopeless."

"Absolutely," Goldie said, her eyes full of waggery, "and that's what makes me the most interesting friend you have."

Blaise had opened her mouth to retort when she and Goldie suddenly melted into the air surrounding them.

"Oopsie-do. Your friends went bye-byes," Parker said, swinging Rafe's hand and arm back and forth like a little girl. Unlike Rafe, she did not at all seem disturbed by the Upons' vanishing act.

"What happened to them?" Rafe asked.

"I don't know." Seamus tightened his grip on his shillelagh, nervously flicking his gaze around the room. "I did not do dat, Madri."

"Neither did I," said Madri Fey.

Next to Rafe and Parker, *The Brushstroke of Time* shimmered. Turning his head, Rafe was shocked to see the items from Alabaster's art studio dissolving into thin air as well.

"Da Sakal?"

"More likely, Araboth," the madri replied. "Listen, Seamus. You should go, and I'll stay with the children. I think it would be best if you remain out of sight and out of mind for a while. We wouldn't want anyone to be tempted to make you disappear, too."

"I can't do dat."

"Why ever not?" asked Madri Fey.

Seamus darted a glance at Rafe. "May I 'ave a word wid ya private like, madri?"

A suspicious furrow in her brow, Madri Fey nodded. She followed Seamus to an unoccupied corner of the attic. Rafe couldn't make out a word of the muffled conversation, but Madri Fey did not look pleased. In fact, judging by her head jerks and sweeping arm movements, she seemed downright mad.

A few moments later, the fairy madri stalked away from Seamus.

"I'm just da messenger," Seamus shouted after her. "I 'ad nothin' ta do wid it!"

Ignoring Seamus, Madri Fey strode to the door of the attic. "Children, follow me downstairs to the dining room. You'll need something to eat before I tuck you into bed for the night. Come on, now. I'll whip up all your favorites."

Wearing an infuriated expression on his face, Seamus tapped his shillelagh on the floor and disappeared.

As the children trickled out of the attic, Baylor passed by Rafe and Parker. "What do you suppose that was all about?" she whispered.

"Your guess is as good as mine."

"*Uh-oh*, it's the Sorceress," Parker said, stepping between Rafe and Baylor. "Please do not talk to my boyfriend, Sorceress. I don't want him to have bad luck."

Gritting her teeth, Baylor's face reddened, and the muscles around her lips twitched. Her dark eyes turned almost black as she glared daggers at both Rafe and Parker.

"I'll talk to him any time I please," Baylor said, her voice dripping with animosity.

"Bay—"

Baylor shook her head at Rafe. "Don't," she warned. Grabbing her brother's hand, she stomped out of the attic, dragging Blake after her.

Chapter Twenty

The Friendship Stump

Stretched out in bed with his hands behind his head, Rafe stared at the ceiling. He wished his thoughts would stop racing around in his head like a bluebottle fly stuck on a windowpane, but unfortunately it was if the blasted things had minds of their own.

Not least on the list of things dashing around his brain tonight was the time of year. Five months of his life had passed without him even knowing about it! The worst of it was he'd missed this year's chance to find a way for the Ryder-Knight students to sneak back to Earth using the Brume Curtain on Halloween.

He'd look for another way to get them all home—the sooner the better, as far as he was concerned. At least he knew his father was still alive and relatively well, thanks to the tree he'd seen in the Keep of Time.

Flipping over on his side with a loud thump, Rafe sighed. *Aauurgh!* Five months! That meant he was five months behind in his soriscope payments to Lydia. He'd have to try to find a way to make it right with her. Maybe the Sakal would tell her it wasn't his fault.

And speaking of the madrikim . . . were they really parents? Why else would they have a picture of two little boys hanging over their fireplace mantel? He'd have to remember to ask Haven and Diadem if the boys might be classmates. If they didn't know, Thomas might.

Oh, no—Thomas! Rafe had promised to attend all the Adomis trials with him this year. If it really was November, he'd missed all seven trials, and quite honestly, those matches were the only things he actually looked forward to seeing in Mystfira.

Sitting up in bed with a frustrated sigh, Rafe swung his feet to the floor. If he were going to be awake, he might as well be up. Snatching his bathrobe, he cinched it around his body before stepping out into the hallway, where he nearly tripped over Leopold.

"Sorry about that," Baylor whispered from behind him. "I couldn't sleep, so I thought I'd go up to the tower room and talk to Sion about a few things."

"I couldn't sleep either."

"Well, of course you couldn't. Snogging a girl will do that to you."

Rafe compressed his lips into a thin line and stuffed his hands into his robe pockets as he fell into step with her. "You Americans should not use that word, and for your information, we were not snogging. Parker kissed me on my cheek, that's all."

"I'm hurt," Baylor said, pretending to look wounded. "She didn't kiss Ebon or me, and we were the ones that actually saved her life."

"How about I give you a kiss on your cheek, you shut up, and we call it even?"

Baylor wrinkled her nose in disdain. "*Ewww.* I'll take a hard pass on that, but I will thank you to tell your new girlfriend to stop calling me the Sorceress."

"We're not—she's not ... we're not boyfriend and girlfriend," Rafe said, gazing at the floor in front of him as they walked along. "She was confused when she came out of the picture, just like Blake was. She probably won't even remember saying that in the morning."

Pausing at the bottom of the spiral staircase, Baylor flapped her hand at him as if he were speaking nonsense. "Which part do you think she won't remember?" she called over her shoulder as she began the climb to the tower room. "Calling me the Sorceress or calling you her boyfriend? I'll bet she remembers both things."

Rafe's mind flew to his time in the leprechaun tunnel with Baylor. She had said one of the reasons she saved Rand was because he had never once called her the Sorceress. The name obviously hurt her deeply.

"I'm sorry, Bay," he said. "I'll talk to her about it. Is that why you wanted to talk to Sion?"

"To tell him someone called me a name? No. Someone is always calling me names. I suppose I should be used to it by now," Baylor said, sinking down onto one of the cushioned window seats. "It was about other things."

"You can talk to me . . . if you want."

"About boring, stupid, uninteresting things?"

"Considering what we've been through lately, I welcome boring, stupid, uninteresting subjects."

"It's nothing really. I got to thinking about Naukiel and wondering if he is all right."

Rafe shrugged and sat down beside her. "Why wouldn't he be? He got to go home, Bay. I'm sure he's happy. But speaking of Nauk, you know what I've been wondering? How did you know what he was saying to you? He wasn't speaking plainly, and I couldn't understand a word he said when we were in that painting."

"Really?" Baylor said, lifting a brow.

"All I heard were grunts, groans, and moans."

"I don't know," she replied. "I understood him perfectly."

"Well, however you did it, I have to say you were a *very* convincing actress. Your cousin had better watch out, or you'll steal the next lead right out from underneath her nose."

Baylor snorted out a laugh. "Deidre doesn't have a thing to worry about. Anyone can act when the stakes are high enough. I'm just happy everyone is back under this roof with us again."

"Me too. So why aren't we sleeping?" Rafe asked.

"I don't know about you, but I couldn't stop thinking about the tapestry in the keep and the prophecy Clariel mentioned."

"Right," said Rafe. "That Champions of the Heavens thing."

Pulling her legs from the floor, Baylor folded her arms around her knees. "I thought maybe Seamus might know more about it than he was saying, so after Madri Fey left, and I had a minute to myself, I used my ring to call him. He still claims he doesn't know anything about it."

"Do you believe him?"

"I do," Baylor said. "He said he'd help me find out, and then he told me about the favor he wants from us. You know, in return for helping us rescue everyone."

"Is it going to get us into trouble?"

"It shouldn't. It's sweet, really," Baylor said, her mouth curving into a smile. "He wants us to help him win a musical contest. I guess he's been trying to win it for years now."

"Don't tell me. Let me guess. The prize is a pot of gold?"

Baylor's eyes twinkled. "It's much more precious than that. If Seamus wins, he can visit Araboth for twenty-four hours to see his wife and daughter. He said the competition is really stiff because so many of the creatures up here enter the contest in hope of seeing their loved ones again. I hope you don't mind, but I promised him we'd think of something fantastic. When Mai told us about Seamus losing his wife and daughter, I don't think I've ever felt so sad," Baylor said, biting her lip and gazing at the stained-glass angel on the domed ceiling above them.

Darting a glance at Baylor, Rafe saw the telltale line of worry appear between Baylor's brows. "Why do I get the feeling there's something else bothering you, and it has nothing to do with Seamus?"

Baylor pulled her gaze from the ceiling, opened her mouth to speak, and heaved a sigh instead.

"Bay?"

"It's nothing important," she said, resting a cheek on her knee and staring at him. "I've just been thinking about the day Mai said our decisions, choices, and actions determine our fate. Remember? When we were at The Treasure Trove with Ebon."

"Vaguely. What about it? Don't you think that's right?"

"I guess, but I've been thinking about what comes before that."

"What do you mean?"

"About what *causes* us to make the choices and decisions we do. I think it ultimately boils down to the amount of strength and courage someone has inside them, don't you?"

"I never really thought about it before."

"Well, don't start. Once you start, I guarantee you won't be able to stop thinking about it."

"I highly doubt that," Rafe said with a chuckle. "Do you spend a lot of time thinking about things like this?"

A strange half smile formed on Baylor's lips. "Normally, no; but since coming to Mystfira, yes . . . and I suppose you're going to make fun of me for thinking of things like this now."

So that's why she wanted to talk to Sion. She could depend on him not to laugh at her or make her feel stupid.

"No," Rafe said, rubbing his fingers against the back of his neck. "You're probably right. When I stop to think about it, guardian angels have to use a lot of physical strength to keep our charges safe."

"True, but don't you think *inner* strength is more important than physical strength?"

"I don't know," Rafe said with a shrug. "I think they're both important, but I guess I would lean toward physical strength being the most important."

"Except inner strength lasts a lifetime and maybe even beyond that, but physical strength won't. It just doesn't . . . at least for humans," Baylor said, shaking her head. "But if you have inner strength, it can never be taken away from you—even when you're old, or sick, or tired. That's the type of strength that gives you the courage to make the hard choices and decisions. Don't you think?"

Rafe blinked. The girl in front of him never ceased to surprise him. He'd never thought about what determined one's fate. All the things that were disturbing his sleep tonight seemed rather small and silly compared to the things Baylor was thinking about. Still, he wasn't sure he really understood.

"So, let me get this straight, you think people succeed or fail in life based on the amount of inner strength and courage they have?"

"No, that is not what I'm saying at all!" Baylor sprang to her feet and began pacing back and forth. "For me, the hard choices and decisions that might spin my life off in a different direction are almost always based on the amount of courage I have, or don't have, at that moment in time."

"Then, you think courage ultimately determines where we end up in life?"

Baylor nodded. "I get that there are outside forces beyond

our control sometimes, too, because that's how we ended up here in Mystfira. But for the stuff we can control, I do think it boils down to courage. Do you see what I'm saying, or do you think I'm crazy?"

Leaning back against the window seat, Rafe watched Baylor continue to pace. If he hadn't been able to change into his angelic body and pull her away from the paint solvent, the courage Baylor had shown earlier in the evening would definitely have determined her fate . . . permanently.

Yes. Using that example alone, Rafe could see how life could change in an instant based on the courage someone had to make certain choices or decisions. "Stop pacing," he said. "You're not crazy."

Baylor whirled to face Rafe. "Really?"

"Really. I see your point."

"Oh, thank goodness," she said, pressing a hand to her stomach and sitting down beside him.

"In fact, when we get back to Earth," Rafe said, "I think you should join the debate team at Ryder-Knight Academy."

Baylor nudged his shoulder with hers. "Now, you're teasing me."

"A little bit. *Uhh*, I see it. There's that smile."

Throwing up both hands, Baylor chuckled. "Fine. You got me. Anyway, that's what I came to talk to Sion about. He's good when I find myself preoccupied with things like this, or when I'm feeling guilty that everyone else is stuck here in Mystfira because of me."

"You need to stop thinking like that. We aren't stuck here because of you," Rafe said, shaking his head emphatically. "If you remember correctly, the guardians of the other Ryder-Knight students knew they were in a battle they could not survive, and they saw an opportunity to save the lives of their charges before their death. Take my word for it—the guardians did exactly what they were trained to do. Everyone here, including me, is safe because your guardian found a way to *save* you."

"But why? I'm nobody."

"That's not true. In this world or any other, Baylor Orion Wingate, *you* are the only *you* that will ever be, and your guardian angels are created for the sole purpose of protecting and guiding you throughout your life."

Baylor confined her laugh to a snort by pressing a fist to her lips. "And yet, here I am alone with a bunch of angry classmates."

"You're getting a new guardian, and as for the others, they'll come around, Bay. I admit I was angry at first, too, but after I assumed my true form in the Valley of Shadows, I understood what your guardian did. I promise you, there's nothing a guardian wouldn't do to save a charge's life. You know what? You *should* talk to Sion about this," Rafe said, getting to his feet and opening the doors to the parapet, "He's one of your guardians. He'll back me up on this. He's got to be hanging around out there someplace."

"Janey Mack, Janey Mack, Janey Mack!" rang through air followed by a heavy repetitive thunking noise.

"Is that Seamus?" Baylor said, dashing past Rafe to look over the parapet.

"It sure sounds like him," Rafe said, following her. "What's going on?"

"I have no idea, but he's banging his shillelagh on the old friendship stump my grandfather carved. I better go see why he's carrying on like that."

"I'll go with you."

Hurdling down the staircases, Rafe and Baylor raced outside to find the leprechaun stomping around the four faces carved into the tree's stump. "Janey Mack!" Seamus exclaimed again.

"Pipe down, Seamus. You're going to wake everyone up," Baylor said.

"I don't care," bawled the leprechaun. "Mai put 'er friend in dis stump fer safekeepin', and I promised 'er I'd get da woman out, but I can't get da stupid ting open. Madri Fey told me ta wait until da Sakal came back and dey would 'elp, but I promised Mai I'd do it as soon as we got everyone out of *Da Brushstroke of Time*, and a promise is a promise. I can't break me word."

"So that's what Madri Fey was upset about earlier tonight," said Rafe.

"Mai put someone in this stump?" Baylor asked. "Who?"

"Some old lady named Jane. She was overcome by smoke on da night of yer corn maze a year ago."

Rafe's jaw went slack as he drew in a sharp breath. "Lady Jane?"

"Dat's it, dat's da name."

"Unbelievable!" Rafe snapped, staggering backwards as if he'd been pushed.

"What's dat boy's problem?"

"Lady Jane is his grandmother."

"Dat's not true. 'Is granny's name is Catherine. Dat's what it said on da tree in da Orchard Room."

"Catherine Jane. She goes by her middle name," Baylor said.

"*Uh-oh,*" said Seamus.

"Yeah. *Uh-oh* is right! Explain to me why my grandmother is in a stump," Rafe said, rubbing his tingling chest with one of his palms.

"Yer granny was unconscious and couldn't tell Mai where she'd like ta be taken, but wind gypsies can read minds by pressin' der lips ta da forehead of a person. Yer granny was dreamin' about dis stump, so Mai put 'er in der fer 'er own protection."

"Brilliant! Put a woman in a stump for safekeeping instead of taking her to a hospital where she belongs!" Rafe said, flailing his arms at Seamus. "I don't understand how that is remotely logical."

"I did not tell ya wind gypsies were logical. Why can't ya just be tankful yer granny's alive and in da stump we 'ave 'ere in Mystfira and not da stump on yer planet?"

Raking a hand over his head, Rafe held his hair away from his face before releasing it.

"I'm sure Rafe is very grateful Lady Jane is here," Baylor whispered, gripping Rafe's arm. "Do you know why she's here and not in the stump on Earth, Seamus?"

"I tink it was just 'appenstance. Near as I can figure, da Blue Star must 'ave been in da process of duplicatin' Cliff house when da wind gypsy was savin' yer granny."

"I cannot believe Homeless Harriet Hobs put my grand-mother in a stump for over a year," said Rafe, shaking his head.

"She goes by da name of Mai up 'ere."

"I don't care what you call her, you get her down here this minute to get my grandmother out of that tree!"

"Dat's da ting. I've called 'er and called 'er. She must be some-place where she's not getting' me messages. And ya shouldn't be gettin' mad at dat poor wind gypsy. She saved yer granny from da fire in da maze."

"By putting her in a tree stump and forgetting about her for a year!" Rafe exclaimed.

"Don't be gettin' all dramatic-like. Der's more space in dat stump den what a genie bottle would 'ave, and yer granny's had plenty to eat. Whatever she tinks she'd like to eat would appear right before 'er eyes."

Rafe balled his fingers into fists at his side. "I don't care! Get her out!"

"What do ya tink I've been tryin' ta do, boy? Paint me fingernails? Usually da only way to undo the magic of a wind gypsy is for the wind gypsy to undo it, but Mai told me I could do it, but she was wrong. I can't."

"Did Mai say how to undo her magic?" Baylor asked.

"All she said was da door ta da stump would open wid a little magic and some love."

Baylor crossed her arms and studied the leprechaun's face. "So why do you think it's not opening?"

"Clearly, I don't have enough love," Seamus said, whacking the tree with his shillelagh with each word he spoke.

"Stop, stop, stop," Baylor whispered, grabbing the top of his shillelagh. "Let me try. Do you have a grain of fairy dust I can use?"

"I think we should call the Sakal," said Rafe. "This is too important. They'll know how to get her out."

"Please, let me try first," Baylor said. "I feel like this is partly my fault. I've been dreaming about Lady Jane being in this stump since we got here. I should have told Madri Isabo. Maybe if I had, we could have figured this out sooner."

"Don't be ridiculous," Rafe said. "Stop shouldering the blame for everything that happens around here. This is not your fault."

Baylor gazed at her feet, trying to hide the tension on her face with her hair. "Will you please let me try to get her out? Please, Rafe."

Stepping closer to the stump, Rafe studied the carving of Lady Jane's face. Her beautiful long hair billowed down toward the roots of the stump. "Go ahead," he murmured.

Seamus fumbled in one of the pouches on his belt and gave

Baylor one glittering grain of fairy dust. Crushing the grain between her fingertips, Baylor sprinkled the glittery powder over the tree stump and chanted:

> *"Liberate our Lady Jane*
> *From this tree stump's bleak domain."*

Rafe's heart hammered as the ground near the tree stump wobbled beneath his feet. The air grew heavy, and the air pressure changed so swiftly and suddenly it caused a painful popping in his ears.

Clapping his hands to his ears, Rafe watched a cloudy vapor seep from the nostrils of the faces carved into the stump until it was completely engulfed. Fast and furious, the mysterious mist whipped around the tree stump like a miniature whirlwind, driving Rafe, Baylor, and Seamus back away from it.

Just as Rafe thought it would tear the stump's roots from the ground, the whirlwind lifted and dissipated, and Lady Jane's carved face swung open like a door.

A sophisticated elderly woman with a delicate face, azure eyes, and a timeless updo stood in the doorway. "Children!" she exclaimed. "There you are!" Gliding across the lawn, she opened her arms to Rafe and Baylor.

Locking his eyes on Lady Jane, Rafe stumbled into her arms with Baylor. "I'm so glad you're here. You have no idea how happy I am to see you."

"The feeling is mutual, my darlings," said Lady Jane. "Is it my imagination, or have you both grown taller since the evening began?"

With a bang, the magic door slapped shut in the stump behind them. Turning in surprise, Lady Jane saw Seamus. "Do I know you?" she asked. "Yes. I think I saw you at the corn maze."

"Dat's possible. I'm Seamus O'Shanahan."

"Pleased to make your acquaintance, Seamus. I'm Jane Ryder."

"And I, yours, Jane Ryder," said the leprechaun. "Since me work 'ere is done, I'll be goin' now." Tapping his shillelagh on the ground, Seamus disappeared.

Lady Jane darted her eyes around in surprise. "Did that little fellow just disappear? My goodness, I must say we hired quite the actors for this year's corn maze. I didn't want to say anything in front of your actor friend, but I'm feeling a bit discombobulated."

"Do you want to sit down," Baylor asked.

"No, I'm not physically tired. Honestly, I've lost a portion of my memory. I can't remember how we got back to Cliff House? Is everyone all right?

"You don't remember being in that stump?" Rafe asked.

"In that stump?" Lady Jane gave Rafe a bewildered look. "Good heavens! No. The last thing I remember was crawling through thick smoke to reach poor Harriet Hobbs. Have you seen the poor old dear? Did everyone get out of the maze safely?"

"Yes, Harriet is fine, and the Sakal told us no one was hurt in the fire at the corn maze," Baylor said.

"That's good news, but I need to get back to the school and see for myself," said Lady Jane, walking toward the backdoor of Cliff House. "By the way, who are the Sakal? Was that the name of the rescue crew called to the corn maze? I'll have to thank them."

"Uh . . . umm . . . no," Rafe stalled. How was he going to explain their whereabouts to his grandmother? Should he break it to her slowly or come right out and tell her? "We can't go back to Ryder-Knight Academy yet," he said.

"Why ever not?" Lady Jane asked.

"It's hard to explain," Rafe said, scratching a temple.

"Has something happened to my car?" Lady Jane asked in a suspicious tone.

"It's not that, Lady Jane. Look up there," Baylor said, pointing toward the sky. "We can't because ... we're not on earth anymore."

Lady Jane's eyes bulged as she stared up into Mystfira's nighttime sky and saw the twelve moons. "Have I died, or am I dreaming?" she asked.

"You're not dead, and you're not dreaming," Rafe said. "We're in a place called Mystfira. It's an angelic training ground between the sixth and seventh heavens."

"Oh?" said Lady Jane, cupping Rafe's chin in her hand and tilting it so she could look into his eyes. "Have you injured your head, my darling?"

"If only it were that simple," Rafe said.

"Let's get you inside, Lady Jane," Baylor said, taking Lady Jane by the hand.

"Yes. Let's do that," Rafe said. "I'll make you a cup of tea, and then Baylor and I will explain everything to you."

"I do hope you remember how to make a good, stiff cup of the stuff because if I'm really awake, as you claim, something tells me I'm not going to like what you two have to say."

Rafe smiled. His grandmother wouldn't like a thing about the predicament they were in, but having her here at his side made him feel one step closer to home.

The End

Glossary of Terms

Found In Mystfira

Adomis trials: considered one of the angels' sacred duties to mankind. Seven times a year specially chosen angels and dark spirits compete against each other at the Rocker for a chance to unleash miracles or disasters onto the Earth. The arena floor is different for each match.

Amber: healing drink the angels use to gain back their strength.

Amethyst Palace: located on the Island of Palades in the first ring of Mystfira. Home to the angelic powers and overseen by Madri Ezekiel, a gifted healer.

Anfar: the language of the angels and fairies.

Angel Slipper: a thick shake-like drink tasting of caramel and almonds.

Araboth: the seventh and highest heaven.

Arcane magic: the type of magic primarily practiced by fairies and leprechauns using magic ingredients, potions, or spells.

Archangels: messengers, protectors and miracle workers; taught by Archangel Michael (formerly taught by Madri Zadeka).

Aurora: an ingredient in amber that has divine healing properties.

Baeldavar: the twelve-ringed training ground of the dark spirits which overlaps the angelic training ground of Mystfira in the arena known as the Rocker.

Blanchilts: tiny insect-like creatures that live in the Ring of Ice and inflict a stinging, burning bite on any exposed skin.

Board of Adjudicators: fourteen angels elected to decide what miracles will be released on Earth when the angels prevail in the Adomis arena. Conversely, fourteen dark spirits elected to decide what torments are to be unleashed on Earth if the dark spirits prevail in the Adomis arena.

Brandire Wood: wood that throws off heat without needing fire or flame. Usually passed down from generation to generation by families in Mystfira.

Brume Amphitheater: magnificent and luxurious outdoor theater in the Fairy Forest with tiered seating levels. Famous for its vividly colored, clamshell seating, marble staircases, curved passageways, tiered fountains, and galleries. Home to the Brume Curtain.

Brume Curtain: a gargantuan green vertical ring with a wispy, gossamer cloud shimmering from its depths, which serves as a fairy portal to other realms and worlds.

Bucklers: in Adomis, the four swordsmen positioned behind the three forward players known as spadroons.

Castle of Reckoning: heavily guarded fortress on one of the Cliffs of Wisdom located in the Valley of Waterfalls in the eighth ring of Mystfira and ruled by Queen Yosoy. In the midst of the castle sits the Keep of Time.

Carrions: the angelic carriers of the dark entities to the underworld; taught by Madri Omega at the Palace of Umber Cascades located in the second ring beneath the Sea of Umber.

Celestial Paints, Pigments, Polishes, and Plasters: an art store on Dressage Street in Truvian Village.

Celestial Spear: similar to a hard breadstick featuring popular meal flavors from both heaven and Earth.

Cherubim: musicians, singers, dancers and artists of the angelic world; taught by Madri Avalon at the Rose Quartz Palace in the fifth Ring of Rocks.

Cuppyducks: yellow flowers found in the Valley of Waterfalls.

Desert ring: the tenth ring of Mystfira overseen by Madri Isabo at the Palace of Pearls.

Dewdrop: a drink in Truvian Village which tastes like ripe peaches.

Divine magic: a type of celestial magic that can only be wielded by an angel.

Dominions: recorders of history and overseers of goodness; taught by Madri Keva.

Druri box: refers to either of the two boxes on either end of the Adomis ring which lift and rotate around the field providing a close up view of the Adomis trials for the Board of Adjudicators.

Druri-glass: the clearest unbreakable glass found in the heavens.

Emerald Sky Palace: the palace of angelic thrones located in the sky of the eleventh Ring of Ashlot and overseen by Madri Saniel.

Fairies: protectors of elements and nature on Earth; taught by Madri Fey.

Fairy dust: are grains of magic primarily used by leprechauns and fairies to perform arcane magic.

Fairy Forest: the fourth ring of Mystfira overseen by Madri Fey at the Tree of Tuatha.

Fairy Wishes: an arcane magic store on Dressage Street in Truvian run by fairies.

Festival of Fajolie: a fairy holiday which falls on October 31st. On that day the fairies are allowed to use their fairy portal in the Brume Theater and visit other worlds. A popular destination with the fairies is Earth to help celebrate what they believe is our festival of disguise known as Halloween.

Festival of Feadh-Ree: a fairy holiday in May which the fairies celebrate with all the children in the twelve rings of Mystfira who wish to participate in the merriment in the Fairy Forest on that day.

Flaming Arrow: a drink found in the Village of Truvian tasting of honey, raisins, and a hint of lemon.

Flaming Flignas: creatures of the Desert Ring whose high body temperature frequently sets themselves and other things aflame.

Floral rain: flower blossoms that fall from the seventh heaven of Araboth sometime between March and April. The floral rain heralds the beginning of the Adomis season with the first Adomis trial held four days after the floral rainfall. The blossoms are collected and woven together into wreaths and necklaces by the jarvartan villagers, as well as the angels, leprechauns, and fairies, and worn to the first Adomis trial.

Foost: or feather snow. White, soft, feathery material that the angelic students use for outdoor pillow fights.

Gadaboot plant: lush green plant with a fragrant red blossom. Famous for uprooting itself and trekking about with its two long roots shaped like miniature boots.

Gargoyles: gruesome winged creatures who can stand so still they look like stone. Protectors of the angels and their palaces in Mystfira.

Glesh: a type of snow in Mystfira. Similar to shards of slivered glass.

Golden Palace: is usually located in the ninth ring of the Jungle of Equinox. It houses the archangels and is usually overseen by Madri Zadeka. Madri Zadeka relinquished her post to the archangel Michael the night the Ryder-Knight students arrived in Mystfira. The Golden Palace has now become part of the Palace of Angels in the Truvian Ring.

Guardians: angelic protectors of humanity; taught by Madri Isabo.

Hell's Tongue: a small plant with extremely long blossoms of shooting flame.

Island of Palades: located in the first ring of Mystfira and home to the power angels who are overseen by Madri Ezekiel at the Amethyst Palace.

Jarvartan: race of beings responsible for assisting the angels charged with protective duties (powers, carrions, archangels, guardians, thrones, and principalities) with their assignments on Earth and in the heavens.

Jelligents: blue flowers found in the Valley of Waterfalls.

Jungle of Equinox: the ninth ring of Mystfira usually presided over by Madri Zadeka at the Golden Palace, but since the Ryder-Knight students arrival in Mystfira, her position has been relinquished and assumed by the Archangel Michael.

Keep of Time: a keep in the Castle of Reckoning full of mazes and puzzles meant to keep people from disturbing the dominion angels at work there—Clariel, Emmiel, and Mortiel. It is the place where the air is spun into the white thread of life and woven into the tapestries of time. A place where magical brushes dip themselves into the vat of time before decorating each thread of the tapestries being worked.

Kohah: clear glass ball in the ceiling of the Celestial Meditation room which will show an angel what the Divine wishes them to see.

Luffkins: a snack which tastes similar to potato pancakes.

Madri: instructor or teacher.

Madri Avalon: leader and teacher of the cherubim students at the Rose Quartz Palace located in the fifth Ring of Rocks. A gifted singer and dancer, she wears rose pink gowns and cloaks.

Madri Estel: leader and teacher of the angelic virtue students at the Winter Blue Palace located in the eighth ring of the Valley of Waterfalls. Overseer of good and giver of strength, she wears pale blue gowns and cloaks.

Madri Ezekiel: leader and teacher of the angelic power students at the Amethyst Palace located in the first ring. A gifted healer and in charge the heavenly infirmary found on the Mount of Mists. Wears purple robe and cloaks.

Madri Fey: diminutive leader and teacher of the fairies. Her seat of power is at the Tree of Tuatha in the fourth ring of the Fairy Forest. She is the most gifted practitioner of arcane magic in Mystfira. She has her hands full with her mischievous fairies. She wears yellow gowns and cloaks, which suit her lovely unnaturally green eyes.

Madri Isabo: leader and teacher of the angelic guardian students at the Palace of Pearls in the tenth ring of the Desert. She is a fierce warrior and gifted empath and psychic. Chosen by Araboth to serve as an archer in the Adomis Trials. When she's not dressed for battle, she wears silver gowns and cloaks.

Madri Keva: leader and teacher of the angelic dominion students at the Palace of Turquoise in the seventh ring of Mukrot. As a dominion she always has her nose in a book and knows the power of words. She wears turquoise gowns and cloaks.

Madrikim: plural for the word "Madri."

Madri Michael: archangel from Araboth who replaced the archangel Zadeka at the Golden Palace in the ninth ring of the Jungle of Equinox the night the Ryder-Knight students arrived in Mystfira. Chosen by Araboth to be a spadroon in the Adomis Trials. Wears gold robes and cloaks.

Madri Omega: leader and teacher of the angelic carrions at the Palace of Umber Cascades in the second ring under the Sea of Umber. Wears orange robes and cloaks.

Madri Roanin: leader and teacher of the angelic seraphim students at the Red Beryl Palace in the sixth ring of the Weeping Woods. Outstanding musician and dancer as well as a superb buckler chosen by Araboth to participate in the Adomis trials. Wears robes and cloaks of crimson.

Madri Saniel: leader and teacher of the angelic thrones students at the Emerald Sky Palace in the eleventh Ring of Ashlot. Fierce female warrior who, when not dressed in battle gear, wears emerald green gowns and cloaks.

Madri Typhicus: the administrator of Mystfira who lives in a house in Truvian. Also chosen by Araboth to serve as a spadroon in the Adomis trials.

Madri Uriah: the leader and teacher of the angelic principalities at the Sapphire Sky Palace in the twelfth Ring of Ice. Fierce male warrior chosen by Araboth to participate in the Adomis trials as a buckler. When not dressed in battle gear, he wears royal blue robes and cloaks.

Madri Zadeka: original leader and teacher of the angelic archangel students who relinquished her position to the Archangel Michael the night the Ryder-Knight students arrived in Mystfira.

Meneteakles: octopus-like plant found in the Ring of Ashlot.

Moodispanks: purple flowering plant found in the Valley of Waterfalls.

Mount of Mists: mountain on the Island of Palades in the first ring. Houses the Theoculus, the angelic infirmary, the angelic gardens, and the entrance to the seventh heaven of Araboth.

Muck Monsters: oozing muddy creatures found in the seventh ring of Mukrot who leave slimy dirt and goo on anything they touch.

Mukrot: the seventh ring of Mystfira overseen by Madri Keva at the Palace of Turquoise.

Mystfira: the largest and most elite angelic training grounds in the universe, and, by far, the most dangerous angelic training facility, situated between the sixth heaven of Zebul and the seventh heaven of Araboth.

Nomi Tree: a tree in Mukrot whose leaves are actually tiny green venomous snakes with nasty dispositions.

Nothing but Notions: store on Dressage Street in Truvian that sells ideas. The fairy proprietor uses disembodied talking heads as her expert sales clerks.

Onks: small creatures found in the twelfth Ring of Ice. They have thick white coats of corded fur and resemble oversized mops.

Ossignio wood: a type of wood that is immune to fire.

Palace of Angels: the palaces of Mystfira have the ability to move and interlock in times of war or trouble. When two or more palaces unite, they are known as the Palace of Angels. The Palace of Angels in our story consists of the archangels' Golden Palace, the guardians' Palace of Pearls, the seraphim's Palace of Red Beryl, and the cherubim's Palace of Rose Quartz. They are locked together in the third ring of Truvian.

Palace of Pearls: the palace of the guardian angels usually located in Desert of the tenth ring and overseen by Madri Isabo, but now one of the four palaces comprising the new Palace of Angels.

Palace of Turquoise: is located in the seventh ring of Mukrot. It is home to the dominion angels and overseen by Madri Keva.

Palace of Umber Cascades: is located in the second ring under the Sea of Umber. It is home to the carrion angels and is overseen by Madri Omega.

Parrot Wind: a wind in Mystfira that learns to speak all the languages it hears in the heavens. The wind is attempting to learn English, but often gets the names of people jumbled up when repeating them.

Patherics: creatures with leech-like mouths, greenish brown skin, golden eye which droop from their sockets, and are without noses, or hair. These creatures feed on the electrical energy from other creatures' brains and are found in the Ring of Ashlot.

Powers: angelic healers and also fierce warriors; taught by Madri Ezekiel.

Presidio: the magnificent round room in the Palace of Angels where the Sakal convene to fulfill their responsibilities. The room also contains the strange living landscape murals. Found in the Red Beryl Palace when the palaces are not joined.

Principalities: male warriors, protectors of Araboth; taught by Madri Uriah.

Quarreling iffbees: creatures found in the sixth ring of the Weeping Woods. They have twelve sets of hands and unless they are all kept busy they enjoy slapping others.

Red Beryl Palace: the palace of the seraphim usually located in the sixth ring known as The Weeping Woods and overseen by Madri Roanin, but now one of the four palaces comprising the new Palace of Angels.

Ring of Ashlot: the eleventh ring of Mystfira overseen by the throne Madri Saniel at the Emerald Sky Palace.

Ring of Ice: the twelfth ring of Mystfira overseen by the principality angel, Madri Uriah at the Sapphire Sky Palace.

Ring of Rocks: the fifth ring of Mystfira overseen by Madri Avalon at the Amethyst Palace.

Rose Quartz Palace: the palace of the cherubim usually located in the fifth Ring of Rocks and overseen by Madri Avalon, but now one of the four palaces comprising the new Palace of Angels.

Rumbrumies: large tree-dwelling creatures of the Jungle of Equinox. Orange-haired beasties known for their excellent sense of smell, wrinkly brown faces, and their long, thick, bushy stalk of hair in the middle of their head. This stalk of hair conceals a retractable elephant-like trunk which serves as their second nose and third hand.

Sakal: the council of eleven angels and one fairy that oversee the training and education of angels and fairies in Mystfira.

Sand Whirlpools: whirling pools of quicksand located in the Desert Ring.

Sapphire Sky Palace: the palace of principalities located in the sky of the twelfth Ring of Ice and overseen by Madri Uriah.

Sea of Umber: is the second ring of Mystfira. Every day the sea is a different shade of red. The Palace of Umber Cascades rests beneath it.

Second Sight Opticals: a store on Dressage Street in Truvian Village featuring lens of all types; telescopes, binoculars, soriscopes and more. Run by Lydia the leprechaun.

Seraphim: joyous musicians, singers, dancers, and artists of the angelic world; taught by Madri Roanin.

Shoosh: the original language of the winds.

Silch: a type of snow in Mystfira. A sticky, grainy substance not unlike thick molasses syrup.

Soriscope: a type of telescope which can see long distances and even through walls!

Spadroons: the three forward swordsmen positioned on the white line in the center of the field at the Adomis trials. When a spadroon touches an opponent ten times that swordsman must leave the field. When the spadroons defeat all the spadroons on the other team they may engage a buckler of their choice.

Sparnot: a stone harder than a diamond.

STOT: shots taken on goal in Adomis trials.

Sweet Dreams: a fairy ice cream and sweet shop in Truvian Village.

The Broken Wing: a fairy store in Truvian which sells new wings as well as repairs and paints old ones.

The Coach and Footman: an establishment in Truvian Village selling clothing and footwear.

The Crooked Curse: a dark magic store on Dressage Street in Truvian Village.

The Full Quiver and Clanking Sword: a store on Dressage Street in Truvian Village that sells all types of bows and arrows and swords.

The Gargoyle's Perch: an oversized eatery on Dressage Street in Truvian Village for the gargoyles of Mystfira.

The Gold Leaf: a popular tavern on Dressage Street in Truvian Village run by leprechauns.

The House of Dew: a magical jungle-like restaurant on Dressage Street in Truvian Village run by fairies. Real trees, plants and flowers form the tables and chairs there. A favorite of the Ryder-Knight students.

The Perfect Perfumery: perfume store in Truvian Village, featuring scents made and bottled by the fairies beneath the Brume Theater.

The Rocker: the large almond-shaped arena, fashioned from a blue diamond of unimaginable size, where the Adomis trials are held. The training grounds of Mystfira and Baeldavar link and overlap only in this arena.

The Sneaky Snake: a tavern on Dressage Street in Truvian Village run by dark spirits.

The Summoning Ceremony: yearly ceremony on October 31st when the new angels and fairies are summoned from the seventh Heaven of Araboth to begin their training.

The Three Sisters: a store on Dressage Street in Truvian Village that sells accessories such as belts and scarves.

The Treasure Trove: a store on Dressage Street in Truvian featuring a collection of various goods, antiques, and other odds and ends. Owned by the leprechaun proprietor, Seamus O'Shanahan.

The Wind and Wings Tavern: a restaurant on Dressage Street in Truvian Village and run by a jarvartan proprietor.

Theoculus: a large, revolving, twelve-tiered building with an unsupported dome featuring an oculus in its top and found on the Island of Palades. The building is the entry point for all visitors to Mystfira and serves many purposes. It is a place for welcome and reception. It serves as a classroom for Celestial Astrology classes and is also the place where angelic award ceremonies take place.

Tree of Tuatha: the place where Madri Fey lives in the Fairy Forest.

Thrones: angelic female warriors, protectors of Araboth; taught by Madri Saniel.

Truvian Ring: third ring of Mystfira containing the Jarvartan Village of Truvian and overseen by Madri Typhicus. Also home to the newly formed Palace of Angels since the Ryder-Knight students arrival in Mystfira.

Truvian Village: the jarvartan village in the third ring.

Upons: fairy tale characters that once actually existed on Earth but removed because they posed a threat to Earth. The fairies changed the real version of our fairy tale stories on Earth so children would not be frightened.

Valley of Shadows: a large valley running from the fifth Ring of Rocks to the twelfth Ring of Ice. Used for angelic training exercises. Also it is the only place the angels are allowed to have their true angelic natures and be free from human emotions in Mystfira.

Valley of Waterfalls: the eighth ring of Truvian overseen by the virtue angel Madri Estel at the Winter Blue Palace. Home of the legendary Cliffs of Wisdom and the Castle of Reckoning with its Keep of Time.

Vesica piscis: almond-shaped area shared by two overlapping circles (like the Adomis arena) that creates a space where great power, love, strength, and intention can exist. It is the shape Rafe Ryder concentrates on to anchor himself to the divine mind of Araboth.

Vexxon: a dark spirit that wants to take over and rule Earth. He is considered the Prince of Tumult and Tempests and is responsible for all earthly chaos, Mayhem, and confusion caused by the elements of wind, water, rain, thunder, and lightning.

Virtues: angelic overseers of good and givers of strength; taught by Madri Estel.

Weeping Woods: the sixth ring of Mystfira overseen by Madri Roanin at the Red Beryl Palace.

Wind Gypsy: also sometimes called a wind walker, a humanoid creature that travels through all galaxies and universes by way of the winds.

Winrup: a sweet, sticky treat, not unlike a donut, but it looks like a rock.

Winter Blue Palace: is located in the Valley of Waterfalls in the eighth ring of Mystfira. It houses the virtue angels and is overseen by Madri Estel.

Woganot: a large winged creature in charge of protecting the Mount of Mists on the Island of Palades and the Brume Theater in the Fairy Forest. The creature's body and wings consists entirely of eyes, which form beautiful and unique patterns on each woganot's body. Their eyes can be sent from their body to peacefully search for someone or something. Their eyes can also transform into razor-sharp blades and be used to defend their posts. Woganots also have a hive-mind. If one woganot knows something, they all do.

Xant: a magical gelatinous air creature the size of a coconut, which when caught by a fairy will become part of them. The creatures enhance magical abilities and protects the fairies' bodies from the elements which harm them in Mystfira. They also excrete xant dust which is an ingredient found in fairy dust. It was discovered that xants would also protect the frail human body from the elements in Mystfira.

Xant dust: protective ingredient found in a grain of fairy dust. If a small amount is breathed in it will make you giddy and happy, but if a larger amount is inhaled, it puts one into a sudden and deep sleep.

Xantman: on Earth the xantman is know as the sandman. He puts people to sleep and brings good dreams by sprinkling magic dust into the eyes of people.

Yaltabolt: artistic dark spirit and brother to Vexxon.

Zebul: the sixth heaven.

Acknowledgements

My deepest gratitude to my team: Jenny Zemanek, Christopher Bell, Kella Campbell, Catherine Jones Payne, Benjamin Guido and Stephanie Guido. Because you pour your hearts and souls into your work, my work looks better than I ever could have imagined. Thank you! Thank you! Thank you!

Thanks to my husband and children for your encouragement, love, and support. I love you more than you know.

Thanks to my brother, Randy, for always making me laugh, and supporting me through thick and thin.

Lastly, thanks to my parents. Let's face it. I exist because of you. Thanks, Mom and Dad.

About tHe AutHoR

L. L. Reynolds is a registered nurse turned middle grade/young adult fantasy writer from Vermont with a husband, three children, two dogs, and anything but dull life!

A labor and delivery nurse for nearly twenty years, L. L. once had dinner with E. B. White, the author of *Charlotte's Web*, and it remains one of the highlights of her life thus far.

She loves tea, children, books, music, art, animals, and lemon meringue pie.

Find out more about her at:
https://llreynolds.com
https://www.facebook.com/llreynolds777
https://twitter.com/llreynolds777

www.ingramcontent.com/pod-product-compliance
Lightning Source LLC
Chambersburg PA
CBHW051326250626
47155CB00007B/2470